Praise for

The Yellow H

and Patricia F

D0103638

"THE YELLOW HOUSE is that great rarity, a book about Ireland written by an American who knows what she's talking about. Intelligently plotted, with engaging characters, the novel offers a fresh view of the highly dramatic Revolutionary Period in Ireland. The well-researched history illumines but never smothers the story line. Small details bring the era to life with stunning clarity. The writing is lucid and accessible, occasionally even lyrical. This is a very rewarding first novel and I look forward to reading more from Patricia Falvey."

—Morgan Llewelyn, author of *Lion of Ireland,*
Pride of Lions, Grania, The Last Prince of Ireland,
and The Irish Century series

"THE YELLOW HOUSE is an eloquently written story of the emergence of hope and love in a time of struggle and confusion in Ireland. It avoids the ever-present pitfalls of drowning us in a history lesson while not ignoring the richness of that very history. With her debut novel, Patricia Falvey breathes life back into an Ireland that has nearly vanished from memory. For that, I am grateful."

—Robert Hicks, *New York Times* bestselling author of
The Widow of the South and *A Separate Country*

"You can often tell where a book's plot and characters are going. But so many times I was astonished to find that what I expected on the next page was a complete surprise to me. Falvey held my attention with suspenseful events that constantly amazed me . . . THE YELLOW HOUSE is a powerful book, full of strongly drawn characters that exemplify vitality, humanity, and passion for life. They are so realistic, that early on I felt like I knew them." —*Irish American News*

"Patricia Falvey draws on her North of Ireland roots to put a human face on the turning point in twentieth-century Irish history. A moving novel and a singular achievement."

—Mary Pat Kelly, author of *Galway Bay*

"This novel delivers the best of both worlds: secrets, intrigue, and surprising twists will keep readers flipping the pages, while Falvey's insight and poetic writing tugs at the heartstrings of the most cynical audiences."

—*Publishers Weekly*

"If you like historical fiction, with great flourishes of families destroyed and remade, this is a classic."　　　　　—*TheReviewBroads.com*

"Falvey tells a good story along the way. A host of interesting characters, surprising but plausible plot developments, and deftly incorporated details of the Irish struggle for independence add up to a debut novel sure to please fans of historical romance."　　　　—*Library Journal*

"Falvey very successfully weaves together the politics, history, and landscape of Ireland in this period . . . Falvey brilliantly illustrates the cultural, political, and economic conflicts that result in erecting Ireland's North/ South dividing border. The well-researched history of the period emerges through the characters, their conflicts, and their choices. The story is absorbing and satisfying historical fiction."

—*Sacramento Book Review* and
San Francisco Book Review

"The early scenes of Eileen's and James's lawless exploits for the Catholic resistance make for thrilling reading . . . The book serves as a provocative reminder of the tangled strings of family, war, and familial war, and also . . . as a splendid example of old-fashioned, minimal-bodice-ripping romance."　　　　　　　　　　—*Dallas Morning News*

"The characters are full, rich, and real and the history of Ireland feels authentic. The author refrains from delineating clearly between the good guys and bad guys. She allows the reader to make their own decisions and I liked that. THE YELLOW HOUSE is a winner. I just can't shake the memory of it and that's a good thing."

—*Minneapolis Insight Examiner*

"[O]ne of the best historical fiction novels I have read in years . . . I simply could not pull myself away from this book. It took me back to classics such as Gaskell's *North and South* and the heroine Eileen had so many of the qualities that I have always loved in dear Tess of Hardy's *Tess of the D'Ubervilles.* When one book can bring me back to two of my favorite books of all time that are both absolute classics, I am in awe. This book kept me emotionally invested until the very end . . . Wonderfully written, magically created, it could only come from a true Irish lass and to be her debut novel . . . amazing. I loved it . . . every page."

—*Stiletto Storytime*

"It is rare for a first-time novelist to tackle historical events in as refreshing a manner as Patricia Falvey does in THE YELLOW HOUSE . . . Falvey controls the story, weaving her characters through the First World War and the Troubles, allowing the characters to be the masters of their own fate rather than falling back on history to guide the plot . . . Readers will be inclined to gluttonously scarf down this novel in one sitting as I did. Take your time reading THE YELLOW HOUSE; you'll be sad to see the last page."

—*Irish America* magazine

"Religious intolerance, political strife, and personal drama combine well in this historical novel whose themes are still relevant today."

—*Hartford Courant*

"Set in the tumultuous years before and after World War I, THE YELLOW HOUSE is an impressive debut that will appeal to readers of Irish family sagas. Falvey skillfully takes major events and reduces them to a personal level, focusing on the effects of World War I and religious unrest in Ireland on one woman and the people around her . . . Falvey steers clear of the stock characters that often plague novels set in Ireland. The love triangle between Eileen, Owen, and James, combined with the historical context, provides plenty of tension and keeps the story moving quickly . . . it's hard not to root for [Eileen] as she fights to reclaim her birthright."

—*Historical Novels Review*

The Yellow House

A NOVEL

PATRICIA FALVEY

CENTER
STREET

NEW YORK BOSTON NASHVILLE

Center Street
Hachette Book Group
1290 Avenue of the Americas
New York, NY 10104

www.centerstreet.com

Center Street is a division of Hachette Book Group, Inc.
The Center Street name and logo are trademarks of Hachette Book Group, Inc.

Printed in the United States of America

Originally published in hardcover by Center Street.

First Trade Edition: February 2011
10 9 8 7

The Library of Congress has cataloged the hardcover edition as follows:
Falvey, Patricia.
   The yellow house / Patricia Falvey. — 1st ed.
     p. cm.
   Summary: "The story of a young woman fighting to reunite her
family and reclaim their ancestral home during the war for Irish
Independence"—Provided by publisher.
   ISBN 978-1-59995-201-7
   1. Young women—Ireland—Fiction. 2. Ireland—History—War
of Independence, 1919–1921—Fiction. 3. Triangles (Interpersonal
relations)—Fiction. I. Title.
   PS3606.A49Y46 2009
   813'.6—dc22
                                        2008053275

ISBN 978-1-59995-202-4 (pbk.)

For my grandmother
Ellen Jane (Hayes) Toner

ACKNOWLEDGMENTS

I would like to thank my agent, Denise Marcil, for her invaluable guidance throughout the development of this novel. I am deeply grateful for the way she challenged me to reach levels beyond which I believed myself capable. Her expertise, experience, practicality, and caring concern are everything an author could ever hope to find in an agent and more. In addition, I would like to thank Anne Marie O'Farrell and Katie Kotchman of the Denise Marcil Literary Agency for their assistance and enthusiasm. I would also like to thank Christina Boys, my editor at Hachette Book Group, for her immediate and sustained enthusiasm for this book. Thanks also to her assistant, Whitney Luken. My appreciation and thanks also go to Alan Tucker, who edited this manuscript with courteous attention and elegant diligence. The manuscript was indeed "ready to meet the queen" when he was finished. Also thanks to Dr. John McCavitt, Northern Ireland historian and author of *The Flight of the Earls*, for sharing his expertise on Irish political and religious history. Thanks also to Dr. Marilyn Cohen, anthropologist, head of women's studies at St. Peter's College in New Jersey, and author of *Linen, Family and Community in Tullyish, County Down*, for her insights into the social conditions in the linen industry in Northern Ireland. Thanks also to Rosemary Mulholland, president of the Bessbrook Historical Society, and Pat O'Keefe, Irish musician, for generously assisting me with my research.

Thanks must also go to many friends scattered throughout the United States and abroad for their support and belief in my dream. They include the Good Eats and Lucky's Gangs in Dallas; the Reno Crowd; Spa Sisters in New York and Pawley's Island; former colleagues at PricewaterhouseCoopers, LLP; and many, many others. I would especially like to thank Marjorie Jaffe, who introduced me to Denise Marcil and so was the reason it all started. Thanks also to my dear friend Susan Grissom for her unflagging optimism and encouragement and for her research assistance. A special thank-you to Bernard Silverman for his sustained caring and support and for all the jokes! And last but not least, my appreciation to my family, especially my beloved sister, Connie, who has kept the spirit of Ireland alive in me all these years.

CONTENTS

Glenlea, County Armagh

1905

I

I remember the summers best, when the days rested in the long arms of the evening and the sounds around Slieve Gullion were as muted as benediction. Only the faint barking of distant dogs cut the stillness as farmers drove their cattle home. Smoke curled from cottage chimneys and children gulped down tea so they could return to play while time hovered between day and night like a gift from heaven.

On such an evening, when I was eight years old, I lay in the tall grass in front of our house with my ear pressed to the ground. If you listened hard enough, Da had told me, you could hear the fairies dancing down below. But this evening all was quiet. I sat up. My brother, Frankie, a year older than myself, was torturing the life out of a worm, hacking at it with a sharp stone.

"Stop that, Frankie," I said.

Frankie shrugged. "I'm only trying to see if it's true."

"What?"

"That it grows itself back again if you cut it in two."

I sighed. Frankie was always doing things like that—cruel wee things. I put it down to his being a boy. I lay down on my back. A brown-and-orange butterfly circled above me. I put up my hands, lazily tracing its flight.

"I wish Da was home," I said.

I heard his voice long before I saw him. His lovely sweet tenor carried from the distance, lilting across the fields that spread out below our house. I scrambled up and raced toward the road. Frankie dropped the worm and followed me. Our old Irish setter, Cuchulainn, pricked up his ears and barked. We shaded our eyes as we squinted into the setting sun. Da appeared at the brow of the hill. He stood up in the cart, his hands loosely holding the pony's reins. His crop of red hair glowed like a halo around his head as the fire of the sun caught it. I imagined him the great Irish warrior Hugh O'Neill himself, returning from the battle, riding out of the sun. How I loved my da.

"Da's coming, Mammy," I shouted back to the house, "Da's coming."

Frankie and I ran toward the cart. Da stopped singing and waved at us.

"Hello, darlin's. Up with you now."

Da was a wiry man of medium height, with a face so full of life that it shone even on the dullest of days. He was dressed today, as always when he went to town, in a brown suit and a white cotton shirt with a clean starched collar. "Dandy Tommy," the villagers called him. He wore no cap, and his curly hair sprang out around his head like a laurel wreath.

He slowed the pony and the cart stopped. Frankie and I clambered up, shoving each other to get in the seat beside Da. Da chucked the reins again, and the pony began to walk. She was a sweet little Connemara pony, gray and white, with eyes like silk.

"On now with you, Rosie," Da said.

Mammy stood at the front door, holding my little sister, Lizzie, by the hand. Lizzie strained to get away.

"Dada, Dada," she crowed.

"She was lovely and fair as the Rose of the summer." Da crooned the words of "The Rose of Tralee." It was his favorite song, one that he sang often to Mammy. The girl in the song was named Mary, the same as Ma, and Mammy always smiled when he sang it. The cart trundled through the gate that led to our farm. It had broken long ago and was never closed. Red summer roses clung stubbornly to the rotted, splintered wood, trailing down over the low stone walls on either side. They were Mammy's roses. She loved flowers.

"What's this, Da?" Frankie said. "What's in these buckets?" Frankie tried to pry the lid off a tin bucket in the back of the cart.

"Wait and see." Da laughed.

Rosie halted in front of the house and we climbed down. Ma came forward, still holding Lizzie's hand. She looked down into the bed of the cart.

"And what in the name of God have you there?" she said. Mammy's voice was always soft and slightly hoarse, as if she had a catch in her throat.

"Paint, my lovely Mary Kathleen," said Da, jumping down from the cart.

"Paint?"

"Aye, paint. Buckets of lucky yellow paint to mark the grand anniversary."

"What are you talking about?" Mammy dropped Lizzie's hand, and the baby toddled forward and wrapped her arms around Da's leg.

"The anniversary of the day my grandda Hugh O'Neill won back this house and the O'Neill family's honor along with it. In 1805—a hundred years ago this very day!"

Frankie and I giggled, while Ma shook her head and sighed. Wisps of long black hair played around her face. She put up her hand to shove them back.

"Will you go on with yourself," she said. "Sure you have no notion of when or even how your grandfather got this house."

Da straightened his back and put on a look of mock outrage. "Don't I know my own family's history, Mary? Didn't I hear the story many's a time from Hugh himself? He won this house back from the Sheridan family . . ."

"In a game of cards," put in Mammy, resting her hands on her hips.

"Aye," said Da, "but the house rightfully belonged to the O'Neills. The Sheridans only had it at all because King James gave it to them. Stole all the land off the Catholics, so they did, and gave it away to the English who were loyal to the Crown, and—"

"Och, we've heard it all before," said Ma, cutting Da short before he could gather steam for one of his big speeches.

"Da, Da. What's the paint for?" Frankie cried. He had managed to lift the lid off one of the buckets with the help of the sharp stone he still had.

Da turned to us. His blue eyes were bright with excitement.

"For the house, darlin's. We're going to paint the O'Neill house yellow. You'll be able to see it from the top of Slieve Gullion itself, so you will. It will be like a giant sunflower standing in the middle of the fields, so bright it would dazzle a blind man."

"Did you bring the meat? And the flour?" Mammy wasn't smiling like the rest of us. I thought maybe she didn't like the yellow color.

Da slapped his forehead. "Ah, love, sure didn't I forget in all the excitement. I'll go back for it tomorrow. But in the meantime I have a case of porter—enough for a good party. P.J. and the boys will be up tonight and we can celebrate."

Da put his arm around Ma, but she pulled away from him.

"The paint was half price, Mary," he said quietly. "I just took the notion and bought it. To cheer us all up, you see. To celebrate."

Mammy sighed. "I don't see much to celebrate."

There were tears in her eyes. She cried sometimes at night when she thought no one was watching. I didn't want her to be sad. I walked over and patted her sleeve. She pulled me close to her.

Frankie stirred the paint in the bucket with a stick. It was the color of daffodils, but it had a sharp smell that made me wrinkle my nose. "Can we start painting now, Da? Can we?" he asked.

Da turned away from Ma and lifted the buckets down from the cart. He lined them up outside the front door like tin soldiers. "Of course you can," he said. "There's still plenty of light. I brought brushes for everybody."

"But Da—it's too high," I said, frowning up at the two-story house with its massive chimneys on each end of a gabled roof.

"Ah, my little Eileen, don't you be worrying your head. My friends and myself will climb the ladders. You just start where you can reach. Here's the brushes. You too, Mary."

Da held out a brush to Ma, but she turned away and shoved me toward the side of the house.

"Eileen, help me take in the washing."

"Och, Ma—"

"Now, Eileen!"

Mammy's voice was sharp. It frightened me. I didn't want her to be mad at my da.

"But we're supposed to be celebrating, Ma," I whined.

"Fetch the basket," was all Ma said. Furiously, she unclipped the pegs from the line, tossing the white sheets into the basket. Her lips were pursed in a thin line. Then she took the basket from me and walked into the house, slamming the door behind her. Da took a stick and stirred the paint in each of the buckets. The golden yellow crust, like the foam on top of fresh buttermilk, dissolved through the rest of the liquid, leaving only bubbles on the top. Frankie had already started slapping paint on the graying white walls of our house, and it dripped down in uneven ribbons.

"He's doing it wrong, Da," I said. Frankie glared at me.

"Ah, he'll get the way of it, Eileen. Here, you start over there."

Even Lizzie had a brush, although she dabbed more paint on the grass than on the walls. She trailed after Frankie, calling his name and laughing. She was the only one of us who could coax a smile out of our Frankie. His brown eyes softened as he looked down at her. "You're a wee pest," he said as he guided her hand so she could dip her brush in the paint. At last Ma came out of the house. Her face was softer now, but tiny red lines ringed her eyes. She lifted a brush and started painting along with us. She smiled at Da.

"Don't be getting paint on my flowers, now," she said, indicating her rows of scarlet poppies, yellow anemones, and blue forget-me-nots planted in a bed along the front of the house and in the window boxes.

Da laughed. "I'll mind the flowers," he said, "but I can't say I'll mind you."

He danced toward Ma and daubed yellow paint on her arm, then danced away.

"Tom!" she squealed. "If that's the way you want it, here goes." She landed a daub of yellow paint on his cheek. Frankie and Lizzie and I laughed, and the knot that had formed in my stomach went away.

I recall that day now through the haze of time and memory. But the yellow has never faded. It is as vivid in my mind as the day we covered the house and ourselves in yellow paint and danced like canaries around the garden.

☙❧

WE LIVED IN the village of Glenlea in the south of County Armagh, in the northern province of Ireland called Ulster. Glenlea, standing at the foot of the grand mountain Slieve Gullion, was one of many villages that ringed the mountain, each village having its particular view of the grand stone duchess. Slieve Gullion was sixty million years old and cradled a sleeping volcano deep within her. In winter, she stood proud and naked like an ancient scarred warrior. In spring, she wrapped herself in green bracken, while bluebells and white hawthorn blossoms cascaded down her great bosom and raced across the fields toward our house.

The night we painted the house yellow, the Music Men came. They came often in the long summer evenings when the pale moon hung in the still-light sky. They came whistling, swinging their fiddles and accordions with stout arms, cloth caps pushed back on reddened foreheads.

Mammy opened the big oak door wide to our guests.

"You're very welcome," she called in her lovely, deep voice.

"God bless all here," said P. J. Mullen.

P.J. was the leader of the Music Men. A fiddle player like my da, he was a short, burly man with coarse red hair and a long red beard that fanned out across his chest. I was sure he was one of the fairies. His voice was so loud, you jumped to hear it coming out of so short a man. P.J. was my godfather.

The men removed their caps and bowed their heads as if entering a church. I shot past them and sat on the wooden bench next to the big hearth in the kitchen, my face warm with joy.

"How's yourself, P.J?" said Ma.

"Fine as the day is long, missus."

"Hello, Fergus, Billy," Ma said, nodding at two of the other men. "How's your ma, Fergus?"

"Not too bad, thanks, missus," said Fergus Conlon. "She'd be great only for her legs."

A bachelor, Fergus still lived at home with his ma, who by all accounts was an oul' witch. Ma often said Fergus was earning indulgences in heaven right and left for having to put up with her.

Billy Craig handed Ma a bunch of wildflowers, his big round face red as a beetroot. Billy, a giant of a man but a bit simple, was madly in love with my ma. Every time he came to the house he brought her a present of some kind, and Ma always made a great fuss over it. She took the wildflowers from Billy, put them right away in a vase of water, and set them in the middle of the table. Billy beamed.

The fourth Music Man was Terrence Finnegan. No one knew much about Terrence. It was whispered he used to be a priest who had fallen in love with a girl and was thrown out of the priesthood. No one ever asked him, of course. We all preferred a good mystery.

Da came downstairs, a broad smile on his face, and shook hands with each of the men.

"Well, I see you didn't get far with the paint job," said P.J. as he dragged a small stool away from the wall. "No bother. The boys and I will be up with the ladders this week to finish the job."

"You'd better hurry," I said. "Great-Grandda Hugh's anniversary will be over."

The men laughed. Da turned his back to P.J. to reach up for his fiddle, which sat on a shelf on the kitchen wall. "She's right," he said.

I watched Da as he took down the fiddle and laid it across his knees. I loved the way he ran his long, slender white fingers along the length of its dark wood. Ma said Da's fingers reminded her of the stems of flowers. Reverently, he brought the instrument up to his shoulder and tucked it under his chin. With his right hand he raised the bow and brought it down across the strings. The sharp, high notes were both sweet and melancholy. I held my breath while the haunting strains ran themselves out. Then Da looked up and flashed a smile at me, and suddenly the fiddle seized on a merry jig. I clapped my hands and laughed.

Da got up again and lifted a small fiddle from a shelf and handed it to me. He bowed. "Would you do me the honor of playing for us, my lovely colleen?" It was a little game we always played before the music session began in earnest.

I stood up and tucked the fiddle under my chin. "Of course," I said in my best grown-up voice. "What would you like to hear?"

"How about 'The Dawning of the Day'?"

I started to play the sad tune, uncertainly at first until I got the feel of it. Then Da and the others joined in. Ma set bottles of porter at the feet of the musicians, who had arranged themselves, each on his favorite stool, around the big fireplace. Even when it was warm outside, we always had a fire going in the kitchen. As the blue smoke from the turf curled up in wisps, I inhaled the familiar pungent smell. A splintered wooden chair stood empty to the left of the hearth, Great-Grandda Hugh's chair. Ma always set a bottle of porter beside that chair as well, and old Cuchulainn would go over and rest his big head on the chair as if he were being petted by an invisible hand.

When we had finished playing, the men laid their instruments across their knees and lifted their bottles of porter.

"To the woman of the house," boomed P.J. He held up his bottle toward Ma and then took a long swallow. "No man would ever go thirsty in this house."

He turned to Da. "I saw John Browne's cattle grazing beyond in your back fields, Tom. Did you lease him the land?"

Ma's head turned sharply toward Da. A knot formed in my stomach.

"Och, no," Da said, looking down at his fiddle. "I sold him a few acres, that's all. Sure I had more land than I could manage."

Ma put down the kettle she had just picked up.

"But, Tom, that's the second parcel you've sold off this year." Her words hovered in the air like smoke. The Music Men fingered their instruments, busying themselves with tuning them. Da looked over at Ma, but she had her back turned to him.

"Will we start with a hornpipe, lads?"

He started a tune on his fiddle, and soon the other men took up their instruments and joined in, following along at the pace set by Da's fiddle. I clapped my hands, and Lizzie crowed and reached up to Frankie to dance with her. Frankie smiled. He rose and set down the skin-faced drum he had been beating with a stick in time to the music. Da had brought the drum, called a bodhran, home for him, and he played it with a fine intensity. Frankie had wanted to learn to play the fiddle like me, but Da said I was better suited to it. Frankie sulked about that for weeks. He was very competitive, our Frankie.

As Frankie walked Lizzie around the floor on her unsteady feet, Ma busied herself making soda bread. She formed the dough into two round batches and etched the shape of a cross with her thumb on the top of each loaf, then put them in a big iron skillet and thrust them into the middle of the turf fire.

The music session took on its own ritual. Da and P.J. set down their fiddles and Terrence his pipes and nodded to Billy Craig. It was his turn to play a solo. Billy wrapped his plump white fingers around his tin whistle and coaxed a sweet, mournful tune out of it. He called it "The Lonesome Boatman." I closed my eyes and imagined a boat skimming across Camlough Lake. The man rowing it was sad. Maybe he had lost someone he loved. Billy may have been simple, but he was a genius with the tin whistle. Da said God often made up for things in odd ways. Billy was the only Protestant in the group, but Da said it made no difference, because when it came to music everybody was equal.

Then Terrence Finnegan took up his uilleann pipes. He strapped the bellows around his waist and right arm and laid the pipes across his knees. Using his elbow, he pumped the bellows, sending air into the pipes. He pushed the mellow sound of "The Cregan White Hair" out of them. The sound was sweeter than that of traditional bagpipes, yet a sound as mysterious as the man himself. A dark man, Terrence was taller even than Ma, with gray flecks in his black hair and intense brown eyes. While he played, he looked around, as he always did, fixing his gaze on Frankie. He hardly spoke to Frankie, but he always stared at him when Frankie wasn't watching. It made me a bit jealous.

Then Fergus, tall and narrow as a stalk, bent over his mandolin and began to play a lovely old air called "The Coolin," his bony, thin fingers stretched across the strings like a crab's legs.

I looked around the room and tried, as I always did, to commit the scene to memory. Something in me wanted to hold on to it forever. From the kitchen window, I saw Slieve Gullion wrapping herself in her evening shawl as the light grew dim. Ma lit the paraffin lamps, and their light joined the glow of the firelight to dance a jig on the walls. All around the white-painted walls were shelves on which sat Da's collection of old musical instruments—uilleann pipes, a banjo, and bodhrans decorated with ancient Celtic designs. There were framed pictures on the walls, too—Ma's handiwork. She loved to sit outside the house and draw the landscape around us. Da framed the pictures and hung them for her. The colorful hooked rugs on the floor were her work as well, and the bright print curtains that flapped at the windows.

I went over to where Ma bent over the skillet in the fireplace.

"Can I help you, Mammy?"

"Aye, Eileen, get out the plates and the butter." Her face was red from the heat of the fire, and her long black hair fell down over one shoulder. She straightened up—a tall woman, with a lovely curved figure and long legs. She carried the skillet to the table and took off the lid. The smell of the soda bread made my mouth water. She slid the round loaves onto a wooden tray, took a knife and cut along each spur of the cross, making eight triangles. She slit each wedge in half and buttered it. The butter frothed from the heat and sank into the belly of the bread.

"Here, Eileen, pass these around."

The men placed their instruments on the floor while they ate and drank.

"Did you hear what those bastards are up to now?" growled P.J. between bites of soda bread.

We all waited. P.J. was a great one for setting up his audience. He took a deep swallow of his porter.

"Those feckers are after forming the Ulster Unionist Council to fight Home Rule. And you can bet your arse they don't mean to fight by civil means."

Billy giggled like a big child, and so did Frankie and I. We always giggled when P.J. cursed. Ma shot us a warning look.

"Home Rule doesn't have a leg to stand on," Terrence said softly. In contrast with P.J. and his bluster, Terrence never raised his voice, but he commanded attention as powerfully as if he had been roaring from a pulpit. "Those fellows down south have been harping on it for years. England will never agree to let Ireland rule itself, and that's the truth."

"Me ma says if Home Rule is ever passed for Ireland, the Protestants here in the north will have the rest of us drawn and quartered." Fergus peered at my ma with the same alarmed look in his eyes that rabbits had when Frankie pounced on them. "No offense, missus, I'm just saying what me ma says, that's all."

Ma smiled. "None taken, Fergus." Ma had been born a Protestant, but she had turned Catholic after she married Da. She was more devout than any of us.

Terrence looked straight at Ma and then scowled at Fergus. "It's all just talk," he said.

"All the same," boomed P.J. as he drained the last of his porter, "them Unionist bastards are getting ready for a fight. They'll not stop until they've burned us all out of house and home. It will be just like the plantation times all over again—they'll take everything we own. Sure there's already been stories of burning up in Belfast. We've not heard the last of it, mark my words."

I shivered as if a sudden draft had entered the room, and I moved closer to Da. I understood some of what they were talking about—Da had spoken of these things often enough. The Catholics in Ireland wanted to be able to rule themselves without interference from the English, but the Protestants were against it, particularly the Protestants in Ulster. They were afraid of the hold the Catholic Church would have on them if they were trapped inside a free Ireland. They were called Unionists because they wanted to keep the union with England. I had heard all this talk before—but tonight it seemed more urgent and more threatening. A frightening thought entered my head and prowled around like a menacing animal. What if, as P.J. said, the Protestants came and took our house back and drove us out? They had done it in the past, and only for Great-Grandda Hugh we would not be living in it now. I swallowed hard and tried to think of something else.

P.J. brushed the crumbs from his beard and said, as he always did, "Will we play one for the road?"

"I'll sing Mary's favorite song," said Da, "the one I courted her with—'On the Banks of My Old Lovely Lea.'"

"Good man," cried P.J.

"Lovely," shouted Billy.

Da began to sing. His tenor voice was high and clear. The years fell away from his face as he sang. Slowly, the Music Men took up their instruments to accompany him. The song was a sweet and melancholy love song. Da looked straight at Ma as he sang, and Terrence followed Da's gaze. Ma sat at the table, smiling at Da. Lizzie had crawled into her lap, and Ma sang the words softly into the child's ear as she rocked her to sleep.

The music ended. The men shuffled to their feet.

"The English took all our land," Frankie put in suddenly. "We learned about it in school. They just came in and took it and gave it to themselves—acres and acres of it." His small face was red with fury, and his dark eyes flashed.

"That's enough, Frank," Ma said sharply. "It's time for bed." Ma always called him Frank when she was annoyed with him.

"The lad's right just the same," said Terrence. "It's a wonder Tom here has any piece of land he can call his own."

Da nodded. "Well, we have my grandfather Hugh O'Neill to thank for that. There were no flies on that man."

I tugged at Da's sleeve. I could no longer hide my anxiety. Frankie had voiced my worst fears.

"Will the Ulstermen come and take our house, Da?" I whispered.

Da stroked my hair. "Of course they won't, love," he said.

"But Mr. Browne has already taken some land, and he's an Ulsterman."

I was sorry the minute the words were out of my mouth. Poor Da's face turned pale. He looked over at Ma. She lowered her eyes and said nothing.

"Ah, sure you do your best, Tom," Terrence said uncertainly. "You do your best."

"Aye," said Fergus. He stood up and put on his cap. "Well, I'd best be going. I have to get started on the bleaching early tomorrow. Ma says the rain is coming. She can feel it in her bones. And there'll be no work to be had when it's raining. Ma says I need to get the work while I can."

"Ah, sure if your ma told you the pope was in the backyard, you'd believe her!" said P.J.

Fergus glared at him. There were times when Fergus turned very dark, as if a dark ghost haunted him somewhere down inside. It frightened me to see it.

That night, after the Music Men left, I climbed the stairs to my bedroom and knelt up on the window seat, as I always did, to bid good night to Slieve Gullion. I rested my chin on my hands and stared at her outline in the pale moonlight.

"Please, Mother Gullion," I whispered. "Please don't let anybody take away our house." The ancient mountain gazed back at me in silence. I slipped into bed and pulled the quilt up over my head, shivering as I waited for the ghosts.

ॐ

THE FIRST TIME Da took Frankie and me to the top of Slieve Gullion to see the house after it was painted, we jumped up and down in delight.

"There it is," shouted Frankie, "I can see it clear as day!" His brown eyes, usually dark and intense, glowed in his small face. It was a look I had seen only once in a while when he looked at Lizzie. I linked my arm in his, and for once he didn't shake me off.

"Didn't I tell you?" cried Da. "Didn't I say you would be able to see it for miles!"

From the summit of Slieve Gullion, it drew your eye like a magnet. Indeed, it would become known far and wide as the Yellow House. When the sun shone it dazzled like a golden beacon, and even on the grayest of days it glowed through the mist like magic. Neighbor or stranger, everyone smiled when they looked at it. I imagined more merry ghosts had arrived to join Great-Grandda Hugh, and for a while the faceless ghosts left me alone.

That crisp, sunny morning in mid-October 1905, we had taken our time climbing up the mountain, as we always did, Da walking ahead of us carrying his blackthorn stick, Cuchulainn at his heels. Frankie scrambled over the rock face to an outcropping called Calmor's Rock, which had a cave beneath it. It was a treacherous climb over to it, but Frankie enjoyed showing off. I made my way more slowly, enjoying the sound of my feet squishing through ditches and scraping over the roughness of the rocks. Mother Gullion's cloak of summer bracken had shredded into tatters, revealing ancient scars and furrows carved from the ice age. A soft breeze rustled the trees, and waterfowl squawked from distant lakes. I breathed in the clean air until I thought my heart would burst.

We stood on the summit at the edge of Lough Berra, which everyone called the Lake of Sorrows on account of some sad story about a young man named Finn who dove in to find a ring for his love and came out—an old man with a gray beard—to find his love gone.

"Aye, Slieve Gullion has seen a lot of sad stories in her time," Da said, "but she keeps all her anger locked up in that volcano at her heart. She's beautiful on the outside but troubled deep down." He sighed. "Just like Ireland."

Frankie pushed me away and danced around, throwing his arms up in the air.

"Will she ever blow up, Da?" he shouted. "Whoosh! Flames and fire everywhere!"

"Let's hope not," whispered Da.

Frankie looked disappointed. He turned to look out over the sweeping landscape below.

"I'm going to own this all someday, Da," he said.

"Sure you've no need to be owning it," Da said gently, "you can enjoy it as much as the next man just by looking at it."

Frankie shook his head. "No, Da. You have to own it."

Da gave Frankie a queer look, and I jumped in to change the subject.

"Tell me about Great-Grandda Hugh again," I said. "Tell me how he won the Yellow House back."

Da smiled. He sat on the bank beside the lake and took out his pipe and lit it. He loved being asked to tell stories. He took two long puffs on his pipe and leaned back against a rock.

"Ah, he was a grand man, so he was," Da began. "He had red hair just like you and me, Eileen, and like the ancient king of Ulster Hugh O'Neill himself. Your great-grandda had green eyes so bright they could light your way on a dark road, and a way with him so convincing he could coax the stars down out of the sky."

Frankie scowled. He hated it when Da said I looked like Great-Grandda Hugh. Da took another puff from his pipe. Cuchulainn raised his head and twitched his ears as a rabbit scurried past, but he thought better of chasing him and lay down again.

"Did I tell you he was a gambler, too?" Da went on. "And he had great luck, so he did. That's how he won our house back from the Sheridans."

We all knew Great-Grandda was a gambler. Da had told us this story a hundred times before. This was his way of having us ask to hear it again.

"Tell us, Da," I said.

Frankie rolled his eyes and picked up a stick and threw it after the rabbit.

"Edwin Sheridan was from a well-to-do family of Quakers, but he was the black sheep," Da continued. "He drank, gambled, ran after women,

and did all the things Quakers are not supposed to do. It was probably
only a matter of time before he would have lost the house anyway. Easy
come, easy go, I suppose. His family had the house granted to them by
the English king. It was O'Neill land before that. There are still Sheridans
living around these parts. They own the big mills over in Queensbrook."
"Will they ever try and take our house back, Da?" I said.
Da shook his head. "No chance of that, darlin'. But if they try, sure
won't you be the one to drive them off? You're marked to be an O'Neill
warrior, love. Those green eyes make you special. You're the one to carry
on the O'Neill legacy."
Frankie, who was busy throwing stones into the lake, swung around.
"I'm fiercer than she is, Da," he shouted. "Why can't I be the warrior?
If the Sheridans ever try to take our house back, I'll fight them and kill
them!"
"Ah, sure you'll make a fine warrior, too, lad," Da said. "Isn't that why
we gave you the name Hugh?"
Frankie shrugged. "It's only my middle name. Why couldn't it have
been my first name?"
Da sighed. "Ah, well, your mother overruled me on that one, son. Said
she wouldn't let me fill your head with all the O'Neill legacy talk. She
wanted you to be your own man."
Frankie rolled his eyes. "I'll always be my own man," he said. "And if I
want to be a warrior, then that's what I'll be. And I'll carry on the O'Neill
legacy better than her," he said, pointing to me.
He was defiant like that, Frankie. I just smiled at him when he went off
on one of his tantrums. I knew that no matter what, I was Da's favorite.
On the other hand, kind and gentle as Ma was with me and Lizzie, she
was always hard on Frank. She expected more from him, always quizzing
him about school and correcting his manners. I supposed it was because
he was a boy and more would be expected of him in the world. I also
suspected deep down that Ma pushed him harder because she loved him
more. It was a thought I always sent away as quickly as it came.
Looking back on it, I can see that Frankie and I acted the way normal
brothers and sisters do with each other. We fought each other at home,
but when it came to outsiders we formed a solid union and defended
each other. I loved my brother, and I knew that deep down he loved me.
We were O'Neills, and no one was going to get the better of us.
A sudden noise of wings beating above us stopped all our talk, and we
looked up.

"It's the geese, Da," Frankie and I shouted together. "Look, it's the geese!"

Da grinned. "Aye, the wild geese."

We strained to see a flock of geese flying in a V wedge over our heads. Every year at about that time, they flew south through a corridor between two mountains known as the Gap of the North, which in olden times marked the division between Ulster and the rest of Ireland.

"There they go," said Da, shading his eyes with his hand, "the flight of the Earls."

"Who were the Earls, Da?" I said.

"They were the great O'Neills and other brave men who fled Ireland in 1607 after nine years of war."

"And where did they go?"

"Spain, Argentina, all points of the globe. But we remember them every year when we see the geese. The geese are a lucky sign to those who see them."

We were all quiet as we descended Slieve Gullion that day, lost in our own thoughts. My imagination ran in circles with visions of fighting O'Neills, and menacing Sheridans, and geese flying to faraway places in the world. My mind eased when I saw the Yellow House and my lovely, smiling ma standing at the door.

"Youse took your sweet time," she said in that husky voice of hers. "I had the dinner ready an hour ago."

My heart swelled with a sudden love for my beautiful ma.

I broke out in a run. "We saw the geese, Mammy," I cried as I threw my arms around her waist.

"I saw them, too," she said.

"Da says they're a lucky sign."

Ma hugged me but said nothing.

2

I sometimes wonder if it's better for the bad things to happen all at once rather than little by little, like blood seeping out of a wound. When they happen all at once, if the shock of it doesn't kill you, you might at least stand a chance of rearing up and fighting back. But when they come on you slowly, one thing creeping after another, it wears you down so that you might as well be dead when they finally end, because you have no strength left to resist.

Our troubles began to creep in on us, stealthy as spirits, one Sunday night late in the following year. We were all in the kitchen waiting for Ma to serve up Sunday tea.

"Will you hand me over the pie, Tom?" she said.

Da took down a towel from a hook beside the fireplace and reached in among the turf bricks to retrieve the iron skillet that held the baked apple pie. He pulled it out by the handle and turned to bring it over to the kitchen table.

Suddenly, the skillet fell to the stone floor. The lid flew off, and hot applesauce and brown pastry scattered out of it. Cuchulainn ran over to sniff the mess.

"Ah, Jaysus," said Da. "I'm sorry, Mary, it dropped out of my hand."

Ma said nothing but took a broom and pan and swept up the remnants of the pie.

"Och, Ma, can we not save any of it?" pleaded Frankie. He loved apple pie.

"We're not that poor yet we have to be eating off the floor," Ma snapped. "Get the dog out of the way."

Da sank back down into his chair beside the fireplace. He studied his right hand, turning his wrist this way and that. "I took a weakness in my hand," he muttered to no one in particular. "It's grand now."

But it was not grand. By the spring of 1907, Da's hands had grown weaker. I could see plainly that they were no longer the hands Da once had—slender and white like the stems of flowers. You would hardly recognize these hands. His fingers grew gnarled and crooked like the branches of an old tree. Hands like these belonged on a workingman, a man who had done hard labor all his life. They did not belong on an artist like my da. I imagined that a bad fairy had come in the middle of the night and stolen Da's hands, replacing them with these grotesque things. I knelt up at my window at night and prayed to Mrs. Gullion to take away the bad fairy's spell.

Ma spent evenings rubbing Da's hands with liniment, cradling them in her own, and humming the tune called "The Spinning Wheel" she used to sing to us as babies. The smell of the liniment was strong, like disinfectant.

Sometimes Da cried, the tears flowing down his thin face.

"I'm sorry, Mary," he said.

"Ssh. Things will be all right."

"I can do nothing on the farm these days." He gazed up at her sadly.

Da had always struggled to make a go at farming, but the truth was that he was not fit for it. He was not lazy, my da, he just didn't have the persistence it took to run a farm. He never got a fair price for his crops or his cattle. He sold off the sheep because he could not stand the thought of slaughtering the lambs every spring. He himself admitted that he was a soft touch. My da was born a dreamer, not a farmer.

"I had to put a mortgage on the house," he whispered one evening as she was rubbing his hands.

Ma dropped his hands. Her face turned white, then red.

"You did what?" she cried.

Da's shoulders sagged. "I'm sorry, love," he whispered. "It was that or sell what was left of the land. It was the only way to pay off the debts from last year and buy new seeds for planting, and give us a bit of money to live on . . ." Da's words trailed off.

Ma picked up his hands again and began rubbing them fiercely with the liniment. I wondered if she thought she could make his hands better. Didn't she understand the real wound was in his heart, not his hands?

"We'll see," was all she said.

ುರ

THE NEXT MORNING, Ma hitched Rosie to the cart and jumped up to take the reins. I had never seen her like this before. Her face was set as firm as granite.

"Get your coat, Eileen, and come with me," she commanded.

Frankie ran out of the door, his face dark. "What about me?" he cried.

Ma hesitated for a moment. Then she said, "No, Frank, stay and help your da mind Lizzie."

"But that's *her* job," spat Frankie, pointing at me.

"It's your job now," Ma said, her voice cold, "and that's enough back talk. Get in, Eileen."

"Where are we going?" I whispered.

"To the bank," she said. "We're going to get this house back."

I climbed into the cart and Ma chucked the reins. Rosie began her slow trot out through the broken gate and down the hill toward the village. It was a blustery spring day. Young buds emerged on trees, holding their ground defiantly against the strong breezes. Pale clouds mottled the sky, and a weak sun shone through their scrim. I wondered why Ma had brought me with her instead of Frankie. It would have been natural for her to bring him since he was the oldest and, as I believed deep down, her favorite. So I was delighted that she had chosen me instead. I stole a glance at her. She sat erect in the cart. She wore her best hat, the one she always wore to mass on Sundays, the one I was told she had worn when she married Da. It was made of brown velvet with silk flowers sewn on the side of it, a brown grosgrain ribbon around the brim. When Ma wore this hat, her back straightened up, as it did now, and she grew an inch taller. The hat transformed her into the person she used to be: the daughter of a prosperous landowner—a person who deserved respect.

I thought we were going to the bank in Glenlea, but Ma drove straight through the village main street without stopping. We passed Kearney's pub at a trot, then Quinn's Chemists and Mary Moloney's grocery shop. Mary was sitting on a chair outside the shop door, and she waved as we passed. I waved back, but Ma paid no attention. Some of my schoolmates, off for the Easter holidays, leaned against the wall, and they waved up at me, too. I waved back and smiled, proud to be seen sitting beside my beautiful mother. Some of the village men doffed their hats, but the women just stared, as they always did. No matter how long she had lived in Glenlea, the villagers still treated her as an outsider. It didn't occur to me then that she was an outsider not because she was not born there, but because she was different. My ma was a lady, and they recognized it. I smiled and moved closer to her.

We drove on to Newry, the biggest town in the area, which sat on the border between Counties Armagh and Down. I had been there only a few times before. The streets were filled with people, carts, and bicycles. It was market day, and people were enjoying themselves. Ma turned off the main road and crossed the bridge over Newry Canal. Bright boats and barges were tethered against the banks, their flags fluttering in the breeze. I craned my neck to look at everything. We drove on into the main part of the town, a large square with a clock in the middle. A big golden tea-pot hung from a wall above one of the shops. I looked up at it in delight, remembering it from past excursions. I had always loved it. I smiled up at Ma, but she paid me no attention. She slowed the cart to a stop and stepped down. I followed her. She called to a young boy and handed him Rosie's reins along with some coins. He led the horse and cart away. I was amazed at Ma's command of things.

The Royal Bank of Newry seemed to my young eyes as big as Newry Cathedral and just as frightening. It was built of granite, with stout stone columns standing on either side of its heavy oak doors. Ma took my elbow and led me up the steps and in the door without so much as a by-your-leave to anybody. I felt her determination burning through my arm where she gripped me. I looked up from the marble floors, past the high arched windows to the carved ceiling, and felt myself shrink. I moved closer to Ma. The customers were well dressed and smelled of perfume and tobacco. They all stood just as erect as Ma, as if they were in a pantomime. Many of them turned to stare at us and whisper as Ma swept straight up to the front of the big room. She stopped in front of a grim, thin-faced woman who sat on a stool high up behind the counter.

"I need to speak to the manager," said Ma, nice as you like.

The woman stared at her. "I beg your pardon?" she said.

"Mr. Craig. I am Mary O'Neill. Please tell him I wish to see him." Ma's tone was sharper than that of any priest giving out a big penance.

The woman jumped off her stool as if she were on fire. "Wait here," she snapped.

Ma and I sat on two wooden chairs at the side of the counter. Customers stared at us openly now. One or two of the men doffed their hats, and Ma nodded back. It was clear to me that they knew who she was even all the way over there in Newry. My ma must be very important, I thought, and I sat up straighter.

After a while, a short, thin man in a pin-striped suit and oiled hair came over. He extended a small white hand to Ma.

"Ah, Mrs. O'Neill," he said, "what a lovely surprise to see you. Why, I remember when you used to come here as a little girl with your father . . ."

Ma put out her hand. She had put on gloves over her callused red hands. Poor Ma, she had not been reared for the rough work of farming. She shook his hand briefly and stood up. "Yes," she said, cutting his blather short, "I am here on urgent business, Mr. Craig. May we speak in private?"

Craig looked at a sudden loss. He was obviously not used to people interrupting him. I stared in awe at Ma.

"This way," he said as he turned on his heel.

We followed him into a big, dusty office. Piles of paper covered the desk and tables and chairs. I wondered how he ever found anything. The walls were covered with black-and-white photographs: men in top hats wearing banners and shaking hands or cutting ribbons; well-dressed couples around a big dining table; drummers marching with lilies in their caps. Protestants, all of them. I clenched my fists as I stood behind Ma and hoped these people would not invade my dreams.

Craig dusted off a chair for Ma and sat behind his desk, peering at us over the pile of papers. "I hear your husband is not well," he said, and clucked his little tongue like a hen.

Ma ignored him. "I understand my husband has taken out a mortgage on our house," she said.

Craig leaned back in his chair. "Yes, yes," he said. "He was lucky to get it. We do not grant mortgages lightly these days, particularly to . . ."

"To Catholics," Ma put in sharply.

"That has nothing to do with things," Craig snapped back, "but it would not have been granted save for your father's connection to the bank."

"I want it removed," said Ma, without waiting for him to finish. "I am prepared to sell off more of our land to meet the obligation and give us some cash. I wish to keep a few acres to graze our cattle and raise the hens, but I am prepared to sell the rest. I am sure buyers can be found?"

Craig sat straight up in his chair. He chuckled, shook his head, and as if talking to a child said, "But my dear Mrs. O'Neill, the remaining land will not bring enough money to pay the mortgage. You see, Mr. O'Neill . . ."

Ma's face turned red. "Mr. O'Neill sold that land to John Browne for next to nothing, and well you know it, Mr. Craig. I intend for you to sell the remaining land at a fair price. This is what I will take and nothing less."

Ma leaned over and lifted a gold-nibbed pen from Craig's penholder, took a pad of paper, and wrote something on it. Then she shoved it toward Craig. "This is the minimum amount I will take per acre," she said.

Craig reached for the pad, read it, and raised one thin eyebrow.

"I, I, er, don't know if we can get close to this. This is a large amount," he said. Then he leaned back in his chair and bared his small teeth in a smile. "Would you not do better to go to your father? I'm sure if he knew the circumstances . . ." He let the words hang in the air, but Ma ignored them.

"I'm sure you can find a suitable buyer, Mr. Craig," Ma said, smiling at him with no humor at all. "I have great faith in you."

Craig barked at the woman behind the counter to fetch some papers. We waited while he made a great show of filling in particulars. When he was finished, he folded the papers and handed them to Ma.

"Mr. O'Neill will have to sign," he said, all business now.

"He will," said Ma, putting the papers in her bag and standing up. She put out her gloved hand to Craig, and he hesitated before he took it.

"Thank you for your time, Mr. Craig," Ma said. "And by the way, Billy is doing just grand, in case you wanted to know."

Craig's face turned pale. He said nothing. Ma shoved me out of the office and pulled me through the bank foyer and out the front door.

"Why would he care about Billy?" I said, unable to picture a connection between this little man and big simple Billy with his tin whistle.

"He's Billy's da," Ma said, a bitter edge to her voice. "Not that you would ever know it. He disowned Billy long ago."

We walked to the corner in silence. The young lad saw us coming and hurried for the horse and cart. We climbed in and Ma chucked the reins.

I was starving all the way back to Glenlea, but I was afraid to ask Ma to stop. For one thing, she was so caught up in her own thoughts that I doubted she would even hear me, and for another thing, I was suddenly afraid I would be showing weakness. So I put my arms over my stomach to stifle the growling and wondered for a while about how so small a man as Mr. Craig could have a son as big as Billy.

I glanced at Ma now and then as she drove. I had always sensed there was something more to her that she kept hidden from us. I had glimpsed it now, and inwardly I wondered if it was my ma and not my da who was the O'Neill warrior. Then I realized the lesson she was teaching me was that a woman can be no less a warrior than a man.

ௐ

DA SIGNED THE papers and the land was sold. The bank removed the mortgage from the house and we settled into our own peaceful world. Ma smiled and talked a lot more than she had ever done, and my da talked less. Ma told us stories about her childhood growing up in the big house outside Newry, a topic she had never touched on before. Frankie and I were bursting with questions, and she answered us patiently, her eyes lighting up occasionally at some happy, silly memory.

The Music Men continued to come even though Da could no longer play the fiddle. Instead he joined in on the bodhran, thumping away at the drum with his broken hands, and although he smiled and sang once in a while, I could tell his heart was no longer in it.

The Music Men brought news from the outside. There was talk of a world war, and fear of it had left Home Rule stalled in its tracks. Republicans, supporters of Home Rule, were getting more and more frustrated and restless, even though their leader, John Redmond, tried to restrain them. Meanwhile, Ulster opposition to a united Ireland under Irish rule continued to fire resentment against the Catholics. There were stories of Catholic tenants being pulled out of their houses by Protestant landlords. But we owned our house free and clear, I told myself, so they could not touch us. I held on to that belief even as faceless ghosts came out of the darkness and laughed at me.

ௐ

AND SO 1907 slipped by softly, and I came to believe that we would be all right, that the bad spirits had done their worst. Ma and Da had made peace with each other. Lizzie had grown into a lovely child. She had blue eyes, and pale gold hair, and a smile so bright she dazzled friends and strangers alike. Old women put the sign of the cross on her forehead so that the fairies would not steal her away. Frankie and I went to school, although I could tell he was growing restless. There wasn't much more they could teach him, and he hadn't the patience to read a book. I, on the other hand, loved school and read every book I could lay my hands on.

In the spring of the next year, Ma's belly swelled, and I guessed another baby was on the way, even though no one had said a word as yet. Da arranged for a friend with a camera to take a picture of the whole family standing outside the house, and Ma set the photo on the big mantel in the kitchen.

I suppose we all get lulled into dreams born of our wishes. At the time, I fervently wished for us all to be happy and live together forever in the Yellow House. But I had been wrong. The bad spirits were not yet finished with us. And while we looked anxiously for signs of trouble outside, trouble itself began from within.

It was coming up on Halloween of 1908. Lizzie had not been herself for days. Her bright smile and chatter dimmed, and she turned fussy and tearful. Even Frankie couldn't coax a laugh out of her. One October afternoon, Frankie and I came home from school to find Dr. Haggerty from the village just climbing down from his pony and trap. His shoulders hunched over with the cold, and he clutched a small leather bag in one hand. I grabbed Frankie's arm, but he shook me off. We followed the doctor through the front door. Ma sat by the fire holding Lizzie while Da held a rag to the child's forehead. Something was very wrong. Ma's face was strained as she rocked Lizzie and sang to her—the old lullaby called "The Spinning Wheel." The song had a gentle, soothing melody that always calmed us as we drifted off to sleep.

Da didn't even offer the doctor the usual cup of tea to ward off the cold. The doctor took off his coat and hat and knelt beside Lizzie to examine her, feeling her head and throat with his fingers, taking out his stethoscope and listening with an intent but unreadable expression. He asked Ma a few questions about how long Lizzie had been sick and what her symptoms were. Sighing, he opened his bag and took out a brown bottle and handed it to Ma.

"Give her a tablespoon of this twice a day. There's not much else I can do," he said hoarsely. "I've been out all over the countryside the last few days. So many children sick. I can come back to look at her in a few days. But I would advise she go to hospital now."

Ma flinched. "But we've no money for a private hospital," she said. "We've hardly enough to pay you."

Dr. Haggerty reached for his coat and hat. "There's always the Fever Hospital, Mrs. O'Neill," he said. "They do not charge."

"But that's part of the workhouse," cried Ma, "where they treat the paupers. God knows what they do to people in there."

The doctor shrugged and tipped his hat. "I'll come back as soon as I can," he said, "but there's so many . . ."

He let the words trail off as he went out the door. I followed him and watched him drive down to the gate, the cart wheels grating on the gravel. The sun had already set, and the short October day had vanished. I turned and went back into the house.

ʘ◊ʘ

THE NEXT MORNING, Lizzie's fever was no better, and Ma handed her to Da. She went upstairs and came down wearing her coat and best hat and gloves. She nodded at Frankie and me. "Get your coats. We're going out."

I looked from her to Da, but Da said nothing. "Hurry now," said Ma.

We were out the gate and on the road to Newry before I dared to ask Ma where we were going.

"On a visit," was all she said.

I wondered if we were going to the bank again to borrow money from Mr. Craig. But the day was Saturday, and I wasn't sure if it was even open. I shrugged and sat back. I supposed I'd know the answer when we got there. It was a fine crisp morning. The countryside was painted in browns and golds, and the leaves fell from trees as we passed, drifting like feathers down to earth. I turned around and looked back at Slieve Gullion. My lovely mountain was shedding her bracken cloak, and here and there patches of scarred granite, like gray wrinkled skin, were exposed amid the mossy grass.

We turned off onto a road that ran around Newry, so I knew we were not going to the bank. The road narrowed to a winding, country road overgrown on both sides by trees and bushes.

At length we turned in through an open iron gate and up an avenue with trees lining either side of it. As we came out into a clearing, I saw a huge stone manor house. The main house was three stories high with a low wing on either end. It looked like a great stone bird sitting there with its wings outstretched. But the arched windows made me shiver. I felt eyes watching me. Ghosts, maybe.

Ma stopped the cart and stepped down, straightening her coat and hat. Without a word she marched toward the house, sighing and clucking her tongue as she looked at the weed-filled flower beds spanning the front of the house. She went up the three stone steps, Frankie and me following at a distance, and raised and lowered the heavy iron knocker on the front door. Ma waited and then knocked again, with more force.

All was quiet except for the rustling of leaves against the grimy windows and the sound of our own breathing. At last the door creaked open and we heard grunting and coughing from behind it. Staring at us was an old man in a hunting jacket that had seen better days. He was stout, with a florid face, grizzly gray whiskers, and small brown eyes. He looked at us with disgust, as if we were some kind of vermin that had arrived at his doorstep.

"Hello, Father," Ma said, her voice quiet but firm.

The old man stared at her, and recognition dawned slowly on his face. But even so, the contempt remained.

"I suppose you want to come in," he said at last, standing back and opening the door wider. He turned on his heel and was swallowed up in the cavernous darkness of the hallway.

Ma followed him, and Frankie and I crept along behind her. I jumped as the old grandfather clock in the hall chimed. The place smelled of the damp and of boiled dinner and brandy. We followed him into a big study with heavy furnishings and thick velvet curtains that let in hardly any light. He sat down in an armchair, picked up a glass from a side table, and began to drink. Two old dogs lay motionless at his feet. He waved his hand at Ma to find a seat. Frankie and I may as well have been invisible. We sat on an old sofa.

"What do you want?" he growled. "If you're looking for dinner, it's the cook's day off. Would you like a drink?"

Ma shook her head. "I have not come for hospitality, Father," she said.

"And what have you come for?" he said. Then he turned to Frankie and me and studied us for a long time. "The girl is an O'Neill brat by the look of her," he grunted, "and the other one, well, who knows who he takes after? Not the Fitzwilliams, at any rate. I hear you have one more at home, and another in the oven, I see!"

"I'm a proud O'Neill," I declared, "and so is my brother!" I don't know where I got the courage to speak up, but I was determined to protect Frankie's pride at that minute. The truth of the matter was that the old man was half-right. Frankie did not look much like the O'Neills, but God help him, he was the spit of the old man in front of us.

"This is Frank and Eileen," Ma said, her voice unusually high, "and I also have another daughter at home."

"Catholics!" he snarled.

He reached for the decanter and poured himself another drink. Frankie glared at him, his fists thrust in his pockets. I put my hand gently on his arm, but he shrugged me off. I shifted on the coarse horsehair sofa and looked around. There were hunting prints everywhere, but on a table in the corner sat a black-and-white photograph of a handsome woman with two young girls kneeling beside her. They were all wearing white lace dresses. I wondered which girl was Ma.

"It is about my other daughter, Lizzie, that I have come to see you," Ma said. "She is sick with the fever and needs medical attention."

"Have you no doctors over in that godforsaken place?" snapped her da.

"We do," Ma said quietly, "but she needs a hospital."

"What's wrong with the Fever Hospital?" he said. "Not good enough for you and your brats?"

Tears welled in Ma's eyes. I could see she was losing her hold on things.

"She'll get no care in that place," she cried. "She needs a private hospital and, well, we have no money for it. That's why I've come to you. Please, Father, will you not help us?"

Ma sobbed full tilt now, but the oul' feller's face did not soften one bit. He was the image of the devil, I thought.

"Please?" Ma said again.

Her da looked at her. "You've some neck on you, girl, coming here for charity after the disgrace you brought on this house. It was your carryings-on that killed your mother, God rest her soul. "

Ma bowed her head. "Mama would have found kindness toward me. She knows what it's like to lose a child."

The old man rose from his chair. He coughed and spat into the fireplace.

"Is it not enough for you that I saved you from being thrown out of your house!" he growled.

"I know you helped Tom get the mortgage, and I am grateful for that, Father," said Ma. "That's why I thought you might . . ."

The old man sighed. "Bring the sick child here and I will see she is taken care of," he said.

Ma's face lit up. But he was not finished.

"On one condition. You leave that fool of a man you married and come back to live here." He glared at Frankie and me. "And bring them with you if you must."

The light went out of Ma's face. She stood up and smoothed out her skirt.

"We'll be going now," she said.

Her da sank back in his chair and grunted. "I suppose you know your own way out," he said. As we went down the hall, we heard him mutter. "You always were an ungrateful girl."

We drove home in silence. Darkness gathered around us long before we reached Glenlea. The strength I felt in Ma when we drove home from the bank that day had ebbed away. Now I sensed she was fragile as a blade of grass, trying desperately to hold herself straight against the wind. I was glad to see the welcoming lights of my beloved Yellow House flickering in the dark. I could not wait to hug my da.

∞

DA ALWAYS SAID crows were a sign of bad luck. They appeared in advance of the banshee, he said, the spirit that comes to carry the dead away. I was afraid of crows. I watched them now as they circled above our cart, swooping and squawking in the spitting rain. I moved closer to Da. All along the road that led to Newry, smoke rose from cottage chimneys and candles flickered on the windowsills. It was Halloween night, and the souls would soon be up and wandering about the land. I felt a strange kinship with them.

Lizzie had grown worse during the previous night. By morning, she lay in Ma's arms limp as a rag doll. By noon, P.J. was sent for. Da was so distracted with grief that Ma thought we needed P.J.'s steady hand. By late afternoon, we were all bundled into P.J.'s cart. Ma sat beside P.J., with Lizzie wrapped in a blanket in her arms. Frankie and I huddled next to Da in the back of the cart, mute as nesting birds. We had all insisted on going, even though Ma shouted at us to stay home. Ma had never before shouted at us. The pain of it hurt more than if she had slapped us.

The Newry Workhouse and Fever Hospital sat high up on a hill just outside the town. I found out later that most workhouses were built high up so they could be seen from all directions by the poor creatures searching for shelter within them. An immense gray stone wall surrounded the building, like a moat around an evil castle. P.J.'s cart was bigger than ours and his horse much stouter than our Rosie, but even he strained in his reins as he climbed the last quarter mile up the hill. He slowed down almost to a crawl, as if he did not want to arrive at this awful place any sooner than we did.

P.J. steered the cart through a tall iron gate and into a courtyard in front of the main workhouse building. He jumped out and came around to help Ma and Lizzie down, the rest of us stumbling out behind them. As we stood in a row looking up at the gray limestone building with its narrow, barred windows, I imagined accusing eyes staring back at me. I moved closer to Ma. Lizzie whimpered softly. Ma swayed backward, and P.J. caught her and steadied her.

"Come on now, love," he whispered.

A heavyset matron met us inside the door. She looked down at Lizzie and heaved a sigh that came out like a pig's snort. She turned and called out to a tall nurse in a white, starched cap, "Another one. Take them into the waiting room."

She walked away from us. I wanted to run after her and pound on her fat back and tell her we were the O'Neills, descendants of the great O'Neill, and we were not to be treated like that. P.J. must have sensed my anger. He put a firm hand on my shoulder and steered me down the corridor. The place smelled of vomit and disinfectant. We shuffled along the worn linoleum, our shadows casting strange shapes on the gaslit walls. The waiting room was filled with people. There was nowhere left to sit down, so we stood at the back of the room. Curious faces turned to look at us. I fought back the bile that rose in my throat at the sight of the thin, whimpering, yellow-faced children with the mark of death clearly on them. I could not imagine what was going through Ma's mind. Her worst fears of the stories of the Fever Hospital were expressed in the sight of the ragged, desperate people staring at us with hollow eyes.

Suddenly Ma straightened herself up and marched up to the desk at the front of the room the way she had done in the bank. My spirits lifted. Surely they would recognize Ma for the important woman she was. But the pinch-faced duty nurse glared at her and pointed to the back of the room.

"You'll wait your turn like everybody else," she snapped.

P.J. went up and put his arm around Ma's shoulder. He led her back to where we stood. He looked so comical, I thought, reaching up to Ma's shoulder like a wee leprechaun. But there was no mirth in the thought. I looked into Ma's eyes, expecting to see her crying, but what I saw was fury. Her eyes blazed as she stared at Da. Poor Da put his head down and twisted his cap in his gnarled hands. Frankie followed Ma's gaze, her fury echoed in his own eyes. I leaned against the wall and stared down at my boots.

At last it was our turn. The tall nurse came in and looked from Lizzie to Frankie and me.

"Is it the three of them?" she said. Her voice was quiet. I sensed a bit of pity in it, and also exhaustion. Instinctively I shrank away from her.

"No," I said, "just her," nodding toward Lizzie.

The nurse put out her arms to take Lizzie, but Ma would not let her go.

"No," she cried, "I will stay with her."

The nurse sighed. "It's not possible, missus," she said gently. "There are so many sick children in the ward, we have it quarantined, you see. Just give her to me now, we'll look after her."

With P.J.'s help, the nurse wrested Lizzie from Ma's arms. The child woke up and began wailing. It tore my heart in two to hear her.

"I'll wait here, then," Ma said weakly. "You'll tell me the minute there is news?"

"It's best if you go home and sleep, particularly in your condition," said the nurse, looking down at Ma's belly. Her voice was firm, but not unkind. "It will be a while before there is any news."

"I will wait as long as it takes."

The nurse shrugged. She turned and walked out of the room carrying Lizzie. It occurred to me later that none of us even got to touch Lizzie before the nurse took her away. We were all in such shock, none of us made a move toward her. We watched helplessly while she was carried out of the room, calling for Ma. We stood there for a long time after she had gone, until P.J. led us out.

"You can stay with us, Mary," he whispered. "You'll be closer than in Glenlea. And I'll be in here every day for word."

Da and Frankie and I said nothing as P.J. led Ma to the cart.

"We'll drive to my house first and let her off, and then I'll take youse home," P.J. said to Da. "After that, I'll send word as soon as we know anything."

We drove home that night in silence. There were no lights to welcome us at the Yellow House. Not even old Cuchulainn came out to meet us.

3

In the days that followed, P.J. came often, but he brought no news.
"Ah, sure no news is good news," he said over and over again.
I went to school, hoping to distract myself. Frankie refused to go. He left the house early in the mornings and did not come back until late. Then he ate his tea in silence and went to bed. I guessed he spent his days climbing Slieve Gullion. In the mornings before school, I cleaned out the henhouse and collected the eggs. In the evenings, I brought hay for the cattle in their stalls. Da hardly moved at all. He sat staring into the fire. I worked in order to exhaust myself, but sleep seldom came. I hadn't even the heart to kneel up on my window seat and talk to Mother Gullion. She knew what was wrong, I thought. She should make Lizzie well without my asking.

Early one Friday morning, I stood in the kitchen stirring porridge for breakfast when I heard the crunch of cart wheels on the frozen ground outside. It was too early in the day for P.J.'s regular visit. It had to be Ma and Lizzie. I dropped the spoon and ran to the door, Frankie scrambling behind me. Da stood up and reached for his jacket and smoothed his hair.

"They're home," I shouted. "They're home!"

Frankie and I pushed each other to get out the door first, Cuchulainn at our heels, the hens scattering from our path. And then we slid to a halt. P.J. helped Ma down from the cart. They both wore black armbands. There was no sign of Lizzie.

"Where is she?" blurted Frankie. "Where's Lizzie?"

I heard Da come up behind us, but I did not look round. P.J. put his finger to his lips to silence us and helped Ma toward the door. We parted to let them pass.

"A drop of strong tea with a dose of brandy, Eileen love," P.J. whispered over his shoulder.

I hardly recognized my ma. She had lost a stone of weight, and her face was white as linen. P.J. eased her into Da's armchair beside the fire and poked at the turf to stir the flames. I hurriedly poured tea and brandy into a mug and brought it to her, but she made no move to take it.

"Here, Ma," I whispered.

I set the mug down beside her and took her hands. They were freezing. I tried to rub some warmth into them.

"Let her be, now," said P.J.

He rose and came over to sit at the kitchen table beside Da. I poured tea and brandy for them. Frankie stood with his back against the dresser, staring from P.J. to Ma and back again.

"They're only after telling us the news last night," P.J. said. His voice was a whisper. "Bastards. The child had been dead since Tuesday, so it seems. They had already buried her by the time they told us. Had to bury them quick, they said, on account of the quarantine."

"But . . . ," I began. Thoughts clashed in my head, but I could not get the words out. Why was she buried there? She belongs here at home with us. They can't keep her there. It made no difference that my tongue was strangled—they all knew what I wanted to say.

"Aye, a pauper's grave," spat P.J. He leaned back and lit his pipe, puffing furiously on it until he was ringed in a cloud of smoke. "Buried down there without as much as a by-your-leave from her family. Sure the poor have no rights at all, none at all." He looked at Da, whose eyes were swimming with tears. "No matter, Tom, we'll find her and bring her home, I swear we will."

Da only nodded.

A chill settled on the house, and I shivered. My teeth chattered and my hands shook. Cuchulainn put his head on Great-Grandda Hugh's empty chair and whimpered. I swore I heard Lizzie's laughter somewhere outside. I jumped and ran to the window, but all I saw was the frozen fields and leafless trees and Slieve Gullion barren and stark. A noise behind me startled me. Ma had risen from her chair and come over to the table. I swung around. She looked like a madwoman. Her hair floated around her white face like a banshee. Her eyes were red and smoldering. She pointed a bony finger in Da's face and screamed.

It was hard to make sense of the words. I heard "pauper's grave" and "money," and I knew she was blaming Da for Lizzie's death. Da stood up and tried to take her into his arms, but she shoved him away and ran up the stairs. There was silence.

"Give her time," whispered P.J. "Give her time."

ৎ৽

MY BROTHER PADDY was born on Christmas Day 1908, a few weeks after Lizzie's death. I thought it would bring the change in Ma we had been waiting for. A baby in her arms was all she would need, or so I thought. But Ma looked down at the baby as if he were a stranger. She would not even touch him. I had to warm milk for him and feed him from a bottle. P.J. brought his wife up to see if she could help. Mrs. Mullen said that women often go a bit mad after they give birth, but they get over it in time. We just had to talk to her, Mrs. Mullen said, and let her know everything was all right. But all the talking in the world seemed to make little impression on Ma. She had gone away from us, a faraway look in her eyes as if she were seeing another world entirely. Her thin fingers ground at her rosary beads, and she muttered words I could not understand. I wanted to shove the baby at her and make her take him. I wanted to shake her and scream at her to come back to us, but it would have done no good, either. She could not even be coaxed downstairs. Da went up and sat beside her and sang to her in the evenings, but she would turn her head away from him. Privately, I cursed her for hurting him that way. Then I prayed for forgiveness.

ৎ৽

MONTHS WENT BY, and then one morning in late August 1909, just after my twelfth birthday, I looked up from the chair by the kitchen fire where I sat feeding Paddy to see Ma standing staring at me. I jumped up. She had not been downstairs in months. And now here she was, dressed in her best coat and gloves and carrying a small suitcase. I was overjoyed, and then as quick as the joy came, it left me. Her eyes were blazing fire.

"Ma?" I cried. "Ma, what's wrong?"

"Nothing's wrong," she said in a voice I did not recognize.

Da came in the back door at that moment, kicking the soil off his boots. When he saw Ma, his face broke into a grin.

"Och, Mary," he said. "Och, Mary." And he went over to her, his arms outstretched.

But Ma backed away. "Get the cart, Tom," she said. "We're leaving. Where's Frank?"

Da dropped his hands. "And where are we going, love?" he said.

"I'll be leaving now, Tom," she said, her voice cool and steady.

Da gaped at her.

"And I'll be taking Frank with me."

Frankie, who had just come down the stairs, jumped as if he had been slapped.

"Why, Ma?" he said. "Where are we going?"

"I'm taking you home."

"But I am home," he said, "and so are you, Ma."

I pitied Frankie for the puzzlement I saw in his face.

"This is not your home, Frank," Ma said. "It never was. And he is not your da."

The words hung in the room heavy as a dying man's last utterance. They struck us as roughly as if we had been punched by an invisible fist. I doubled over from the pain of it. Then I looked at Frankie's face and all thought of myself disappeared. I will never forget the look of hurt and confusion and anger that settled on him. Tears filled his eyes, and then fury raged.

"Whose son am I, then?" he cried. "Whose?"

He swung around from Ma to Da. "Who's my da?" he cried. "Tell me!"

Ma remained calm. "It doesn't matter," she replied. "You are not his. You are my sin, and that is why God punished me by taking away Lizzie. They told me so."

"Who told you, love?" Da whispered gently.

"The voices," she said.

I had a sudden awful feeling. I stood on the edge of a world about to crumble.

"Is Da my da?" I cried.

Ma nodded. "Yours and Paddy's and Lizzie's." Then she sighed. "You can come with me, too, Eileen," she whispered. "I love you. But I can't bring Paddy. God is waiting to punish me again. God will take him, too."

I looked at my parents, studying them as if I had never set eyes on them before. What choice was this I was being given? Leave my poor da alone? Let my ma go away without me?

Da came over and put his arms around me. "Sure she doesn't know what she's saying, love. She's astray in the head with grief. She'll come to in time and we'll forget all this."

I knew even as he said it that we would never forget it.

"I'll stay with Da," I whispered.

"Fetch the cart, Tom," said Ma. "Take me home."

"But this is your home, Mary," whispered Da.

Ma looked at Da. Her eyes were flat and empty. "I'm sorry, Tom," she said, "but I had no right to be here. It's time I went back where I came from. Come on, Frank."

She picked up her bag and led Frankie out to the cart. Da followed, looking over his shoulder and nodding at me. "Just give her a wee bit of time," he said again.

I watched from the door as Da hooked Rosie up to the cart and started down the road toward the gate. Neither Ma nor Frankie looked back. Frankie's slight frame was stiff as a board, but I could see by the way Ma's shoulders moved that she was crying. Something didn't look right about her. Then I realized she was bareheaded. I looked up and saw it still hanging on the peg by the door.

"She left her hat," I cried out—but there was no one to hear me.

☙☙

THAT NIGHT, I thought back to Frankie's worms. When you split them in two they grow themselves back, he had said. Would the O'Neills grow themselves back? I wondered.

☙☙

THE WINTER OF that year was unremarkable. I had expected the skies to open and floods to wash away the land, or snow to come and freeze the whole world in place so that nothing moved. I had expected the birds to stop singing, the foxes to bury themselves in their holes, and the sun to refuse to rise. But none of this happened. Life and its rhythms went on as usual. Farmers tended their land, shops and pubs opened and closed, and the Music Men still came to the Yellow House. At first I was resentful. How could everything go on the same when Lizzie was dead and Ma and Frankie had gone away? Then I was angry. Why didn't anyone else seem to care what had happened to us? Why were other people allowed to laugh and dance and carry on while Da and I cried in our silent house?

In time I managed to separate my own grief from the outside world, and in time I allowed the world in again. When I turned thirteen, I stopped going to school. This small rebellion gave me the illusion of control over my life. I argued with Da that I had too much to do around the house and farm, and besides, I was not learning anything new at school. Da hadn't the strength to argue much.

"Your ma wouldn't hear of it," was all he said.

"Well, she's not here, is she?" I snapped.

ço

IN THE FIRST days after Ma and Frankie left, Da and I took turns standing at the window or door, listening for the sound of the cart that would bring them back. But no one came, and in time we stopped listening. P.J. had gone to visit them at Ma's daddy's house, but she refused to leave. Although I was angry with Ma for leaving us, part of me yearned to go and see her. I pestered P.J. to take me with him, but all he did was shake his head.

"She's in a bad way still, darlin'," was all he would say. Eventually, I gave up and stopped asking him. Surely she would be back with us before long.

Da and I did not speak to each other of what had happened for a long time. Paddy was a convenient diversion for us, as were the requirements of the farm. "Are the cows milked?" "The hens are slow laying the eggs this year." "The child is after spilling the food on himself."

One morning, about a year after Ma and Frankie left, I fought my way to the surface of a dream. The devil had me in his grip and turned the vise so tight that the pain burned like a welding torch deep into the core of my being. I awoke. The dream vanished, but the pain remained. The curse had begun. I recognized it right away. Ma had warned me about it when I was younger. Back then it had seemed like a vague thing, a thing to be borne in the future when I grew up, a thing that Ma would ease with her gentle voice and touch. But Ma was not here. Every month, she had said. Every month! I got out of bed and found a stray piece of paper and pencil and marked down the date. I passed the rest of the day in a trance, staying as far away from Da as I could. Anger and fear mixed in my mind, and I cursed Ma for leaving me alone. The child I had known was leaving. I did not know who I would become. I trembled on the threshold of the rest of my life. I allowed the child her final farewell that night, as she pulled the covers over her head and wept for her ma.

ço

I GREW TALLER and stronger. I became nearly as tall as Ma, and I had her build—long legs and a strong back. My red hair fell in a thick braid to

my waist. Unloosed from Ma's constant watch, I felt myself grow reckless. I became willful, refusing Da's orders and pleasing myself. I stopped
going to mass. I began to swear, enjoying the guilty pleasure of the ripe
words rolling on my tongue and the sour looks of the old biddies who
heard me. I delved into the excesses of my nature with robust curiosity:
I found I was quick to anger, quick to judgment, intolerant of stupidity
and arrogance, and impious. I was also playful, quick to laugh, and raven-
ous for life.

P.J. was the first to remark on the changes in me. "She's growing up,
Tom," I heard him say. "She'll need a strong hand to keep her in line."

"Aye," Da said, "maybe when Mary comes home . . ."

Like me, Da still held out hope that Ma and Frankie would one day
come home.

The Music Men provided diversion, and they all put up a good show
when they came. But something had changed that I couldn't put my finger
on. Terrence spoke less than usual. Fergus smiled a secret smile, as if to say
now we knew what trouble was like. Billy Craig was the only one to show
his true colors. He scowled at Da, his red face bloated with anger. He believed that Da had sent Ma away, and no one could tell him any different.
He banged around the room and grunted so much that the boys told him
to control himself or stop coming altogether. He did not come back.

One night after a music session, I sat down by the fire and looked
at Da.

"Tell me about Frankie," I said.

Da looked up at me, surprised. He started to wave his hand to dismiss
the question, and then he thought better of it. "What do you want to
know, Eileen?"

"Who is his da?"

"I don't know."

Rage roared up in me. "Don't lie to me, Da."

He gazed at me. "I'm not lying, darlin'. I don't know who his da was.
All I know is that I was in love with Mary, and when she came to me and
said she was in trouble and would I marry her, I never thought twice."

He paused and lit his pipe, stoking the tobacco with a gnarled finger.

"I knew there was a baby coming, but it was no matter to me. In fact, I
loved that baby for bringing Mary to me." He leaned toward me. "I loved
Frankie," he whispered. "I could not have loved him more if he was my
own flesh and blood. He was part of Mary, and he was the reason Mary
came to me."

Tears welled in his eyes and he blinked them away.

"But did you never ask her?" I whispered. "You know, about his daddy?"

"Ah, sure it made no difference to me," said Da. "If Mary had a mind to tell me, all well and good, and if she didn't, it was no matter." He sighed deeply. "Och, Eileen, we were so happy. You know, child, there's always one in the pair who loves more than the other, and that makes it enough for two. And anyway, I think your ma loved me just a little bit."

I was crying now. I sniffed back the tears. "She loved you a whole lot, Daddy," I whispered. "I saw it in her eyes every day."

"Aye, until the last day."

"She was astray in the head the last day. You said so. And I could see it for myself." I leaned forward and took his hands in my own. "She loves you still, Daddy," I said. "I'm sure of it."

I looked at Da now as if seeing him for the first time. His lovely red hair had turned white. In the months since Ma left, I had not noticed my da turning into an old man.

๑๑

WE NEVER FOUND Lizzie's grave, so P.J. and the boys arranged to have a headstone put in the field next to the house where Da's da and grandda were buried. Two angels were carved on the stone, and it faced out toward Slieve Gullion. I knelt there often in those days, talking to Lizzie, telling her not to be afraid.

While the days coming up to Christmas of 1912, and Paddy's fourth birthday, passed quietly and slowly at the Yellow House, the thunder of trouble rolled across the Irish landscape. P.J., Terrence, and Fergus talked of nothing else. The promise of Home Rule was fading under the growing threat of a world war. The English hadn't time for Ireland and her problems, Terrence said they were too worried about their own skins. Meanwhile the Ulster Unionist Covenant had been passed, declaring its fierce opposition to any kind of Irish rule in the North of Ireland. The growing rebellion down in the South was spilling over into the North, and the Ulster Volunteer Force, a quasi-military organization known as the UVF, was formed to oppose any rebellion in the North. There were stories of them throwing Catholics out of their houses and businesses and burning property. P.J.'s predictions were coming true—the violence was not just around Belfast anymore, but was drawing closer—Newry, Camlough, and Rostrevor.

"It's heating up," P.J. warned. "It's only a matter of time now."

"Until what?" I ventured.

P.J. bent and tapped out his pipe on the hearth. "Until the flames of war are all around us," he said.

"Och, don't be scaring the girl," Terrence said.

"I'm not scared," I said.

But I was. That night, the faceless ghosts came again to haunt my dreams. This time they carried torches of fire. I put my head under the sheets, but I could not blot them out.

∽⊙

THEY CAME IN the early hours of the morning of March 17, 1913, the feast of St. Patrick and a Holy Day of Obligation. St. Patrick's Day was a solemn day marked by mass and a closing of the pubs. To wear a shamrock or carry the Irish tricolor flag in Ulster was to invite trouble, even though the Protestants were free to bang their drums as loud as they wanted on their own day of celebration, the twelfth of July. So St. Patrick's Day usually passed quietly like any other religious feast day. But the one in 1913 was an exception.

I lay in bed, restless as always, waiting for the sun to rise over Slieve Gullion so I could get up and distract myself with work. At first I heard voices in the distance and the dull thud of feet on the road. I thought maybe I was still dreaming and sat up just to be sure. I looked over at Paddy in his bed beside mine, but he slept peacefully. Da must have heard the noise. The bedsprings creaked in the next room as he got up, and I heard the shuffle of his feet on the floor as he pulled on his trousers. I tiptoed to the door of my room and opened it. Da felt his way along the landing in the dim light.

"Who is it, Da?" I whispered.

He swung around and put his finger to his lips. "Och, probably just some young fellows home after a night on the drink," he said, "making up for the pubs being closed tomorrow. Go back to bed now, darlin', and watch Paddy."

But I did not believe him, and I knew he did not believe it himself. I waited until he was down the stairs, and I crept out onto the landing. The dying embers still glowed in the hearth and cast shadows on the walls. Cuchulainn roused himself from his place beside the fire and padded to the front door behind Da. I held my breath and waited.

A loud thud broke the silence as a stone hit the front door. Da jumped back.

"Who's out there?" he shouted.

Voices grew louder, male voices, shouting and cursing.

"Open the door, Tom O'Neill," a voice called. "It's your friend Billy come to visit you."

"Jesus," Da muttered, "what's that eejit doing at this time of night?"

I relaxed. It was only simple Billy Craig come to play a trick on us. He had not come back to the house at all after the other Music Men told him to stay away from the music sessions. I supposed he was still angry with us over Ma's leaving. He had never been right in the head. He'd probably been out drinking and was egged on by some blackguards to come up and scare the daylights out of us.

Da opened the door. "What in God's name do you think you're doing at this hour, Billy," he began. "It's home in your bed you should be—"

Thud! Another stone hit the front door as Da spoke. Billy jumped back and looked around.

"We've come to teach you a lesson, Tom," he said, his voice high with excitement, "a lesson for sending Mary away. Haven't we, boys?"

I crept to the bottom of the stairs and could see Billy plainly. The earlier relief I felt had fled. In its place was a sinking, heavy fear deep down in my stomach.

"Come out, Tom," shouted Billy.

"Don't go, Da," I cried.

Da swung around. "Get upstairs, Eileen," he shouted. "Now!"

I had never heard Da raise his voice like that, and it startled me.

"Now!" he repeated.

I turned and fled up the stairs, but I stood on the landing to watch. I saw Da run into the kitchen and return with an old and rusty rifle that had rested for years on the mantel above the fireplace. It had belonged to Da's da. I had never seen Da touch it. I always supposed it was there as a keepsake only. I raced back down the stairs and hovered behind Da. The voices grew louder, and burning torches scorched the darkness. I saw the outlines of thick bodies running toward the house. A flame shot through the air and hit a window. It was followed by another, then another.

"Burn the fecking place," cried a voice. "Burn the fecking papists out."

A sizzling sound made me swing around. One of the torches had caught a curtain at an open window, and flames roared upward toward the ceiling. "Ma's curtains," was all I could think to say. "They're burning Ma's curtains."

Suddenly Da was just outside the door. His voice roared above all the others.

"You'll not take the O'Neill house as long as I'm standing," he shouted. "Youse'll have to kill me!"

A voice screamed, "No!" It was a scream from purgatory. I realized it was mine.

I watched Da fire the rifle, his gnarled hands gripping the metal, bullets flying helter-skelter into the darkness. I put my hands to my ears to drown out the noise. I watched his face glow in the flames as bright as the day he had ridden out of the sun carrying his lucky yellow paint. I watched him clutch his chest and fall backward from the open door into the hallway. I watched Cuchulainn run to him and stand whimpering over his limp body. I watched the look of horror spread across Billy Craig's big face as blood pumped from Da's chest. I watched it all as an observer watches a scene of horror from a distance, separate and apart, with no emotion and no involvement. I watched Billy bend, sobbing, over Da.

"I didn't mean for this, Tom," he cried, "only to frighten you a bit. I didn't mean for this." And then he shook Da like a rag doll.

Flames were everywhere now. I smelled scorched grass and bitter smoke. As if in a dream, I went upstairs and put on my coat over my nightdress. I didn't bother with my boots. Then I took Paddy from his bed and dressed him quickly. I led him downstairs and stood at the open door beside Da's body.

Paddy strained to get away. "Da," he cried. "Da."

Billy Craig shook me to my senses.

"Get out now, Eileen, and take the child. If they realize you're here . . . Come on now."

His big hands turned me around and shoved me into the kitchen.

"But Da," I cried. "I have to stay with Da." I pushed against Billy, but he would not move.

"I'll see to your da. Out the back door, and stay low. I'll distract them." He looked at me, his big face twisted with grief. He turned and reached for Da's fiddle from the shelf on the wall and the black-and-white photograph of the O'Neill family outside the Yellow House. Then, as an afterthought, he snatched Ma's hat from its peg. He shoved everything at me. "Here, darlin', take these. Go to P.J.'s house. Go on now, for God's sake."

The grass was wet under my bare feet as I stumbled away from the house in the direction of Slieve Gullion, one of my arms around Paddy and Da's fiddle and the photograph under the other. Paddy clutched Ma's hat. I got as far as Lizzie's headstone before I fell down. I lay down behind the low stone wall that enclosed the graves and cradled a weeping Paddy under my coat.

"Ssh, love," I whispered. "Ssh."

He quieted, as if he knew the danger. I watched as flames engulfed my beloved Yellow House. Never had she looked as bright as she did now, flames swirling in every window like giant kaleidoscopes. Da always said she should be a beacon of light in the darkness. If he could have seen her tonight, I thought. Maybe his soul was watching her along with Great-Grandda Hugh and the merry ghosts.

Looking back now, odd as it sounds, I remember I felt a flood of relief that night as I watched the Yellow House burn. All my worst fears had come true. Even the bad spirits must be out of tricks now. They had done their worst. The waiting was over. I remember hearing the distant bells of the fire brigades as they rushed toward the burning house. I remember lying flat in the grass as heavy boots thudded past me, making their escape. I remember the pride I felt that my da, Tom O'Neill, had died a warrior, and as his soul entered mine in that moment, a new warrior was conceived inside me. The legacy of the O'Neills had been passed on. I held the fate of my family, and my beloved Yellow House, in my hands.

Queensbrook Linen Mill

1913

4

Early on a May morning in 1913, I rode the tram from Newry up to Queensbrook to start work at the Queensbrook Spinning Mill. Paddy and I had moved in with the Mullens after we fled from the Yellow House. Now P.J. was taking me to start my first job. He sat with me, looking out the window and remarking on the lovely fields of flowers and how grand the mountains were. But I paid scant attention to him, lost as I was in my own thoughts. It had been a spring morning such as this when I rode with Ma to the Royal Bank of Newry and she had saved the Yellow House. How happy and proud I had been—the O'Neill family had overcome their troubles and would have a new beginning. Now I no longer believed the blather about spring and new beginnings and hope. I straightened my back against the hard wooden seat of the tram and followed P.J.'s gaze.

The tram, an electric one installed by the mill owners to bring in workers from outlying towns, rattled up a hillside as we approached Queensbrook. When we reached the top, I looked down on a lovely valley ringed by the Camlough Mountains and saw in the distance my beloved Slieve Gullion. But as the tram descended, dozens of gray buildings rose like hideous granite beasts out of the early morning mist. The tallest were four stories high, with gabled roofs and rows of windows marching in formation along the front. Chimneys, like cathedral spires, clawed the sky, belching clouds of gray smoke. Surrounding the cluster of buildings was a river, sparkling and innocent as the morning itself.

"There's a lovely wee village down there where the local workers live,"

P.J. said, ignoring the look of horror on my face. "It's a model village built by the mill owners. You'll see it better when you get the chance to walk around. Protestants and Catholics live in it side by side nice as you like, and not a hint of trouble. There's everything you'd be in need of there," he continued, "shops, churches, schools." He smiled, his red face crinkling up with merriment. "Ah, but there's no pub," he said, "and no police station or pawnshop, either. The Sheridans who own the mill are Quakers, and they don't believe in the drink. And without the drink, they're thinking there's no need for the pawnshop or the police station. A queer lot, the Quakers. Good people in their own way, I suppose, but they just don't understand the Irish."

I shot a look at P.J. Sheridan? The name sounded an alarm somewhere down deep inside me.

"Wasn't Sheridan the name of the boyo who lost the Yellow House to Great-Grandda Hugh in a game of cards?"

P.J. looked over at me. "Aye"—he nodded—"one and the same, an ancestor of the family that owns the mill."

The sick feeling of the worried child washed over me again. "I always thought they would come to take it back," I whispered.

P.J. patted me on the knee. "It wasn't the Sheridans as took it, darlin'," he said gently, "it was a crowd of Ulster blackguards." He shook his thick red mane. "Them and that eejit Billy Craig."

The men with the torches had all been caught. They were rogue members of the newly formed Ulster Volunteer Force, whose intent was to preserve Ulster for the Unionists and to fight with force any attempts to impose Home Rule. The band who attacked the Yellow House had been acting without orders. They were all jailed, except for Billy. His da, Mr. Craig at the bank, had managed to get him off. Some said Craig did it only to save himself from the embarrassment of having a son in jail and not because he had any love for Billy.

"They're all one and the same," I muttered, "Sheridans, Ulster Volunteers, Billy, they're all feckin' Protestants."

We left the tram and walked through the main gate of one of the buildings and up to a hut where a guard sat.

"This is Eileen O'Neill. She's to see Joe Shields," P.J. said. "He's arranged for her to start today."

Joe Shields managed the spinning mill, and P.J. knew him because he sometimes played with the Music Men at a pub in Newry. "A Protestant fellow," P.J. had said, "and brilliant on the accordion."

P.J. put his hand on my arm. "I'll be going, Eileen. You know how to find your way back on the tram now?"

I nodded. I was suddenly sorry to see him go. I wanted to call out after him not to leave me. But that would have been childish, and I was no longer a child. Instead, I grasped the tin lunch box P.J.'s wife had given me and followed the guard into the mill building and up the stairs.

The heat assaulted me even before we arrived at the top of the stairs. The guard led me into an enormous, noisy room filled with machines and workers. The heat in the room was stifling, and sweat began to ooze out of my skin. The smell of oil sickened my stomach. As I followed the guard to a small office in the corner of the room, I tried to take in everything I saw, but it was a blur.

"A new one for you," the guard said to a fat man seated behind a desk, "I forgot her name."

"Eileen O'Neill," I said more sharply than I intended. "P. J. Mullen sent me. I'm to see Mr. Shields."

The man behind the desk had a round face with cheeks streaked pink and purple. His black hair had receded, leaving bumps exposed on his white forehead. His arms were fleshy, and his fat white hands looked soft as a baby's. I supposed he hadn't done much hard work in his life, just sat here on his fat arse giving orders. He looked me up and down, eyeing the lemon cotton dress and white peep-toe shoes I wore. Mrs. Mullen had been delighted when she gave them to me. "We want you to look as well as the next girl up there, love," she said.

"I'm Joe Shields," he said at last, waving a fat arm at the guard to leave. "Sit down." He pointed to a chair. "So, I see you have no experience. If you had, you would not be coming here in a getup like that."

I looked down at my dress, unsure of what he meant.

"No matter," he continued, "I told P.J. I'd do him the favor. I'll give you a start. One week only. We're not the Sisters of Charity here. You'll have to show you can earn your keep."

I stuffed down the anger that rose up in me. A hundred defiant answers raced through my head, but I took a deep breath and lowered my eyes. "I'll do my best, sir," I said.

"Good," said Shields. "You'll start as a doffer. That's how all our young girls start. You'll be responsible for keeping the bobbins on the spinning frames going. You'll take off the full ones and put up empty ones. And you need to be fast. We don't want you slowing down the spinners." He stood up. "I'll get Miss Galway. She's the doffing mistress. She'll get you started. Wait here."

He went out, and I stared at the empty chair where he had sat. Spinning frames? Bobbins? It was a foreign language. I had no idea what he was on about. Sweat poured off me. Jesus, it was hot in there.

I soon found out what was wrong with my clothing. Miss Galway, the doffing mistress, looked at me in horror. Her thin lips opened wide, revealing buckteeth that put me in mind of an old donkey we once had at the Yellow House. I had to stop myself from smiling.

"Oh, that will not do!" she exclaimed. "Will not do at all!"

I looked up at her. She was a tall woman, six feet surely, reed thin and bony. She had a long face and a chin as sharp as a shovel, her black hair pulled back in a bun. She wore a long gray dress with a white collar, a heavy black apron, and laced-up brogue shoes. The shoes had seen better days, I thought; they were battered and shapeless.

"Come with me," she commanded.

I followed her out into the main spinning room, clutching my tin box. I saw now that the wooden floors were wet from the water that sprayed out from the spindles on the spinning frames. I hadn't noticed it earlier. Most of the women and girls were working in bare feet. They all had their hair tied up in scarves and wore the same heavy black aprons as Miss Galway. I looked down at my lovely lemon frock with its white collar and buttons all the way down the front, and my white peep-toe shoes, and blushed.

"Will you look at the cut of the frock?"

"Aye, and the shoes. She must think it's a garden party."

"I'll give her a day at the most!"

Raucous laughter followed me as I walked the length of the room to Miss Galway's office. I squared my shoulders and looked straight ahead. I noticed younger girls—some could not have been more than twelve years old. They scattered when they saw Miss Galway coming. There were a few boys as well, around the same age, gawking at me. I wanted to ask them what they were looking at, but I kept silent. I learned later that these children were half-timers, working mornings in the mill and going to school in the afternoons.

"Now then," Miss Galway said crisply, "here's an apron for you. I would advise you to take off your shoes and leave them here. And here's the picker to remove the bobbins." She handed me a queer-looking tool the shape of a spoon. "Josephine!" She motioned to a girl a bit older than me, with black matted hair and a pale face. "This is Eileen. She will follow you today, and you will show her how to change the bobbins."

Miss Galway turned to me with a thin smile. "Josephine is one of our most experienced doffers, aren't you, Josephine?" The girl gave her a surly nod. "You will do well to learn from her."

The girl scowled at me. She was in no mood to be teaching anybody, I could see. She shrugged and walked away toward a row of spinning frames. I followed her. The spinning frames were wide iron contraptions with rows of spindles that grinned out at me like grisly teeth. Two rows of spinning bobbins around which the flax threads were wound ran the length of the frame. The spindles spat out boiling water like devils hissing from hell. The frame clanked and roared like an animal that defied taming. A young woman, about twenty, operated two side-by-side machines. She was surprisingly calm as she glided back and forth along the length of the frames, smoothing the threads and spreading oil on hanks of flax waiting to be spun. I watched her, fascinated. I wondered if I could learn to run such a monster. I made up my mind that I could, and I would.

At lunchtime a whistle screeched, and the machines ground into silence. I picked up my lunch box and followed the crowd down the stairs and outside. The sun shone, but I shivered. Coming out of that hot, humid hellhole into the fresh air left me light-headed. I sat on a low brick wall that ran along the river and opened my lunch box. The cheese sandwich was dry as cardboard in my throat. No one spoke to me. I watched the crowds of workers come and go. Some sat along the wall by the river. Others spread themselves out on the grass near the mill pond. The women chatted and laughed. Men sat in small clusters, smoking and watching the women. It struck me that I had seen no men in the spinning room. Like anywhere, I supposed, all the men had the soft jobs bossing around the working women.

The afternoon passed slowly. The younger workers left, but Josephine stayed on. She never smiled once. I wondered how long she had been there doing that same job. I picked it up quickly. My height and my long arms made it easy for me to reach the top row of bobbins. By the end of the day, I did the work while Josephine watched me, hands on her hips. Miss Galway came over to give me her nod of approval.

"Well done, Eileen," she said. "I shall have a good report to present to Mr. Shields."

I suppose I should have been pleased, but I really wanted to tell her to go feck herself. Her smug voice sent shivers down my back. I was relieved when the closing whistle blew at six o'clock.

ରଡ

I SURVIVED THE first week at Queensbrook. Each day, the routine became a little easier. I got over the shock of the blast of heat and the smell of oil that slapped me each morning as I climbed the stairs to the spinning room. I swapped my lemon frock for one of Mrs. Mullen's gray smocks and a green head scarf. I wore my old boots but took them off as soon as I reached the spinning frames. I lined up the boots alongside all the other shoes in a dry corner of the big room. Miss Galway nodded her approval.

As the week wore on, I continued following Josephine around. I removed full bobbins and replaced them with empty ones while she stood there with one arm as long as the other. It didn't take long before I realized she was a bit simple. She had been a doffer for eight years—ever since she started as a half-timer. The younger girls giggled at her and teased her. She should have moved up to a spinner long before now, they said, but she wasn't fit for it. I suppose I should have felt sorry for her, but I just shrugged. She was one less person ahead of me in the queue. I was determined to move up to the spinner's job as fast as I could. I watched the operators carefully, memorizing their every move so I would be ready when the time came.

We worked shifts from seven in the morning until six at night, with an hour off to eat lunch. That hour didn't count toward our shift. On Saturdays, we worked from seven until noon. We were off on Sundays. On the first Saturday morning, as I joined the other workers on our way up the stairs, I noticed that the mood was lighter. The girls and women smiled and joked. Some even tossed a smile at me—the first time that week. When the closing whistle blew at twelve o'clock, the machines ground to a halt and the women raced to snatch up their shoes. They flew down the stairs, jostling and pushing one another good-naturedly. As they ran, they tore off their black aprons and dull smocks and rolled them into balls, tucking them under their arms. They smoothed their bright summer dresses and chirped and laughed. I thought of the butterflies that used to swarm around the Yellow House in summer. Da had explained that they had transformed from wee brown grubs into beautiful creatures decked out in all their finery, but that they lived for only one day. I felt a stab of sadness as I thought of these gay, colorful girls creeping back to the cave of the mill on Monday, brown and dull as worms.

I stood aside and let them rush past me. I felt only a distant connection with them. I recognized my place among their gender, but I would not share their fate. I was no ordinary girl. I was Eileen O'Neill, and I was a warrior.

Joe Shields stood behind a table set up in the entryway, calling off names from a list. As their name was called, each worker came up to take an envelope from him and sign the list. I noticed that one or two of them made only a squiggle. What kind of people could not spell their own name? When my turn came, Shields held up the pay envelope in front of my face like a bone to a dog.

"Well, Miss Eileen," he said, "d'you think you deserve this?"

I wanted to scream at him that I deserved twice that much. I had worked like a slave all week. But I bit my tongue and lowered my head. "I hope so, sir," I muttered.

"The reports I have are very good," he continued, looking over at Miss Galway, who stood, arms folded, overseeing the proceedings. "I've been watching you myself. You catch on quick. I think we'll keep you for another week."

He grinned, exposing yellowed, uneven teeth. I suppose he thought he was a real comedian, torturing anxious young girls who needed the money.

"Thank you, sir. I'm grateful, sir" was all I said.

Satisfied, he handed me the pay envelope. "Don't spend it all at once, now."

I took it from him and hurried outside before my anger could explode. I ran across the bridge spanning the river and sat on the low brick wall to wait for the tram. Emotions buzzed through me. It was not in my nature to swallow my pride the way I had done with Shields. Even a year ago I would not have been able to do it. But now, I realized, there was something at stake. If I wanted the job, and the money it brought, I would have to keep my head down and my mouth shut.

I opened the envelope and slipped my fingers inside. I felt for the shillings and sixpences and the threepenny bits. I traced the raised outline of the queen's image on the coins, like a blind person reading Braille. I looked down and saw my name written on the envelope. Eileen O'Neill. Eileen O'Neill. An unfamiliar feeling flowed through me, warm and strong and alive. I realized it was pride. I had a job! I had earned money all on my own! Och, Da, can you see me now? Ma, Frankie? I'll come and take you away from that evil oul' man's place soon. The flush of pride

fueled my hopes, and suddenly they were boundless. I would work hard. I
would put up with the long hours and the heat and sweat. I would move
up from a doffer to a spinner. Maybe I would buy a sewing machine and
take on finishing work at home at P.J.'s house—hemming handkerchiefs
or tablecloths—for extra money. I would spend nothing. Soon I would
have enough to make a home for Paddy and Frankie and me and Ma. And
in time I would have enough to repair the Yellow House. I was giddy
with the thoughts. I smiled for the first time in months. I realized I was
happy. I was even happy with God. I looked up into the clear spring sky.
"Thank you," I said.

☙

ONE DAY, P.J. told me that Ma's da had put her in the insane ward at
the hospital. P.J. said news of Da's death had sent her over the edge, and
her father could no longer take care of her. I snorted angrily at that one—
oul' bastard cared for nobody but himself. I asked P.J. about Frankie, but
all he would say was that Frankie was still at the Fitzwilliam farm and
doing grand.

Soon after, on an early summer Sunday after mass, I went with P.J. to
visit Ma. It had been almost four years since I had seen her. I could hardly
believe so much time had passed. I had long ago given up pestering P.J. to
take me to see her at her father's farm. Then I had gone through a period
of such anger with her for leaving me that I had told myself I didn't care
if I ever saw her again. It wasn't true, of course, but it had been easier
to bury the pain under rage than to accept her abandonment. Now I
was afraid of what I would find. If her da had put her in the asylum, she
must be in a bad way. I clutched a bunch of white daisies in my hands
as I rode in the cart beside P.J. up toward the hospital. Ma's hat, which
I had kept with me since that awful night of the fire, sat on my knees. I
looked down at the daisies and thought of how just a short time ago their
small shoots had thrust themselves out of the frozen, hard ground just
when you might have given them up for dead. And within weeks they
blossomed, as if to say, "Had you no faith in us at all?" Today I was filled
with faith—faith in myself, faith in the future, aye, and even faith in God
Himself.

I shuddered as we approached the building that housed the Fever
Hospital, workhouse, and ward for the insane. I tried not to think of
the night we had carried Lizzie here, not knowing that we would never
see her again. It all seemed so long ago, and I thought I had buried the

memories deep in the back of my mind, but they reared up again now, raw as ever. I shook off the uneasiness and pinned my eyes on the hospital straight ahead of us. It was a three-story stone building, square and grim. P.J. stopped the cart and helped me down. We walked in through a big arched door to a reception room that smelled of wax and disinfectant. P.J. led the way over to a nurse sitting behind a big desk.

"Hello, Nellie," he said.

She looked up, her round face creased in a smile. "Well, hello, Mr. Mullen, it's grand to see you again."

"And yourself, Nellie. You look lovelier every day."

The nurse blushed under P.J.'s charm. I smiled in spite of my nervousness. P.J. had been coming to see Ma about once a fortnight, so he knew the way of things there. But for me it was a strange and forbidding place. I inwardly cursed my grandfather for putting Ma there. This was the last place she would ever want to be.

"This is Eileen—Mary O'Neill's daughter. She'd like to see her ma."

The nurse looked at me and sighed. Her face was kind, but her eyes were sharp. She looked up at P.J.

"Are you sure she's old enough? We don't let children under sixteen into, er . . . that particular ward."

P.J. nodded. "She's close enough, Nellie. Besides, she has more sense in her head than girls twice her age."

The nurse looked doubtful. "Well, as long as you go with her, I suppose . . ."

"I want to go alone!" I said without thinking. I turned to P.J. "I'll be all right—I just want to see her by myself. It's the first time . . ." My voice trailed off.

P.J. stroked his beard as he always did when weighing things up in his mind. "I understand, love. But come on back down if you need me. I'll sit myself right here next to this charming Florence Nightingale." He beamed over at the nurse.

An older, very stern nurse led me up two flights of stairs. She reminded me of Mary Galway at the mill. She walked as if she had a poker up her arse.

"You're not to be staying long," she said over her shoulder. "Visitors have a way of upsetting the patients."

"She's my mother," I retorted. "How would I be upsetting her?"

She did not answer.

"Does she have many visitors?" I asked suddenly.

The nurse pursed her lips. "Well, there's that very forward man, Mullen. He comes twice a month or so. And her father's representative comes every month to pay the room fees and speak with the doctor. And of course there's Mr. Finnegan."

Mr. Finnegan? I had no notion of who Mr. Finnegan was.

We reached the top floor. I followed her down the middle of a large ward. Women, old and young, lay or sat on single iron beds, watching us intently. Some cackled and made dirty gestures, while others cursed aloud.

"Pay no attention," the nurse said.

I tried to keep my eyes off them, but I could feel their presence, like ghosts, all around me. I was suddenly terrified of seeing Ma. She was kept in a private room at the far end of the ward. The nurse opened the door, and I crept in behind her.

"You have a visitor, Mrs. O'Neill," the nurse said briskly. And then to me she said, "Keep it to a half an hour," and left the room.

I walked over to Ma. She sat in a chair by the window, staring down at the people coming and going in the courtyard below. She was thinner than I remembered. Her long black hair had streaks of gray, but it was brushed and tied back in a pink ribbon. She wore a long pink dressing gown over a flannel nightdress and had soft slippers on her feet. I wondered idly who had bought the clothes for her. I knelt and handed her the flowers and her hat. "Hello, Ma," I said. "I brought you these flowers. Remember how you always loved daisies? And here's your lovely hat. You forgot it when you left." She turned toward me, a startled look on her face.

"Thank you," she said politely, as if to a stranger.

She made no attempt to take the flowers or the hat, so I laid them in her lap. She looked down but did not touch them. I got up and pulled over a chair and sat down facing her. She looked straight at me with dull eyes, and I realized with a shock that she did not recognize me. I tried to tell myself it was because I had grown so much in the last four years, filled out, become stronger. I was no longer a little girl. But my heart sank anyway. Any mother in her right mind would know her own daughter, no matter how long it had been since they had seen each other.

Anger rose in me and fell. I began to talk, racing from one subject to another, my voice rising hysterically.

"They burned the Yellow House, and Da died defending it. You should have seen him, Ma. You would have been so proud of him." Tears stung my eyes. "Paddy and I escaped harm. We're living with P.J. and his wife. Mrs. Mullen is awful good to Paddy." I sniffed back the tears. "I've got work now, Ma. I'm a doffer up at Queensbrook Mill. I earn my own wages every week." I pulled an empty pay envelope out of my pocket. "Look, Ma. You see, it has my name on it. Eileen O'Neill. Isn't that grand? I intend to save as much as I can so I can fix the Yellow House and we can all go home. You see, it didn't burn to the ground, Ma. It might have if Da had not chased them off, but it can be repaired. Won't that be great, Ma?"

Ma stared at me, a small frown on her face.

I reached over, grabbed her wrists, and shook her violently. "For God's sake, Ma, look at me. Talk to me!"

She stared at me in confusion. Sighing, I dropped her hands and knelt and put my arms around her instead. She was brittle and fragile in my embrace. I kissed her left cheek, dry as parchment. "I'm sorry, Ma," I said. "Here, let me put the flowers in water."

I stood up, took the flowers from her lap, and thrust them into a jug of water that stood on a bedside table. Then I took her hat and hung it on a peg on the back of the door. When I looked at her again, she was back to staring out the window. I wonder how old you have to be until you don't need your ma to love you anymore. I wanted my ma back—my lovely, elegant, smiling ma who doted on me. I wanted to feel again the stroke of her hand on my hair and the brush of her lips on my cheek when I brought her a present—fistfuls of buttercups from the garden, a pretty stone from the beach at Warrenpoint, a picture I had drawn for her.

I walked to the door and looked back at her. P.J. had warned me that she was changed, but I hadn't believed it. Even now, I refused to believe she would not get better. Surely if she was brought home to her old surroundings with her family around her, surely she would be better. I realize now that I needed that hope more for myself than for her.

I closed the door gently and walked back through the ward where the women sang and taunted and screamed. My ma was not like these women. She would never be like these women. I hastened my step and ran down the stairs until I was back in the front office. I ran directly to P.J. and buried my head in his shoulder.

"Take me home, P.J.," I murmured.

"Aye, love."

5

A fortnight before my sixteenth birthday, on a sweltering Saturday evening in August 1913, I stood on the stage in the Ceili House pub in Newry, holding my da's fiddle. The Music Men surrounded me—Terrence, Fergus, and P. J. Mullen. A new young fellow named Gavin had replaced Billy.

That morning, P.J. had come into the kitchen and thrust the fiddle into my hands.

"It's about time you took it up, girl," he'd said, "or the poor thing will get warped from lack of use."

"But I hardly know how to play," I had protested.

P.J. had waved me off. "Sure it's in your blood, child. God will guide your hand." And then he'd winked at me. "There's money in it for you."

I stood now, my knees trembling, as I looked out at the crowd. The Ceili House, the most popular pub in Newry, drew people from miles around. Da used to play there often. I tried to see it through his eyes. The room was bathed in a yellow glow from the gas lamps set along the walls. A mahogany bar ran the length of the room on one side. On it, pints of black porter stood in a row, waiting for the white foam to settle. Behind the bar was a cracked, dusty mirror. Shelves filled with bottles of spirits reached to the ceiling. Two men, the owner and his son, red-faced and jovial, moved swiftly among customers, their broad, beefy hands slapping bottles and glasses on splintered wooden tables. A toothless old woman sat on a stool at the end of the bar, sucking a tobacco pipe.

Along the wall opposite the bar was a row of tiny rooms with curtains drawn across them. They reminded me of confessional boxes, but these were the snugs where people sat for privacy—a boyo with a woman not his wife, maybe, or a pair of women so respectable that they would not dare be seen in a place like this. The wooden floor was stained black from spilled ale and dirt, and worn from the tramp of a thousand pairs of feet. The place smelled of spilled whiskey, stale beer, and smoke. There were no windows; the air stirred only when someone opened or closed the front door.

The boys played here often, and even though I had called them the Music Men since I was a child, they performed under the name of the Ulster Minstrels.

"And it's my pleasure to introduce to you now Miss Eileen O'Neill. Most of you remember her father, Tom O'Neill, God rest his soul." There were murmurs and quick signs of the cross as P.J. mentioned my da. "Miss Eileen is playing with us in public for the first time, so please give her a big hand."

Hands clapped and there were a few raucous cheers. The sweat poured off me, and I thought I might faint. P.J. led off with his fiddle, playing the same tunes we had played back in the days at the Yellow House. I raised my bow and brought it down on the strings and slowly coaxed out a sound. I felt Da's hands on mine, strong and sure, and gradually I relaxed my grip and let the music flow freely through me. Ah, so this was what Da felt—the thrill of the music throbbing through your body like something alive, voices singing and feet thudding on the floor, and yourself in the center of it all, casting a spell over everything and everyone. How powerful this music that can mesmerize men and women into a trance of lightness and joy! I smiled and silently thanked Da for this miraculous gift.

We played for almost two hours without stopping, jigs and reels followed by slow laments. As I watched the crowds move to and fro, I noticed a young man standing at the back of the room, his cap pushed back on his thick black hair. Frankie, I thought, my God, it's Frankie! I turned to P.J. "We have to stop," I whispered.

We finished the tune and I put down my fiddle and flew off the stage, pushing my way through the crowd. Stale breath and yellowed teeth leered in my face.

"Grand wee fiddler, so you are. You'll be as good as your da one day!"

As I neared the door, I knocked into a tall, fair-haired chap.

"Excuse me," I said as I pushed him aside.

He leaped back, a look of concern on his face. I thrust open the front door and ran outside. I looked up and down the street, but I could not see my brother. "Frank?" I called out hopefully. "Frank?" But there was no sign of him. I was sure it had been him—didn't I know my own brother? Why had he left so suddenly? My earlier pleasure in the music sank, and I trailed back in through the door.

"I'm really enjoying your music."

"What?" It was the fellow I had nearly landed on his arse in my rush to get out the door. "I'm sorry," I mumbled.

"What for?"

"For nearly knocking you to the ground."

He looked at me and smiled. Even in the dim light, I saw that his eyes were striking. They were the color of heather.

"Can I get you a drink? Lager, or lemonade, perhaps?"

His accent had an English tinge to it—cultivated. He seemed out of place in this pub.

"No, thanks," I said automatically.

He looked let down. "But you look very hot and thirsty. Please?"

I nodded. "A lemonade would be grand."

He ordered the drink from the barman. I watched him. His movements were smooth and confident. He was my height, with a slender build, and he wore an open-necked fine white linen shirt and khaki trousers.

He handed me the lemonade. "O'Neill," he said. "Where is your family from?"

"Glenlea," I said absently. I stared at the door, hoping that Frank would return.

"Any relation to Tom O'Neill? He lived in that bright yellow house at the top of the hill."

I swung around to face him. Sudden anger welled up in me. "Did you not hear the announcement earlier, or are you deaf?" I snapped. "Yes, he was my father. He's dead!"

I supposed by the look on his face that my abruptness caught him by surprise, but I didn't care.

"Forgive me," he said, "I'm so sorry. Of course I heard what happened to him. Terrible tragedy. I used to enjoy our walks up on Slieve Gullion." He paused. "Oh, where are my manners? I'm Owen Sheridan."

He held out a smooth, slender white hand, but I left it hanging there. Sheridan? I had come face-to-face with the devil himself. I stared at him in horror. He dropped his hand and went on. "You know, I think I met you once when you were a small girl. You were climbing Slieve Gullion with your father. He seemed to dote on you." He smiled a smug, confident smile. At that, I let loose.

"How dare you talk to me about my father? It's the likes of youse persecuted him and killed him. How can you live your soft life when my own poor family has been torn asunder? It isn't fair. None of it is fair!" I didn't care how nice and polite he was. The lemonade turned sour in my stomach. "I have to go," I said.

He reached out and put his hand on my arm. I shook it off.

"I am truly sorry for your loss, Miss O'Neill," he said, "but I assure you neither I nor my family are to blame. We are Quakers. We do not believe in violence."

I looked at the glass of ale in his hand. "I thought Quakers didn't believe in drink, either?" I snapped.

His smile returned. "Well, I suppose I'm the black sheep of the family."

He looked me up and down, the smile of amusement still on his face, as if he were enjoying a conversation with a wayward child. My cheeks reddened under his gaze.

"Where do you live now, Miss O'Neill?"

I almost told him it was none of his fecking business, but I wanted to end the conversation, so instead I said, "I live with P.J. and his wife, and I work up at Queensbrook Mill."

He arched an eyebrow. "Really? I can't say I've seen you there—but then again I don't often visit the mills. Are you in the spinning mill or the weaving mill?"

"The spinning mill. I'm a doffer." And before I could stop myself, I added, "And I enjoy tramping around every day up to my arse in water, and nearly catching my death when I come out of an evening."

He laughed aloud, a full, hearty laugh, and his eyes lit up. He was enjoying himself, the bastard, I thought, taking my words for a fine joke, making a mockery of me. I wanted to reach over and wipe the grin off his face. But before I could do anything, P.J. shouted down from the stage.

"Eileen? It's time we were starting up."

I turned on my heel and marched up to the stage.

"I like your spirit, Miss O'Neill," he called out after me.

"Who was that you were talking to?" P.J. asked.

"Nobody special."

I took up my fiddle again, but now anger had replaced my earlier nervousness. It took a while for it to seep out of me and let the rapture of the music replace it. Silently I again thanked Da for his gift to me. It might be the only thing that would help me hold my temper—and I was, I realized, in desperate need of that.

☙

I CAUGHT MY breath when I saw Owen Sheridan walk onto the spinning room floor that following Monday morning. Now I was done for. My temper had got me in trouble, and my job was about to be over almost before it started. I hovered behind a spinning frame in the corner, pretending to adjust the bobbins. The frame operator scowled at me. I watched Sheridan walk, hands behind his back, his head bowed, listening to whatever it was that Joe Shields was whispering in his ear. I hated Shields for bowing and scraping to him like he was feckin' royalty. But I had to admit he looked well just the same. His hair was blonder than I remembered from the Ceili House, and he carried his tall, slender frame with a mixture of arrogance and grace. He was a man you would look at twice. The other women obviously agreed with me. The frames slowed as they turned to gape.

"Who's that fellow?"

"I think that's the owner's son."

"Och, isn't he lovely?"

"It will be well for the woman gets him—looks and money and the whole lot."

"Maybe it'll be yourself, Maureen—sure don't you look grand in that apron?"

"I hear he's a rake. There's women in three counties mad for him, but not one of them's been able to land him. Black sheep of the family, so he is. I hear he's fond of a drink and gambling as well."

"Well, he must do his drinking outside of Queensbrook—he'd be famished with the thirst for all the pubs we have in this town."

"Aye. No pubs, no pawnshops, no police station," they chorused, echoing the words P.J. had said that first morning on the tram.

The women laughed and joked. He turned and smiled, nodding at each one of them as if she were the only woman there, saying, "Good morning," and, "How are you?" in that refined voice of his. He stopped in front of a frame where the steam spat water on him. He moved back, brushing off the front of his jacket. Serves him right, I thought, but I bit my lip. Why hadn't I kept my mouth shut? I watched as he talked to the operator. Blushing, she pointed down at her bare feet and the puddles of water on the floor. I slipped out of the corner and edged closer so that I could get a better look. He swung around as if he had eyes in the back of his head.

"Ah, Miss O'Neill," he called aloud, "there you are!" His voice was pleasant enough, but I cringed. I waited for the ax to fall. "You see, I took your comments quite seriously. I decided to have a look for myself."

Joe Shields stood beside him, glaring at me. "I agree these are regrettable conditions," Sheridan went on, "however, I don't know what can be done about them. I intend to speak to my father on the matter. Perhaps some other mills have found ways of containing the water. Do you have any ideas, Miss O'Neill? You seem like a bright young lady."

He wore that same smile of amusement he'd had in the Ceili House. He was mocking me again. I wanted to lash out at him, but I just stood there like an eejit with no tongue in my head. Most of the spinning frames had stopped as the workers turned to stare at me. I flushed red to my ears.

"Well, good-bye, Miss O'Neill," Sheridan said at last, "lovely to see you again. Let me know if you have any more concerns."

He walked away with Shields at his side. Then he turned and said over his shoulder, "Oh, and you have no need to thank me."

And he was gone.

The women started in.

"Well, some of us have friends in high places, don't we?"

"Little doffer's a dark horse, isn't she?"

"Will you put a good word in for me, love? I could tame a man like him."

I didn't know whether to be angry or relieved. I suppose I was both. I was so sure that he had come to sack me that I couldn't take in that I was still there. Shields was a different kettle of fish, though. I had earned no points with him at all. Finally I shouted back at the women who were cackling away at my expense.

"Look, all I told him was the truth, that we were drowning up to our arses here in this feckin' water."

There was silence for a minute, and then the laughter started, and a few of them even clapped their hands. "More power to you, darlin'. There's not many would have the brass to speak up to the likes of him."

Miss Galway came up behind me. "Back to your work," she said sharply. She was not laughing with the rest of them.

"Yes, ma'am," I said. But I knew I had not heard the end of it. I would

have to pay for causing Owen Sheridan to interfere with their operations. I would be labeled a troublemaker, and they would watch me like
a hawk.

ର∞

I BECAME A regular with P.J. and the Ulster Minstrels at the Ceili House.
My confidence as a fiddle player grew, and soon I was playing solos. I
never saw Frankie there again after that first night, but Owen Sheridan
appeared once in a while, always sitting near the back by the door. I
did my best to avoid him. I couldn't trust myself for what I might say
to him and get myself in trouble again. I suppose I should have at least
thanked him. He had arranged for splash boards to be installed on the
spinning frames, and while they did little to ease the puddles of water on
the floor, at least they stopped the spinners from getting drenched with
the spray from the spindles. I earned the respect of the other women for
speaking up, but Joe Shields and Miss Galway were spitting mad over my
interference. I was not about to suggest any more improvements to Mr.
Sheridan.

6

ꙮ

One Sunday in late September, I took it into my head to go and see Frankie. He had been weighing on my mind since the night I had seen him at the Ceili House. I needed to know that he was all right. Something told me he was hurting desperately, and I could not bear to think of that. On the other hand, I didn't know what kind of a welcome I would get, but I made up my mind that wasn't going to stop me. I had survived worse than Frankie's angry looks. P.J. wasn't so keen, however.

"Sure I told you the lad was in fine fettle the last I saw him," he said.

"Maybe. But I'll go and see for myself."

P.J. rubbed his cheek. "You may not get such a warm welcome."

"I'll take that chance."

P.J. sighed. He knew I was not to be talked out of it, although I didn't quite understand why he was trying to do so. We threw my old bicycle in the back of the cart and drove to mass. It was agreed that after mass P.J. would drive me as far as the village near the Fitzwilliam estate. He would wait in the local pub, and I would cycle the rest of the way up to the house. I wanted to visit Frankie alone.

It was a gorgeous late summer day as I rode out from the village. The last of the summer field roses bloomed wild along hedgerows, creamy clusters of meadowsweet and clumps of red clover painted the fields, the grass was a fresh, moist green, and everything seemed lush and ripe. Men passing me on the road touched their caps in greeting. Children laughed and waved. I waved back. But as I came in sight of the massive stone wall that surrounded the estate, my heart began pounding. I rode through the open gateway and dismounted, wheeling the bicycle beside me as I approached the big house. It looked as foreboding as ever, like a haunted house in a fairy tale. I felt soulless eyes watching me from the high arched windows. I looked down at the flower beds. No beautiful late summer blossoms grew there. Instead, dead brown twigs and weeds covered the ground. I dropped my bicycle and climbed the broken and cracked stone steps to the oak door. I squared my shoulders, lifted the heavy iron knocker, and let it fall. I waited. Eventually, I heard the squeal of locks being released and the grunt of the door as it opened.

"What do you want?"

My grandfather looked smaller than I remembered. He stooped forward and his clothes hung on his frame like a coat on a scarecrow. The change in him shocked me.

"I'm Eileen," I began.

"I know fine well who you are," he snarled. "What do you want? Your ma's not here."

I swallowed down a sudden anger. "I'm here to see my brother," I said.

He looked me up and down, his rheumy eyes taking in every detail. I shivered. Then he opened his dry lips and let out a laugh that sounded more like a croak.

"Mr. Frank O'Neill, is it? I believe you'll find that gentleman beyond in the stables where he belongs."

Before I could answer, he stepped back and shut the door in my face.

"Oul' bastard!" I swore out loud.

I backed down the steps, picked up my bicycle, and wheeled it along the path that ran around the house. I assumed the stables were somewhere behind the main house. So Frankie was out tending the horses? I winced, remembering how he disliked animals. God spare the horses, I thought. The path ended suddenly at the side of the house, but in the distance across a rough patch of grass, I saw a cluster of white buildings. As I walked toward them, wheeling my bicycle, I saw the stables. The buildings stood in a square around a wide, stone-flagged courtyard. A couple of horses peered over latched half-doors, and straw was scattered around the ground. As I approached, one of the half-doors opened and Frankie appeared, wearing overalls and carrying a bucket and a shovel. He did not see me right away, and I stopped and watched him. He had grown, although he was still a good six inches shorter than myself. His skin was brown from the sun, and new muscles stood out on his bare arms. He walked with his head high and his back straight, defiant despite the load of dung I guessed he carried. He was still the old Frankie. My heart soared at the sight of him.

"Frankie," I called.

He stopped when he saw me, and the look he gave me made my heart squeeze shut. His dark eyes, like those of a missionary priest, seared into me. He set down the bucket and shovel and sauntered toward me, coming to a standstill so close to me that I could smell the sweat and dung off him. His sneer reminded me of my grandfather's.

"Well, well," he said. "The high and mighty Miss Eileen O'Neill, daughter of the great O'Neills, has come to see the bastard son."

His words cut through me. I was about to lash back at him when I remembered his poor, frightened face the day he rode off from the Yellow House with Ma.

By this time, two stable hands had stopped their work to stare at us. They elbowed each other and giggled.

I turned on them. "I'm his feckin' sister," I yelled.

They giggled louder. I turned back to Frankie.

"Can we go to your room up at the house? I'd like to talk in private."

He laughed—a low, mirthless sound. "You can come to my room if you like," he said, "but you'll have to watch out for the dung on your nice, shiny boots. My quarters are in there along with the horses."

I gasped. "What?" I said.

"Aye. Quarters fit for a bastard like myself."

"Och, Frankie, will you stop calling yourself that."

"Frank to you, miss. The old Frankie's long gone."

I fidgeted with my bag and brushed my skirt. I had dressed in the long black skirt and white blouse I wore to play in the band. I had polished my boots that morning and brushed my hair until it shone. I wanted to look nice for Frankie. But now I felt overdressed and embarrassed.

"Can we walk a ways, then," I whispered, "away from here?"

He shrugged but began walking across the courtyard and out toward the open fields beyond. I followed him. When we came to a stone stile over a brook, he sat down, and I sat beside him.

"I'm sorry, Frankie—er, Frank," I said. "I didn't know it was like this."

He said nothing. A sudden anger shot through me. "How could Ma have let him treat you like this?" I exploded.

Frank waved his hand. "Sure I was her sin, don't you remember? No punishment was too good for me." His voice was sharp as acid.

"But it wasn't your fault," I said. "You had nothing to do with it."

He shrugged. "I was here all the same. A reminder of the curse God had put on her." He shoved his hands in his pockets and stared out at the sky. "Anyway, she went astray in the head after that."

"I went to see her," I said. "She didn't even know me." Tears pricked my eyes. I turned to Frank. "Why didn't you come to Da's funeral? I needed you there."

Frank snorted. "And why would I go to that oul' eejit's funeral?" he shouted. "He was nothing to me."

"He was your da in every other way," I said.

"Not in the way that counts." Frank paused and laughed. "And since when did the proud Eileen O'Neill ever need anything or anyone?"

"That's not fair," I said.

We sat in silence. In the distance, horses' hooves clattered in the stable yard, and dogs barked. The sun was high in the sky. Frank pulled his cap down over his eyes.

I sat erect and cleared my throat. "I have a job now," I said, "at the Queensbrook Mill. And another job playing with the Ulster Minstrels."

"Aye, I saw you once," whispered Frank

"It was you, then," I cried out in delight. "Why didn't you stay?"

Frank shrugged.

"And I've a good bit of money put away," I went on. "The Yellow House didn't burn to the ground that night in spite of what the bastards tried to do, and when I have enough saved I'm going to get it repaired and move us all back—Ma, Paddy, you, and me—"

Frank's laughter cut me short. He stood up and faced me.

"Will you listen to yourself," he said. "Jesus, will you just listen to yourself. The great Eileen O'Neill is going to make the world right for all of us!"

"I'm serious," I yelled.

Frank stopped laughing. His face turned dark despite the sunlight. He felt in his pocket and pulled out the stub of a cigarette and a match. He struck the match on the ground and lit the stub, inhaling long and hard and blowing the smoke into the air. He coughed.

"Well now, I have a surprise for you, miss," he said, looking straight into my face. "The Yellow House belongs to me. Isn't that a joke? Oul' P.J. came and told me that being as I'm the oldest surviving son, it's to pass to me when I come of age. That eejit Billy Craig's father beyond at the bank is holding all the papers on it."

"But . . . but you're not even an O'Neill," I blurted out. I was sorry the minute I said it, but the shock had knocked all sense out of me.

"No, I'm not. And that's why I'll be selling it as soon as I'm able. Good riddance to all it stands for."

"No!" I cried. "Ah, Frankie, no. You can't mean that." I reached out my hand to his. He shook me off. "But what about the O'Neill legacy?" I said.

"I don't give a shite about the O'Neill legacy."

"But you used to," I cried. "You believed in it as much as I did. We used to fight over who would make the best warrior. Remember? Remember?"

He said nothing and turned to go. I caught his arm and wrenched him to a stop. "You can't do this," I cried. "This is my dream. This is what keeps me going."

"You'll just have to find another dream, then, won't you?"

He strode off toward the stables.

"Have you no loyalty?" I shouted after him.

He turned briefly. "None at all," he said.

I sat on the wall and watched him go. My body felt heavy, as if I had been thumped and pummeled by some marauding animal. I did not think I could move again. I rode the emotions that flowed through me: anger, sadness, shock, pity, fear—I could take my pick. Eventually, I picked anger, and I turned it on P.J. P.J. had known about the house ever since Da's death, yet he had let me blather on for months like a fool about how I would restore it and reunite us all. Now I understood why he had not wanted me to see Frankie. He knew the truth would come out. The fury gave me energy, and I jumped on my bicycle and pedaled across the grass, past the stables, down the avenue, and out the gate. I had to get away from that evil place. It was cursed. I pedaled down to the village, the rosebushes a blur beside me, the greetings of strangers unheeded. I marched into the pub and tapped P.J. on the shoulder.

"I'm ready to go now," I announced.

P.J. did not press me. He knew by the look on my face what had happened.

"We'll go home, so," he said.

"No," I said. "Take me up to Glenlea. I want to see the Yellow House."

∞

I SAT ON Calmor's Rock, an outcropping halfway up Slieve Gullion, where Frankie and I played as children. Images of the small boy grinning in triumph after he scrambled ahead of me and claimed the rock for himself brought unwanted tears. How could I stay angry with him? I could not hate him for clutching the small staff of power that fate had handed him and lashing out with it at everyone who had hurt him. I would likely have done the same myself. But I also knew myself well enough to know that I could not give up my rage. Rage is what had fueled me all this time. If I let it go, what would become of me? Would I become like all the other women beyond at the mill—passive, powerless, destined for a life of slow, creeping despondency that even marriage and children could not cure? No. I had been baptized a warrior. I was born to fight. And I needed rage to drive me forward. But where was I to find it now?

I stared down at the ruins of the Yellow House far below me. No longer did she stand glinting gold in the afternoon sun. She stooped instead like a spent warrior, the damaged, scarred symbol of our broken family. Och, Da! I am so tired of fighting. Why can I not forget the glow of your face that night as you fought to save our house? Why does your ghost keep bringing me back here? I'm just a girl, Da. I'm only sixteen. What do you want me to do?

A wet nose poking against my knee startled me. I looked down to see a rust-colored Irish setter with big brown eyes staring up at me. My heart jerked at the memory of our own old faithful dog, Cuchulainn. He had died the day after Da and was buried beside him near the Yellow House. This dog was more like Cuchulainn had been in his prime, lively and alert. I smiled in spite of myself and bent forward to pet him.

"Hello there, lad," I said, "and where did you come out of?"

The young dog wagged his tail and put his head on my knee. A voice called out from the bushes.

"Rory? . . . Rory? . . . Come back here, boy. Heel!"

The dog pricked his ears, then turned and ran toward the main path. Still smiling, I watched him go. My smile faded when his owner came into view. Owen Sheridan. What the feck was he doing here? Could a body not have a bit of peace when she needed it without the likes of himself bursting in on her? I scowled at him as he tipped his cap to me.

"Why, Miss O'Neill," he said, "what a pleasant surprise."

Pleasant surprise my arse, I thought, but I said nothing. I hoped he would go on about his business, but instead he stood for a moment looking at me, then scrambled across the bushes and gravel until he was sitting beside me, bold as brass, on the rock. Rory ran in circles around us, panting and looking as delighted with himself as his master.

"So Calmor's Rock is one of your secret places, too," Sheridan said, paying no heed to the dirty looks I gave him. "I used to hide out here when I was a lad. I didn't think anyone else knew of it."

"Protestants don't own everything in the world," I snapped.

He ignored me. Instead he gazed around us.

"Is there ever a time of year when Slieve Gullion is not beautiful?" He sighed, removing his cap and scratching his close-cropped hair. He turned his eyes on me, and they were filled with delight.

Eejit, I thought. I shrugged.

"I particularly love her at this time of the year, though," he went on.

I also loved Slieve Gullion best in the late summer, although I was not going to tell him that. Her summer robe of bracken so thick now would soon be in tatters, exposing the scars and furrows on her surface. Crevasses formed millions of years ago by the ice age would be exposed, crossing her face like ancient wrinkles. But now the last of the summer flowers and grasses clothed her in a colorful robe. A rabbit darted past, and in the distance waterfowl cried from the many lakes. As I had climbed up today, I had paused at the ash groves in the Valley of the Fews, also called the District of Songs on account of all the poets said to have lived and walked there.

As if reading my mind, Sheridan said, "I come here to read poetry when I am in the mood. I always hope the ghosts of the poets will inspire me to write something beautiful someday. But no such luck yet."

I said nothing but looked off into the distance, hoping he would go on about his business. Instead he turned to me.

"My poor Miss O'Neill," he began. "You seem troubled today."

"I wasn't troubled until you came along," I snapped.

He paused, then stood up. "In that case, I will leave you in peace," he said. "I came seeking some solitude myself, although I often think brooding on our troubles can make them seem greater."

I shrugged. What could he know about troubles? He whistled for Rory, and the two made their way back over to the main path. But just then, out of nowhere, I didn't want them to leave. I supposed he was right. Thinking about things often made them more painful. I needed to move.

"Wait," I shouted, "are you going to the top?"

A grin creased his face. "We are," he said.

"I was going up there, too," I said, "but I was wanting to go alone."

He grinned more widely, flashing white teeth in his tanned face. "Well then, Rory and I will go ahead, and you can follow in your own time."

Cheeky bastard, I thought as he began to climb. Rory fell back and walked beside me. I studied Sheridan as I walked behind him. He wore a tweed jacket, linen trousers, and stout climbing boots. He was a fine figure of a man, I had to admit. He was about as tall as myself, and well built, but he had a fineness to him that made his movements graceful. As he climbed, he whistled, swinging his blackthorn stick in time to the tune. I realized he was putting on a show for me because he knew I was watching him. He had a bob on himself, did this one. Still, I found myself smiling because he put me in mind of Da, who used to swing his stick in the same way on our excursions up the mountain. For a moment, a chill crept over me. When I asked you what you wanted me to do, Da, I said to myself, I didn't expect you to send me a Protestant as the answer to my question. What are you playing at, for God's sake?

I followed Sheridan up to the summit of the mountain. He stood motionless in the weeds at the shore of Lough Berra, the Lake of Sorrows. I clambered up behind him and stood erect. As always, the beauty of the landscape that swept out and around Slieve Gullion took my breath away. Slieve Gullion herself was ringed with a range of smaller mountains known as the Ring Dyke. Beyond the dyke, valleys and plains spread out as far as I could see, stretching green and gold and gray and purple all the way to the horizon. I turned in a circle as I did when I was a child, standing on my toes like a dancer, and stretched out my arms to greet the land. I had forgotten about Owen Sheridan until I heard his laughter. I swung around and scowled at him. He looked at me in a queer sort of way that made me blush.

"Beautiful, isn't it?" he said.

"Aye," I said. "Do you know the story of the lake?" I added, as much to break the odd spell that had overtaken me as for any desire for conversation.

"I do indeed." He nodded.

As if in answer, a sudden breeze blew across the lake, leaving ripples in the water. Rory plunged in.

"Here, boy!" Sheridan called.

"Afraid his hair will turn white?" I quipped.

I was referring to the legend that anyone who swims in the lake will come out with their hair turned white.

"No," he said, "but I wouldn't want to risk it all the same. Your Irish legends can be pretty powerful."

I stared into the lake, inhaling the salty smell of the marshes. Da always said Finn's hair turned white from sorrow because he lost the thing he loved most. Poor Da. His hair turned white from sorrow as well.

Tears pricked at my eyes, and I turned away from Sheridan. I looked down at the ruins of the Yellow House, and my tears flowed freely. I felt a touch on my shoulder. Sheridan stood so close, I could smell his tobacco and the fresh scent of his hair. He said nothing, only stared down with me at the Yellow House.

"I'm sorry," he whispered.

"I loved that house. And I loved my da," I said before the sobs took over.

We stood there for a long time. His hand lay gently on my shoulder like a warm balm. As its warmth spread through me, my sobs gradually eased. He reached in his pocket and pulled out a flask.

"Would you like a drink?" he said, and then, smiling, added, "Don't worry, it's only water."

As I took the flask, a rush of wind overhead startled us.

"It's the wild geese," I exclaimed through my tears. "Look, it's the wild geese! They've come early!"

I was a child again, standing beside my da, pointing up at the graceful birds. They usually came in late autumn, flying over Slieve Gullion on their way south.

"They're not due for another month!"

Owen Sheridan watched them, too, his face upturned, smiling.

"Did you know that two of them flew over Da's funeral this past March?" I said with pride. "I think they came to escort Da to heaven. Da says great luck will come to those who see them!"

He smiled at me. "I hope your da's right," he said. "I could use some good Irish luck just now."

I wanted to ask more, but for once I held my tongue. A shadow crept over his face and then was gone. "Well, shall we go?" he asked, all business.

He insisted on escorting me down the mountain. Now that the earlier spell had been broken, I wanted to shrug him off, but the press of his hand on the small of my back was warm and comforting. The sun was setting in the west, taking its warmth with it. I shivered slightly, and my old irritation with Sheridan's presence returned.

"How are you getting home?" he inquired.

"No bother of yours," I said. "I have my bicycle."

"And where is it you live?"

Jesus, it's a nosy bugger he is, I thought. "Newry!" I snapped.

"But you can't cycle all the way to Newry. It will be dark soon."

I turned on him. "I have walked it in the middle of the night, half carrying my young brother," I said. "I can surely ride a bicycle there without harm."

We had arrived at Kearney's Pub in Glenlea village, where I had left my bicycle. I had told P.J. not to wait for me, but I saw him now sitting outside the pub, drinking a stout with Shane Kearney, the pub's owner. I was grateful to see him. If nothing else, it would shut up Sheridan's blather.

P.J. raised an eyebrow when he saw us. "Och, Eileen! And Mr. Sheridan now."

Sheridan tipped his cap. "Owen, sir. Mr. Sheridan is my father."

"I ran into this eejit on the mountain," I snapped, ignoring P.J.'s questioning look. "A body can't get a bit of peace anywhere these days."

P.J. drained his glass. "Well, I'll bring the cart around so," he said with a grin. "Mr. Sheridan . . . er, Owen lad, can I be giving you a lift, too?"

Sheridan grinned. "Ah, no, thank you, sir. There is a certain lady in these parts waiting to give me dinner. So I'll be off. Good night, Miss O'Neill."

I glared at him as he lifted his bicycle, which had been leaning against the wall of Kearney's Pub. So it was right what the women said about him, that he was a bit of a rake.

P.J. grinned back. "Well, enjoy yourself."

I watched Sheridan cycle away, his blackthorn stick across the handlebars and Rory trotting beside him. Strange feelings crept up inside me, but I was too tired to dwell on them. I'd had enough emotion and confusion for one day. All I wanted now was to sleep.

❧

IN THE DAYS after my visit with Frankie, I tried to keep my head down and my nose clean. I was afraid if I thought too hard about things, I would fall apart. For the moment, I fixed my rage on my circumstances. I was female and I was Catholic and I was poor. Well, I could do nothing about the first two, but I could do my best to make money. Without money, I realized, I had no power in the world at all. So I went to the mill every day determined to be a model worker so they would have no cause to sack me. I hoped to move up soon to spinner; I had spent enough time as a doffer. I played every chance I could with the Ulster Minstrels. I bought a sewing machine and took in mending and dressmaking work. P.J. used his connections to get me bundles of handkerchiefs to hem with lace—clean, tidy work that was usually given to Protestant women.

I did my best, but the truth was I had no talent for it. My hands were too big and clumsy, and I had no patience for the delicate work. I gave up eventually, sold the machine, and took a job serving whiskey and stout in the Ceili House two nights a week. Every Saturday, I brought home my pay envelope and gave half my wages to Mrs. Mullen to pay for Paddy's and my keep.

"I'm only taking it to save your pride," she said, "but there's no call for it at all."

I put the rest of my wages from the mill and the money I earned from the Ceili House in a big glass jar I kept beside my bed. I loved looking at the coins piling up. One day, P.J. took me to the post office on Hill Street in Newry and helped me open an account.

"It's safer in here, darlin'," he said, "and it will be earning interest for you."

I took the passbook home and sat on my bed holding it reverently between my two hands like a Communion host. When I had enough, I told myself, I would buy the Yellow House back from Frankie. I had a few years until he was twenty-one and old enough to sell it. Surely he would sell it to me if I met his price. New hope fueled my energies.

I clung more and more to my brother Paddy. Looking back on it now, I see that it was not fair to the child. He had only just begun to stand on his own feet again after months of refusing to sleep by himself and crying after me every time I went out the door. But my family was slowly slipping away from me, and I just could not chance losing him as well. At night, I told him stories about the Yellow House. In the beginning he had been all ears, asking questions and laughing at my stories about Great-Grandda Hugh and the merry ghosts. He wanted to know when Da was coming back—in his mind, Da was just away visiting heaven. I'm afraid I encouraged him to think that way. I wanted him to keep asking me when I was going to take him home. I didn't want him to forget. I even took him once to see Ma, but she backed away and screeched so hard when she saw him that I had to rush him out the door. I didn't take him back after that.

He looked more and more like Lizzie every day. He had her same blond hair and wide blue eyes. It sometimes made me sad to look at him. I wanted him to grow up strong and happy, but just now I realized I needed him more than he needed me. If I let him go, I would have to let go of my dream. So I suffocated the poor child with hugs and kisses and tears. During those days I swear he was wiser than I was, the way he looked at me with a queer sort of patience and pity.

It was only when the Mullens put him in school in September that we all realized the depth of the anger that was raging in Paddy. At the end of the first day when Mrs. Mullen went to collect him, he had bruises on his cheek and his sleeve was torn. Paddy refused to talk to her about what happened. The next day she went to see his teacher, who told her Paddy had been in a fight in the playground. It wasn't unusual for a child to be in a fight on his first day, the teacher explained, and once he settled in, things would be grand. But things were not grand. Within a week, Mrs. Mullen was called to the school and told to take Paddy out. He had been picking fights with other children, even though many of them were much older than him. They would not let him back in until the next term, they said, until he was older and had learned to behave himself. I was as shocked as the Mullens.

"For God's sake, Paddy, what happened?"

I crouched down in front of him and looked into his face. He stared back at me but said nothing. Instead of Lizzie's sweet face, I suddenly saw Frankie's defiance, and my anger exploded. I shook him by the shoulders.

"What do you think Da would say to this behavior?" I shouted.

"Da's dead," he said.

His words were like a shower of cold water. Shocked, I dropped my hands from him. "What?" I whispered.

"Da's dead," he said again.

A torrent of sadness washed through me. Oh, the poor wee lad. It had finally sunk in that his da was really dead and not just "visiting heaven," as he used to say. As for his ma—I shuddered at the image of her screaming at him like a banshee to get away from her. Jesus, no wonder the boy was angry. I reached out and crushed him against me. He didn't resist.

"I'm sorry, love," I whispered. "I'm so sorry."

I leaned back and clutched his shoulders between my hands. "I promise I'll not leave you, Paddy," I said. "I'll bring us all back to the Yellow House."

After that, neither I nor the Mullens questioned him. We went on about our lives as if the school incidents had never occurred. At home, he was a good child, quiet and helpful. Mrs. Mullen took it on herself to teach him to read, and it turned out he loved books. P.J. taught him to play simple wee tunes on the fiddle, and I took him to mass with me on Sundays—just the two of us. Afterward we would go for lemonade, and I would buy him a picture book. I think those outings kept us both sane.

7

The quiet routine of life suited me. I had no need of friends. But it turned out God had other ideas. A few months after my sixteenth birthday, He arranged for a girl named Theresa Conlon to interfere with my life and turn it upside down.

Theresa came to work at the mill and started, like the rest of us, as a doffer. She was a year younger than me. I was put in charge of teaching her. If anyone could be called great *craic*—the Gaelic word for fun and good company—it was Theresa. She was always joking and laughing, and she did a wicked imitation of Miss Galway. On top of that, she could swear better than me. I couldn't help liking her. It turned out she was the sister of Fergus Conlon, the tall, reed-thin Music Man who used to play the mandolin with the group at the Yellow House and whom I played with nowadays in the Ulster Minstrels. When she invited me to her house, though, I didn't know what to say. First of all, I had heard all the stories from Ma about what a harridan oul' Mrs. Conlon was, so I was in no hurry to meet her. Even more to the point, I had never had friends, and I was sure I did not want any—they would only interfere with my purpose. But Mrs. Mullen was so delighted at the prospect of my having a friend that I hated to disappoint her. When I told her I had been invited to tea, she went into a dither of what I should wear, what I should bring, and all the rest of it.

THERESA AND I must have looked an odd pair as we walked down the hill from the spinning mill toward the village of Queensbrook. I had grown to six feet tall, with big feet and hands and hair that fell in a long auburn braid down my back to my waist. I was slender, thank God, but strong as a horse. My new friend Theresa, by contrast, was only five feet in height, and she walked with a limp on account of being born with a club foot that left her with one leg shorter than the other. She was a lovely girl all the same, with long, wavy brown hair, big hazel eyes, and a smile that would light the road at night.

I had never seen the village up close. I had no interest in exploring the place; when work finished I always made a beeline for the tram. Now I saw it as P.J. had described on that first day we rode the tram to Queensbrook. It was like a toy town. Small, tidy houses with red geraniums in window boxes stood shoulder to shoulder in two big squares. In the middle of each square was a green where men bowled, and children played while mothers sat on wooden benches watching them. Trees and shrubs grew here and there. The pavement that ran around the greens and in front of the houses was clean and smooth. Along the main road that linked the squares stood two churches, a community hall, a library, and two schools. Well-tended shops sold meat and vegetables and dry goods. As P.J. had said, there was not a pub to be seen.

Theresa watched me as I gazed around. "Have you never been to the village?"

"No."

"It was built by the Sheridans. By the way, I hear you know the son." Theresa's eyes blazed up at me. I had found out already that she was a terror for the gossip. I decided to stay clear of it.

"Not really," I said.

Theresa shrugged. "Anyway, it's all mill workers that live here. My brother Fergus is a bleacher. My da was a hackler before he died. Ma's convinced the dust killed him, and so is my other brother, James. He hates the mills. But I don't mind it. I'm just glad that Ma's finally let me out of the house."

"What about your brother?"

"Fergus? He lives here, but we don't see too much of him between his work and playing at the Ceili House."

"No. The other one."

"James? Well, he's studying to be a priest. He's away at the seminary down in Dublin at the minute. Ma sent me to work to help pay for his school fees."

I had known from Ma that Fergus worked as a bleacher at the

Queensbrook Mill and that all his wages went to pay the school fees of his younger brother, James. Now I learned that Mrs. Conlon had put Theresa to work in the cause of James, too. I was prepared to hate this James on sight.

She pushed open the front door of a house halfway up the right-hand side of the second square and pulled me in after her. "Ma? We're here," she called.

A small woman, thin and short as Theresa, came into the parlor. Her steel gray hair was cut blunt around her head and secured with clips. She had a sharp beak of a nose, thin lips, and cheeks dotted with red blotches. Around her neck hung a silver crucifix. I had expected a much bigger woman. I suppose, to be fair, I was not what she was expecting, either. She fixed her little brown eyes on me.

"You're a tall one, aren't you?" she said by way of greeting. Her voice was surprisingly strong given her frail appearance. "My James is tall like you," she went on. "Theresa now, she took after me. Our Theresa's the runt of the family."

"Ma, this is Eileen O'Neill," said Theresa, ignoring her mother's remarks. "Sit down, Eileen. Make yourself comfortable."

I looked around the parlor. I didn't see how anybody could be comfortable in this room with its stiff furnishings, not to mention the pictures and statues of Jesus, his Mother, and the pope staring out at you. I chose a small red armchair beside the fireplace.

"Oh no, not there!" Mrs. Conlon blurted out.

I jumped and Theresa giggled. "I forgot to warn you," she said. "That's James's chair. You know, the prince has to have his throne."

"But I thought he was away," I said, confused.

Theresa sat on the sofa and patted the seat beside her. "Sit here," she said.

I handed the tin of biscuits Mrs. Mullen had sent to Mrs. Conlon and sat down beside Theresa. I looked around the room again, trying to avoid Mrs. Conlon's glare. The odor of wax on the floors and furniture nearly choked me, and I smelled bleach off the curtains and the tablecloth. A fluffy gray cat sat on an outside windowsill and meowed. I supposed the oul' bat wouldn't even let the cat in for fear it would dirty the place. I wondered that she had not told me to take off my shoes.

"Do you have the tea made, Ma?" said Theresa, kicking out her legs and sighing. "We're famished with the hunger."

Mrs. Conlon turned her eyes up toward heaven. "Och, why don't you make the tea, Theresa? My legs are killing me. I was on my hands and knees all day."

Theresa winked at me. "She says the rosary. For penance, you know."

Mrs. Conlon bristled. "Somebody has to pray for the sinners of this world."

Theresa hauled herself up off the sofa and went into the scullery, dragging her club foot behind her. Mrs. Conlon made herself comfortable in the armchair that sat on the other side of the fireplace from James's chair. "So you're up at that oul' mill, too? It will probably kill youse, like it did her da." She sniffed. "Of course, there's them that's lucky enough to get married and out of there that might survive, but I wouldn't put you among them. Her neither—" She nodded toward the scullery, where Theresa was banging around cups and pots. "The deformity, you know." She paused and sighed. "Och, well, we all have our cross to bear."

"But why did you send her to the mill, then?" I blurted out, astonished.

"She can earn more there than working as a shop assistant. And we need the money for James's fees. What our Fergus earns is not enough. It's a sacrifice worth making to have the great blessing of a priest in the family." She stared heavenward again and crossed herself.

As long as you're not the one making the sacrifice, you oul' bitch, I thought.

Theresa came in from the kitchen carrying a tray of tea and sandwiches. Her mother looked at what she had set out and sniffed. "I was saving that ham for tomorrow," she said.

"Eileen plays the fiddle at the Ceili House in Newry," Theresa said. "She knows our Fergus."

Mrs. Conlon blessed herself again. "That den of devils!" she shouted. "That's where our Fergus went astray. Lord save us from the drink. There was never a drop of it in this house. And, praise the Sheridan family, not a drop of it in this village."

Theresa rolled her eyes, and I thought that her poor da could have done with a drop now and then to put up with this old harridan.

"I'll say a novena for you," Mrs. Conlon added, "that you may be spared a life of the drink."

I didn't know whether to laugh or hit her.

"O'Neill?" she said, settling in for the inquisition. "Are you a relation to that Tom O'Neill as was shot?"

"Ma!" cried Theresa.

"He was my father," was all I said.

There was silence as we chewed on the ham sandwiches and drank the tea. I noticed some of the spirit had oozed out of Theresa.

"Is your son long at the seminary?" I said, trying to steer the conversation.

Mrs. Conlon brightened, and the red spots on her face glowed like stigmata. "Two years this September," she said. "He's eighteen now. He has years yet to go."

"If he stays," muttered Theresa.

Mrs. Conlon shot up in her chair. "And why wouldn't he?"

Theresa shrugged. "Maybe he'll join the army," she said sourly. "The English are talking about a war coming soon. And then there's the unrest that's happening around Ireland. Maybe he'll leave and fight for the Revolution!"

Mrs. Conlon rose to the bait. Her face turned scarlet, and she clutched her crucifix.

"He'll be a soldier of Christ," she said shrilly. "That's what he was born to do. And mind your manners, miss."

"Would you like more tea?" said Theresa, holding out the pot to me.

I saw my chance and stood up. "No, thanks, I should be going." I nodded toward Mrs. Conlon. "It was nice meeting you. Thank you for the tea." God forgive me, I thought, for the lies I'm telling.

Mrs. Conlon did not get up. "Well, Theresa's never had many friends," she said. "I'm glad to see she's finally made one."

Theresa pushed me out the door. She stormed down the pavement, dragging her leg behind her. "No friends my arse," she muttered. "She drove them all away, that's why. Sanctimonious old bitch." She looked back at me. "I'm sorry I didn't warn you."

I shook my head. "No bother," I said. "I've met worse."

Theresa giggled. "Well, if there's worse, I'd like to meet them."

We both laughed. She waited for me to catch up, and she linked her arm in mine.

ॐ

AS I RODE the tram home, I thought about the evening. I felt sorry for Theresa, cooped up in that house with that old hypocrite. And as for the James fellow, well, I was prepared to hate him, too, priest or no priest, letting his sister and brother work like slaves to pay for him. But there was another feeling inside me: So this is what friendship is? I thought of the girls I had seen at the mill or on Hill Street in Newry, arm in arm, giggling at everything in front of them. I always thought that they were eejits. But I had to admit that beneath my scorn there lay another feeling—envy. Now, as I considered this new feeling of friendship, I turned it over and over like a stone in my hand and felt something creep into my heart. It wasn't as strong as joy—I realized I was not yet ready for joy—but it was a warm feeling just the same. I leaned back against the wooden seat of the tram and smiled.

ဆာ

AS CHRISTMAS EVE 1913 approached, I was in very bad form. For months I had been asking to be promoted to spinner. I knew every inch of the job, I said, so there was no reason I should not move up. I had been a doffer for eight months. Even the slowest of them usually moved up within a year—except for the likes of Josephine, who was not fit for anything else. But every time I opened my mouth, Shields turned me down. "It's not time," he would say. "There's others more deserving ahead of you." I was supposed to swallow that and go back to my corner. I knew fine well that the real reason was that I had complained to Owen Sheridan about the conditions in the mill. Shields was getting even with me, and Mary Galway was going along with him.

I had saved a fair few pound already, but it was slow going. I could save twice as much working as a spinner. My plan was to spend a couple of years proving myself as a spinner and then move over to the weaving mill and run a loom. Weaving was considered a higher skill than spinning, and the workers were paid by the piece instead of by the hour. I was a hard worker, so I knew I could do well there. I'd also have dry feet for a change, I thought, even though I'd be exchanging the hot, humid conditions for pouce—the name the weavers gave to the flax dust that clogged their lungs.

"What would you want to go to that oul' place for?" Theresa said when I mentioned it to her. "Sure it's so noisy over there the weavers can't even talk to one another. They have to use sign language. And the pace is so desperate they don't have time to scratch their arses. There's no *craic* over there at all."

"I can do without the *craic*," I said. "The money is what's important."

"Life's what's important, Eileen," she said, "enjoying yourself while you're young. You're going to be an old woman before your time."

In early December, Theresa ran up to me full of excitement.

"Are you going to the ball, Eileen?"

"The what?"

"Och, do you never pay attention to anything? The Spinners' Ball. It's going to be a big do on Christmas Eve. All the girls are talking about it. I'm in charge of the committee. The Sheridans have agreed we can use the Community Hall, and they will pay for a band and all the food. No drink, of course, but it will be great *craic*. There'll be a lot of fellows there from all around and there'll be dancing, and—"

"But can you dance?" I blurted out. I could have bit my tongue off. I sounded just like Theresa's ma.

Theresa grinned at me. "Och, aye. I just drag this old thing around after me," she said, looking down at her club foot.

I felt a rush of admiration for her. "I don't think I'll be going, Theresa," I said. "I'm not one for social events."

"Well then," said Theresa, "we'll just have to book the Ulster Minstrels."

The day before the ball, Theresa presented me with a white satin blouse she had made. It had a low neckline and wee pearl buttons on the sleeves. Unlike me, Theresa was a great hand with a needle.

"It'll go well with your long black skirt," she said, pleased that I liked it. "And for Jesus' sake wear some jewelry. I'll lend you one of my necklaces. It's only glass, but it's a lovely green color—it'll match your eyes."

I thanked her and laughed. There was no opposing Theresa. Small as she was, she always got her way. I promised I would wear whatever she gave me, even though I would feel awkward all decked out and drawing attention to myself. Wasn't my size enough to cause remarks, without lighting myself up like a bloody Christmas tree?

◌◍

ON CHRISTMAS EVE night, I rode in the tram to the party along with P.J. and Mrs. Mullen. I had persuaded P.J. and the boys to play, even though P.J. was scandalized that there would be no porter to wet the throat. I wore Theresa's white blouse, a necklace of glass emerald-colored stones, and a green ribbon threaded through my braid. The band uniform was black trousers and white open-necked shirts, so I wore a long black velvet skirt. Mrs. Mullen got tears in her eyes and said I looked lovely.

We joined the crowd of people walking toward the Community Hall in the middle of the village. The night was chilly, and there were flurries of snow. People were wrapped up in mufflers and hats, and everyone talked away a mile a minute. When we entered the hall, I gasped. The place was like a fairyland. It was lit by gas lamps and lanterns. Streamers of green, white, and red crisscrossed the ceiling. Holly wreaths with red berries and dusted with white hung around the walls. Bunches of mistletoe hung here and there. Dozens of round tables covered in white tablecloths and adorned with candles and colorful Christmas crackers ringed the hall. On one side of the room, a long table was piled with roast beef, ham, bread, fruit, and pastries, along with big bowls of fruit punch and cider.

Theresa rushed up to us, her face glowing. "Och, you're here," she breathed. "Isn't it lovely? I designed all the decorations myself."

"It's grand, Theresa," I said, "and you look well."

She blushed and looked down at the jade velvet dress she wore. It was low cut in front, with a lovely long full skirt. The color of the dress made her hazel eyes shine. Her dark hair was coiled up on top of her head. She looked elegant. The club foot seemed a faraway thing at that moment.

"Me ma says the dress is scandalous." She giggled. "She said a rosary for me before she came out of the house tonight, to save me from the devil. The blouse looks well on you."

I touched the smooth sleeves. "It's lovely, Theresa. Thank you, even though you could choke a horse with this necklace." I fingered the emerald beads.

"Nonsense," said Mrs. Mullen. "It's beautiful on you."

P.J. looked around the room. "So this is the place?" he boomed. "I never thought I'd be playing for the Temperance Society. No matter . . ." He paused and patted the pocket of his coat. "I have a wee drop of insurance with me in case I faint from the thirst."

Mrs. Mullen gasped. "Och, P.J. Don't let them be seeing you with that!"

"Never mind, darlin'. They'll turn a blind eye, or they'll do without the finest fiddler in Ulster!" P.J. puffed out his chest. He looked like a rooster strutting the walk. Mrs. Mullen and I both laughed out loud at him.

We threaded our way through the crowd toward the stage to set down our instruments. Many of the women from the mill waved and called hello. I didn't recognize some of them without their scarves and aprons. They wore a rainbow of colors, their hair arranged just so, their cheeks red from the cold air. The men looked awkward in jackets and tight collars, their hair brushed back and smoothed with oil.

Mrs. Conlon sat in state at a front-row table, clutching her walking stick, her little eyes roaming over the crowd. She nodded toward me but said nothing. Terrence, Fergus, and Gavin were already seated on the stage. They each patted their coat pockets and nodded toward P.J. Jesus, I thought, I hope they don't disgrace me. I sat down and we waited for the crowd to settle themselves. A tall, elegant, dark-haired woman in a lovely bonnet came in holding the arm of a gray-haired man with a craggy, stern face.

"Them's the Sheridans themselves," whispered P.J.

A younger, pale blond woman along with a ruddy-faced middle-aged man followed them in. I shifted my eyes away from them and stared toward the door. I realized I was looking for Owen Sheridan and was vaguely disappointed when I didn't see him. I busied myself tuning up my fiddle. And suddenly there he was. His family was already seated when he came in the door, shaking snowflakes off his overcoat. I tried not to watch him, but I couldn't stop myself. He looked well in a black tuxedo suit, white shirt with a high, starched collar, and black bow tie. His blond hair was longer than last I saw him, and he ran a slender hand through it to shake off the snow. He stood rod straight and flashed a smile at Miss Galway as she made a beeline for him. She took his arm and escorted him in the direction of the Sheridans' table. The oul' bat was making sure none of the mill girls could get close to him. He nodded and smiled around at the crowd. My throat tightened. I saw now what the women meant—he was indeed a handsome man. He must be ten years older than me, I thought, a fact that should have made him more interesting than the fellows my own age. But the truth was I did not know what to make of him. Then he saw me. Surprise lit his face. He must not have realized I was going to be there. I tore my gaze away and went back to tuning my fiddle.

Joe Shields was in his element as the master of ceremonies. He almost burst out of his tight, shiny black suit. His chest and belly formed an arc under his white linen shirt. All in all, he looked like a fat seagull. He cleared his throat and looked down at the notes he clutched in his pudgy hand. Stupid eejit, I thought, he can't even remember the names of the people without help.

"Welcome one and all to the first annual Spinners' Ball," he boomed.

There was loud applause.

Shields pointed toward the Sheridans' table. "I'd like to thank the Sheridan family for their kind patronage in making this event possible . . ." He went on, spreading the compliments thick as butter. Mrs. Sheridan lowered her eyes and stared at the table, as did Owen and the other couple. Only old Mr. Sheridan seemed ready to take his bow—he nodded around at the assembly, although no smile cracked his stern face.

"And last but not least," Shields went on, "I'd like to thank the workers' committee, chaired by Miss Theresa Conlon. I think you'll agree they
made a lovely job of it."

I looked over at Theresa and caught her wide smile. Her mother sat
next to her, glaring straight ahead.

"And now, it's my pleasure to introduce to you the Ulster Minstrels,
featuring our very own Fergus Conlon on the mandolin, and Miss Eileen
O'Neill on the fiddle."

As the applause rose again, Owen Sheridan grinned widely at me. Our
eyes met briefly, and his mother followed his gaze. Then, as P.J. tapped
three times with his foot, the Ulster Minstrels began to play.

☯

THERE'S SOMETHING ABOUT a holiday party, no matter how crowded,
that makes you fiercely aware of the people missing from your life. As I
watched the dancers, I imagined Ma and Da twirling around the room,
Da's bright red hair springing out in all directions as he smiled up at
my lovely, graceful ma. I wondered if Great-Grandda Hugh's ghost was
there, enjoying the *craic*. I wondered how Frankie was that night. I pitied
him crouched in the cold stables, alone with his anger. I thought about
Lizzie. She would have been almost ten and not old enough to be there,
but Da would have brought her anyway. I imagined her dancing with
Da or Frankie in a pretty blue dress, her long blond hair tied in matching ribbons. And Paddy—lonely, troubled child—I wondered if he would
ever grow up and enjoy flirting with the girls like the young chaps there
tonight.

Theresa whirled in front of the stage in the arms of a young, fresh-
faced fellow not much taller than herself. She waved at me and winked
over his shoulder. I smiled back. Oul' Mrs. Conlon's glare followed Theresa, her mouth set in a prim line, while she fingered the silver cross at
her throat. Mrs. Mullen had made the mistake of sitting beside her. She
looked up at me and rolled her eyes. The Ulster Minstrels had the place
hopping—people clapped their hands and tapped their feet and cheered
us after every set. I had long ago overcome my shyness on the fiddle,
and I was in great form. When the time came for a break, I was exhausted
and covered in sweat. I climbed down from the stage and pushed my
way through the crowd toward the door to get a breath of air. I stepped
outside and bumped straight into Owen Sheridan.

"Miss O'Neill!" he said, as if surprised to see me. "Are you finished playing? I was hoping to hear more. You have developed into an accomplished musician."

I shook my head. "Och no, sure we're only taking a break. P.J. and the boys are back in there taking a little refreshment."

"Punch, I assume?" he said with a laugh.

"Aye," I said.

I shivered a little and wrapped my arms around myself. He took a cigarette out of a silver case for himself and then offered me one. I shook my head no. He snapped the case shut, lit the cigarette, and inhaled deeply. His movements were slow and graceful.

"You smoke, too, I see," I said. "I wouldn't take that for a Quaker habit, either."

He laughed. "You have me again, Miss O'Neill. I'm the prodigal son. I assume you have no bad habits to speak of?"

"Oh, I take the odd stout once in a while," I said, "and I can curse a blue streak. Besides that, I'm as close to a saint as you can get."

I didn't know what had come over me. I tried my best to sound relaxed, but the truth was I was shaking more with nerves than from the cold. "It's time I went in," I said.

He put a hand on my arm. "You've not had a chance to dance . . . ," he began.

"I don't dance," I said quickly.

"Nonsense. All the Irish dance. It's in their blood. Like poetry. Would you do me the honor of dancing with me?"

I shook my head furiously. "I can't," I said. "I have to play."

"Och now, we can do without you for one dance, love." P.J.'s voice boomed out from behind me. I swung around and glared at him. He winked back at me.

The boys struck up a Viennese waltz as Owen Sheridan escorted me into the hall, his hand resting on the small of my back as it had done weeks before on Slieve Gullion. My face burned as he turned me around, placed my hand on his shoulder, and took my other hand in his. I thought of how I used to waltz with Da when I was a little girl, but the image faded as we moved to the music. Everyone in the hall was watching us. I knew what they were thinking—it was scandalous for one of the gentry to be dancing with the likes of me. But it didn't seem to bother Owen Sheridan. He was the black sheep, after all. He smelled of clean soap and mild cologne. I felt the fine thread of his jacket through my fingers on his shoulder. Heat radiated on my back where his hand pressed lightly against it. My face was even with his, and I stared directly into his eyes. They were dark tonight, almost violet. As we spun to the music, I felt a grace I had never known before. Suddenly my hands and feet were not as big, my body not as taut. I was no longer primed for battle. I closed my eyes and flowed with the music to some distant place. I held my breath.

"So, you are still at the mill?" His voice cut through my trance.

My awkwardness returned and my guard went up. "And why wouldn't I be?" I snapped.

He looked as if he were sorry he had spoken.

"Well, while Mr. Shields tells me you are happy being a doffer, I'm not sure I believe him. I took you for a more ambitious girl."

I stopped dead in the middle of the dance. "That bloody bastard!" I cried. "He's refused to move me up even though I've asked a dozen times." I was glad of the anger. I was back on safe ground. "It's because I interfered—about the splash boards."

Owen Sheridan caught my hands again with a sudden strength and forced me to dance. I was aware of stares. "Surely not," he said mildly.

"You don't feckin' know him," I said, tightening my grip on his shoulder.

He nodded and smiled toward the other dancers, deflecting their stares. "I will speak to him," he said.

"Oh, don't do that," I said, "you'll only make things worse."

He smiled. "Worse than being condemned to be a doffer all your life?"

The music ended, but he held on to my arm. "Shall we get some punch?"

"I should get back to the band."

"They seem to be doing quite well without you. Shall we sit over here, near the door where it's cooler?"

He led me to a chair and then went to fetch the punch. The mill women winked over at me and whispered among themselves. I tried to look unconcerned. Theresa brushed past me, her dance partner in tow, as they made for the door. "You'll tell me everything next week," she whispered.

He came back carrying two glasses of punch and sat beside me. He looked around the hall. "I shall miss all this," he said.

I shot a look at him. "Why, where are you going?"

"I'm leaving for England after the holidays. I have accepted a commission in the army."

"Why in the name of God would you be doing that?" I blurted out.

He smiled. "Because England will be at war soon. They will need good leaders."

"But you're a Quaker," I insisted. "I thought Quakers don't believe in fighting."

He grinned. "Ah, you have me yet again, Miss O'Neill. But I believe in doing service for my country, even if it requires taking up arms."

I swallowed some punch. Then the devil danced into my head. "Och, you're probably just looking for a bit of excitement," I said.

His eyes flashed. "You think me that shallow, Miss O'Neill? I am sorry I have given you cause for such a low opinion of me." Annoyance filled his voice. So he had a temper after all! He wasn't always the cool, calm, and collected fellow he made himself out to be. For reasons I did not understand, I was pleased.

He caught himself then. "I am joining up because I hope to make some difference in the world," he went on more calmly. "God knows I'm not contributing much with my present way of living." He looked at me and sipped some of the punch. "Or, as you say, maybe I am just looking for some excitement."

He looked toward the head table where his parents sat. "I haven't told my parents the news yet," he said. "It's going to be a difficult conversation. My mother in particular abhors violence."

"Have you no wife to knock some sense into you?" I said.

He looked back at me. "No. I don't."

Jesus. I had gone too far again. "I'm sorry," I said quickly, "that was forward. This tongue of mine will be the death of me."

He laid a hand on my arm. Again, I was aware of his slender fingers, so like my da's. He smiled. "On the contrary, it's refreshing to meet a woman who speaks her mind. Although I was rather hoping that you would simply say that you would miss me."

I was pondering the notion of being called a woman when a shrill voice cut in.

"Oh, Mr. Sheridan, I have been looking for you. I'm going to take you up on that dance offer." The shadow of Mary Galway rose above us, her buckteeth bared in a false smile.

Owen Sheridan stood up, and I stood with him. "Forgive me, I must go," he said. "Thank you for the dance, Miss O'Neill, and Happy Christmas." Then he leaned over and brushed his lips across my cheek.

I stood stunned. My cheek burned. I looked up and saw a sprig of mistletoe hanging from the ceiling. Slowly I walked toward the stage, ignoring the smiling and winking mill women. It was only a Christmas kiss, I told myself. He'll probably be pecking away at old Mary Galway's cheek in a minute. No matter, I had no time for men or for their foolishness. I had my life all sorted out.

I reached the stage and gave P.J. a dirty look, as if everything were his fault. Then I took up my fiddle and began to play with ferocious energy.

War

1914–1918

8

On the fourth of August 1914, Britain declared war on Germany. As Ireland was under British rule at the time, that meant Ireland was at war as well. The newspapers were full of reports of Irish boys, Catholic and Protestant, joining up. There was no conscription, but for a variety of reasons they volunteered anyway. About fifteen thousand men of the Ulster Volunteer Force, the Protestant paramilitary organization, joined to show their allegiance to the mother country. Catholic nationalists who had been pushing for Home Rule for Ireland were committed to the war by their leader, John Redmond, on the grounds they should support Belgium, which had been invaded by Germany. He called Belgium a small Catholic country in bondage, just like Ireland. He said this move would help cement Home Rule for Ireland.

Some Catholic boys joined because the money was good. An unskilled worker could more than double his pay in the army. Others were simply after the adventure—to see what war was like and to feel like grown men. Theresa's brother James turned out to be one of these.

"He's left the seminary!" Theresa screeched one morning as we walked up the stairs of the mill.

"Who?" I said.

"James!" she cried. "He's enlisted. Me ma's destroyed with worry."

I shrugged. I could not see that there was much to choose between the seminary and the army. One was as bad as the other. But I felt sorry for Theresa all the same.

"Och, he'll be all right," I said. "He probably just wanted to see a bit of the world."

Theresa bit her lip. "Me ma's on her knees praying morning, noon, and night," she said. "I don't know how I'm going to put up with it."

"At least you can leave the mill now. You won't be needing to pay any more school fees."

Theresa looked horrified. "I'd rather go to work in hell than listen to Ma crying all day long."

"Aye."

☙❧

AS TIME WENT on, word came of other boys joining up. Tommy Mc-Parland, Theresa's dance partner at the Spinners' Ball, volunteered and they took him even though he was only five feet three inches in height. I supposed the government didn't care as long as you could carry a gun. A number of other men around Queensbrook volunteered as well, even some who had the skilled jobs. I made inquiries about Frank. He was eighteen now and old enough to join up. I thought maybe he would jump at the chance to escape from the Fitzwilliam estate, and I would not have blamed him. But P.J. reported that he was still at the farm. I was relieved that he was safe but wondered what had kept him there.

"If conscription comes, he'll have to face it, though," P.J. said.

The war was good for the linen industry. Demand went up, and Shields and Mary Galway drove us like slaves to produce more. I was moved up to a spinner right after Christmas. You should have seen Shields's face when he told me. He would rather have given the job to the devil than to me, but I knew he had no choice. I had opened my mouth again to Owen Sheridan, and Shields had been told to promote me. I shrugged. Feck him, I thought, I hardly needed the likes of him as my friend. The whole atmosphere on the floor changed, though. Because spinners worked on time and not by the piece, they had been used to a certain pace that let them slow down once in a while and enjoy the *craic* or celebrate the occasional birthday or engagement. Sometimes an operator would leave a few loose threads flying on the spinning frame while she enjoyed a break, and the management would not pass any remarks. Now, though, the minute Shields or Mary Galway saw this happening, one or the other would swoop down on her like a vulture. She was to tie the threads immediately and not be slowing production. Those two had eyes in the backs of their heads. Women were threatened with the sack if they gave any guff. There were plenty of women whose husbands were in the war that would be glad of their jobs, Shields would say.

The worst of it came when Mary Galway announced we would be fined if we were caught talking, singing, laughing, or even straightening our hair. Bloody nerve of them! If I wanted to live in silence, I would have joined the Carmelite nuns. The trouble was, we had never heard of unions. If we had, we would hardly have put up with the conditions as they were—working in that hot hellhole until the color drained from our cheeks and we caught our deaths from pneumonia. Now they wanted to take away what little comfort we had. What added insult to injury was that Mary Galway herself, being the only woman in management, refused to speak up for us.

I was fit to be tied when I told P.J. about the change the first evening.

"Are these fines even legal?" I shouted.

"No. But what can you do, darlin'?" he said. "Sure a strike is the only answer. But you've no organization, and you'll not get one at that place— the Quakers are antiunion. You'd have to get them all to follow you out at the one time, or you'd be sacked as a troublemaker."

"I'm already a troublemaker," I said.

P.J. put more tobacco in his pipe and tamped it down, then lit it and inhaled slowly as he always did when turning things over in his head.

"Aye, but you don't have Owen Sheridan around to protect you now he's away in the army."

I flared up at the comment. "I don't need his or anybody else's protection," I said.

But I knew P.J. was right. Even though I had never admitted as much, there was always the thought in my mind that if I needed something at the mill, I could go to Owen Sheridan, and as long as it was a reasonable request, he would get it done. He was my weapon against Shields, who would sack me as soon as look at me. I wondered, not for the first time, how Owen Sheridan was faring in the war. Had he gone to the front yet? The sensation of his kiss on my cheek on Christmas Eve had long since cooled, folded away in a chest of sweet and childish memories. He had said he hoped I would miss him. The truth was I did. I had not seen him since the Spinners' Ball, and his absence caused a new and unexpected void in me, tiny as a pinprick, which I filled with work and single-minded focus on my dream. I said a silent prayer for his safety.

"You've a fair bit saved now?" P.J. said.

I smiled and nodded. "Aye. I've a long way to go before I could think

of buying any house, let alone the Yellow House. But I know one day I'll
be able to do it."

P.J. said nothing. He knew by the question he had set my mind in
motion. Was I willing to risk my dream to get justice for the mill girls?
Wasn't I better off keeping my head down and my mouth shut? The
O'Neill warrior inside me wanted to strike out and lead the charge. But
then I thought of Ma sitting in that old place surrounded by madwomen.
I had made her a promise. And I had made a promise to Paddy. I couldn't
risk letting them down.

I sighed. "You're right, P.J."

He nodded. "You have to learn to pick your battles, girl."

As I lay in bed that night, Da's face appeared to me. "You're a warrior,
darlin', a descendant of the great O'Neills." I fought back tears.

"I'm not the warrior you wanted me to be, Da," I whispered. "I'm sorry
I'm letting you down."

ON A SEPTEMBER Sunday in 1914, about a month after war was declared, I strolled down Hill Street in Newry, holding Paddy by the hand.
We had been to late mass at Newry Cathedral. It had become our habit to
go together to the twelve o'clock mass. I craved this time alone with my
brother, and he seemed willing enough to go with me each week. He was a
quiet lad, so we never talked much, but it was lovely just the same to kneel
beside him in the church and then take his hand in mine as we dandered
along the street, stopping every so often to look in shop windows.

Old Father Dornan had given a long, boring sermon on our obligation
to pray for the boys going to war, no matter what their religion, that they
might come to no harm. He could have got it across in five minutes, but as
was usual for him, he made a bloody big meal of it. The oul' blatherer loved
hearing himself talk. I was parched with the thirst from listening to him.

"Will we go and get a lemonade, Paddy?" I said.

He looked up at me, blue eyes suddenly bright, and nodded.

I reached up and took off my hat. Unlike Ma, I hated hats and wore
one only to mass. Paddy pulled off his cap, too, and stuffed it in his pocket.
I shook out my long braid and inhaled the soft, cool September breeze.

"Ah, freedom." I laughed. "Shall we go?"

I grabbed for Paddy's hand again and swung him around so that we
could walk in the direction of the café. As I did so, I collided with a man
in a British Army uniform. Startled, I jumped back.

"Please excuse me, sir," I muttered. "I wasn't looking where I was going."

"Well, and if that isn't the nicest apology I've ever had from you," said a familiar voice. "In fact, I think it's the *only* apology I've ever had from you."

Owen Sheridan beamed at me from beneath an army lieutenant's peaked cap. I swallowed hard, as if I'd had the wind knocked out of me. He was thinner than I remembered—not thinner, exactly, but more lean and taut. He stood erect, the sun glinting off the buttons of his jacket. I forced my eyes away from him and looked down at Paddy instead.

"This is my brother," I said, "Paddy O'Neill. Paddy, this is Mr. Sheridan."

" 'First Lieutenant Sheridan,' if you please. I didn't go through all that training not to get my full title." He smiled as he spoke, the old teasing kind of smile I remembered.

I shrugged. "Lieutenants are nineteen to the dozen these days."

Paddy tugged on my arm and gave me a wistful look. I remembered the lemonade.

"I, er, I just promised Paddy I would take him for a lemonade," I said. An odd feeling had come over me. I wanted to get away from Owen Sheridan in order to collect myself, but at the same time I didn't want to say good-bye. I had been thinking about him on and off for months, and now here he was big as life and me at a loss for words.

"Wonderful idea!" he said. "Please allow me to accompany you. It will be my treat."

Without so much as a by-your-leave, he stepped to the outside of the pavement and linked his arm in mine, urging me forward.

"Morocco's Café, I assume?" he said, nodding and smiling at passersby as if he were the cat who got the cream. I kept my head down as people turned around to look at us. I recognized many of them from the mill or as customers of the Ceili House. There would be quare gossip about this. The talk about his dance with me at the Spinners' Ball had only just died down; now it would start up again. I held on so tightly to Paddy's hand that he finally wrenched himself free and skipped on ahead.

"Fine-looking boy," said Sheridan.

"Aye," I said.

We wound our way through the crowds that filled the pavement. Many were families with a young man in army uniform in their midst. Young soldiers were everywhere, eager and ready for adventure.

Morocco's Café was a popular meeting place in Newry. It had an exotic appeal with its gold-lettered signs, walls covered with paintings of faraway landscapes, and an owner of unknown origins. Mr. Morocco, if that was his real name, was dark-skinned and spoke little English. His Irish wife translated for him. She was not from Ulster, either. Their two daughters were as dark-skinned and mysterious as their father. When you entered the café, it was as if you were transported to an enchanted and slightly dangerous world.

Paddy raced in ahead of us and claimed a table and three chairs near the window. Owen Sheridan escorted me over to the table, his hand on the small of my back radiating warmth. When Paddy and I were settled, he went over to the counter to order. I watched him as he walked up and down, inspecting the pastries and breads set out on big wooden trays and pointing to the ice-cream bin in the far corner. He chatted easily with the owner, who smiled when he saw him and reached over to shake his hand. Funny, I never took him for one who would come to a place like this. I always imagined that he would be taking high tea in some posh hotel, but it was obvious that Mr. Morocco knew him. I set my hat on the windowsill behind me and unbuttoned my dark green jacket. I was glad it was Sunday and I had worn the best clothes I owned. I was not one for style like Theresa. If I was not wearing my mill apron, I wore my band uniform— except for Sundays. I don't think up to then I could have told you what giddiness felt like, although I recognized it sometimes in the mill girls. But now the fluttering in my stomach and the racing of my seventeen-year-old heart confirmed that even I, Eileen O'Neill, was not immune to it.

Owen Sheridan returned with a tray loaded with food and drinks: lemonade, steaming tea, wedges of cake with pink icing, and three paper cones filled with ice cream. Paddy's eyes widened and he clapped his hands. Dimples creased his cheeks. He stared at Sheridan in awe.

"Thanks, mister," he said.

"Thanks, Lieutenant," I corrected, grinning. "Jesus, you bought out the shop."

Sheridan grinned back. "I was born with a very sweet tooth."

We ate and drank. Between bites, I learned that he was home on leave before shipping out to France. He had two days before he left. Paddy, having overcome his shyness and stuffing in all the cake and ice cream he could manage, asked him a lot of questions about being a soldier. Sheridan answered politely, leaning back in his chair, his long legs crossed at the ankles.

"And have you ever killed anybody?" asked Paddy.

"Jesus, Paddy! That's an awful question to be asking."

"A fair one, just the same," said Sheridan. His smile faded and he sat straight up in his chair. The earlier ease had gone, and now he was tense as a rabbit sensing a fox.

"I have never killed anyone, Paddy. But I do not doubt that I shall when I get into the war."

"You don't seem too keen on it," I said, finishing off the last of my cake.

He stirred his tea in an absentminded way. "No, I'm not," he murmured, "but it's inevitable. I have wrestled with the thought for months."

He looked at me and his eyes clouded. "I just hope to God I'm doing the right thing."

The mood at the table had turned somber. Owen Sheridan became lost in his own thoughts. I was annoyed that things had taken such a turn. I didn't want to talk about the war. I wanted to talk about lighter, happier things. This dark talk did not fit my mood. Paddy began to fidget. I pressed some coins into his hands.

"Go and pick out a cake to bring home to Mrs. Mullen for the tea," I said. He jumped down off his chair and ran up to the counter.

"Damn it, I had to do something!" Sheridan's sudden outburst startled me, and I sat up straight. "I couldn't go on the way I was living—shallow, without any purpose. I had to find something I believed in. I had to find a way to give my life meaning, to make a difference."

It was as if he were talking to himself.

"The mills give my father purpose, but I find no pleasure in them. They are horrible, sordid places."

I wanted to pass a rude remark, but for once I curbed my sharp tongue.

"I've considered teaching," he went on, "someday, perhaps, but not now. What life experience and wisdom do I have to pass on to young people? How to rebel against your parents?" He gave a snort and lit up a cigarette.

"How did your parents take your decision?" I said, not just for want of something to say. I was truly interested. This was a side of the man I had never suspected. Doubts? Search for a meaning? Even in my young mind, I felt in that moment we had much more in common than I would ever have thought.

"Well, Father was stoic as usual, but disappointed. And Mother cried for days. Not only because I'm going to the war and she fears for my life, but because I am committing the final rebellion against everything they stand for. They abhor violence. And here I am going off to kill men." He sighed and took a long draw on his cigarette. He finally looked at me, as if just realizing I was there. "The irony is that this rebellion is different. I am not going against their values just to show them I can do it, as I did when I was younger. This rebellion is necessary to save my soul."

I was so mesmerized, listening to him, that I jumped when Paddy came back and dropped a huge chocolate cake on the table.

"You didn't eat your ice cream, Eileen," he said.

"Oh, right," I said absently, and brought the paper cone to my mouth. The ice cream had melted, and some of it ran down my chin. Paddy started laughing, and I blushed in confusion. Owen Sheridan reached into his pocket and pulled out a white linen handkerchief.

"Here, let me," he said softly, and reached over and wiped my chin as if I were an infant. I sat motionless while he did it. Echoes of Ma's soothing voice as she bathed a scratch on my small cheek drifted into my head. How long had it been since someone had taken care of me? I had forgotten what it was like. When he was finished, he folded the handkerchief and replaced it in his pocket. He stood up.

"Well, I must be going, Miss O'Neill. Big family farewell dinner tonight." He winced. "Not that I shall have much of an appetite."

"Not surprising," I said, looking at the empty dishes on the table. I tried to make my voice jaunty in hopes of raising his spirits, the way I sometimes did with Ma or Da. I also wanted to shake off the memories that had just come over me.

Paddy ran out into the street. I lifted my hat from the windowsill and buttoned up my jacket. Sheridan studied my hands as they closed the buttons. I hoped he did not notice the mended buttonholes or the frayed cuffs. Suddenly he put out his hand and touched my sleeve.

"Would you do me the honor of writing me a letter now and then, Miss O'Neill?" He smiled. "I understand soldiers always welcome news from home. You can address the letters in care of Queensbrook House."

I was stunned. My thoughts and emotions jumbled themselves up, and I could not wait to get out the door to clear my head. I allowed my sharp tongue to come to the rescue.

"And what makes you think I know how to write?" I said. "After all, I'm just a poor mill girl."

He smiled. "Ah, no, Miss O'Neill. You are much more than that."

As he walked off down Hill Street, I made a big show of buttoning Paddy's coat and fiddling with his cap to let him get well ahead of me. I watched him until he disappeared into the crowds. He did not look back.

9

The war was supposed to be over by Christmas. All the news reports said so, and they were all wrong. By 1915, Japan had allied with Great Britain, and Turkey had joined the Germans in the conflict. Fighting was taking place on land and sea. It was clear the war was going to continue for a long time. In May, the fight struck close to home. First, the luxury passenger liner the *Lusitania* was sunk by the Germans off the coast of County Cork, and then London was bombed by the German Zeppelin airships. By 1916, the British government introduced conscription for men between the ages of eighteen and forty-one, although, thank God, it did not extend to Ireland. I assumed that Frankie must be fighting, but when P.J. came with word that Frank said he hadn't signed up on the grounds that he was the sole support of his sick mother, I went into a rage. I had seen neither skin nor hair of my brother since that one time at the Fitzwilliam stables. Now I wanted to go back there and confront him. How dare he say he was supporting Ma! When I calmed down I changed my mind, of course, but I still didn't understand why he would prefer life with our grandfather over going into the army. Frankie had always loved the notion of battles—he would have been in his element in the middle of a war.

In July 1916, one of the bloodiest battles of the war took place in France: the Battle of the Somme. Twenty thousand British troops perished on the first day. The newspapers were full of the story. Almost six thousand of those killed had been members of the Ulster Volunteer Force. The sorrow in Ulster was so great that the Orange Order, a Protestant organization, canceled their annual celebrations commemorating the 1690 victory of King William, Prince of Orange, over the Catholic king James of Scotland at the Battle of the Boyne, an important event to the Protestant community.

I could not get Owen Sheridan's face out of my mind. I had never written to him. I had started a dozen or more letters, only to have my pen slow to a halt after the first few sentences. What was I to say to him? What could I tell him that his family and friends could not? How could I tell him that I missed him for reasons I myself did not understand? And then I thought of the looks there would be on the Sheridan family faces when they saw a letter from me addressed to him at Queensbrook House. Could they have stopped themselves from tearing it open and reading it? I would be disgraced—a poor Catholic upstart at the mill who got above herself and had the cheek to write to the likes of Owen Sheridan! And so I gave up the idea. I convinced myself that I had no obligation to write to him—after all, he had no notion of writing to me. Still, I kept my ear to the ground, hoping to get some news of him at the mill.

At home, political unrest increased. The Irish push for Home Rule had been put on hold when the war started, but a small band of frustrated nationalists, who had ignored a call by John Redmond, Home Rule Party leader, to join the British Army, formed the Irish Citizen Army and began planning a rebellion against British rule in Ireland. On Easter Sunday 1916, some eighteen hundred volunteers seized the General Post Office and various other major buildings in Dublin and proclaimed the Irish Republic. Led by poet and schoolteacher Patrick Pearse, they proceeded to shoot it out with the British Army, holding out for a week before they were forced to surrender.

Around Queensbrook, as in the rest of Ireland, there was little sympathy for the rebellion, particularly after it was discovered that they had tried to smuggle in arms from Germany. It was only after the leaders were publicly executed in English jails and their bodies brought back to Ireland for burial that the tide of opinion turned. The English had failed to understand the power of Irish funerals. A man might have been a schemer or chancer all his life—but put him in a box and parade him down to the graveyard with bagpipes, and toast his passing at a wake, and suddenly he was the greatest fellow ever lived. So it was with the rebels. They were idealized as martyrs overnight, and a great shift in the Irish attitude toward the English developed as surely as if there had been an earthquake.

I had grown up knowing that as a Catholic I was in the minority in

Ulster. I learned that the Protestants had been planted in Ulster by the English government, and many Catholics had been thrown off their land. Da had always been great for stories about those times and the battles that had led to the flight of the Earls and the wild geese. I took for granted that the best jobs at the mills went to the Protestants and that in general the Protestants were better off than the Catholics. It was a way of life to me, and it had not occurred to me there was much to be done about it. I planned my life on what was available to me based on my religion and status. I could be a spinner. Maybe I could be a weaver. But I could not get a job in the finishing shops doing embroidery or hemming linens. In the same way, Catholic men rarely got skilled work in the mills, let alone management jobs. The number of Protestant women who had to go out to work was small compared with the number of Catholic women. Protestant men had the better jobs and could afford to keep their wives at home.

I suppose if I had been a Protestant in Ulster at the time, I would have been more than a bit afraid of becoming part of an independent Irish Republic, where I would be in the minority. I would not only lose my privileged advantage, but I might be forced to follow the rules of the Roman Catholic Church. So I couldn't say I totally blamed the Protestants for getting more and more nervous as the movement for Home Rule gained support. They were practical enough to know that if they could not stop Home Rule, they could at least fight to keep Ulster out of it. But as they united behind the idea of a partitioned Ireland, it turned out they were thinking about more than a political solution. The Ulster Volunteer Force, organized in 1912, was armed and ready to fight.

Stories trickled out about clashes between Catholic and Protestant workers in Belfast and other towns around Ulster. Catholic workers on their way to the shipyards were pulled off buses and beaten. Riots broke out, policemen were waylaid and shot, and the papers were full of predictions of doom. For the first time since Da's death, I began to put what had happened that night in the larger context of the religious and political divide in Ulster. Slowly a picture of the enemy emerged in my mind. Was this the direction in which I should turn my anger? Was this emerging sectarian war my personal war as well? The possibility of it chilled me, and I put the thought away at the back of my mind.

At the mill, we were under even more pressure. The war had left them short of skilled male workers, and we were expected to make minor repairs to our own machines where we could. The system of fines was still in place. Poor Theresa paid half her week's wages in fines. She could no more keep her mouth from opening than she could keep the rain from falling from the sky. The women were all in bad form, and at lunchtime they sat on the wall swearing and complaining. They talked halfheartedly about striking, but I knew they would not go through with it. It was then that the devil danced into my head, as he often did. What if we didn't exactly strike, but slowed down? What if, when Theresa blurted out a word or the bars of a song, we all talked or sang at once? What could Shields and Mary Galway do to us? They could hardly sack us all—they needed every worker just now. There would be no obvious ringleader to pin it on. Even if they suspected me, they couldn't prove it.

I grinned with delight the first afternoon we tried it on for size. The look on Mary Galway's face when we all started singing "The Star of the County Down" along with Theresa was worth the price of the fine. She stalked up and down the rows of spinning frames, her face scarlet with sweat and indignation.

"Youse are all fined!" she shrieked like an old crow on a wire.

We all nodded and laughed.

Then Theresa blurted out, "Och, I'm sorry, girls, I couldn't help it."

We all turned to her and answered her out loud:

"Don't worry, Theresa."

"No bother."

"Sure what's a tongue in your head for, anyway?"

We kept it up all afternoon and all through the next day. At the same time, we worked slow and steady, and production dropped. Shields was fit to be tied. But we waited him out, and by the end of the week he announced that he was suspending the fine system.

"But youse better put your arses into the work again," he bellowed, "or so help me I'll swing for the lot of you."

A cheer went up throughout the room. We had won our point. And I had won my first battle.

◎◎

ABOUT A WEEK after our victory at the mill, Joe Shields called me into his office. I'm done for now, I thought. Maybe someone had told him it was my idea to join in the singing and talking with Theresa. It would not have taken much to convince him, given my reputation for troublemaking. I squared my shoulders. I would not let him see that I was afraid.

"Sit down," he growled.

I did as he said and waited.

"You're the cheekiest girl that's ever set foot in this mill, Eileen O'Neill," he said as he eased himself into his chair. "Where you get your brass from I don't know. And now this!"

I was right, I thought, sweat pouring down the back of my neck, I'm going to be sacked. With a shiver, my whole life passed in front of my eyes the way they say it does when people are dying. I saw Da firing the rusty rifle at the intruders outside the Yellow House; I saw Ma's and Frankie's faces as they left our house for the last time; I saw Paddy's innocent eyes looking up at me as I promised him I would get back our home and bring us all together. Och, all the promises, all the dreams, they were slipping away like shadows in the night.

"Miss O'Neill!" Shields's voice cut through my thoughts. I shot straight up in the chair. O'Neill was holding up an envelope in his broad, stubby hand.

"And now this!" he said again. "I almost can't believe this!"

"What?" I said. Annoyance began to surface. "What's that?"

"What's this?" Shields's face burned crimson, and bumps stood out on his bald forehead. "This is a fecking letter addressed to you from Owen Sheridan."

"But he's away in the war," I said.

"So he is. But they can still write letters from over there. And this is addressed bold as brass to yourself care of me at Queensbrook Mill!"

I reached over to take the envelope, but he snatched it away. "You've gone too far this time, girl," he said. "You've got above your station. Who do you think you are corresponding with the likes of Sheridan? How dare you interfere with your betters!"

Anger and confusion rose up in me. "I didn't ask him to write to me," I shouted, "and what business of yours is it if I did?"

His anger matched mine. "It's my fecking business if you're going behind my back and telling him stories about what is going on here in the mill—if you're telling him rumors and lies about me and—"

"Och, don't flatter yourself," I cried. "If I was writing to him, I think I'd have better things to talk about than the likes of you!"

I thought he was going to slap me. He stood up, his whole body shaking, and raised his hand. But he must have thought better of it. Instead he pushed the envelope across the desk toward me. I picked it up and inspected it.

"I'm surprised you didn't open it and read it for yourself," I muttered.

Shields remained standing. "I would not stoop that far, miss," he said,

his voice more even now, "but I can tell you that you are in for a big fecking surprise if you think this fellow has any interest in you at all. He's a
rake, and you're just one more foolish woman throwing herself at him.
Oh, I've heard all about it—walking arm in arm with him bold as brass
down Hill Street in Newry. Well, when the time comes he'll marry his
own kind, mark my words. And then the high and mighty Eileen O'Neill
will get her comeuppance! Now go on, get out, and don't be reading that
thing on company time!"

A thousand answers ran through my head—words I wanted to shout
at him. Marriage? What the feck was he on about? I never thought of
Sheridan that way. And what I did was my own business. I didn't have
to answer to him or anybody! But in the shock of it all, I said nothing. I
thrust the letter into my pocket for fear Shields might snatch it away and
went back to my spinning frame.

◯〉◯

WHEN I GOT home that night, Mrs. Mullen told me I looked pale. I
seized on the excuse to go straight to my room. I lay down on the bed
without even taking off my boots and stared at the ceiling for a long time.
I went over in my mind everything Shields had said to me. Could he have
been right? Was I throwing myself at Owen Sheridan? Did I have hopes
of something more than a friendship? A faint shame crept over me as I
recalled the playful, girlish dreams I had allowed to dance into my mind.
But it was only a bit of fun, I told myself, it was nothing serious at all.

I sat up and shook off the shame, replacing it with my usual anger
at Joe Shields. I examined the envelope. The postmark was France, and
the date on it was July 15, 1916. Jesus, here it was almost September.
Had that oul' bastard Shields been holding it back all this time? And I
wouldn't be a bit surprised if he'd opened it and read it and resealed it,
no matter that he had denied doing anything of the sort. I sighed. And
why was Owen Sheridan writing to me, anyway? I had not written to
him. The cheek of him, I thought, taking it upon himself to write to
me without so much as a by-your-leave. And look at the trouble he had
caused me. I was good and angry by this point, and I tore open the envelope without another thought.

My Dear Miss O'Neill:
  I hope you will forgive my impertinence in writing to you. I had
hoped to receive a letter from you which would more easily justify

my writing a reply, but no letter came. I suppose I never really ex-
pected one, but it would have been lovely all the same.

I hope you are well. I get much news from family and friends at
home, and so am aware of the changes taking place all over Ireland.
I suspect much of the unrest suits your restless temperament—but
I hope you will resist any urge to be brought into it. I realize I have
no right to give you advice—not that you have ever shown any in-
clination to take advice from me or anyone else! You are your own
woman, Miss O'Neill—it is what I admire most about you. Perhaps
it is for this reason that I believe I can write things to you that I can-
not put in words to my family or friends.

But first let me apologize for letting my black mood destroy our
last meeting. I had no right to burden you with my troubles. You were
only a young girl enjoying a pleasant Sunday outing and I cast a
dark shadow on the day. Yet you listened bravely and without judg-
ment, and I am grateful for that. I'm afraid I am about to cast more
dark shadows in this letter, Miss O'Neill, so I will not blame you if
you do not wish to continue reading.

You have no doubt heard by now about the Battle of the Somme.
I never thought to see hell while I was still alive, but that is what
it was—smoke and fire and torment. Men died in my arms, Miss
O'Neill. In all, almost 6,000 of our own 36th Ulster Division per-
ished. Do you know that many of them stormed the hill toward
the enemy bearing their bright orange sashes—the symbol of their
loyalty to England? Was that loyalty misplaced? Was the death of
all these poor creatures a fair price to pay to forge a new order in
Europe? I'm afraid I have no answer. All I can be sure of now is that
there is no glory in war.

I thought war would give me my chance to create some mean-
ing in my own life—a way to fill the emptiness which has always
stalked me even as I played the carefree prodigal son whose only goal
was amusement. But I was wrong. There is no meaning to be had
from war, let alone any glory. There is no meaning to be had from
killing other human beings as I have done. War is an abyss which
sucks in souls both brave and desperate and spits them out again
dead or disillusioned.

As I sit in this ditch under the French moon, my leg throbs with
pain, but it does not compare with the pain in my heart. I worry
now that our own dear Ireland is creating its own abyss into which

valiant and resolute men will march. I can hardly bear the thought of it, Miss O'Neill.

You know, there is an old Quaker philosophy that says there is truth to be found no matter what the source, and we must be open to it. I believe I have found my truth here in hell. Take care, Miss O'Neill, and I wish you well in seeking your own truth.

Sincerely,
Owen Sheridan

I read and reread his letter, the flimsy paper clutched in my hands. A range of emotions coursed through me in wave after wave—joy, anger, pride, pity, and sadness among them. Tears clouded my eyes, and I set aside the letter and lay down.

Poor man! He had sounded so wretched. Sadness filled my heart as I remembered his face that day in Morocco's Café. He had so much wanted this war to be the thing that changed his life. Obviously it had, but not in the way he expected. And while I was too young and inexperienced to understand the true depths of his despair, I felt a warm pride that he had chosen to bare his soul to me. I had bristled with annoyance at his attempts to teach me some lessons—but there again he recognized I was not one to be taking advice. I smiled when I read that. I was not sure I agreed with him on the uselessness of fighting, though—particularly given what was going on in Ireland. I would make up my own mind about that when the time came.

I folded the letter and put it back in the envelope, gently rubbing my fingers across my name on the front, imagining him spelling out the letters in the moonlight. I got up and went to the drawer where I kept the photograph of the Yellow House. I slipped the letter in underneath it. It was in that moment I realized that a bond had been forged between Owen Sheridan and myself, and that no matter what else happened or what other people came into our lives, it would never be broken.

❧

AS 1917 DAWNED, the war in Europe still raged on and unrest at home continued to mount, but I minded my own business. When thoughts of Owen Sheridan came into my head, I chased them away. I had not replied to his letter. What would I have said? I did worry for his safety, but I decided God would do whatever He was going to do without my help or my prayers. My job for now was to keep my head down and my mouth shut as best I could and save my money. I had Ma and Paddy to think about.

Paddy had finally made his Holy Communion in March of that year. He had just turned eight. The priests had made him wait a year on account of his bad behavior at school. Although it had improved from the time he was first enrolled, he still had outbreaks of temper every now and then and lashed out at whoever got in his way. The priests said he couldn't make the sacrament until he understood the difference between right and wrong. I was convinced he knew the difference fine well, but he just couldn't control himself. Eventually the priests gave in, mostly because he was too clever to keep holding him back in school.

He looked so well in his Communion suit, with his hair brushed back and his shoes polished, that I had to wipe away tears. He looked like a proper young man. I missed the feel of his small hands around my neck as he nestled his head in my shoulder the way he did when he was a baby. He was reserved these days, polite but distant—the most I ever got was a kiss on the cheek.

I decided now was the time to bring up with the Mullens the subject of moving Paddy and me into our own house. I could afford the rent, and I would put Paddy into the Catholic school in Queensbrook. The Mullens were defiant. Paddy should go to the Christian Brothers' school, they said, and then maybe, God willing, to the seminary. All the teachers said he had the makings of a priest. Sure he would grow out of his temper in time, they said, and such brains as his belonged in the priesthood. I raved and cursed at them. He was my brother—I would make the decisions.

Mrs. Mullen reached over and took my hand. "I know you want the best for him, love. I know you think it's your duty to take care of him."

"It is," I cried. "We're all that's left of our family."

"Aye, maybe so, but you're a young woman now, Eileen, and entitled to your own life. You've no need to be saddled with a young lad."

"It's not like that," I persisted. "I want to make a home for us. I've saved up for it. I can afford rent now. I know I promised I would take him to the Yellow House one day, but this is a start . . ." I let the words trail off.

Mrs. Mullen shook her head. "It's not your business to be doing that, love," she said gently. "Your business is to make a home for yourself and your own children someday. That's what God wants. That's what your ma and da would want."

"I'm never getting married," I said fiercely.

Mrs. Mullen laughed. "No? A fine-looking girl like yourself? You'll see—when the boys come home from the war, they'll be lined up. You'll have your pick, so you will."

I shook my head.

"Och, you'll change your mind soon enough." She sighed. "Now, about Paddy. You know he's better off here. The poor child has had it hard enough without uprooting him again. He's settled. And P.J. and I are delighted to keep him." She smiled wistfully. "He's like the child we never had."

"Well, why don't we ask him, then?" I shouted. "Just see who he thinks he belongs with. Just see if he'd rather be with strangers than with his own sister!"

I saw by the look on Mrs. Mullen's face that I had hurt her, and I was sorry.

"I've lost everyone else," I said more gently. "I have to keep Paddy and me together. It's all I've thought about. It's what's kept me going."

Mrs. Mullen went out of the room and returned with Paddy. He was still wearing his Communion suit. I walked over to him and took both of his hands in mine. He stiffened.

"Paddy," I whispered, "you know I love you, don't you?"

He nodded. His pale face was solemn.

"You know I want to look after you and keep you safe?"

He nodded again.

"Well, I've found a lovely house in Queensbrook where you and I can live. And there's a fine school there where you can make new friends, and . . ."

He was shaking his head from side to side before I even finished speaking.

"No," he said, "no."

"But I'm your sister. I've always looked after you."

"No," he said again. He pulled away from me, dropping his hands by his sides and balling them into fists. "I want to stay here, Eileen."

"But—" I began.

"You only want this for yourself," he cried, "it has nothing to do with me. Nobody ever asks me what I think! Nobody! Well, I won't go, and you can't make me!"

In horror, I watched the transformation before me. My beautiful, gentle Paddy had turned into a devil before my eyes. His face was red with anger, and his blue eyes were ice. Mother of God, I thought. Is this what the teachers have been talking about? His temper is worse than Frankie's ever was. Stunned, I backed away from him.

Mrs. Mullen took him gently by the shoulders. "C'mon now, lad," she said, "let's get some tea."

As she led him out of the room, he turned and looked at me over his shoulder. The gentle, solemn Paddy had returned.

"We can still go to mass together on Sundays," he said softly.

That night, I took out the photograph of the Yellow House. It was wrinkled and a little torn from all the wear and tear of the years I had carried it with me. White cracks zigzagged across the black-and-white image. I rubbed my fingers over it gently, staring again at Ma and Da and wee Lizzie and myself, all of us smiling out at the camera. I touched Frankie's solemn face and a tear fell on my hand. I would not let my dream be over—not yet—but it was dimmed and tarnished as the photograph itself.

ⴰⴰ

AFTER THE DECISION was made about Paddy, a loneliness I had not known before settled over me like a heavy shawl. I went on living with the Mullens. I went to work each day at the mill, but my legs and arms felt heavy as I tramped up the stairs. Suddenly I wondered, what was the point of it all? My dreams were being ripped into shreds. What was I killing myself for? Why didn't I just give in and put my mind to finding a husband like all the rest of the mill girls? But the thought of myself got up in a fancy frock and high heels and wiggling my arse every time a man walked by was so ridiculous, I almost laughed. I'd be more suited to a nun's habit than that, I thought. Wearily, I went about my work at the spinning frames, resigned to whatever life God had in mind for me.

As it turned out, what God had in mind was James Conlon.

10

The first thing I noticed about James Conlon was that he was clean. He looked as if the grime of ordinary life had never touched him. His tanned face glowed with health, and his thick, brown wavy hair fell back in shiny ripples from his broad brow. Even the cotton bandage and sling that held his injured right arm was as snowy white as a priest's robe.

He came home in late 1917 after taking a bullet in France. Theresa, giddy from the minute he arrived, pestered me until I came to visit.

He sat in the small red armchair beside the fireplace in the Conlons' house, his long legs stretched out toward the hearth. On his lap sat the big gray cat that I had seen often before, but always outside on the windowsill. As he stroked it with his free hand, it purred loudly.

"James. This is my friend Eileen I was telling you about," said Theresa.

He looked at me with clear gray eyes. It was a direct look that gave no hint of his opinion. I found it more unsettling than if he had leered at me. I pushed down a vague sense of anger.

"Eileen O'Neill," I said evenly, returning his gaze.

He set down the cat and, resting his free hand on the arm of the chair, eased himself up. I thought how ridiculous it was for a man that tall to be folded into a wee chair like that. When he straightened up, he was a couple of inches taller than me. He was too big for the room, like a giant in a doll's house.

"I'm very pleased to meet any friend of Theresa's," he said. "I'm sorry I can't shake hands."

His voice was deep and musical, with the lilting cadence common in the speech of natives of South Armagh.

"No bother," I said, looking at the sling.

"O'Neill," he said. He grinned, showing a full mouth of white teeth. "A descendant of the great O'Neills, then." It was a statement, not a question.

"So I'm told," I said.

Theresa bustled out to the scullery and came back carrying a tray of tea and sandwiches. I sat on the sofa and studied him as Theresa set a cup and plate on a small table beside him. He smiled up at his sister. He was a powerfully built man—and even though he was only twenty-one, a year older than me, he had the bearing of someone much older. His face was broad, with a firm jaw and full lips. His long nose had a wee bump in the middle of it. You would have thought the bump on the nose would interfere with his looks, but somehow it made him even more attractive. He was a handsome bugger—there were no two ways about it. I supposed the women must all be mad for him. He wore a crisp white cotton shirt and gray trousers with a crease so sharp, it could have cut butter. You could have seen yourself in the boots, they were polished so well. And yet he was as at ease as if he had been wearing a pair of old overalls.

Even old Mrs. Conlon was smiling. When she came in from the scullery and sat beside me on the sofa, she looked at James as if she were seeing the beatific vision.

"Isn't he the grand chap, Eileen?" she said to me.

A bit of a smile played on his lips. "Aye, Ma, the grandest chap to desert the army," he said.

Mrs. Conlon shot straight up. "Don't be saying that," she cried. "Sure weren't you over there two years and took a bullet for them." She looked at me. "They discharged him fair and square. Don't be listening to his nonsense. He's only codding you."

James sipped his tea. "Well, let's say then I couldn't wait to get back to Queensbrook and go to work at the mill." There was a trace of sarcasm in his voice.

Again Mrs. Conlon turned on him. "But you're going back to the seminary, lad. You'll be taking up where you left off."

James shook his head. "Now, Ma, you know I'm not. I was never cut out to be a priest."

Mrs. Conlon raised her hands in exasperation. "Sure it's that oul' war has turned his head," she said to me. "He'll come around after he's been home awhile."

I almost felt sorry for her at that minute. It was clear to me James meant what he said.

"There'll be plenty of work at the mill," I said. "Many of the men have volunteered. You could get on there easy, I'm sure."

It was the worst thing I could have said, I realized, after I saw the look of disgust on both their faces.

"I always thought I'd go to hell before I went there," spat James. His eyes darkened as if a sudden squall had disturbed their calm. "That place killed my da."

"Now, James . . . ," began Mrs. Conlon.

"Don't 'now, James' me, Ma," he said, anger rising in his voice. "You know I'm right. And look at our Fergus—his hands are destroyed from the bleaches. It won't be long before he'll have to give up the mandolin." He paused and said more quietly, "I suppose I may have to go for a while until I get myself sorted out. I have other plans, but they may take a while to organize."

I was about to ask what other plans he had, but a glare from Theresa stopped me.

"James, why don't you tell Eileen some of the great stories you were telling us," said Theresa. "You know, about all the people you met. Or maybe about the ladies in Paris." She turned to me. "James says they all have great style."

We passed the rest of the evening pleasantly enough. James was a great storyteller. He reminded me a bit of Da the way he dressed things up for the sake of the story. He had a fine sense of humor, and by the end of the night, his eyes brightened and were calm again.

Theresa walked me as far as the tram stop.

"Didn't I tell you he was lovely?" she said, grinning.

I nodded. "Aye, there'll be quare *craic* at the mill when they see him coming," I said, and I believed it.

Theresa shrugged. "Aye, well, he's always had girls after him. It's nothing new to him. But I think he liked you."

She gazed up at me, her big eyes shining in the dusk. "I told him you played the fiddle, and he was very interested. He might come to hear you at the Ceili House."

It was my turn to shrug. "The admission's free," I said.

As I rode home on the tram, I thought about James Conlon. He was not at all what I had expected—a spoiled, pious little mother's boy. No, James Conlon could give me a run for my money. He could well have been an

O'Neill. I recognized the warrior in him as surely as I knew it in myself. I had seen it in his eyes. There was a fire inside him just like the fire inside my beloved Slieve Gullion. An image of Owen Sheridan drifted before me. There was no sign of the warrior in him, I realized, even though he went into war. James Conlon, on the other hand, would kill without a second thought if it served his purpose. Unlike Owen Sheridan, James Conlon would never doubt his war. I knew him as well as I knew myself—James Conlon and I were two of a kind. I shivered slightly, as if someone had just walked over my grave. I would do well to steer clear of him, but even then I knew I was being drawn to him as surely as a moth to a flame.

∞

AS I HAD predicted, the women went wild when they caught sight of James Conlon. He showed up on the spinning room floor on a Monday morning in March 1918, and all work stopped. He was immaculate in a white cotton shirt, black trousers, and a black waistcoat. His shirtsleeves were rolled up to the elbows, exposing strong brown forearms flecked with dark hairs. The sling was gone from his right arm. He nodded at me as he walked past but ignored the other women. I suspected he was enjoying the attention all the same. Cocky bastard, I thought.

"Hello, Eileen," he said in his lilting voice.

I looked down at my bare feet, suddenly embarrassed by their nakedness. He followed my gaze. His smile dimmed. "I see conditions haven't improved much since me da's day," he said. "Theresa told me about this, but you have to see it to believe it."

I shrugged. "You get used to it," I said.

He strolled to a machine at the far end of the room and set down his toolbox. He had been taken on as a mechanic—tenters, they called them—on account of he was good with his hands and had had some experience with it in the army. I thought to myself that they wouldn't have given tuppence for his experience if there had been a Protestant fellow around. Skilled jobs like this never went to Catholics. But the war had changed things, and they took whoever they could get. Theresa beamed with pride as she watched him.

"That's me brother," she announced.

She had hardly a need to say it. They all knew full well who he was. Word had spread within a week of his coming back home. There wasn't a woman for miles didn't know he was Theresa Conlon's handsome brother. Now they licked their lips and clucked like hens at laying time.

"Would you ever come over here and look at my frame, love, it's running very stiff. Maybe you could liven it up for me?"

It was surprising how many machines suddenly broke down that March.

ഇരു

"I NEVER SEE your brother at the Ceili House," I said to Theresa as casually as I could one day as we sat on the mill wall. My curiosity had got the better of me.

A shadow crossed her face. "I wish that's where he was," she murmured.

I knew right then something was wrong. "What d'you mean?"

Theresa sighed. "Well, it's just that he's been very secretive lately. He goes out every night and doesn't come home till all hours."

"Probably has a woman somewhere," I said.

Theresa played with her sandwich. "I want to think that," she began, "but if it was a woman, James would be boasting away about it. And anyway, women with him are nineteen to the dozen. He's never satisfied with just one."

"So what does he tell you?"

"Meetings," said Theresa. "He says he's been to meetings. And Ma's climbing the walls. She thinks he's involved with politics."

"Politics?" I was more than curious now.

"Aye. You know there's a lot of trouble down in the South. They want a free Ireland. The movement may be taking hold up here, too."

"Och, so what if he goes to a few meetings," I said, trying to reassure her, "what's the harm in it?"

Theresa shoved her uneaten sandwich back in the bag and wiped the crumbs off her apron. "I don't know. Me ma's afraid he'll do something stupid and get himself shot again. He hasn't been the same since he came home from the war. He met up with some fellows over there from the South and they told him all about the troubles down there, and now it's all he seems to talk about." Theresa's eyes were wide as she looked up at me.

I patted her arm. "I'm sure it's nothing," I said. "It will all die down."

"Sometimes he stays away the whole night," Theresa went on. Her eyes flashed with sudden anger. "If we'd known he was going to go on like that, me ma would have had no need to put our Fergus out in the shed."

"What?" I said.

"Aye, Prince James had to have his own bedroom, and there's not enough room in the house for all of us. I sleep in the granny's room off the scullery. So Fergus was put out in the back shed with only a bed and no heat. He can come in for his meals, but that's all. Some nights when they're asleep or James is not home, I bring him in to warm himself by the fire."

"And James let this happen?"

"Aye, well, it was Ma's doing. But to tell you the truth, I don't even think James has realized it—he's too preoccupied with his own business." Theresa shrugged. "Ma never treated our Fergus well—came from him not being her own son, I suppose. Fergus's own ma died when he was young, and his da married my ma. She always resented having to rear another woman's child."

Poor Fergus, I thought. I understood now why there was always something secretive about his nature, as if he carried a deep resentment toward the world. And he had been in particularly bad form at the Ceili House the last few weeks. I wanted to smack oul' Mrs. Conlon, and I wanted to shake his brother.

ତ୨ତ

ONE EVENING NOT long after my conversation with Theresa, I found myself alone with James. Theresa had invited me over to tea, but her mother had insisted she go with her to hear a priest from the African missions. Missionary priests, with their firebrand tales from faraway lands, were great sport, and the churches were always packed on mission nights. Theresa apologized, but I told her to go on, refusing the offer to go with them.

"I'll just finish my tea," I said. "I can get the seven o'clock tram."

I was just leaving my cup down in the scullery when James came banging through the door.

"They're away to hear the missionary," I said in response to his questioning look. "I'm away home myself now."

I reached up to the wall peg to get my coat. He came over and stood beside me. Again I was aware of how big he seemed in this small house.

"Could you stay on and have a cup of tea with me?" His voice was quiet, and I could read nothing in his face. I was wary just the same.

"I've had me tea," I said. "I'll just be on my way."

He put his hand on my arm. "Will you not stay, Eileen?" he said. "I'd appreciate the company."

His grip tightened on my arm, and I looked down at his broad, brown hand and then into his eyes. What I saw in them was neither arrogance nor anger, but a cool control that made me reluctant to cross him. I shrugged, dropped my coat on the sofa, and walked into the kitchen.

"You'd think a big fellow like yourself could make his own tea," I said as I bustled about with the kettle.

He stood at the door of the kitchen and grinned.

"Aye, but sure when you're the favorite son in the house with two women fussing over you day and night, you have no need to learn to do for yourself. It's helpless I am without a woman around."

"Aye, the favorite son who lets his poor brother sleep outside in a cold shed while he enjoys his creature comforts." Anger tinged my voice.

His face registered surprise. "Who told you that?" he demanded.

"Your sister," I retorted, "and don't tell me you didn't know."

"I didn't," he said. "I never would have let—"

"Well, your sainted ma thought it was good enough for him."

"I'll speak to her," he whispered.

"You do that. And now get out of my way and let me do my woman's work." I made sure he caught the sarcasm in my voice.

I made tea and sandwiches and brought them into the sitting room on a tray. James sat on the sofa, his long legs stretched out to the hearth, his feet propped up on the fender. I nodded toward the red chair. "You're not on your throne tonight."

He laughed aloud. "Och, sure it's the most uncomfortable seat in the house, but I haven't the heart to tell Ma that it cuts the circulation out of my legs every time I squeeze my arse into it."

I smiled. "You do look like a quare bird when you're all hunched up."

He took a cup of tea off the tray. "It wouldn't suit you either, miss," he said. "You're almost as tall as myself."

"I wouldn't dare sit there," I said. "I made that mistake once and your mother almost turned me to stone."

I sat in the other armchair and sipped my tea. James attacked the sandwiches like a starving man, washing down the mouthfuls with hot tea. The fire blazed in the hearth, and the mantel clock chimed half-past six.

"No meetings tonight, then," I said.

He looked up, startled. "Meetings?"

"Aye. Theresa says you're out every night till all hours."

He didn't answer for a while, but sat chewing on the last sandwich. "Did she say anything else?"

I shrugged. "No. Well, except your ma's worried you've joined up with the Republicans." I laughed to put a bit of lightness in the comment because his face had turned dark.

"Maybe I have," he said.

"It's your business."

We both sat and stared at the fire. I had a feeling that something important had been unearthed and that if I didn't leave now, I might be pulled into it. I put down my cup and stood up.

"Don't go," he said. It was not a command this time.

"It's late. Theresa and your mother will be back any minute, and wouldn't I look a right eejit if I was still here after saying good-bye two hours ago?"

I stacked the dishes on the tray and lifted it. He jumped up—light on his feet for such a big man.

"Let me take that. I'll walk you to the tram."

I shoved the tray at him. "There's no need. I can find my way there blindfolded."

Hurriedly, I put on my coat and scarf and walked to the door.

"Cheerio," I called into the kitchen.

"Wait." He came into the sitting room and over to the door where I stood. We looked at each other in silence. "Well then," he said at last, and opened the door for me. "Safe home. And thanks for the company."

I ran up the street toward the tram stop. I was in an awful state and didn't understand why. I had the sense of narrow escape—from what, I did not know. All I knew was that I had come close to entering a place that was so unsettling, it had all my nerves rattling. I breathed deeply as I slumped down on the bench to wait for the tram.

11
ಞ

During the next few weeks, I spoke to James only occasionally. At lunchtimes he sat on the grass in the middle of a circle of young fellows from the mill. They looked up at him with such reverence, you would have thought he was Moses giving them the Ten Commandments. He was clearly the leader of the band. I suspected it all had to do with politics, and part of me wished I could sit and listen to him as well.

My own interest in politics grew, and I had to admit much of it was on account of James. I read about the Irish nationalist movement that was catching steam. Militias known as the National Volunteers, the Irish Volunteers, and the Irish Republican Brotherhood numbered well over one hundred thousand. A man from West Cork named Michael Collins was stirring things up in the South. He was by all accounts a firebrand, inciting crowds at rallies with his fine oratory. His picture was often in the newspapers. He was a handsome fellow.

One lunchtime my curiosity got the better of me, and I strolled over to where James sat with his followers. He looked up when he saw me. I could see he was surprised, but I could not tell if he was pleased.

"Hello there, Eileen," he said politely.

The young fellows around him elbowed one another and grinned. I glared at them. I supposed they thought I was just another love-struck mill girl trying to get James's attention.

"Can I sit in?" I asked.

James arched an eyebrow. "We were just finishing up," he said. He stood up and nodded to the other men to leave. Then he turned to me. "What did you want to talk about?"

"I want to know more about this Collins fellow," I said firmly. "I've been reading up on him."

A brilliant smile lit his face. "Michael Collins, is it? Aye, he's a handsome fellow all right. There's plenty of women flocking to the cause of Irish freedom on account of him."

My cheeks reddened. I wanted to slap the grin off his face. "Well, I'm not one of them," I said sharply, "I'm only interested in his politics."

His grin stretched even wider. "Well then, you'd be a rare one, Eileen O'Neill."

I shrugged. "Being different is nothing new to me."

He put his hand on my arm, and I let him lead me across the green toward the mill buildings. His hand was rough on my arm, as if a fire seared my skin. I thought of the warm glow Owen Sheridan's touch always caused. Just now I liked the fire more. James was silent for a minute, as if making up his mind about something. Then he stopped and turned to face me.

"If it's serious you are," he began, "you can come and listen to him yourself. There's a rally below in Dundalk next Thursday night. The boys and I have hired a car to take us down. There's room if you'd like to go."

He waited to see if he had called my bluff.

"All right," I said, rising to the challenge.

He grinned again. "Meet me at my house after work," he said.

He strode away toward the weaving shed. I watched him go, his long legs striding easily across the grass. He carried himself well, I thought, like a man who knew who he was and what he was about. For myself, I had no idea what I had just got myself into—but I wasn't going to back down.

∽

I RODE DOWN to Dundalk squashed between three of the mill boys in the back of a motorcar. James sat in the front beside the driver. I had never set foot in a motorcar before, and I was giddy with the experience. Dundalk lay in County Louth, partway between Newry and Dublin. I had never been that far south before. I realized what a sheltered life I had led—Newry to Queensbrook and back every day and mass on Sundays—it seemed so dull now. I craned my neck, looking out the window, ignoring the taunts and winks of the red-faced youths beside me.

As we neared the hall, crowds appeared, streaming down the main street. There were men and women, old and young, well dressed and poor. Among Collins's followers, I knew, were laborers and clerks, teachers and doctors, and poets. We all crowded into the small hall where a podium was set up, behind which was hung the green, white, and gold Irish tricolor flag. People greeted one another with handshakes and salutes. Several men came up to greet James as if he were an old friend. I squeezed into a row near the front. James sat to my right. I was aware of his body close to mine, the heat from his arm that brushed my own, and the rhythm of his breath. I sat as straight up as I could, trying to contain myself in my own space.

A cheer went up as Collins strode onto the stage and stood behind the podium. He was an impressive-looking man—tall and broad-shouldered, with wavy brown hair brushed back from his temples. He was so well dressed, he could have given James a run for his money. There was a hint of a swagger in his walk that spoke confidence but not arrogance. I glanced at James, who was standing and applauding as loudly as the rest of them. He glanced back at me and smiled. There was a shuffle of feet as the crowd settled and the applause died down.

"Dia dhaoibh achan duine. Agus fáilte romhaibh!"

As Collins welcomed the crowd in Gaelic, such a roar went up that it could have lifted the roof off the hall. And then he mesmerized us.

"We gather here tonight because a great change is coming over our land—over our beloved Ireland. For too many years we have suffered under the bondage of our oppressors. They have stolen our land. They have crushed our language. They have starved us. They have imprisoned us. But yet they have not broken our spirit. Our spirit today is as strong as was our fathers' and grandfathers'. Every generation before us has fought to rid our land of English tyranny. I promise you tonight that we will not ask our children to take up the struggle. The fight stops here—with us—with every man and woman in this hall and all over this glorious country of ours. We are the ones who will finish the job!"

Cheers went up from the crowd. How Da would have loved this, I thought. When the noise died down, Collins went on.

"How many promises have we heard from Westminster that one day the Irish will be free to rule Ireland? How many promises have been postponed or forgotten or denied? How long must we wait for Home Rule? One year? Ten years? One hundred years? I will tell you. The waiting is over. We will wait no longer. We will listen to no more promises, no more excuses. We will act now. We will take up our cause and take our country back, by force if necessary, but take it back we will."

Applause broke out, and people stomped their feet. I sat on the edge of my chair, drinking in every word.

"On Easter Monday of 1916, that action was begun. Valiant men stood up and declared a free Ireland. The oppressors herded them on cattle boats and into British jails. But they did not break their spirit. They executed their leaders. But still they did not break their spirit. Instead, they awoke the giant sleeping spirit of Ireland herself—her ghosts rose up, her mountains thundered, and her seas roared. And that roar will echo until Ireland is free."

In answer, a deafening roar filled the hall. And then, as if the audience sensed what was coming, they bowed their heads.

"May the prayers of our saints and the wisdom of our scholars guide us. May the bravery of our great warriors stouten our hearts. May our poets inspire us. And may God bless our cause."

Feet stomped, and hands clapped, and cheers roared around the hall. The man was brilliant. He preached revolution with the words of a poet. Like everyone else there that night, I came away in love with Ireland and with Michael Collins.

It was a fine late summer evening when we all poured out of the hall. Electricity ran through the crowd—an excitement that you could feel in your body as well as your mind. I had never known a night like it. It was breathtaking and frightening.

James came up from behind me and took my elbow. He was smiling.

"Come on," he said.

"Where?"

"To meet the big fellow himself."

The "big fellow" was the nickname many used for Collins. James pulled me through the crowd to where he was standing, a small group of men pressed close around him.

I was suddenly shy. "Ah, no," I said. "Sure what would I say to him?"

James ignored me and strode up to the group, pulling me by the arm. When Collins saw him, he smiled and put out his hand to shake.

"James," he said. "I'm delighted to see you." Collins's Cork accent was even more pronounced than when he was onstage. "I thought 'twas yourself I saw. And who's this fine-looking woman now?"

"This is Eileen O'Neill, a friend of mine from Queensbrook."

Collins gave me a brilliant smile. "A pleasure to meet you, Miss O'Neill."

His hand was large and firm, and I felt my own trembling in his grasp.

"It's her first meeting," said James, smiling.

"And what did you think of it?" said Collins.

I struggled to speak. "I thought," I said, "that it was pure poetry." My face reddened, and sweat trickled down the back of my neck.

Collins beamed. "And poetry aside, do you agree with what I had to say?"

Sudden anger filled me. "It was Unionist bastards killed my da. We owe it to him and those like him to take our country back." And then the devil danced into my head. "But you and your boyos would make a better job of it if you let the women fight instead of making fecking sandwiches!"

I was mortified once the words were out. They hung suspended in the air. I held my breath. For a second Collins said nothing, then his face broke into a wide grin.

"Ah, James, now there's a woman with a head on her shoulders. I'd hang on to her if I were you."

He gave us a nod and moved off to speak to some older men who were calling him. I was afraid to look at James. He was probably fit to be tied over my cheekiness to Collins.

"Come on, let's find the lads," was all he said as we pushed through the crowd to the street where the car was parked.

James was silent all the way home, while the other lads recounted every word of Collins's speech. I think they would have taken up arms there and then if they could and made a run on Belfast—they were that carried away. Young eejits, I thought, out for sport. Did they really understand what this was all about? I was uncomfortable listening to them, but at the same time I sensed a great change was coming all over Ireland.

The driver let me off in Newry outside P.J.'s house. The young lads were up for making a night of it at the Ceili House. James said they could go where they wanted as long as they took him to Queensbrook first. If he said good night to me, I did not hear him. I climbed out of the car in a hurry. I needed to get away and think. Life was suddenly moving too fast for me, and I was afraid I was losing control of it. I could not do that. Control was all I had.

℮⁐

JUST AS WHEN water floods the land it forever alters the landscape, so the tide of Republicanism in Ireland slowly eroded old beliefs and accepted orders. In the weeks that followed my meeting with Michael Collins, I began to see life around me through new eyes. I looked at the mill girls and saw the narrowness that bound their futures. There was no hope for them to make a life for themselves beyond the option of marriage and labor in the mill until they became too old or sick to go on. What opportunities did they have for advancement, education, a better life? None that I could see. And the hard truth was that I was one of them. I began to understand my brother Frank's passion for owning land. Instinctively, even as a child, he had known that without land you had no control of your life. Anger stirred in me. What right did the English have to come all those centuries ago and put us off our land? And what right did they have to come and kill my da? The distinction between the English and the Ulster Protestant thugs who had come that night along with Billy Craig to burn down our house became blurred to me.

For the first time, rightly or wrongly, I put a face on all my troubles. It all stemmed from the actions of the English—taking away land, treating Catholics as second-class citizens, giving them no say over their own affairs. Michael Collins was right—we needed to get them out of Ireland once and for all. These thoughts fueled a new sense of purpose in me. I realize now that I feared my old dream of reuniting my family was fading and that I needed a new dream. The warrior in me had found her war.

I marched over to James Conlon one day and told him I wanted to join the Irish Volunteers.

"And don't think I'm signing up just to bring tea and sandwiches to the meetings the way most of the women do," I said. "I want to train, and I want to learn to fire a gun."

James stared at me, and then he scratched his head and laughed.

"I can see you've your mind made up," he said, "and if I say no, it's another battalion you'll be joining. You may as well join with me so I can keep an eye on you—I think it would be safer!"

Within a week, I was out in the fields at night, drilling with the men. I learned to shoot a rifle. As it turned out, I had a steady arm and a good eye. I could have blasted the head off anybody from two hundred yards away. James was careful, though. He must have sensed the force of my newly focused anger and realized I might be more reckless than was good for me or for anybody else in the battalion. And so I was forced to earn his trust through less risky assignments. At night I rode my bicycle over the small, dark winding roads of South Armagh and South Down, picking up and delivering messages to red-faced men in farmhouses, sallow men behind bank counters, and old, toothless women wrapped in shawls sitting on rocks beside rivers. I never read the communications, but I knew

they contained information on the movements of the police, the Ulster
Volunteer Force, and the British Army, as well as plans for Republican
actions both in Ulster and elsewhere. During the day, I went to my work
at the mill and kept my mouth shut. Theresa eyed me with concern, but
I gave her a look that told her to keep the questions to herself.

☙

IN NOVEMBER 1918, World War I was declared over and there was
great celebration around the country. Irish soldiers, wounded and able-
bodied alike, returned in droves. Tommy McParland came home, and
he and Theresa made plans to be married. Other women in the mill
announced their engagements as well. The atmosphere was giddy. Mr.
Sheridan, the mill owner, announced that the Spinners' Ball, which had
been canceled during the war years, would be held on Christmas Eve in
honor of the returning soldiers. I wondered if Owen was among them.
For the first time in two years, I allowed myself to think about him for
more than a fleeting moment—to remember the heat of his hand on
my back as he waltzed me around the floor, the tingle of his kiss on my
burning cheek, and the gentle way he wiped the ice cream from my chin.
It was only a foolish schoolgirl crush, I had been telling myself, and the
truth was I was embarrassed by it. I didn't have time for such foolishness.
But now the memories resurrected themselves from their long slumber
and pounded on my heart for escape. I thought about his letter. I had
read and reread it so often, I could recite every word of it. I wondered if
he was sorry he'd sent it. Would he be angry I had never written back? In
spite of all my resolutions to forget about him, I was anxious to see him.

And so it was that I played again at the Spinners' Ball on Christmas
Eve of 1918, along with P.J. and the Ulster Minstrels. The scene was
much the same as it had been five years earlier. Theresa once again led
the committee. The hall was gaily decorated, and long tables were piled
with food and punch and cider. As before, there were no spirits served,
but this time it was more than just the band that smuggled in their wee
drop of insurance in their pockets. James sat at a table near the front
beside his mother, who beamed with pride at everyone who walked by.
Young men home from the war were determined to erase the dirt, the
fear, and the brutality from their memories. God help them, though; if
they had expected to be treated as heroes, they were to be disappointed.
Their sacrifice had dimmed to insignificance in the brilliant light of Ireland's recent homegrown martyrs. Now they hovered in that bright but

brief limbo between their escape from the past and their fear of the future.

I tried to imagine myself as I had been five years before—at sixteen—old in some ways and still a child in others. Now, at twenty-one, I knew I had changed. My dearest dream of returning to the Yellow House had grown dim, kept alive only by childish stubbornness and sweet, pale memories. I was infused now with a dream equally passionate but far less innocent. The resolute, brave child now slept within me, while the fierce O'Neill warrior took center stage.

I wondered if I looked different. I had already reached my full height of six feet well before my sixteenth birthday. My dark red hair still fell to my waist in a thick braid. I wore the same black velvet skirt and white satin blouse that I had worn five years earlier. But I sensed that I carried the clothes differently. The stranger who had crept into my body when the monthly curse first arrived was no longer a stranger. She was a woman.

As I played, I let my eyes wander over the crowd, searching for Owen Sheridan. The minute I saw him, a shiver ran through me. He came in through the door, as he had done before, shaking the snow off his coat and out of his blond hair. Then he lifted his face toward me and we held each other's stares until I could stand it no more and looked down at my fiddle. People raced up to shake his hand, and he turned away from me. I watched him walk toward the front table where his family sat. Something was different, I thought, and then I saw what it was: He was limping. It would not have been noticeable if you were not staring at him closely, as I was. But it was unmistakable. He dragged his left leg a bit stiffly as he walked. So that had been what was wrong with his leg when he said in his letter that it throbbed with pain. He had taken a bullet, and now he had a limp. He sat down at the table with his parents and two young women I supposed were his sisters. I had seen one of them along with her husband at the last ball, but the other one, a pretty curly-haired blonde, had not been there. They all stood up to kiss him.

When it was time for a break, I made my way through the crowd to get a breath of air outside. A number of young fellows lounged outside the door, drinking from flasks and laughing. They called out to me, and I answered them. One of them elbowed the other and whispered. The rumors had spread that I was involved with James and the resistance. I denied them, of course, but there was a part of me liked the respect it earned me. I walked on past them and stopped a little way down the street near a lamppost. As a UVF armored lorry rumbled by, the young men jeered at it.

"We meet again, Miss O'Neill."

I swung around. "I see you still have the habit of creeping up on a body," I said.

The cheeky grin I remembered appeared. "It's wonderful to see you, too."

Owen Sheridan shook my hand, and a tingle ran up my arm. Under the light of the gas lamp, I saw lines etched deep on either side of his mouth and across his forehead. Gray flecks streaked his blond hair. He had changed. I knew he was about thirty-one, but he looked like an older man.

"I'm glad you're home safe," I said quietly.

"Thanks," he said. "And how have you been?"

I shrugged. "No complaints," I said.

"You look well." He hesitated. "Married by now, I suppose?"

I glared at him. "Is that what you think all women want?"

"Forgive me. I forgot that you are your own woman, Miss O'Neill. I believe you did tell me that before." He smiled at me, and his eyes shone violet in the shadows of the streetlamp. "You never wrote." It was not a question, but his voice had a touch of sadness.

I shrugged again. "I told you I wasn't good at writing." A silence hung between us. "I got your letter," I began, "and—"

"So this is where you are hiding." James's lilting voice rolled over my shoulder as he put his arm around my waist. Startled, I moved away from him, heat searing my face.

"Er, this is James Conlon," I said to Owen. "James, this is Owen Sheridan, the mill owner's son." My voice was calm, but I was shaking inside with a sense of foreboding.

Owen bowed politely but did not move to shake hands with James.

"I've heard of you, Mr. Conlon," he said.

"And you'll be hearing more, no doubt," said James.

"James works at the mill, and his da before him," I put in. Jesus, what was wrong with me at all? I was blathering on like an eejit. Where had these nerves come from?

"I'm surprised he has time," said Owen, and there was no mistaking the ice in his voice.

"James took me to hear Michael Collins. He's a grand orator." Jesus, would I ever shut up?

"So I hear," said Owen. "There was a time, I suppose, back in my more profligate days, when I would have admired him myself." He looked straight at James, and his voice filled with anger. "But I have been in a real war, Mr. Conlon, and I have seen what violence does. It is never the answer."

"I served in the war, too," James shot back, "and this is as real a war as that was."

"No. It is not. It is merely an uprising by a few who are not patient enough to wait for the political process to take its course."

"Political process my arse!" shouted James.

I stepped in between them and tugged at James's sleeve. "Come on, James, it's time I was getting back."

But James shrugged me off. He moved closer to Owen, planting his feet squarely in front of him. Owen did not move.

"And who controls the political process but the likes of yourselves?" James was shouting now, and a crowd began to gather. "You'll stamp out the Catholics like those that came before you. Is the political process going to give us back our land or a fair chance at jobs?"

There were rumblings of, "Good man," "You're right there," from the crowd. But Owen remained calm.

"You have a job, Mr. Conlon, and a well-paid one. As does Miss O'Neill here."

Sudden anger hit me. I forgot my earlier nerves. "You needed us all during the war," I shouted. "Who knows how many of us will be sacked now that the soldiers are home? Anyway," I finished lamely, "it's not that well paid."

Just then the young curly-haired blond woman who had been sitting at the head table came up and caught him by the arm.

"Owen? Owen darling. You'll catch your death out here." Her voice was English, polished, and Protestant.

Owen turned around. "I was just coming in, Joanna," he said. "No need to fret."

He turned toward me. "Miss O'Neill," he said, his voice formal, "this is Miss Joanna Wharton, my fiancée. Joanna, this is Eileen O'Neill."

The woman nodded her head. "Oh yes, I know. I think you are a wonderful musician, Miss O'Neill. It's such a pleasure to have you entertaining us." She turned to Owen. "Come along, darling, it's freezing out here."

Owen Sheridan turned back to me and bowed. "Good evening, Miss

O'Neill. I would give you a piece of advice about keeping dangerous company, but I have always known you to be a woman with a mind of her own, so I doubt that anything I say could change it."

He bowed curtly to James. "Mr. Conlon."

I watched him walk away with Miss Wharton, his hand resting on the small of her back as he guided her toward the door. I was suddenly aware of the cold, and I folded my arms across my chest to warm myself. As I watched them go, a cold, empty feeling settled inside me. Joe Shields's words came back to me. What a fool I was. How could I ever have thought? Thought what? That Owen Sheridan would have an interest in the likes of me? There, I had admitted it: the lingering, faraway, childish fantasy that I had never allowed to grow but had nursed just the same. And I had been stupid enough to think she was his sister! The cold feeling inside of me melted under the hot weld of my shame.

By the time I had linked James's arm and marched with him into the hall and up to the stage, I was ablaze with anger. When Owen Sheridan and his fiancée had seated themselves at the head table, I pulled James toward me and kissed him long and hard on the mouth. By the time the whistles and applause from the crowd had died down, I mounted the stage erect and confident. All doubts were gone. I opened my arms and embraced Eileen O'Neill, warrior.

Insurrection

1919–1920

12

The rifle thudded heavily against my thigh as I walked back and forth across the Newry Canal bridge. I held it hidden under my coat, its barrel cold in my hand. It was a strange and dangerous thing, like an extra limb that grew out of me of its own accord. I wondered at its power—to protect and to slaughter. I wondered would I have the strength to control it. I glanced down at the Customs House on the embankment below. James and his men crept toward it under cover of darkness, carrying bricks, paraffin, and matches. The building was dark. I prayed there was no one inside. Outside the black water lapped at the moored ships, sending them creaking as if ghosts walked their decks. A cold wind wailing around them, like a cry from the deep, sent shivers down my back. The strong smell of oil wafted up from the canal. I thought back to the day I had ridden with Ma to the Royal Bank of Newry and marveled at the colorful ships with their flags stirring in the breeze. How excited I had been. How innocent.

I quickened my step as a stranger approached from the other end of the bridge. It was a man, not too steady on his feet. He tipped his hat to me.

"Good night, missus," he said, his voice shaky with the drink.

"Good night," I said, and hurried past him.

I wore a long coat and heavy boots, my hair tucked up under a hat. James had appointed me the lookout on account of the fact that a woman seen walking over the bridge late at night would arouse less suspicion than a man.

It was February 1919, and tensions had grown all over Ireland. After the general elections held in December of the previous year, a majority of those elected refused to take their seats in the Parliament in London. Instead, they formed their own parliament in Dublin, called Dáil Éireann, and declared the Irish Republic. This new—and unlawful—body was led by a fellow named Éamonn de Valera, whose political party was called Sinn Féin, Ourselves Alone. At the same time, the various militias that had fought under the banner of the Irish Volunteers formed a new military force called the Irish Republican Army (the IRA) and were recognized by Dáil Éireann as the official army of the Republic. Under the leadership of Michael Collins, the IRA vowed to fight for full independence from England for the entire island of Ireland. This set the British Army and police in motion to our south, while the Ulster Volunteer Force went into action in Ulster. The Anglo-Irish war had begun in earnest, and James began receiving orders from the IRA leadership. Burning the Customs House was our first big assignment.

"You know what to do," James had said before he left me on the bridge. There was an edge of nervousness in his voice.

"Of course I know," I snapped. "Haven't we been over it a dozen times?"

"Three quick shots," said James. "That's the signal."

"I know!"

He nodded his head. "Aye, all right, then."

As he signaled the rest of the men and started down the embankment, I called out after him, "Good luck."

I watched the drunken man stagger away over the bridge, and all was quiet again. I strained my eyes for the sign of any police cars or Ulster Volunteer boyos in their armored lorries. We had picked a Sunday night on purpose, thinking there would be fewer people about than on a weeknight. It seemed we had made the right decision.

The silence was broken by several thuds followed by shattering glass. James and his men threw bricks through the Customs House windows and scrambled through the openings. They had rehearsed over and over how they would carry things out. I held my breath and waited. Within minutes, black smoke poured from the open windows, curling into the air. Then balls of flames, like devil's tongues, lapped at the sky, lighting up everything around in their red glow. I watched them, mesmerized. A mixture of fear and excitement rose in me. The flames shot higher, exploding in showers of sparks over the moored ships. In the midst of the flames, I saw Ma's gaunt face and Lizzie's wide, feverish eyes. I saw Da's gnarled hands and Frankie's lost, soulless stare. I wanted to toss all the bad memories into the fire and watch them burn down to ashes.

A sliver of light caught the corner of my eye. I snapped myself back to the present and swung around. Jesus, they were coming. The police were coming. I froze as I watched the two circles of light draw closer. I watched myself, as if in slow motion, take the rifle from under my coat and point it toward the sky. I squeezed the trigger and jerked back from the impact of the shot. Twice more I squeezed, and the reports echoed through the air. I watched as the car screeched to a halt. Two policemen jumped out and raced down the embankment toward the fire, while I stood rooted to the ground in the middle of the bridge, the rifle dangling at my side.

Suddenly a hand grabbed my arm and tugged me forward.

"Run, Eileen. For Jesus' sake!"

James dragged me to the other side of the bridge and down the far embankment. He plunged me into the middle of a pile of empty flour sacks that were stacked on the quay. He threw himself on top of me and pulled a tarpaulin over both of us, then made a small hole in the pile where we could look out and watch the Customs House as it was consumed in the flames.

"Will you look at that," breathed James. "Isn't it a grand sight?"

I opened my eyes and looked out. My whole body quivered from fear and excitement. James smelled of smoke and oil and sweat.

"Did they all get away?" I whispered.

"I hope so." He chuckled. "Jimmy Traynor threw himself in the canal, and Paddy O'Keefe jumped in after him. They may have to swim all the way to Camlough."

"Why didn't you go with them?" I breathed.

"Because you, my darling Eileen, were standing like a statue on the bridge waiting to be lifted by the police."

My cheeks burned. "I was going to run."

"Aye, and pigs might be going to fly." Then, in a gentler voice he said, "It's all right, love. It was your first job. You did well. Without your warning we would have been sitting ducks."

We lay side by side in silence, watching the Customs House burn. Bells clanged as the fire brigade arrived and began dousing the flames in a frenzied effort to save it.

"I suppose this is just the beginning," I whispered.

James rolled over and looked at me. "Aye." He smiled. Then he leaned forward and kissed me on the lips. It was not how I ever imagined my next kiss with James would be—if I had imagined it at all, it certainly would not have been in the middle of a pile of flour sacks, almost choking for air. His lips were soft and hot as they pressed hard on mine. All thought left me. I kissed him back as violently as he was kissing me, matching him gasp for gasp. I kissed him until I had no breath left in me. Then we tore at each other's clothes. I felt a cold rush of air on my bare thighs, then James's hot limbs on top of mine. The raw cloth of the flour sacks clawed at my buttocks as James thrust inside me. My cries pierced the night air, fusing with the urgent, shrill wails of the police sirens and the clamor of fire brigade bells, creating a strident harmony that soared to the heavens. I knew at that moment that a bond had been forged between James and me that would be there forever. I thought briefly of another bond and another man before I closed my eyes.

James pulled away at last. "We're in this together now, darlin'," he whispered. "We might be spending a quare amount of time in places like this." He paused. "So—I suppose you'd better marry me."

"I suppose I should," I said.

✷

ON THE EVE of my marriage to James, I rode out to the Yellow House. I leaned my bicycle against the wall and looked west into the setting sun. I imagined Da riding again over the brow of the hill in the little pony cart with the sun behind him. I heard his lovely tenor voice singing "The Rose of Tralee" as clear as if he were there again beside me. This was the first time since that awful night that I had ventured so close to the house. Skeletal black rafters clawed the sky. The pungent smell of burning wood still lingered in my nostrils, and the sharp pops of exploding fire echoed in my ears. I went closer and pressed my palms against the rough, scarred walls, trying to feel for some pulse of life. But there was none. The jagged shards of broken windowpanes, sharp as fangs, snarled at me, and I shuddered and drew back. Whatever ghosts stalked this place now, they were not the merry ghosts of old. These ghosts were angry and evil. Without thinking, I made the sign of the cross on myself.

I lifted a bunch of lilacs from the basket of the bicycle and walked away from the house. I crossed the gravel and weeds, where once Ma's flowers had bloomed, toward Da's grave. Slieve Gullion watched me with stately grace. A small arc of black marble marked where Da lay. P.J. had arranged for it to be placed there. Da's name and dates of birth and death were etched on it in gold lettering, and a fiddle and bow were carved beneath. A small plaque in the ground nearby bore the name of his old dog, Cuchulainn, who had died the day after Da. Lizzie's wee white marker with the two angels on it sat nearby, facing out to Slieve Gullion. I knelt beside Da's grave, holding the sprays of lilac in my hands.

"Och, Da, why did you have to die on me?" I whispered.

I sat back on my heels, playing absently with the lilac.

"I'm getting married, Da," I said aloud. "P.J. is giving me away. It won't be the same as having yourself there. You'd like James. He's a warrior worthy of the O'Neills. I think he's a braver one than I could ever be. I'm trying to live up to the O'Neill legacy, Da. I'm fighting for the Cause. You should have seen the Customs House go up in flames—such a grand sight." I paused, remembering the rush of passion I had felt. I wondered then if the Unionist boyos had felt the same passion when they burned our house.

"I have to fight for something, Da. You always said that's what we were born to do. I've been fighting to keep our family together. To bring us back to this place. I'm still saving what money I can. But Ma's gone into her own world, and Frankie wants his own life, and Paddy wants to stay with the Mullens. I don't know if I can do it—or if it's even possible. Och, Da, I don't want to lose the dream." I rubbed away tears with my sleeve. I took a deep breath. "Anyway, Da, now I'm fighting for the Cause as well. I'm fighting the bastards who killed you and destroyed our house. You'd be happy about that. I know you would."

I leaned over and placed the lilacs on his grave, then knelt in silence for a while. I stood up and looked over at the house. It was aglow in the flame of the afternoon sun. I smiled and looked back at the grave.

"I won't lose the dream, Da. I promise."

I brushed the grass and leaves off my skirt.

"Pray for me, Da," I whispered, "and play a tune for me at my wedding."

ॐ

THE WEDDING WAS a small affair. James and I were married in St. Jude's chapel in Glenlea on Easter Sunday 1919. I was twenty-one years old. P.J. gave me away. Theresa was my matron of honor, and Fergus was James's best man. Fergus told me he was happy I had married James because now he could have a room in the house again. James would, of course, be moving out since we had been approved for a house in Queensbrook village a few streets over from where Mrs. Conlon lived.

"But didn't James tell his mother to bring you back a long time ago?"
I said.

Fergus shook his head. "He must have forgotten," he said.

Mrs. Mullen and Mrs. Conlon both wept throughout the ceremony, although I suspected for different reasons. Theresa's new husband, Tommy McParland, was there as well. Ma was not allowed to leave hospital to come—not that she would have known what was happening anyway—but her absence left a hole in my heart. The invitation to Frankie had been returned unopened. But Paddy was there, carrying the wedding rings on a white satin cushion, solemn as a priest.

I wore an ankle-length cream satin dress that Theresa had designed and made, and I carried a bunch of blue forget-me-nots. James wore a navy blue suit with a white shirt and blue tie. Everybody said we made a handsome couple. As we walked down the aisle, James put his hand on the small of my back, but it felt rough and heavy. I remembered the warmth and steadiness of Owen Sheridan's hand and stepped quickly away from James. The reception was at the Ceili House, of course. The Ulster Minstrels played. Some of the girls from the mill came along with their husbands or boyfriends. None of the boys from James's battalion came; it would have been too dangerous to have us all in one place.

James hired a car to take us to the seaside town of Warrenpoint, where we booked into a small Victorian guesthouse overlooking Carlingford Lough. I had changed into a daytime dress.

"Will we go for a walk?" I said. "The strand is lovely."

James gave me a sharp look but nodded in agreement. I supposed he thought I couldn't wait to jump into the bed and make love to him. But I needed time.

As we strolled along the promenade, I looked down at the gold wedding band on my left hand. It felt heavy and strange, as if this new identity were crushing me. I tried to smile. I looked up at James. He had taken off his tie and jacket and rolled up the sleeves of his white shirt. He was a handsome man, there was no doubt about that. Women young and old eyed him as they passed by, and he nodded back to them. Why was I not on top of the world? Any other woman in my place would have been. But I was not any woman. I was Eileen O'Neill. But, no, she was gone. And in her place was Eileen Conlon, wife, eventually even mother. My skin tingled as if someone had stepped on my grave.

That night, James and I made love for the second time. It was a far cry from that February night when our passions burned along with the Customs House. This time James took charge of things, moving according to his own needs, forcing me to match my rhythms with his. When it was over he rolled off me and fell into a heavy sleep. I lay as if alone, stiffening and relaxing my body with the rhythm of the sea, which swelled and ebbed outside our window, until I found the release I sought.

ॐ

WE MOVED INTO a mill house in the village on the next square over from James's mother's house. The house was small—a parlor, a kitchen, a scullery, and a wee room off the scullery known as "the granny's room," all on the ground floor, and two bedrooms upstairs. We were lucky that James's job as a tenter got us a house with a parlor—such grandeur was usually reserved for the higher-paid workers. Even so, with two people the size of James and me in it, it seemed like a dollhouse. How some of our neighbors managed to squeeze two parents and several children into one of them, I could not imagine.

The houses were solid and well built and laid out in such a way that every house got the sun at some time during the day. I was not much of a housekeeper, but I tried to make it cozy by hanging pictures on the walls and lining the shelves with bright crockery. If I'd had Ma's way with flowers, I would have filled the window boxes with bright geraniums the way others did, but as it was I left them empty. Theresa had sewn up some bright curtains, and I told myself that was enough color. We bought a few sticks of furniture: a couple of armchairs for the kitchen, along with a table and chairs, and a cheap rug and a sofa for the parlor. I'd thought of bringing in some of the pieces that had been salvaged from the fire but couldn't bring myself to do so. Those pieces did not belong there, they belonged in my real home, the Yellow House. I kept the place tidy and cooked the meals on time. James turned out to be a fussy bugger. Besides his clothes having to be washed and pressed every day, everything in the house had to be in its right place. Well, it might have suited his ma to wait on him hand and foot, but I had no intention of it.

ॐ

THE REPRISALS FOR the Customs House burning were swift and fierce—and random. Innocent people were pulled out of their beds, just as Da had been, and made to watch their houses or shops burn to the ground. All the Volunteers succeeded in doing was turning more and more Catholics against them and against the police. Peace-abiding people were turned into rebels overnight. Even those who did not take up the fight supported James and the rest of us silently.

Assignments came to our battalion thick and fast, and James and I were out almost every night. I acted as lookout for a while but then demanded more responsibility. I know now that I was trying to relive the passion I had felt that night at the Customs House—not just at watching the flames, but the passions aroused in myself with James. And so I sought out more and more danger: setting fire to police stations, blowing up railway tracks, ambushing UVF lorries on dark country roads. And on those nights when it was over, James and I would go home to bed, rip off each other's clothes, and make love again just like that first night.

We held our meetings in a room above the Ceili House. James and I gathered there along with his lieutenants and the Ulster Minstrels. P.J. always sat at the head of the table. He loved the limelight, and we let him blather on about the state of things. But Fergus and Terrence were another matter. Fergus had become dark and sullen. He turned out to be not only brutal but reckless. He would just as soon kill a Protestant as look at him. I thought that he was only releasing all the resentment he had built up over the years, but I worried that he would get us all in trouble before long. On the other hand, Terrence, the mysterious uilleann piper who had played with the Music Men, turned out to be a skillful negotiator. He had contacts all over the country and was trusted with the most sensitive information by the highest IRA command. I thought sometimes James was a bit jealous of Terrence, but Terrence never gave him any cause for anger.

It was a warm July night in 1919 when we gathered as usual in the attic above the Ceili House. The building was more than two hundred years old, the attic a dome of gray stone walls, damp and uneven. The stone floor of the attic was cold and covered in dust. The only light came from a small window at the top of narrow stone stairs, but even so we draped it with a cloth so that no light would shine out on the street. A splintered wooden table and mismatched chairs were the only furniture. We did not turn on the single naked electric bulb that hung from the ceiling but instead lit a couple of candles. The landlord's son brought up a bottle of Paddy whiskey, some tumblers, a jug of water, and a pile of sandwiches, then went down the stairs and locked the door behind him. One of James's men stood guard, rifle in hand, at the foot of the stairs.

Terrence came over and smiled at me. "Hello, Eileen," he said in his deep, calm voice. "I saw your ma last week. She's put on a bit of weight. That's a good sign."

"Aye," I said. I had realized after my first visit to Ma that the Mr. Finnegan the nurse said visited her was no other man than Terrence. I wondered why he went, but I never asked. He was free to do what he pleased, I supposed.

"Any word from Frank?" It was a question he asked often.

"No," I snapped. "And why would I care? He wouldn't even come to his own sister's wedding."

Terrence sighed. "Ah, don't be so hard on him, Eileen. Sure life dealt him a cruel hand, so it did."

"No worse than the rest of us," I snapped back.

P.J. brought word once in a while that Frank was doing well. He had been seen around Newry wearing brand-new clothes and looking every inch the gentleman farmer. I grew nervous. Maybe he had sold the Yellow House and was spending the money like a drunken sailor. P.J. assured me the house was not sold, so where Frank was getting the money remained a mystery. I suspected that whatever the source, it was far from legal.

P.J. took his seat at the head of the table as usual. He never took part in any of the raids, but we allowed him his place out of respect. Terrence and James joined him at the table, but the rest of us—me, Fergus, and James's two lieutenants, Jimmy Traynor and Paddy O'Keefe—sat as usual behind them in a row of chairs along one wall. P.J. poured whiskey for those who wanted it and raised his glass.

"God bless all here!" he boomed, reminding me of the greeting he always used to call out when he came to the Yellow House.

"And may God bless Ireland," we chorused.

James and Paddy O'Keefe drank water. I took a drop of whiskey, as usual, and then filled my tumbler with water. P.J. stoked his pipe, lit it with his usual ceremony, and inhaled the smoke.

"I hear they burned Tommy Tumulty out of house and home last night," he began.

"He's not the first, and won't be the last," said Fergus. "Sure there's running battles in the streets every night of the week."

"It's a desperate situation altogether," continued P.J. "The War of Independence is surely under way now. Did you hear they brought the British Army into it up here in the North? I heard that Owen Sheridan fellow is leading them here in Newry."

I could not help the cry that came out of me. Where it came from, I don't know. It was as if I had placed my hand on a hot stove. James swung around to look at me.

"Aye, Eileen's old friend," he snapped.

I swallowed some whiskey. "He's no friend of mine," I said, but I could feel the flames scorching my cheeks.

Terrence cleared his throat. "I have information the police are going to be instituting a curfew within days. They're talking about wanting every-body off the streets by nine o'clock at night."

James gave Terrence the queer look he always did when Terrence had information that was new to him. "You mean they want the *Catholics* off the streets," he snapped. "Their own kind will be able to go about as they please."

"Aye, you can be sure of that," P.J. said.

"But what will that do to us?" I cried. "How will we get the jobs done?"

James swung around again and glared at me. I didn't know what had put him in such bad form tonight.

"We'll do what we've always done, and more," he said, his voice cold. "And if it's too dangerous for you, then you can stay at home."

I glared back at him. Anger and hurt fought within me. "I . . . ," I began, not knowing what to say.

Terrence came to my rescue. "Will we get to the orders?" he said quietly.

As I watched the men study the documents and maps on the table, I felt a sickness rising inside me. The whiskey had turned my stomach. Suddenly, sweat poured off me. I clutched the rifle that leaned against my knee as if for support. Sounds of laughter from the downstairs pub grew muffled in my ears. Then the room spun around me and everything turned black.

13
↬

Our daughter was born in January 1920, the beginning of the most violent year in the struggle so far. I called her Aoife, after a famous Celtic warrior princess. While I knew that James had badly wanted a boy, I thought at least the name would please him.

"What kind of a name is that?" he snapped. "Sure I wouldn't even know how to pronounce it."

"It's pronounced Eeffa," I said, "EE-FF-A. And it's Irish. What kind of a rebel are you when you can't even pronounce your own language?"

It was an unfair remark, I knew, but I didn't care. Neither James nor I, both brought up in Ulster, had been taught the Irish language. I had picked up a few words from Da. I had come across the name Aoife in one of P.J.'s books. Terrence was the one who told me how to pronounce it.

"She fought the famous Ulster warrior Cuchulainn, you know." He smiled. "And would have won had it not been for a trick her sister played on her. She was a fine, brave woman, just like yourself, Eileen."

So I had thought that if I ever had a daughter, I would name her Aoife.

"Ma expected you'd name her after your mother and herself. Mary Margaret. It's the custom," said James. "Besides, they're both saints' names."

"Feck your holy ma," I said through gritted teeth. "She's my child and I'll call her what I like."

James said nothing. I knew he was disappointed the child was not a boy—another soldier for Ireland. "No matter," he had said, "there'll be a boy next time."

I thought he might be waiting a long time if I had my way. I had no interest in a big family. Having a brood of children following me down the street would not give me the same pride it gave other women. One would be enough.

"She's the image of you, anyway," I said, looking down at the shock of brown hair on the child's head and the shape of her nose and chin.

She looked back at me, and I could already see defiance in her eyes. She would not be an easy child to rear. I had a vague uneasiness that she knew what I was thinking. Her arrival marked for me a sense of loss. Up until now I had still held on to my old, tattered dream of putting my family back together in the Yellow House—the way it used to be—although for years now I had known it was hardly possible. Da and Lizzie were dead, and Ma and Frank may as well have been dead. And now Paddy was living his own life with the Mullens. It was foolish, I knew, but the dream had still given me comfort on the long, lonely evenings when I lay in bed, heavy with the child, waiting for James to come home. Now that Aoife was here, my fear of loss had turned into resentment toward her, this child who was forcing me to put the past behind me and look to the future.

The Ulster Minstrels had come to the hospital one by one, bringing flowers and chocolates and pronouncing the child the most beautiful wee lassie they had ever seen. Fergus was delighted when I asked him to be her godfather. His poor, drawn face lit up like a Christmas tree. Had no one ever done anything nice for him before? I wondered. Then, late one evening just before visiting hours ended, I saw Billy Craig creeping down the ward toward my bed. I was trying to nurse Aoife, but she kept fussing and crying. Billy came over and stood like a big, awkward child beside the bed.

"Hello," he said. "I brought this for the child."

He thrust out his big, beefy hand, and in it was a tiny tin whistle. "I made it for her. And I'll teach her to play it."

Aoife stopped fussing and looked directly at Billy. I didn't know what to say. Memories of Billy kneeling over my da that awful night came flashing back, and then in a blur I saw Billy thrusting Da's fiddle at me and pushing myself and Paddy out the back door.

"I'm sorry, Eileen," he said. Tears streamed down his big face, and he began to sob. The other women in the ward stared at us. A nurse came over to see if I was all right.

"Aye," I said. "He always cries when he sees babies." Then I turned to Billy. "Sit down, you big eejit, before you get us both thrown out."

"I loved your ma," Billy said through his tears, "and I loved your da, and I loved everybody. I meant no harm."

I looked at him sitting there, his big face crumpled up, and my heart melted. Poor Billy had suffered enough. Even though his da had managed to get all the charges against him dismissed, people in the town still shunned Billy. And he was no longer welcome to play with his beloved Ulster Minstrels.

"I know you didn't mean to harm us, Billy. It's all right."

As suddenly as they had come, Billy's tears stopped and his face stretched in a wide grin. He looked at Aoife. "Can I hold her?" he asked, eager as a boy.

Reluctantly, I slipped Aoife into his big arms. He gazed down at her in delight.

"She's the image of your ma," he said.

"I thought she looked like James," I whispered.

Billy shook his head back and forth. "No," he shouted, "your ma!"

"Ssh," I said. "You're right, Billy."

He smiled down at the baby again and waved the tin whistle in front of her. "I'll teach you to play it when you're older . . . "

He looked up at me in sudden dismay. "I don't know her name," he gasped.

"It's Aoife," I said, "after a Celtic warrior."

"Aoife," he said, pronouncing the name perfectly, "Aoife."

ᕪᕤ

THE CHILD WAS christened a week later. They liked to hurry it up in Ireland in case the devil got to her before God. I was not allowed to be there. Women who had given birth had to wait four weeks before they were allowed to set foot back into the church, and even then only after attending a few sessions with the priest. It was as if we were dirty creatures that had to be cleansed all over again. The whole business set my teeth on edge, and if it weren't for the scandal it would cause, I would have refused to have Aoife christened at all and would not have set foot in a church again. As it was, Theresa was the godmother and Fergus the godfather. It hurt me that Frankie had ignored yet another invitation. I missed Ma as well and, of course, my da. I felt very alone.

The reception was held at James's mother's house. Everyone arrived from the church, Mrs. Conlon in front carrying Aoife like a trophy. "Such a grand wee girl," she crowed, "not a peep out of her the whole time." She glared at me. "She's much better behaved when she's with strangers."

It was a dig at me and the fact that Aoife was very fussy when I held her. And as if to prove her right, the child bawled as soon as I took her in my arms. Theresa stepped in to the rescue. "Come on now, Mary Margaret," she cooed, taking the child in her arms. "You can't be crying on your christening day."

"It's Aoife," I snapped.

"Not anymore," said Mrs. Conlon, her thin voice high with triumph. "She was christened Mary Margaret after the saints, like any good Catholic child."

"But her name is Aoife," I cried, turning to look at James. "You know that."

James shrugged. "I couldn't go asking the priest to christen her with a pagan name, now, could I?" he said. "And anyway, Ma would have been scandalized."

"Feck your ma!" I cried. I turned around to P.J. and Fergus. "And you went along with this?"

Fergus gaped at me and then glared at James. P.J.'s face turned red. He threw up his hands. "Sure what was I to do, Eileen? Mary Margaret was the name on her birth certificate, and her da here made no objection."

Anger seared through me, and tears burned my eyes. I swung back to James.

"You betrayed me," I shouted. "You fecking bastard. Why?" I started to pummel him on the chest. He grabbed my wrists and pushed me away.

"Have you lost your bloody mind, Eileen?" he said. "Sure it's only a fecking name. There's more serious business in this world to be worrying about."

My brother Paddy came over to me and took my hand. "Aoife's a nice name, Eileen," he whispered. I pulled him close to me, but I could not stop shaking.

"Ah, she's just emotional," said Theresa. "They say a lot of women get that way after a birth. She'll get over it."

But she was wrong. I would not get over it. It was a small betrayal, I know, but it is the first betrayal that hurts the most. It is the first betrayal that slays innocence and leaves a scar that is never forgotten. Just as a physical scar fades with time but can still be felt when fingers are laid ever so softly over the place where it was, so too with the emotional scar of betrayal. I sensed there would be more betrayals to come. My poor heart had set up a lookout for them. And there would be more scars. And in time, there would be so many scars to be avoided that there would be no place left to touch.

❧

I WENT BACK to my job at the mill. When I refused to leave Aoife with his mother, James sighed and told me to suit myself. I found an elderly neighbor who was delighted to keep the child. James kept working as well. It was best not to draw attention to ourselves, he said, and I was happy enough to be living on his wages so I could keep building my own savings. The savings account, in my own name, was my one piece of independence I was not giving up.

After Aoife was born, I hardly went out on any assignments for the IRA. Things had become very dangerous. But there was a part of me still yearned for the excitement of it. I admit that it fueled my resentment toward the child. Not only was she forcing me to give up my dream of reconstructing the past, but she had also forced me out of the action that I had come to thrive on. I sighed as I looked at her—what kind of a mother would I be if I already resented the child in my life? I prayed it was only a passing mood. When Aoife was a bit older I would go back to the fighting, I told myself. In the meantime, in spite of James's objections, I continued to go to the meetings.

❧

"WELL, IT'S A great night for Ireland," boomed P.J., holding up his glass and grinning at all of us. We were gathered in the room above the Ceili House. It was a May evening in 1920, and word had come down that the Unionist politicians had lost the majority of their seats in elections in Londonderry. It was the first time an election had been held in the United Kingdom under a system of proportional representation, and the Unionists had the shock of their lives. The new councillors pledged themselves to the Irish Republic proclaimed by Dáil Éireann.

"We have Derry back in our hands again," shouted P.J., his face red with excitement.

"There'll be quare trouble now," Fergus muttered.

"Och, can you not take pleasure in the news?" shouted P.J. "Do you always have to be the wet blanket?"

"I'm just saying," said Fergus, scowling.

"He's right," said Terrence. "They won't take this lying down."

James was silent. I could see the thoughts racing through his head. He was never one to rush to judgment. He was weighing things, as he always did. Then I saw the set of his jaw, and I knew what he was going to say before he opened his mouth.

"We'll need to be prepared." His voice was calm and quiet. Everyone turned to look at him. "You may expect to see battles raging in the streets. It's not just the UVF and the RIC and the army that will be in it. Every feckin' Prod in the North will be fancying himself a vigilante."

"There'll be hooliganism on all sides," put in Terrence.

"Aye, but the Prods still have the numbers and the power on their side," said James. "We'll need to have eyes in the backs of our heads. And there'll be trouble in the mill before long, mark my words." He shot a look at Terrence as if to say, "You're not the only boyo with advance information."

The thud of the lookout's rifle on the attic door startled us. We stopped talking and stiffened, holding our breath. Then, like clockwork, we shot into action, clearing away the maps and documents and the extra tumblers and cups. James and his men dove through a small trapdoor at the top of the stairs. P.J., Fergus, Terrence, and I spread ourselves around the table, trying to look natural. The door opened and boots scraped on the wooden stairs.

"Ah, sure good evening to yourself, Sergeant Hamilton," said P.J. in his sweetest voice. "Will you and your man join us for a bit of refreshment— or is it against your orders?"

Sergeant Hamilton and his man were with the RIC—the Royal Irish Constabulary. There were no strangers around Newry. Everybody knew everybody.

"You know fine well it's against orders," said Hamilton, an overweight, red-faced man, sweating from the effort of climbing the stairs. "What are youse doing here?"

P.J. smiled. "We could ask you the same thing, Sergeant. As for my friends and myself, we are taking a break from the commotion downstairs. We're so popular our fans won't leave us alone for a minute, so we come up here to clear our heads."

Hamilton sniffed. He knew P.J. was lying, but what could he do? He walked around the room, hitting his baton against the walls and the floor. "I hear youse spend a lot of time up here," he growled.

P.J. nodded. "Aye, we do so."

Hamilton completed his inspection. Terrence and I looked down at the table, but Fergus watched the men as they prowled around the room. I could see he was sweating. Hamilton came to a sudden halt in front of him.

"Fergus Conlon?" he snapped.

"You know fine well who I am," muttered Fergus.

"Stand up, then. We have orders to take you in for questioning."

"On what charge?" cried Fergus.

The younger policeman snickered. Hamilton shot him a glare. "We don't need charges. Suspicion is enough. Up with you now!"

Hamilton grabbed Fergus's shoulders and heaved him to his feet.

"We can do this with or without handcuffs. I don't suppose you'd want your . . . er, fans to see you led away like a criminal."

I thought Fergus was going to spit in his face. Instead he said, "Feck you," and walked toward the door. We watched in silence as he went. Then he turned to us.

"Save my place," he muttered through clenched teeth.

"Take your time, lad," said P.J. "Sure we can do without you for one night."

We sat in silence as they trundled down the stairs and slammed the attic door shut. At last James and his men crawled out of the trapdoor. Then, out of the blue, Terrence blessed himself and murmured something in Latin. I had never seen him do that before. Maybe he had been a priest after all.

P.J. must have known what I was thinking.

"We're going to need more than God on our side, Terrence."

∽

AFTER THE SCENE at the Ceili House, James was proved right. Things became more troubled all around. Street violence spilled over from Belfast and Derry into Newry. The curfew was ignored, and you took your life in your hands if you were on the streets after dark. Fergus had come back but was very tight-lipped about what had happened. His face was covered in bruises and his arm bandaged. There was a fury in his eyes I had not seen before. What he told James I don't know, but after that James seemed to take him more into his confidence. James no longer shared as much information with me as he used to. He said it was best for my sake and the child's. I knew better. It was just another way of letting me know I was not his equal, never was, and never would be.

After the troubles escalated, James was often away overnight, so when he didn't come home one night in June, I didn't worry. Aoife was in one of her crying moods, and I was preoccupied with her. I went to work at the mill the next day expecting to see him, but there was no sign of him. Shields came over and asked me where he was. I gave him a wise answer.

"How should I know? Women are supposed to let men go about their own business, aren't they?"

He scowled. "Don't get cheeky with me, lassie. Production's behind. I need to know where he is."

"He's sick," I said. "He'll be back tomorrow."

But he wasn't back tomorrow or the next day. I talked to some of the lads in his squad. They were tight-lipped. "He's away, Eileen," was all they would say.

"Sure I feckin' know he's away," I shouted. "I want to know when he's coming back. I have a child to feed."

But they were silent. I supposed James was out on some secret assignment. My disappointment about being left out turned into anger. I was steaming mad. How could he go off and leave me and the child and not a word? I worried, too, about how long Shields would hold open his job. A week went by, and on the Monday next when I went to the mill, I saw a strange fellow kneeling down repairing a spinning frame. I marched up to him.

"Who the feck are you?" I demanded. "That's my husband's job!"

He leered at me, two yellow teeth protruding from his gums. "It's mine now, lassie. Your husband's loss—fine woman like yourself. Charlie Fagan at your service." He bowed like an oul' eejit and tried to take my hand. I pulled it away and walked straight into Shields's office.

"What's going on?" I demanded. "Why is that eejit out there?"

Shields fixed me with a stare. His face was stone. "I have a factory to run," he said, "and James Conlon is off about his own business. Now get you back to work, or there'll be no job for you, either."

At first I had been so angry, it had not even occurred to me that James might be in danger or, God forbid, even dead. But as time went on, I began to fear the worst. My anger subsided and worry set in. Every noise, every knock at the door, sent me jumping. Aoife was anxious, too. She cried nonstop. Then one night I heard a scraping at the back door. I was afraid to open it at first. I stood in the dark listening, my heart pounding. Then I heard my name.

"Eileen!" came the whisper. "Eileen, let me in, for God's sake."

Shaking, I opened the door. There was James, stooped on his knees, a two-week growth of beard on his chin, his clothes in tatters. He looked like the devil. If I hadn't known it was him, I would have been looking down at his feet for the cloven hoof.

My relief turned immediately to anger. "What in the name of God?" I shouted. "Where the feck have you been?"

"Let me in, Eileen," was all he said. "I'm famished with the cold."

As he sat warming himself by the fire, he told me that he had been on the run from the Constabulary since a job had gone badly astray.

"We were to kidnap Lord Brooke," he said, "but the oul' bastard got a tip we were coming and set up the alarm."

"Lord Brooke," I breathed. "Is it mad in the head you are?"

James grinned—a weak imitation of his old smile. "Sure you have to be bold, Eileen," he said. "Anybody less would be hardly worth the trouble. Anyway, we'll get him one of these days. He'll be enjoying bread and water soon enough."

Lord Brooke was one of the men who had called for the formation of the Ulster Special Forces to combat the nationalist activity. The worst of this group were the B-Specials, Ulster volunteers who numbered, some said, one hundred thousand strong. As far as I was concerned, they were thugs with a free license to kill and maim.

I bathed James's bruises and pulled thorns from his bare feet. I made him strong tea with a shot of whiskey and gave him a blanket. He sat by the fire and sipped his tea. He looked up at me with those misty gray eyes of his that always softened my heart.

"I'm sorry, Eileen," he said. "I've given you a lot of trouble, I know. But it's all for a better—"

"Stop," I said before he finished. "I know what you're going to say. But I don't believe it, James. How can abandoning your wife and child be for the better? I don't give a feck what you say about the cause of Irish independence. Your place is here with me and your daughter."

James looked surprised at the mention of Aoife. It was as if he had forgotten she existed.

"How is she?" he whispered.

"A holy terror," I replied. "Just like yourself. She's been raising ructions since you left."

I couldn't resist a small smile. James smiled, too, and reached for my hand.

We made love that night—sweet and hungry and anxious. Later, as

I lay in his arms, I found myself thinking back over my life. How had I ended up here? Here in this bed with this man of passion and moods, a man with his own demons? If I had been looking for security and safety, James Conlon was the worst choice I could have made. And yet something in his restless nature had called to me; I recognized my own self in him. And together we had created a restless, rebellious child. Tiredly, I turned away from him and fell into sleep.

James was awake before dawn. I got up with him and made tea. We sat at the wooden table in the small kitchen, a gray light creeping through the window.

"What now?" I said. "Shields gave away your job."

"I know," he said. "I can't go back in any case. There is too much to do."

"But, James," I blurted out, "for God's sake, what if we can't win this way? Isn't it enough we have made headway in the elections? Surely in time the political process—"

I stopped as soon as I realized I was repeating Owen Sheridan's words. It was the first time I had expressed any doubt, and it surprised me as much as it did James. He grabbed my wrist.

"It's not over, Eileen. Not until we have a united Ireland. Too many good lads have died for it."

He took a swallow of his tea and went on more gently, "Do you want us and Mary Margaret to live the rest of our lives in a place where we are treated like dogs, where we have no rights at all, where we have no jobs and no say in the government? In a place where the Ulstermen march with their drums banging in our ears, and give their righteous speeches ridiculing our religion? Is that what you want?"

For once I ignored his use of the child's other name. "No," I said. "It isn't. But for God's sake, James, why do we have to be the ones to make all the sacrifice?"

He looked at me solemnly. "Somebody has to, Eileen."

He got up and put on the clean clothes I had washed for him. "I have to go now," he said. "I'll try to get money to you when I can. Kiss the child for me."

He kissed me lightly on the cheek, took up the packet of sandwiches I had made for him, and was gone. I sat for a long time staring after him, until Aoife's wails finally stirred me.

14
∾

I saw James only once in a while after that. He came to the back door like a thief in the night, always looking like a cat dragged through a hedge backward. He was a far cry those days from the dandified James I had first met. I would clean him up and make him sandwiches. It occurred to me then that I had become just like the women I had complained about to Michael Collins: relegated to making sandwiches while the men fought. James brought money on occasion, and I never asked where he got it. It was well enough deserved, I thought, given the sacrifices we were making. But still and all, money was scarce, and without my job we would have been out on the street. I could no longer add to my savings account; in fact, I worried that one day I would have to draw it down. I kept to myself at the mill, avoiding Shields and keeping my mouth shut. The new fellow in James's job did his best to get my goat, but I stared him down, and he finally gave up.

Word of the Troubles filled the newspapers. Killings on both sides were reported, and Belfast appeared to be in a state of near riot. It was no time to be Catholic in the North, and certainly no time to be an opinionated one. I prayed for James and cursed the Ulstermen.

I suppose I knew at some point they would come looking for him. One night in late August, an almighty rap on the front door made me jump straight up in bed. On cue, Aoife started bawling. I grabbed her from the cot and went downstairs, carrying her in my arms. Two uniformed men stood on the doorstep. B-Specials, the bastards, I thought as I recognized their uniforms. They had their rifles drawn, and one was pointed straight at me and the child.

"Is this the house of James Conlon?" barked one of them. "Is he here?"

"He's not."

"When was he last here?"

The one that was doing all the talking was a big, burly customer with a head on him the shape of a bullet, pointed on top.

"He's not been here," I said. I was defiant, and I knew it was not good for me.

He angled his rifle and pushed it against my neck. I felt the cold, raw steel against my skin. He pushed me backward, and I almost lost my balance.

"No lies, missus, or you'll get what's coming to you. You can go to jail or worse for harboring a criminal."

"Youse are the criminals," I spat.

A younger fellow stood beside him, laughing under his breath. "She's got a mighty mouth on her, Georgie," he said. "Maybe we should teach her a lesson."

Aoife squirmed in my arms and bawled louder.

"Shut that child up," said Bullet Head, pushing me farther back on the doorstep.

I opened my mouth to shout at him, but a voice from the shadows startled me into silence.

"Leave the woman and child alone, Campbell," he said. "Back away now. And lower your rifles, the both of you."

Owen Sheridan stepped into the light. He wore a British Army captain's uniform, and his voice was soft as a kiss. They minded him, though, the two of them backing away, growling beneath their breath. He stared at me, shock evident on his face. So he was here by chance, I thought. He had no notion this was my house.

He took off his peaked cap. "I apologize for my men, Mrs., er . . . ?"

"Conlon!" I snapped.

He knew rightly who I was, but I guessed he did not want the bullies to know that. He looked straight at me, his eyes bright in the lamplight.

"I will need to ask you a few questions about the whereabouts of your husband. May I come in?"

The question hung in the air.

"You can come into the kitchen," I said at last, loud enough so the other two could hear me. "I have no need of the neighbors knowing all my business. But I won't be offering you a chair."

"Thank you," he said, and turning to the others, "You two go to the end of the street and wait for me there. We do not want to be tarnishing Mrs. Conlon's good name."

He followed me into the house, and I turned on the gas lamp. I hoped he did not see that my hand was shaking. But he missed nothing. He laid his hand on my arm.

"I'm sorry, Eileen," he said softly. "Those ruffians should be court-martialed for treating you and your baby that way."

I shook off his arm. "It's 'Mrs. Conlon,'" I snapped, "and it would take more than the likes of them to put fear in me."

He stepped back and bowed, formal again. I supposed he could see the way of things; after all, we'd left each other that Christmas Eve night with no love lost. It all seemed so long ago now. But the old resentment had risen back up inside me. Or was it hurt? I did not want to think about it. Instead I looked him up and down. The gold wedding band on his finger glinted in the light.

"Still in the army, I see," I snapped. "I thought you gave it up after the war gave you that limp."

It was a cruel thing to say. He looked down briefly at his leg.

"And promoted to captain as well," I went on. "You must be a fine soldier after all." Sarcasm filled my voice.

"It's easy enough to gain promotions over the backs of dead soldiers," he said, "it takes no talent at all." He paused and looked directly at me. "I had indeed retired out," he went on evenly, "but when I came home and saw what was happening in the streets of our own country . . . well, I couldn't stand idly by."

"Couldn't stand by and watch the likes of yourselves torturing the rest of us, is that it?" I snapped. "Wanted to be part of the action?"

"On the contrary, Mrs. Conlon, I felt that these volunteers needed some army discipline. Otherwise who knows what atrocities they might commit."

"It's a bit late for that," I retorted.

He nodded. "I do what I can," he whispered.

Aoife stopped crying and eyed him with interest. He smiled at her and offered her his hat. She reached out and took it in her chubby hands.

"A fine child," he said. "She took after her father, I see."

There was an awkward silence. He looked around the kitchen. It was hard to read his face, but it softened as he took in the bright dishes on the shelves and the fire in the hearth. For a moment, he seemed lost in thought. I waited. Aoife let out a cry of protest as I pulled his hat away from her just as she was about to suck on its brim. Her cry startled him. He took out his notebook and a pencil and got down to brass tacks.

"I need to ask you a few questions. Would you not be more comfortable sitting?"

"I'll stand, thank you."

There followed a string of questions about James and his doings. I suspected he knew a lot more about that than I did. As it was, I told him nothing of importance. I said I did not question James on his activities and he never discussed them with me. No, I had not seen James since he disappeared two months before. He knew, of course, that I was lying. He nodded and put away the notebook. I opened the front door to let him out, and he paused on the doorstep.

"You know, you could be in danger, Mrs. Conlon. The more we know, the more we can protect you. If there's anything you want to tell me that might have slipped your mind—"

"I've forgotten nothing," I interrupted.

"Well," he continued, "should you have more to add, you can find me at the barracks most evenings." He put on his hat. "Good night to you now. And lock the door."

I slammed the door on his heels and turned out the light. I watched from behind the curtain. He stood for a moment looking up at my house. He crossed his arms in front of his chest and rubbed them as if he were cold, although it was a mild evening. Then he squared his shoulders and limped away on down the street and around the corner. I watched him until he was out of sight.

I went back into the kitchen, cradling Aoife in my arms. All sleep had been driven from me, but at least the child had drifted off. A strange confusion crept over me. I should hate that man, but I could not raise the feeling inside me. I should be frightened as well. He clearly knew more than he was letting on about James and me. Yet I felt safe knowing he was there. It made no sense to me. I sighed. This whole bloody business was driving me astray in the head. I thought maybe Ma was just as well to be where she was, wrapped up in her own private world. I looked down at Aoife, who was peaceful now, smiling in her sleep. They say babies see angels when they dream. I hoped they were good angels. Maybe they would drive away the bad ghosts.

࿔

AS JAMES HAD predicted, trouble began to fester at the mill. Rumors spread like fire that the Protestants were going to picket at the gates to stop the Catholic workers from going in to work. The same thing had been happening up in Belfast at the shipyards and at other mills around the province. It was estimated that ten thousand Catholics had been put out of their jobs. The Sheridan family had never discriminated against Catholics in employing unskilled workers, so no one believed they'd sack us just because we were Catholic. But it was clear our Protestant co-workers were out to make our lives miserable for us.

The rumors came true of a Monday morning in October a couple of months after Owen Sheridan had come to my house. Myself and dozens of the other workers found our way barred by a line of picketers at the mill gate. It was only a dozen or so of them, but they were carrying signs and cursing at us as if we were animals. I hovered about with the rest of the women, not knowing what to do. Surely the police would come and break it up. But after fifteen minutes, there was still no sign of them. Some of the women fled away down the street, crying. My temper rose. How dare these bastards stand in our way?

When I could stand it no more, I braced myself and marched to the front.

"Let me pass," I demanded. "I'm late for work."

The fellow leading the protest, the foxy oul' Charlie Fagan who had taken over James's job, laughed.

"Will you listen to her, boys? 'I'll be late for work.'" He mimicked me in a high-pitched voice. "And where is your fine husband? He's not here to protect you now, is he?"

The picketers were all men.

"He has better things to do than fight with the likes of you," I shouted. "You should be ashamed of yourselves trying to put the fear of God into innocent women."

"Innocent, is it?" His grimy face was inches from mine. "Well, maybe some of them are, but not you, my girl. From what I hear, you've been in the thick of it."

"Leave it alone, Eileen." I heard Theresa's voice behind me. "We'll go home and leave the police to sort it out."

I was rigid with anger. "We're coming in," I said to Fagan. "And if you

as much as lay a hand on us, you'll not only have the police to answer to,
but James Conlon's men as well!"

He backed away. I could see he had not expected any of us to put up
a fight. There was a murmuring among the other men. One by one, they
put down their signs. I turned to the women behind me.

"C'mon," I said. "We'll be docked for the lost time as it is. No sense
losing any more money on account of these ignorant louts. Come on,
Theresa."

Theresa linked her arm in mine. She was shaking. She looked back at
the others, and one by one they linked with one another and walked past
the picket line. The men backed off, but they yelled curses at us.

"Dirty papists! You've no right to our jobs."

I held my head high and marched in the gate with the rest of the
women behind me. As I punched my card in the time clock, I saw Shields
snooping from his office door. Bloody coward, I thought.

The police arrived that afternoon. Lot of good they'll do now, I thought.
They asked me questions and I answered them. I gave them the names
of every man on the picket line, making sure to point out that Fagan was
their leader. The other women nodded at my statements, but only Theresa was brave enough to give her account as well. After the police left,
cheering broke out among the women.

"They'll get what's coming to them now," they said.

"Wait till my Eamonn hears about this."

"We'll have peace now. They'll not try again."

Their camaraderie was infectious. Mary Crowley started singing the
Republican national anthem, and the rest joined in. The threads were left
spinning loose on the spindles, and the bobbins dropped as they joined
hands. Shields came roaring out of his office, his face red as a rooster. He
banged on a table, but with little effect. He glared at me.

"See what you started?" he muttered.

I wanted to remind him it wasn't me that started it at all. But what
good would it have done? I was going to be blamed no matter what. And
the sad thing was that not one of the women thanked me for taking a
stand.

That night, I went over in my mind what had happened. Was I wise to
do what I did? Well, it was too late now, and besides, somebody had to do
it, or they would not stop until we all quit. I felt a small sense of triumph.
The old passion was back. I realized how much I had missed the action
of the fight, the churning in my stomach as we set up the ambushes, the

close calls, the flames licking the sky, the torrid lovemaking afterward. And not that I wanted to be called a hero, but I was raging that not one of the girls said thank you. Not even Theresa. I supposed they were all either suspicious of me or afraid to be seen talking to me. I was becoming like those untouchable women in India I'd read about in one of P.J.'s books. A pariah—was that the word? At least I could show James that I had not lost my nerve. He was not the only one in the family who could stand up to the oppressors.

ଓ

"WHAT THE FECK did you think you were doing?"

James stood over me, shaking with anger. He had arrived at the back door in the early hours of the morning. For once I was really delighted to see him. I couldn't wait to tell him my news. But as soon as I began, he held up his hand. He had already heard about it. I should not have been surprised the way news like that traveled around the country. I was more shocked at his reaction. I stared at him with my mouth open.

"What d'you mean? Sure wasn't I standing up for our rights the way you do yourself?"

James shook his head in disbelief. "You stupid woman," he cried, "don't we have enough troubles without you drawing attention to yourself?"

James had never called me stupid before, and his words stung.

"And what would you have had me do?" I yelled. "Lie down and let them walk all over us? Or run home with my tail between my legs like the rest of the women?"

James let out a sigh. "Do you not see," he said quietly as if talking to a child. "It's your name is on the complaint, now. And it will go to the Sheridans. And besides getting the label of a troublemaker, you could lose your job, and the police will be watching the house more than before."

"Complaint? What complaint?"

"Fagan and his crew have lodged a complaint with the mill and the police stating you threatened them with bodily harm."

I laughed out loud. "Bodily harm? Sure there's no one in their right minds would believe that. And the Sheridans should be happy I stood up to them, otherwise they would have lost a day's work from all of the women."

James shook his head, exasperated. "Do I have to spell it out? Do you think that Fagan, who hasn't the brains he was born with, came up with this idea on his own? Do you not think it was the Sheridans put him up to it? They don't want to get the reputation of sacking Catholics. They know they'd have to answer to us if they did. But if they allow the pressure to be brought on us to quit, then they can still keep their holier-than-thou Quaker reputation intact."

"That's nonsense," I said. "Who would do the work if we all quit?"

"There's plenty of Protestants would be glad of the jobs. Some of the other mills have closed. There's plenty of people out of work between here and Belfast."

I said nothing in reply. I sat down and stirred the fire, mulling over what James had said.

"The Sheridans would not do that," I said at last. "They're good people."

James stared at me. His face was dark. "Is that so?" he said. "Why don't you ask your fancy friend Owen? Push comes to shove he'll not be protecting you. Blood's thicker than water."

I felt a flush rising on my cheeks. Had he heard that Owen was at the house?

"You're dreaming," I said. "I'm no more friendly with Owen Sheridan than the man in the moon."

"That's not what I hear."

After James left, I sank down on my knees. James had betrayed me again. He had turned on me as if I were the enemy. He had accused me of things that were not true. And he had called me stupid. I blinked back tears before they could fall. Stupid, is it? James Conlon would regret the day he ever called me that. The anger powered through me, and I got up. The energy was enough to get myself and Aoife dressed and out the door. But it faded as I made my way over to the mill. All I could think of was another scar somewhere on my poor heart, another place that could never be touched.

ơᴓ

JAMES'S THIRD BETRAYAL followed swiftly. On the Saturday morning following the incident at the mill, I stood in the line as usual to collect my pay packet. As always, the mood was light, the women joking back and forth with one another, making plans for their Saturday night out. When it was my turn to sign for my pay, Shields pulled me aside. The look on his face was hard to describe. Satisfaction? Triumph? A cold feeling washed over me.

"Make this one count, lassie," he growled. "It's your last."

My hand froze on the envelope.

The women stopped laughing and looked at me, but they said nothing. Mary Galway stood prim as ever behind Shields's shoulder. She waved a bony hand at me.

"Move along now," she said without addressing me by name. "You're holding up the line."

For once in my life, I had no words. Sacked! I'd been sacked! For all my brave talk, I had never really believed it could happen. I looked down at the envelope in my hand and clutched it like a drowning man. A shove behind me knocked me forward. Then a fire roared through my legs and I ran as fast as I could out of the mill, across the courtyard, out of the gate, and down the hill. I thought I heard Theresa's voice calling behind me, but I paid no heed. I had to get away. Shame blanketed me. My face was hot and red. I jumped in front of the Newry tram just as it was pulling out, and the conductor caught my arm.

"Where's the fire, lassie?" he called.

I ignored him and slumped down on the wooden seat. I could not think. My life passed before me as if I were drowning. What was I to do? What about Aoife? What would James say? I got off the tram at the Newry station and ran to the post office. I had no idea what I was going to do there. I could not deposit the money in my pay envelope. I needed it for me and Aoife. I had not made a deposit in weeks. I didn't even have my passbook with me. A tight spiral wound through my gut, and I could hardly breathe. Somehow I had to know what I had in the post office was safe. I had to know my dream was still protected.

A guard stood at the door as I rushed in. "We're closing in five minutes, missus," he said. "You'd better make it quick."

The room was filled with last-minute customers buying stamps and cashing money orders. The buzz of conversation and laughter and the clank of the clerks' machines swarmed in my ears. I heard the clack of screens as one clerk after another closed their windows. I raced to the far end of the long counter to the savings window. Mary Dunn, the clerk, stood there talking to a big fellow who was wearing an overcoat and a hat. She was flirting with him, her fat country face lit by a stupid smile. I never liked the girl. She had a crafty way about her. But at least she was in no hurry to shut down. I still had time. And then I slid to a halt. I had caught the sly look in Mary's eyes, and instantly I knew all. The man was James. And he had taken my money!

I threw myself on James and wrenched the small red savings book from his hand. I touched its frayed edges and rubbed my fingers across the faded lettering on its cover. Tears blurred my vision. My fingers shook as I rifled through the pages, and there, on the last page, was what I knew I would find: "Balance, October 16, 1920, Five Shillings and No Pence."

James watched me silently. I lifted my eyes to his face.

"Five shillings?" I blurted out. "How can it be five shillings? I had over four hundred pounds in there. How?"

Even though I knew well how it had happened, I turned on Mary Dunn.

"Why did you give it to him?" I shouted. "You had no right."

She shrugged her plump shoulders and gave me a cunning look. "Mr. Conlon is your husband," she said, her tone mocking me with its sweetness, "and besides, he had your passbook."

James spoke up. "The Cause is desperate for money just now, Eileen. I'll pay it back. That's why I left the five shillings to keep the account open. And anyway"—he put his hand on my arm and grinned—"it's not as if it was that much."

A red fire burned in front of my eyes. I tore at James's sleeves, scratching the rough cloth with my fingernails. He took me by the shoulders and tried to push me away, but I clawed at him more, scratching small furrows of blood down the skin on the backs of his hands.

"Not that fecking much?" I screamed. "It was all I fecking had. It was every penny I've been scraping together for the last eight years!" I choked back the bile that had risen up from my belly. "It was for the Yellow House," I whimpered. "You know it was. Och, James, how could you do it?"

A pair of hands grabbed my shoulders from behind. "Come on, now, missus," said the guard. "You're causing a bit of a scene."

I shook him off and lunged at Mary Dunn, who was trying to bring down the screen on her window. I grabbed the screen and pushed it up again.

"You feckin' eejit," I screamed at her. "D'you know what you've done?"

Her small eyes grew wide with fear. Gone were the slyness and the smugness.

"I'm sorry, missus," she muttered.

James and the guard took me between them and, almost lifting me off my feet, dragged me to the door and out onto the pavement. A black motorcar idled at the curb. James pulled me toward it.

"Get in!" he commanded. "You'll have the coppers here with your carrying on. And I have no intention of being caught."

I wrestled against him. "No!" I screamed. "I'll go nowhere with you ever again."

James shrugged. "Suit yourself," he said, and got into the car.

As the car sped off, a sudden sweat drenched me, and the world began to spin.

When I came to, I was sitting on a bench outside the post office, sipping water, my coat open and my blouse unbuttoned at the throat. The guard knelt beside me, patting my hand.

"You'll be all right now, love," he said. "Sure you just took a bad turn."

I nodded. "Aye."

"Can we send word for somebody to take you home?" he said.

"No." I shook my head.

"I'll be going, then."

I watched him walk away down the street. I was in a daze. Something had happened. Something awful. But what? I couldn't remember what. Slowly, I got up and stumbled in the direction the guard had gone. I had no idea where I was going. A loud buzzing clogged my ears, and a wicked headache almost blinded me. As I walked, passersby nodded. I nodded back. They acted as if I knew them, but I didn't. I wasn't sure I rightly knew who I was myself.

The October day was closing in. Soon it would be dark. I buttoned my coat against the chill and kept walking. I arrived at the edge of Newry and stood looking out on the Belfast road that led out of Newry to the north. What was I doing? Did I intend to walk to Belfast? Why? I knew nobody in Belfast. Dear God, what was happening to me? As tears streamed down my face, I wiped them away with my fist. An awful sadness descended on me, so heavy that my knees buckled. I sank down on the pavement and gave myself up to sleep.

"Move along, there, missus. You're violating the curfew!"

A sharp stick poked me in the ribs.

"Get on home with you now."

I opened my eyes and stared up at the policeman who bent over me. He peered closer at me. "Are you all right, missus? Have you been on the drink?"

I shook my head.

He took out his flashlight and shone it in my face. I shrank back at the shock of the light in my eyes.

"Well, if it isn't Eileen Conlon," he crowed. "Watching out for the hus-band, is it?" He cackled. "Fine lookout you are, falling asleep on the job."

He pulled me roughly by the arm. "Get up out of that now and go home before I take you down to the station."

My tears began to flow again.

"I don't have a home," I sobbed. "I don't have anything."

He let out a curse under his breath. "Another O'Neill gone astray in the head," he said. "Stay there. I'll send for P. J. Mullen to come and get you off the street before you disgrace yourself altogether."

I slumped down to wait. As I did, memory slowly slithered into my body, smooth and venomous as a snake. James. James had taken every-thing I had. Ever since the night he had taken my innocence, I had known he would not stop until he had taken my dreams. Then the betrayals would be complete.

Truce

1920–1921

15

∞

Loneliness lay upon me heavy as a stone. I sat at night stirring the fire, lost in my thoughts. I worried that I was turning out like Ma. Soon I'd be staring out in the distance with no recognition of anybody or anything.

It was Aoife who preserved my sanity. At almost a year old, she was already walking and babbling a blue streak of half-formed words. She needed her own way in everything and stood, tiny hands on her hips, crying out her demands. Her face might have belonged to James, but her personality was all mine. I recognized myself in her stubbornness, the way she planted herself in front of me and would not move until she got what she wanted. There was no ignoring Aoife.

Maybe it took losing everything for me finally to embrace my daughter. Up until now I had always carried a deep, shameful resentment toward the child. She represented to me the death of my past and the birth of my future. Now I realized that with my dream in shambles, Aoife, my little warrior, was here to force me to keep living. She would not let me give up either on my dream or on my future because she was part of it, not separate from it. In Aoife, James had unknowingly given me a gift more powerful than he could ever have imagined.

Billy Craig came often, a foolish smile on his big face. He brought sweets for Aoife and fancy cakes for me. He would sit on the floor and play with Aoife, who was delighted with his attention. When she fussed he soothed her with tender notes from his tin whistle. As I watched them, I envied their innocence.

Fergus came at times, on his way home from work. He would sit drinking tea, his dark eyes blazing brighter than the flames in the hearth. Over
and over, he apologized to me for what James had done, each time his
anger growing more intense. I tried to play things down in front of him; I
was afraid his anger would boil over and he would kill James.

Terrence came as well. He brought me news of my mother, even
though it was always the same: She was in good health, but no, her mind
was not back yet. I did not go as often to see Ma anymore. Once, when I
brought Aoife to see her, she had turned her face to the wall and begun
to weep. She upset the child—and me.

Terrence was more than willing to talk about Ma, but I had to drag
information out of him about Frank. P.J. was a better source of news.

"Ah, he's the quare fellow all right," P.J. said, drawing slowly on his
pipe. "Nobody can tell what side of the fight he's on, but he's profiting
from it just the same. He's been seen parading through Newry in the best
of finery, carrying a big walking stick like he owns the town."

"If you're saying he's smuggling over the border," Terrence said fiercely,
"I'm sure you've got it all wrong. Frank was not brought up to be a turncoat." Terrence's black eyes blazed. I wondered why he was so quick to
defend Frank.

P.J. shrugged. "Think whatever you like. But a stable boy doesn't get
that kind of money shoveling dung!"

A desperate thought entered my head. "He hasn't sold the house, has
he?" I cried.

P.J. and Terrence both turned to me. "No, love," said P.J. "He's asking
such a fortune for it nobody sane would ever buy it."

Terrence and P.J. also brought me money that they said came from
James. I didn't believe them, but I took it all the same. P.J. brought Paddy
every now and then. The boy's quiet presence was a comfort in the long
evenings. No sign of his temper showed these days. He appeared to have
grown out of it. I still went to mass with him on Sundays and took him
and Aoife for lemonade afterward. I could hardly afford bread in the
house, but I would not give up the small pleasure of spending an afternoon with my wee family. It kept me sane.

Word came to me from James once in a while. A young fellow would
show up at the back door, the way James had done, and shove a note or a
fistful of pounds into my hand and away like a rabbit before I could speak
to him. The notes said little, just that he was alive but could not come to
the house because he was in hiding. I stuffed the pounds in my pocket

and ripped up the letters. I didn't care much whether he was alive or dead. If it weren't for Aoife's sake, I wouldn't care at all. I read newspaper accounts of incidents—soldiers ambushed, farmers taken out and shot because they were suspected of informing, and the like. I knew James was involved with much of it. The country was in turmoil.

Worry gradually replaced my anger. What was I to do? The money came less often from James, and the pounds were fewer. As long as the Cause needed it more, there would be none for me. There were no jobs any- where—certainly not for Catholics. I still went to the Ceili House, even though it took all the courage I had to stand up and play in front of all those people as if nothing had happened to me. The little bit of money it brought kept Aoife and me from starving. There was always the workhouse, I thought grimly, the gray, ugly building that loomed over Newry and made everybody shiver when they walked past it. No. I would not see Aoife and myself in that oul' place. James's mother was dying to take the child. She didn't give a tinker's curse about me, but she kept sending Theresa over to the house to ask would I let "Mary Margaret" go down to her until I got settled. Poor Theresa. I slammed the door in her face. I worried about the house as well. It belonged to the mill, and neither James nor I worked there anymore. It was only a matter of time until they put me out.

I thought about going to see Frank, but I realized he wouldn't help me. If anything, he would get pleasure out of my predicament. Frank had not changed. If he had, he would have come to my wedding or to Aoife's christening. And if P.J. were to be believed, he was up to his neck in no good. I assumed he was biding his time at my grandfather's farm until he could make his own way—if he had not left already. My grandfather! Now there was a laugh. I would dig ditches before I would lower myself to go and beg from that old git the way my mother had done. But where else was I to turn? The Mullens had done enough for me already. The more I thought about it, the more it became clear to me. I had to go to Owen Sheridan. He was my only hope.

☙

ONE NIGHT LATE in December 1920, I shined my boots, put on my best coat and hat, left Aoife with Billy, and rode my bicycle up to Queensbrook House, where the Sheridans lived. I had seen the house often enough from a distance but had never gone close to it. It stood on a hill overlooking the mill yards, a sprawling granite manor surrounded by a low stone wall.

The house was dark. It had not crossed my mind that Owen might be away for the coming holidays. As far as I knew, there was to be no Christmas Eve celebration on account of the Troubles. Maybe he had gone away to London with his fine blond wife. Sweat drenched me in spite of the cold. How would I ever get up the nerve to come here again? It had taken many sleepless nights to get myself to this point. I was coming to the English manor house to beg, just as so many of my ancestors had been forced to do in times of trouble and famine. A deep shame washed over me. If he wasn't in, I told myself, it would be just as well. I would find another way.

I leaned my bicycle against the gate and walked up the pathway to the front door. It was a beautiful night, clear and frosty, and the moon lit the ground around me as if it were day. It was very quiet up there on the hill. I looked down and saw the outline of the mill buildings like hulking shadows crouched together in sleep. I remembered the first morning I had come in to Queensbrook on the tram with P.J. and saw the ugly buildings and chimneys in the first sunlight. But now they looked docile, almost comforting in their slumber.

I sucked in a deep breath, pushing my pride down into my stomach, and walked up the steps to the front door. I took the bell pull and heaved on it. The sound echoed away into silence. I stood back and waited. Eventually, a light flickered on the side panels of the door, casting yellow shadows on the tempered glass. A young girl in a white apron curtsied when she opened the door.

"Good evening," she said, and then her jaw dropped.

She straightened up quickly and looked me up and down, an expression between disgust and curiosity on her broad, red face. She recognized me, and I her. She was Mary Galway's young cousin up from the country. I had seen her at the Christmas Eve balls and occasionally at the Ceili House. She was thick featured, but with the same sharp black eyes as her cousin. She knew me straightaway.

"What is it you're wanting?" she said. How servants everywhere loved it when they could let down the polite pretense and take out their frustrations on one of their own. "D'you have an appointment?"

"Appointment my arse," I began, but before I could go on, Owen Sheridan's soft, firm voice drifted up behind her.

"Show the visitor in, Kathleen, there's a good girl."

The girl glared at me and stood aside as I entered a dark, paneled hallway. The place smelled faintly musty, and there was a portrait of a sour-looking oul' fellow on the wall. A bit of a shiver crept over me. Owen Sheridan appeared in the hallway. It had been a while since I had seen him out of uniform. He was wearing a worn tweed jacket over a white linen shirt and fawn-colored trousers. He looked every inch a Protestant country gentleman.

"Eileen . . . er, Mrs. Conlon," he said. "How pleasant to see you." He was a cool customer, I thought. He showed no surprise at all at seeing me on his doorstep. I wished I had his control. "Kathleen, bring us some tea, will you?"

The maid bobbed a curtsy at him while throwing me a daggers look and then disappeared down the hall. He showed me into a big room at the back of the house with floor-to-ceiling windows that looked out onto the garden. Gas lamps washed everything in a mellow light. A fire glowed in the fireplace. Family photographs crowded the yellow mantelpiece. Two chairs covered in a faded, flowered print sat on either side of the fire, with a low wooden table between them. A daybed draped in an embroidered quilt sat against the window. The carpet, red and blue and gold in a swirly pattern, was faded and a little threadbare in places. I supposed it must be an antique, but I wouldn't have given it house room. There were books everywhere, crowded on shelves, lying on tables, and stacked on the floor. He moved some off one of the chairs so I could sit down.

"Here, let me take your coat."

I removed my coat, my hands trembling with nerves, placed it on the back of the chair, and sat down.

"It's a wonder your head's not sore with all this reading," I said without thinking.

He smiled. "Books are my passion," he said. "And I have difficulty throwing them away. I suppose they have stacked up, haven't they?" He looked around as if faintly surprised. He shrugged. "My family leaves this room to me. It's become my study and"—he sighed—"I suppose my sanctuary."

Sure what would he need sanctuary from? I thought. Hasn't he the fine life? But I said nothing.

We made small talk for a few minutes. He asked about Aoife. I told him a friend was minding her. He seemed faintly disappointed at that.

"She would have been very welcome," he said.

Kathleen brought in the tea. She banged white china cups and saucers with gold rims on the table along with a matching milk jug and sugar bowl. There was also a plate piled with sandwiches cut in white triangles with the crusts trimmed. If he noticed her rudeness, he said nothing.

"Oh, the child would have been a holy terror in here," I said truthfully. "She'd have the place torn apart in minutes."

He smiled. "That would have been something to see."

He poured the tea, added milk and sugar, and handed me a cup. His hands were white, not the hands of a workingman, I thought. I wondered suddenly what they would feel like on my body. I was shocked to blushing that such a thought had entered my head. I choked briefly.

"Is it too hot?" he said, concerned. "Let me add more milk."

"It's grand," I said sharply. "I'm just not used to drinking from cups made for dolls."

I put down the cup and smoothed my dress. I had fought with myself over what to wear. Why should I bother dressing up for the likes of him? But I told myself that good manners required I should at least wear what I would wear to mass. I had settled on a dress of dark green wool that Theresa said matched the color of my eyes. I had lost weight in the past month, and it was a bit loose on me, but I cinched it with a leather belt and it looked well enough. I had brushed my hair and braided it again so no stray wisps escaped. The familiar motion of plaiting the hair through my fingers had calmed my nervousness. Sheridan stared at me, saying nothing. I began to get agitated under his gaze.

"I . . . er, I . . ." I could get no words out.

"Take your time, Mrs. Conlon," he said.

"I thought you might be away in London with your wife," I blurted, for want of something to say. It was none of my bloody business, and I knew it.

He gave me a sharp look. Jesus, I was done for now, and I hadn't even had the time to get out the words I had come to say.

"Mrs. Sheridan is indeed in London, visiting friends," he said quietly. "She finds Ireland rather boring these days and"—he paused—"that appears to include myself. Apparently I've become a far cry from the cavalier and amusing chap I was before the war."

I had no ready answer. "Well, I suppose you're away a lot," I stumbled, "what with the Troubles and all. Just like my own husband."

He nodded. But I knew that line of conversation was over.

I gulped down more tea. I stiffened my shoulders and looked straight into his eyes. It was now or never. "I came to ask you for help," I said. "I was sacked from the mill, and James is not able to give me any money." I was not about to tell him what James had done to me. "And I'll probably be put out of the house," I went on, "and Aoife and myself will be on the street. So if you could see your way to helping me find another job, I'd be very grateful—sir!" I spat the last word, a tiny defiance even as I begged for my life. Sweat poured off me. I felt like a schoolgirl after confession waiting for the priest to pronounce penance.

He put down his cup and picked up a sandwich, chewing it slowly. He took his sweet time about answering me. Couldn't he just say no and throw me out and get it over with? My annoyance grew. I clenched my fists in my lap. At last he wiped the crumbs from his fingers and set down his plate.

"Well, that's quite a litany of troubles," he said blandly. He was a piece of work, this boyo. He knew how to take control of a situation.

He leaned back in his chair and stared directly at me. "How long have I known you, Mrs. Conlon? Five years? Seven? And in all that time I have known you to be an intelligent, ambitious, and brave woman. But you are also a hothead, and you look for trouble." His voice grew sterner. "And, of course, I know about your more recent involvements with the uprising, although I'm willing to put most of that down to the influence of your husband."

Red flashed in front of my eyes. "I'm under nobody's influence but my own," I shouted. "I joined the uprising of my own free will and for good reason."

"No reason is good enough to maim and kill," he said, his voice rising.

"I never killed anybody," I protested, "at least not knowingly." And then, because I could never keep my mouth shut, I added, "But I would if I had to. Those bastards killed my da."

"Killing them won't bring him back," he said.

"Well, I can see this is no use," I said. "I must have been astray in the head to come here." I stood up. "Thank you for your time, Mr. Sheridan. I'll not be bothering you again."

He jumped up and put a hand on my arm. "Not so fast, Mrs. Conlon. There are a few home truths you need to hear, and then you are free to stay or go as you wish."

The anger in his voice startled me, and I sat back down. I had never heard this tone from him before. Gone was the calm, controlled manner. Owen Sheridan had a temper that could equal James's any day of the week.

"Do you have any idea," he shouted, "how often I have pleaded your case to Joe Shields and my father? Do you?" He left me no time to answer. "Of course you don't. I have saved your job for you more times than you can imagine. But this last time you went too far."

I bristled. "Those friggers wanted to put all of the women out of their jobs, just like down in Belfast. Somebody had to stand up to them," I shouted.

"And it had to be you?"

I shrugged. "I suppose so."

"As I said, you are a hothead. It is time you grew up and thought about the consequences of your actions. After all, you have a child to look after now. You cannot come running to me every time you get yourself in trouble. I am not your savior. You must give up your reckless ways, Mrs. Conlon, or—"

"I'll not inform, if that's what you mean," I cried.

"I would never dream of asking you to do that," he said. "First of all you would never do so, and if you did, it would put your life in grave danger and I would not do that."

I was silenced. He was right, of course. Informers were found every day of the week with their throats cut and a placard around the necks with the word *Traitor* written in big, black letters.

"What I meant," he continued, "is that I need your word that you will give up all your violent activities. You will not so much as take or deliver a message. You will attend no meetings. You will harbor no known insurgents—"

"I'll not turn against my husband!" I protested.

He raised a pale eyebrow. "Such loyalty, after the man has effectively left you and his child to starve."

And worse than that, I thought. I hated James for what he had done to us, but I was not going to admit it to him. "He's still my husband," I said.

"Quite so, and to bar him from the house would put you in danger. I would not expect you to do that. But if I am to go back to my father and make another plea on your behalf, I must be able to assure him that you have given up your life of violence." He paused and looked directly into my eyes. "And," he continued with a faint smile, "if you were to agree to some volunteer work, I'm sure my father would be gratified to hear it."

Silence fell as we both stared into the fire, thinking our own thoughts. What he was asking me to do was not that unreasonable, and besides, it had been a long time since I'd been out on any missions. Something in me kicked and screamed at being told what I could and could not do. Eileen O'Neill, warrior, would never have put up with it. But I was also Eileen Conlon, mother, and I had my child to think about. I would have to swallow my pride for the child's sake.

"But I promised my da," I whispered, "that I would fight for the O'Neill legacy. I promised I would get our house back and bring us all home."

The tears escaped now, and I brushed them away roughly. Sheridan leaned forward and took my hands gently in his.

"Sometimes promises are made rashly," he whispered, "and to please others. Surely your father would not want to see you putting your life in danger. And anyway, I don't see how ambushing armored lorries will get you back your family home."

He was right, of course. When you said it outright and logical, it made no sense. How was I to explain that I was so mixed up between revenge and anger and helplessness that I had to hold on to something? I could not let the warrior die as well.

As if reading my mind, he went on, "I know that there are many who feel helpless to change things, and see violence as the only answer. But believe me, it is not." He sat back and looked into the fire. "I saw horrors in France that I would not wish on my worst enemy. There was no glory in the mud and mutilation on the battlefield. I realized the Quakers had been right all along. Problems must be solved by peaceful means."

"But you still joined up again," I said. It was more of a question than an accusation.

He nodded. "I believe I explained that to you when we last met. I am trying hard to contain the violence. Tempers are raw on both sides, and there is little discipline." He sighed. "I hope I am making some difference."

We lapsed into silence again. He stared into the fire. I stared at my rough, red hands. Aoife, I thought. I have to do it for Aoife.

"All right," I whispered.

Sheridan jumped as if he had forgotten there was someone else in the room. "Pardon?" he said.

"All right! All right!" I shouted. "Do you want me to sign it in blood, too?"

He smiled then. "That won't be necessary," he said.

☙

LATER THAT NIGHT, I heard from Terrence that the Government of Ireland Act had been passed in England. The act called for two parliaments to be set up, one in Ulster and the other in the South of Ireland—both parliaments to be tied to England. The act had been proposed by a fellow called Walter Long, a Unionist leader in Belfast. Under pressure from Ulster Unionists, six of the nine counties of Ulster were partitioned from the rest of the island to form Northern Ireland, a new territory separate and distinct from the rest of the country. The Unionists accepted the new Northern Ireland parliament. Meanwhile, the Republicans in the South refused to take their seats in the newly created Southern Ireland parliament and vowed to continue to fight for a free and independent Ireland. Would freedom for Ulster continue to be included in that fight, I wondered, or had the betrayal of Ulster begun? And, I wondered, had my own betrayal of my warrior self also begun?

CHRISTMAS CAME AND went, with no word from Owen Sheridan. My shoulders slumped in shame every time I thought about what I had done. I had lowered myself and begged—something I was sure my da would never have done. Certainly my ma, when she was in her right mind, had never done so. I remembered the time I slouched behind her as she strode into the Royal Bank of Newry, bold as brass in her best hat, and had put Mr. Craig in his place. She wouldn't even bend to her oul' da when he would have forced her to leave her husband. She had turned on her heel and walked away, pride stiffening her shoulders. I was ashamed of myself. What kind of an O'Neill was I at all? I could not shake the faint sense that I had betrayed myself and Da.

Finally, word came in mid-January 1921 that I was to go back to the mill for my old job. I had hoped to get a place at the weaving mill or the finishing factory, but beggars can't be choosers. I imagined Owen Sheridan's self-righteousness as he thought of how I would have to lower myself and go crawling back to the likes of Joe Shields and Mary Galway. He probably thought it would be good for me. Well, I would not give any of them the satisfaction. I would march in like Ma with my head high and my shoulders straight.

ON THE FOLLOWING Monday morning, I walked up to the mill. The crowds of workers seemed like ghosts hurrying through the gates as the horn blew. I felt like a stranger in my own skin. Where had my nerve gone?

"Help me, Da," I whispered.

Shields came out of his office as soon as he saw me.

"You're back," he said, eyeing me up and down.

My temper exploded. "And who do you think it is," I snapped, "a feckin' ghost?"

He nodded. "I see your time off has done nothing to curb your temper, missus. Well, there'll be no place for that here. You'll keep your nose clean and your mouth shut. You're on trial only, no matter what your fancy boy has told you."

"Fancy boy?"

"Don't get cute, missus. We all know you were up at the house. And who knows what you were willing to do to get back here. After all, we all know Sheridan's reputation for the ladies. And you the great Republican! And him a Protestant!" He spat tobacco on the wooden floor, missing my bare feet by inches.

I marched over to my old spinning frame. I made a big show of tying on my apron and arranging my tools. The place was silent. All eyes were on me. I tried to keep my hands steady as I oiled the flax and wound it onto the spindles and started the machine up. My heart pounded. I looked at nobody. I was more shocked than angry. Of course it should have occurred to me that the whole town would know I was up at Queensbrook House. Mary Galway's cousin would not have waited to spread the gossip. But to make those accusations! God knows what she had said. God knows what these people were ready to believe.

A cold foreboding crept through me. Had James heard about this? Had Theresa told him? Would he believe her? I pushed down the fear and let anger rise so that I was back on solid ground.

Feck him, I thought. It was his doing drove me to beg. And if that meant I might have had to sleep with Owen Sheridan to get food for my child, what right did he have to judge me?

All the same, bitter tears stung the back of my eyes at the thought that people were ready to believe I could have done such a thing.

I worked steadily the rest of the morning. When lunchtime came, I tried to avoid Theresa, but she caught up with me, tugging at my sleeve. Her eyes were bright and she was bursting for news.

"I heard you were up there," she said. "I didn't believe it at first. But now you're back here, I suppose it must have been himself got you the job?"

"Aye," I said. "And believe what you like about how I got him to do it."

Theresa fell into step beside me. "Och, don't mind them busybodies. Sure if there's no scandal, they'll make it up for the *craic*."

Well at least Theresa was ready to give me the benefit of the doubt.

"Anyway," she went on, "I'm more interested in the house. You know, the furniture and all?" Her eyes widened and her mouth dropped open, ready to take in everything.

I shrugged. "Nothing to write home about. I've seen better in a tinker's caravan."

Theresa's mouth turned down in a pout. "Och, come on, Eileen. Give us the details. I'm dying to know."

I snapped then. I turned on her. "Well, isn't it the desperate empty life you have, Theresa, when all you care about is how the gentry live."

Her face crumpled like a child's. I knew I had hurt her, but I couldn't help myself. Poor, innocent Theresa. What harm had she done me?

The rest of the afternoon dragged on. When the closing whistle blew, I was the first one out.

That night, I dreamed about the Yellow House. I had dreamed of it before, usually about happier times when we were all together and the music played. But this time it was a nightmare. I saw the burned skeleton of the house standing under a shrouded moon. I heard the cries of babies coming from inside while soldiers surrounded it and fired shots through its windows. I saw Da at the door, calling for help and then collapsing from a bullet. Frank was there among the soldiers, and I couldn't tell whether he was firing at the house or defending it. James was in the dream, too; he rushed out from behind Da carrying Aoife, ignoring my cries to stop. He disappeared into the night. In the dream, I sat on a low stone wall across the road and watched. The grass in front of the house was trampled, and cigarette butts and other debris littered the path that led to the front door. A cold feeling came over me, as if I were looking at a corpse.

16

Shortly after I started back at the mill, I heard Owen Sheridan had gone back to England. I supposed he was trying to mend his marriage. He was gone longer than I expected. Miss Joanna Wharton must be taking a good bit of persuading. By March, however, he was back and spending more and more time at the mill. Word was that his da had fallen into bad health. I saw him often in Shields's office, going over papers, Shields glaring down at his bent head. When he inspected the factory floor, I noticed that he was walking straighter, the limp barely noticeable. He often wore his army uniform and strutted with his hands behind his back. The women watched him with a mixture of hostility and fascination. He had aged in the last few months. His fair hair was more tinged with gray, and more lines etched his face than when he had first come back from the war. I had to admit to myself that the changes suited him. He looked more handsome now and mature—a far cry from the cocky, grinning fellow who openly admired the women as much as they admired him.

He nodded in my direction now and then when he was on his visits. I was grateful he didn't single me out. I had enough suspicious eyes on me as it was. But one day Shields came out of his office and barked at me.

"You're wanted in the office!"

The spinning machines slowed down, and heads went up all over the floor. My face flushed. "Mr. Sheridan wants to talk to you," he said aloud, and then, leaning into my face, he growled, "And don't go getting above yourself, missus. I'm watching you."

I slowed my frame to a stop and went into Shields's office. Owen Sheridan stood up from behind the desk. He smiled.

"Ah, Mrs. Conlon. Shut the door, will you, and sit down."

Shakily, I pushed the door shut and sat down opposite him. He stared at me, and the flush on my face grew deeper. My discomfort set me on edge. I assumed he wanted to talk about whether or not I had kept my bargain and stayed out of James's activities, so I decided to strike first.

"I've not been involved in anything," I snapped, "although it's hard to stand by while you and your bloody volunteers run roughshod over innocent people. It's time youse went home and minded your own business."

"I wish we could, Mrs. Conlon," he said calmly, "but the other side won't let us. They refuse to honor the Government of Ireland Act."

"They won't back down, if that's what you mean," I said, the steam out of me now. "They believe in what they are fighting for."

He leaned back in his chair. "Indeed," he said. "However, I did not ask you in to discuss the political situation."

I waited.

"You remember when you came and asked me to give you back your job?"

I began to sweat. Jesus, he was going to change his mind.

"If you recall, part of our bargain was that you would perform some volunteer work. It was obvious that you were not keen on the idea at the time, so I have waited until you were settled in again at the mill. But the need continues to grow, and now I am afraid I must collect on the promise."

His words spun around in my head. "Volunteer? Promise?" But there was no mention of the sack. My shoulders sank in relief.

"If you are free on Sunday afternoon," he continued, "I would like you to accompany me up to the Newry Hospital."

"I, er, is there not some other place I can go? My baby sister, Lizzie, died in there."

Thoughts of the hospital made me shiver. I went there, of course, to see Ma, but I had to admit my visits were fewer now than before. And I hadn't set foot near the fever wing since Lizzie had been brought there.

He raised an eyebrow. "I'm sorry, I did not know you had difficult personal memories associated with it," he said quietly, "but I think you could perform a great deal of good. I often find that volunteer work has personal rewards greater than one could imagine."

There was to be no changing his mind, I could see that.

"All right," I said. "I'm a woman of my word. I'll keep to the bargain."

He smiled. "Excellent! Shall we say Sunday, about one o'clock? Er, I assume mass is completed by that time?"

"Your guess is as good as mine," I said. "If that old blather Father Dornan is up there, the pubs could be open and closed again before he's finished."

He grinned at me. "Shall I collect you at your house?"

I shot a look at him. "Is it astray in the head you are? Sure what would the neighbors be saying at the cut of myself stepping out on a Sunday with the likes of you? Believe me, the heads would be bobbing behind the lace curtains to beat the band. Anyway, I still have to take Paddy and Aoife for their lemonade. I'll meet you at the hospital main gate at two o'clock—although the thought of going up to that hard oul' place again leaves me cold."

He leaned over and patted my arm. "I know, Mrs. Conlon, and I appreciate your willingness to go. But keep in mind we are trying to help those less fortunate than ourselves."

He stood up and dusted off his trousers. "I will see you on Sunday, then."

"Aye," I said.

He walked around the desk and opened the door. "I'm finished here, Mr. Shields. Thank you for the use of your office."

Shields came in, scowling at me.

"Get back to work!" he barked.

∽

THE FOLLOWING SUNDAY, I left Aoife with the Mullens. All I told them was that I was going to visit Ma; there was no need for them to know more. Then I walked up the hill that led to the hospital.

I shivered in the damp, breezy air and pulled my coat tight around me. March had come in like a lion. "There'll be no summer at all this year," people said. "Sure no sun would shine in the midst of all the Troubles." I climbed the hill slowly, looking down at my feet as I always did when I went to visit Ma in the insane wing. I never wanted to look directly at the grim old workhouse or the Fever Hospital itself. I remembered too well the painful ride all those years ago with Lizzie sick in Ma's arms. Instinctively, I looked up in the sky for crows. Eventually, I reached the courtyard. I looked up at the cluster of gray, limestone buildings with their narrow, barred windows. I wondered, Was Ma watching me? Was poor Lizzie's ghost staring out from behind one of them? Rain began falling. I shivered and hurried in through the tall arched doorway into the main hall.

Owen Sheridan was waiting for me. He stood up and smiled when he saw me. He wore a tan raincoat over his uniform. He had no hat, and his fair hair glistened darkly from the rain.

"There you are, Mrs. Conlon," he said, holding out his hand.

It seemed an odd thing to shake hands with the man at this stage. I had seen him enough times before and never done so, but I supposed he was showing good manners. His hand was surprisingly firm, even though the long fingers had always struck me as delicate. As soon as the thought came over me, I dropped his hand as if it were on fire. I was suddenly all business.

"Well, where do you want me to start?" I asked.

He nodded. "Indeed. Well, I thought we could start on the men's ward in the main wing. That is where most help is needed. So many chaps are being wounded in the fighting." He sighed. "I thought you could meet Sister Rafferty."

"Right," I said.

I followed him up a dim, winding stairway. The smells of disinfectant and urine brought my memory into sharp focus. I swallowed down the bile that rose in my throat. A nurse in a white uniform passed us, her shoes squeaking on the floor. As we reached the second floor, the low drone of coughing and moaning grew louder. Owen Sheridan pushed through the swinging doors and greeted a nurse who stood just inside the ward.

"Ah, Sister Rafferty! I'd like you to meet Mrs. Conlon. She has graciously agreed to become a volunteer."

Graciously agreed my arse, I thought, but I smiled politely. Sister Rafferty wore a dark uniform and a tall, white starched cap, signifying that she was the head nurse. She was not an old woman, but she looked worn out. She sighed.

"Ah, Mr. Sheridan, you are our guardian angel." Then she turned to me. "Welcome, Mrs. Conlon. We need every pair of hands we can find. Let me show you through the ward."

We followed her down the ward between rows of single iron-framed beds. As I looked from one bed to the next, I expected to see old men. But instead they were mostly young, some only a few years older than my brother Paddy. Some were missing arms, others were missing legs.

Some were bandaged so you could hardly see their faces. Some grinned and waved, some moaned, others lay still as the dead. On the wall over each bed hung a medallion—blue for Protestant, red for Roman Catholic, Sister Rafferty explained—so the priests and the ministers would know which fellows to pray over. I tried to do a quick count. The reds and the blues looked to be about equal.

"We are getting so many poor lads in every day, we can't take all of them," said Sister Rafferty. "If they're not so bad, we patch them up and send them home. Or if there's nothing we can do for them . . . Well, there's no sense taking up a bed."

"Are there no visitors?" I said suddenly.

"Ah, no. Only the clergy. They're too sick in here to be bothered by all the blather of visitors."

It seemed odd to me. Would not the sight of a wife or mother ease their suffering? But I said nothing. I thought of my own ma. I had a sudden urge to see her.

"Our nurses can use any sort of help you want to offer," Sister Rafferty said to me. "It would even be a great help if you would just sit and talk to the patients, so the nurses can get on with their other duties."

I nodded. A strange feeling crept over me as I looked around. All of a sudden, it didn't seem to matter to me so much whether there was a blue or red medallion above their beds—they were all just young lads in awful pain and in need of comfort.

"Of course." I nodded. "I can manage one night a week, and a couple of hours on Sundays."

"That would be grand, Mrs. Conlon. Will we expect you this week, then? Maybe Friday? Friday's a hard day to get volunteers. The young girls like the dances better than coming here."

I was about to say I played at the Ceili House on Friday nights, but something stopped me. Instead, I smiled. "I can give up the dancing for one night," I said, and Owen Sheridan broke into a grin.

When we were back in the corridor at the top of the stairs, I said suddenly, "I'll leave you here now. I need to go see my ma."

Owen Sheridan bowed. "Ah, of course, your mother is here, isn't she?"

I shrugged. "In the wing for the insane," I said sharply.

"I will accompany you, then," he said.

I started. "No. I'll go alone."

He smiled. "I'm afraid you won't be let in without me, Mrs. Conlon, unless you want to wait until six this evening for visiting hours to begin."

He was right, of course. Visiting hours in the insane wing were very limited. Jesus, the last thing I wanted was for him to meet my ma in the state she was, but I had such a strong urge to see her, I would have to give in.

"All right," I said.

When we reached the main hall of the insane wing, Nellie, the round-faced nurse P.J. always talked to, sat at her desk. She looked up in surprise.

"Why, Miss O'Neill," she said, "it's been a while since we've seen you." She looked over my shoulder. "Is Mr. Mullen with you?"

I had never corrected her on my name. I suppose I liked hearing myself called O'Neill every now and then. "No," I said, and her face fell in disappointment.

"Well, I'm afraid you're far too early for visiting hours."

Owen Sheridan strode over to her and put out his hand. "I am Captain Sheridan, Nurse," he said smoothly. "I was hoping you would allow Mrs. Conlon a short visit with her mother. I shall accompany her, of course."

I watched him in awe. It must be grand to be able to take over any situation just like that and have people do your bidding. Nurse Nellie flushed under his gaze.

"Ah, well, since it's yourself, sir, I would say there's no problem. Shall I fetch a nurse?"

"No," I put in sharply. "I know the way."

She watched us go. Whoever Nellie knew would get a grand story out of this, I thought. It would not be long before it got back to the mill.

We mounted the stairs to the top floor and went into the main ward. I led the way. The same women were there, cackling and cursing. When they saw Owen Sheridan, some of them made dirty gestures and loud kissing sounds at him. I didn't turn around to get his reaction but kept walking toward Ma's room at the far end of the ward. I opened the door slowly and peered around it. I expected to see Ma in her usual chair by the window, but today she was lying in bed. She looked like a ghost, her face the color of bleached linen and her long graying hair spread out wildly on the pillow. I choked back a cry. I went over to the bed. I heard Owen Sheridan close the door, and I could hear his breathing in the stillness of the room.

I bent down. "Ma?" I whispered. "Ma, it's me, Eileen."

She opened her eyes. They glistened with tears. "Have you been crying, Ma? What's wrong?"

In answer, tears rolled over her cheeks. I took her hands. "Och, Ma, don't be crying. Everything's all right."

I tried to lift her up. Her bones felt loose inside her skin. I set her against the pillows and smoothed her hair. She stared at me. I knew that she recognized me, but only as the woman who came to see her sometimes and not as her daughter. I fought back my own tears. Suddenly, she looked around the room and then down at my hands.

"What is it, Ma? What is it you want?"

"Flowers?" she whispered. "Flowers?"

My tears let loose then. "Och, Ma, I didn't bring flowers, I'm sorry. I didn't know that I was coming. I'll bring some next time."

But she closed her eyes again and turned away from me. I had lost her.

⁓

"I WILL GIVE you a lift home," Owen Sheridan said when we reached the open courtyard. The wind gusted now, and the rain beat sideways. I shook my head.

"I have to collect Aoife at P.J.'s," I said, "then I can get the tram home."

"I will not let you ride on the tram in your present state," he said firmly, "you are much too upset. We will stop at the Mullens' and I will explain the situation. I'm sure they will keep the child overnight. Then I am taking you home."

He led me to his motorcar and opened the door for me to get in. I sank down on the soft leather seat. The car smelled strongly of wood polish and faintly of tobacco. Idly I recalled the first time I had ridden in a car, when I went with James to hear Michael Collins. But this time there was no excitement in me over the novelty of it. I was in too much pain. We stopped at the Mullens', and I waited in the car as Owen Sheridan knocked on the door and went in. He was gone only a short time. I wondered what P.J. and his wife were making of the whole thing, but I was too tired to care. As we drove on toward Queensbrook, the steady rhythm of the rain beating on the windshield sent me into a numbing trance. Between seeing all the young fellows broken and crippled in the ward, and then seeing Ma the way she was, I was suffocated with feelings I could not identify. I was in a fog as thick as the one that surrounded the car. When we reached my street, I thought I should tell him to leave me off there, and I would walk home. But I could find no words. There was no alarm in me over what the neighbors would think. All I felt was weariness.

He parked the car and walked behind me into the house. I sank onto a chair at the kitchen table. He found the kettle and filled it with water. Then he bent and lit the bits of wood and newspaper that lay in the grate. I watched him in silence.

"Do you have any whiskey?" he said.

I nodded toward one of the cupboards.

"Good."

He made tea and poured it into two cups, along with a shot of whiskey in each. He handed me one and sat down at the table beside me. His presence was oddly comforting. I should have been scandalized, I realized, having this man in my kitchen making me tea, and him a British Army soldier, and me a married woman with a child. But somehow none of it mattered. I took the teacup from him and sipped it, trying to thaw the numbness that enveloped me. I said nothing, and neither did he. Instead, he looked around the kitchen, studying the pictures on the wall and in particular the framed photograph of the Yellow House. He stared at it for a moment. Then he got up and cleared away the cups and stirred the fire.

"I'll be getting along now," he said. "Will you be all right?"

I nodded. "Thank you, Captain Sheridan."

He looked down at me, his eyes filled with concern.

"It's 'Owen,'" he said. "I think we know each other well enough now for you to call me that."

I nodded. "Thank you, Owen," I said. I liked the feel of his name on my tongue.

He came over to me and put his hand lightly on my shoulder. My tears came again.

"I should have brought her flowers," I whispered.

He stood for a moment, his hand still on my shoulder.

"I'm sorry, Eileen," he said. And then he was gone.

☙❧

AS EXPECTED, IT took no time at all for news of my visit to the hospital to get around the mill. On Monday night, Theresa caught up with me as I was walking out the door. She linked my arm and looked up at me, her eyes bright. I knew what was coming.

"There's a lot of talk about you today, Eileen. I thought you should know."

"I don't give a tinker's curse what they're saying," I snapped.

I had not slept at all the night before. I sweated as if I had the fever, and when I got up I was soaked to the skin. I thought maybe madness had overtaken me, just like Ma. It was in the family, after all, wasn't it? I had always been a strong woman, but my energy had ebbed away, and it took everything I had to get out of bed. I had no emotion at all, not anger, not sorrow—just a hollowness that left my heart rattling around inside me.

Theresa sniffed. But she carried on as if I'd not spoken at all.

"They say you're stuck like glue to that Sheridan fellow. And I'd say they're right. First you went to his house. And yesterday you were seen up at Newry Hospital with him. Nellie Leonard that's a nurse up there is a sister to Mary Leonard, the doffer, and she was telling all." Theresa stopped to draw a quick breath. "And then his motorcar was seen outside your house last night."

I stopped and faced her. "Look," I said, "I ran into him up at the hospital when I went to visit Ma. He gave me a lift home because it was lashing rain."

Theresa looked doubtful. "Nellie Leonard says you came too early for visiting hours, and if it wasn't for his nibs, she would not have let you in at all."

Theresa folded her small arms in front of her chest and looked up at me, waiting for an explanation.

"Will you whisht, Theresa," I interrupted her. "I don't need to be giving you or anybody else a minute-by-minute account of my doings."

Theresa pouted at being cut short midstream. She shrugged. "Suit yourself. But I'm only telling you—the walls have ears."

"Aye," I said.

We walked on awhile until it was time for Theresa to turn off for her street. She hesitated. "Tommy's away to Donegal on a delivery. Will you come down for the tea?"

I looked at her. She was still looking away from me, but I could sense something in her voice besides satisfaction at her news. Loneliness, maybe? Her husband, Tommy, drove a delivery van for the mill and was often away overnight.

I thought about going home to my own empty house.

"I have to collect Aoife," I said.

"Come down after, then," she said, "and bring her with you."

Theresa and Tommy had been married for two years, but there was still no sign of a child. I was surprised. All Theresa ever talked about was a family of her own. She would have six or more, she said, if God granted them to her. Well, apparently God was not in a giving mood when it came to that, no matter how many novenas her mother made. Her mother told her it was a cross to bear and seemed to take an odd satisfaction in Theresa's misery. Twisted oul' bat. I think she was happiest when there was misery about, for all the praying and kneeling that she did.

☙☙

THERESA WELCOMED US at the door of the tidy little house. You could eat off her floor, it was so spotless. I always had a twinge of guilt when I went in there, my own house being not as clean as it could be.

"The kettle's on," she said. "Sit yourself down. Why, hello, wee doll. How's my lovely girl?" She bent and picked up Aoife, who gave me a look as much to say, "I'll be able to get away with murder now. My aunt Theresa loves me." She was right, of course. Theresa doted on the child. It broke my heart sometimes to watch her.

We sat down to bowls of savory stew, fresh bread, and hot tea. Theresa set everything out as you would see in a magazine.

"This is lovely, Theresa," I said. "You shouldn't have gone to such trouble."

She smiled with pride. "Not at all," she said. "Tommy and I eat like this every night when he's home."

I passed no remarks but ate and tried to stop Aoife from picking up her bowl of stew to drink from it. Later, we took our teacups and sat by the fire. Aoife sat on the floor, playing with a new doll Theresa had bought for her.

"I'm sorry, Theresa," I said at last.

"What for?"

"For cutting you short that time—the time you asked about Queensbrook House."

Theresa waved her hand. "Och, that! Sure I forgot about that weeks ago."

I knew, of course, she still held it against me, but I smiled all the same. Theresa took her opening.

"But speaking of the Sheridans," she said, "I just want to warn you, Eileen."

Jesus Christ, I thought, would she never drop it? But I knew Theresa too well.

"Warn me about what, Theresa?" I said.

Theresa swallowed a drink of tea and straightened up in her chair. She was in her element. I sat back and waited.

"Well," she said, "you know I'm not one for gossip, but it's all over the mill about you and his nibs. Like I said, they know you went to his house, and yesterday you were seen meeting him up at the hospital, and afterwards he was seen escorting you home. The word is he goes to your house late at night and you let him in." Theresa's eyes were wide. "Is that true, Eileen?"

I shrugged. "If you've all these witnesses, then it must be," I said sharply. "But you left out the times I was seen fornicating with him in the middle of the street outside the mill!"

My temper was gathering. These people would rather believe the lies, so what was the point in denying any of it? Theresa looked shocked.

"Don't be talking like that, Eileen. Sure they'll believe you."

"I don't care what they believe. Nosy oul' biddies, the lot of them."

Theresa drank some more tea. She looked at me solemnly.

"There's them that's saying you're informing, Eileen. I know myself it's not true, but you have to admit it looks suspicious. Captain Sheridan is in charge of a brigade of B-Specials."

"And my husband is a known freedom fighter," I retorted.

"Aye, right enough. But they're saying you're getting even on James for stealing your money and deserting you. Even Ma thinks that . . ."

"Who cares what that sick oul' woman thinks!" I cried. "And how do they know about the money? Did you tell them?"

Theresa looked more than a bit frightened. "Why would I tell something like that on my own brother?" she cried. "It was Mary Dunn down at the post office told Maggie Sheehan, and she told—"

"Shut up, Theresa," I shouted. "I want to hear no more of it."

I was raging. Aoife looked up from her doll and started whimpering.

"You've frightened Mary Margaret," said Theresa.

"Her name's Aoife!" I snapped. "Anyway, we need to go. Thanks for the tea."

"Any time."

I pushed Aoife out the door, ignoring her screams. I rushed home as fast as I could, half carrying and half dragging the poor child by the arm. I needed to get into my house and close the door as fast as I could. What was wrong with all these people? Couldn't an innocent body go about her business in peace? But underneath my anger, a small voice was telling me that I could not ignore them. Was I going to have to stop seeing Owen Sheridan? Not that I was one to let people tell me what to do. And not that I was afraid of any of them, I told myself. But I had better battles to fight than over the likes of him. I could get along without his company. Somehow, the thought left me feeling a little hollow.

17

I went to the mill every morning, my head high, ignoring the stares and the gossip. I tried to make it up to Theresa for my bad temper. I bought her a lovely green scarf, but she sniffed and said she had enough scarves to hang herself with. I sighed and gave up. She was going to make me work to earn her forgiveness.

The nightmares about the Yellow House kept coming back. Not since I was a young child had so many ghosts haunted my dreams. But I was not a child anymore, and after a while I made up my mind to face them. One Sunday afternoon in April, I asked P.J. to take me up to Glenlea and the Yellow House. As we drove, Paddy sat up in the seat between me and P.J. He held Aoife on his knee. I looked down at them and smiled. Paddy was still a solemn lad. You would have thought Aoife would be too active for him, but something in his mild presence calmed her down. She sat peacefully staring out at the scenery around her. I followed the child's gaze to the budding hawthorn bushes that lined the road, and a rush of memories, sad and joyful, flooded back to me. I wiped away a stray tear as I looked out over the fields and up at my beloved Slieve Gullion. She had draped herself once more in a cloak of bracken and adorned herself with wild blossoms.

"Look, Aoife," I said, "look at the beautiful mountain."

As we rounded the corner past Kearney's pub, I stiffened my shoulders and straightened my back, preparing myself for the spike of pain my first sight of the house always brought. But the pain did not come. Instead, my mouth fell open in disbelief. Where had the ugly, charred skeleton gone? As we climbed the hill, I stared at the house. Surely I was imagining things. Maybe the clouds were distorting my view. But it was a clear, sharp day and there was no mistaking what I was seeing.

"Jesus, Mary, and Joseph, will you look at that?" cried P.J.

"Jesus, Mary, Joseph," cried Aoife, clapping her hands.

"What's happened, P.J.?" I whispered, afraid the vision would disappear. "Is it the ghosts playing tricks on us?"

P.J. let out a loud belly laugh. "If it's ghosts, darlin' girl, it's the good ghosts."

He pulled at the reins on the pony and jumped down from the cart and ran to the house, his arms outstretched as if to touch it. I sat in the cart and stared. The skeleton was gone. New walls had been built and whitewashed. The roof had been restored. New panes of glass glittered in the sunlight. Planks of fresh new wood were stacked in the front yard beside troughs of gravel and cement. Wheelbarrows stood in silent witness to the miracle that was under way. P.J. poked his head through a window and then stood back, his hands on his hips.

"It's almost as good as new, darlin'," he called.

By now, Paddy and Aoife had struggled out of the cart and were running toward the house. I could not bring myself to move, afraid I would break the spell. I crossed my arms on my chest and breathed deeply. Did I dare believe it? Och, Da, how could I have ever thought of giving up the dream?

After a while, P.J. escorted the children back to the cart.

"Will you not come and see it for yourself, Eileen?"

I shook my head, smiling. "No. It's enough I can see it from here," I whispered.

P.J. nodded. "Aye, a shock for you, love. A shock for all of us."

"Frankie," I whispered. "Frankie changed his mind. Thank God."

P.J. gave me a sharp look as he climbed into the cart.

"How can you be sure it's his doing, love?" he said.

I turned to him. "But it has to be," I said.

P.J.'s face turned solemn. "He could have sold it, lass. This could be the work of a new owner."

"No. No." I shook my head firmly. "Da would never have let Frankie sell it."

"But your da . . . ," began P.J.

"I know," I snapped. "But he still talks to me, and I know he must talk to Frankie." I shook my head. "Anyway, if it had been sold, we would surely have heard word of it, wouldn't we? I mean, it would have been in the newspaper. Or someone would have told us."

P.J. nodded. "You may be right, darlin'. But no one told us about the rebuilding, either. We'll go in below and see what Shane Kearney knows."

He turned the cart around and started down the hill. "No," I said suddenly. "No. Leave us back to Newry and I'll ride out and see Frankie. I want to thank him."

P.J. gave me a queer look. I ignored it. I'm right, I thought, I must be right. Da would not see it sold to strangers. It was Frankie who'd had a change of heart.

 observ

IT WAS WITH a light and glad heart that I rode my bicycle out to my grandfather's farm later that same April Sunday. I rode fast as the wind past the lush hedgerows and wildflowers that lined the road. Like the late summer day so long ago when I had ridden this same road, I smiled and waved at old people and children out for their Sunday stroll. Even as I approached the massive stone wall that surrounded the estate, my heart did not sink. Instead, I flew through the open gateway like an excited child, my feet hardly touching the pedals.

As I approached the house, my mind recorded some changes. The broken bricks had been replaced, the flower beds were filled with rows of sweet violets and bluebells, and the shutters had been painted. I circled around the pathway and across the patch of grass toward the stables. As soon as I reached the courtyard, I jumped off my bicycle and laid it on the ground. I rushed toward a young lad of about thirteen who was coming out of a stable carrying a bucket of dung and a shovel. I had a vision of the last time I had seen my brother in this same exact place, and my heart was fit to burst.

"Is Frank O'Neill about?" I called urgently.

The boy dropped the bucket and came closer. He wore a sly smile, but his eyes were sullen. "There's nobody here by that name," he growled.

"Of course there is," I said. "Can you find him, please?"

The boy's smile faded. "And just who would you be?" His tone was accusing.

My temper flared. "I'm his feckin' sister," I snapped, "not that it's any of your business, you wee git!"

"What's the trouble, Aidan?" a voice came from behind. I swung around. I recognized one of the stable hands from before.

"I'm looking for my brother, Frank O'Neill," I said.

The fellow looked me up and down. I wanted to lash out and hit him.

"Well, well," he said, "there's no Frank O'Neill here at the minute, miss."

He looked at the boy. They were enjoying a joke at my expense. I was ready to explode. "What the feck do you mean?" I shouted. "You know fine well he's here."

The older fellow shrugged. He took a long draw on his cigarette. "Now, if you were to tell me you were looking for a Francis Fitzwilliam, then I'd tell you you'll find him right enough beyond at the big house. But the fellow Frank O'Neill that used to work in the stables is not here any longer."

The boy snickered.

"Suit yourselves," I said, frustrated. I picked up my bicycle and turned on my heel. I wheeled my way toward the house. What the feck were they on about? I wondered. "Eejits!"

I pulled hard on the heavy iron knocker. I supposed I was going to have to face my foul old grandfather after all. I'd been hoping to avoid him. When the door opened, it was a small, bird-eyed woman who peered out from behind it.

"Yes?" she said.

"I'm Eileen O'Neill . . . er, Conlon," I said. "I'm Mr. Fitzwilliam's grand-daughter." Jesus, the words caught in my throat. "Is he about?"

She stiffened. "He's not up to visitors," she said.

"Well, actually, I was really looking for my brother Frank," I said.

"Who is it, Rose?" a male voice came from somewhere behind her.

"A woman who says she's your sister," called Rose with surprising force.

"Bring her in, then."

She stood aside and let me into the dark, musty hall that I remembered. It was still dark, but it smelled now of wax polish and lemons. I walked toward the sound of the voice.

Frank sat at a wooden table in the kitchen, hunched over a plate of meat and steaming potatoes. He looked up and his fork froze in the air.

"What is it you want?" he growled.

"Fine greeting for your sister," I said, my earlier good mood almost gone. I pulled out a chair and sat down. The woman hovered in the background. Frank waved his hand at her.

"Get her some tea, then leave us alone."

"Yes, sir."

I watched in amazement as she set a cup of scalding tea in front of me and quietly left the kitchen. I turned to Frank. "Sir?" I said.

Frank shrugged. "She's new here. It's nice being waited on for a change," was all he said.

He had grown darker and stockier since I had last seen him. There was no trace of a boy left in him. To my horror, I realized he was the image of old Fitzwilliam himself.

"What is it you want?" he said again. "If it's money, you may as well leave now, because you'll get none from me."

I suddenly remembered why I had come. My good mood returned. I laughed and put my hand on his arm. "Och, Frankie," I whispered, "I'm here to thank you."

He frowned. "What for?"

"For not selling the Yellow House after all. For repairing it instead. Ah, Frank, I was up there today and it looks grand, so it does. You've made me so happy. And Da, too, I'm sure of it."

Frank's dark eyes pierced my face for a moment, and then his frown disappeared and a grin of understanding took its place. He put down his fork and laughed.

"Jesus, that's a good one!" he cried, slapping his knee. "Ah, now, that's the best one I've heard in many's a day." He laughed until his face turned red. I stared at him, waiting, while a slow, dull spit began to turn in my stomach.

When he was all laughed out, he shook his head. "Jesus, Eileen. I took you for a lot of things, girl, but never for this much of an eejit. You really thought . . ." The laughter threatened to erupt again. I stared at him, the sickness growing inside me.

Frank leaned back in his chair. His dark eyes were cold. "Did you not understand what I told you before? I hate the O'Neills. I owe them nothing." He grinned again. "I even changed my name."

"What?" I said, confused.

"Aye." He put out his hand as if to shake mine. "Francis Fitzwilliam, at your service."

I ignored his hand. What the feck was he talking about? I wondered for a minute if he had not gone astray in the head.

"You see, darlin' sister, our grandfather began to get frightened that the rebels would come and burn down his house and everybody in it.

Of course, I fanned the flames a bit, as you might say—got some of my friends to come up here with torches and scare the daylights out of the old bastard."

He kept talking as if I weren't there.

"In time I got him convinced I was the only one could save him. I told him I hated the Catholics as much as he did, and wasn't I a Protestant at heart and by blood just like himself. He took a bit of persuading, but he gave in. Signed everything over to meself as long as I would change my name and my religion. Small price to pay, wouldn't you say?"

I stared at him. He had gone astray in the head. I was convinced now.

"After all," he went on, smiling to himself, "there was nobody else for him to leave it to. Ma's only sister died young and she had no brothers. I assured him I would keep the Fitzwilliam line going and his fortune intact. Ah, I have the devil's tongue on me, so I do. You'd almost think I was an O'Neill. Are you not proud of me, Eileen?"

I could not take in what he was saying. Frank had connived his way into owning the Fitzwilliam estate? He had turned Protestant?

"Don't be looking at me like that, Eileen," he sneered. "Ma was a Protestant. You're half a one yourself, no matter how fine a Republican you think you are."

"You're a bloody turncoat," I hissed at him.

He shrugged. "I have no interest in either side. They're all the same as long as it means money for me. And as for fighting for the bloody Cause the way you and your husband do—that's for eejits altogether. If you're going to lie and burn and kill, you may as well do it for your own profit, not for some feckin' vision of glory! Look at what it's done for you—a slave beyond at the mill, and your husband with a price on his head." He grunted. "At least I have land to show for my actions. What have you?"

I was growing weary. I wanted to jump up and beat him with my fists and yell and scream. But all the energy had drained out of me.

"What did you do with the Yellow House?" I asked, my voice flat.

Frank's face broke out in a wide grin. "Ah, now that, my girl, was a masterstroke!" He laughed aloud. "Ah, that did my heart good. I sold it indeed, Eileen, and you'll not guess in a thousand years who I sold it to."

I waited.

"Och, be a good sport, Eileen. Go ahead, guess."

I said nothing. He stopped laughing, but the sly grin remained.

"I sold it to Owen Sheridan," he crowed. "Isn't that a good one? I sold it back to the people the O'Neills stole it from in the first place. Isn't that the greatest joke you ever heard?" He was cackling now, an evil, awful sound. "I took the O'Neill legacy and I shoved it up their arses."

I don't recall how I got home that night. My eyes were a blur of tears. My mind was numb with confusion. I felt no emotion—not fear, not anger, not sadness. It was as if the very core of me had been ripped out and all that remained was flesh and bone.

∞

IN THE DAYS after my visit to Frank, I feared I would lose the last threads of my sanity. My money was gone, the Yellow House was gone. What had I left? It was Terrence who helped me hold on by stoking my fury. When he heard what Frank had done, he turned into a man I had never seen before. Gone was the sitting and staring into the fire on long quiet nights. Instead he paced the floor, cursing Frank and the Sheridans and James and anybody else he could name. He scared the daylights out of poor Billy so much that he fled up the stairs with Aoife in his arms and would not come down.

"He'll pay for it, Eileen. Mark my words, Frank will pay for his sins! He should burn in bloody hell for this."

The strength of Terrence's anger shocked me. He had always been such a quiet, thoughtful man—no matter that I always sensed there was something passionate burning deep down inside him. What surprised me was that it was Frank's actions that had unleashed that passion in him. I'd always thought Terrence secretly admired my ma, but what Frank had done made no difference to her. The world could blow up around her and Ma would be none the wiser.

No matter. I seized on Terrence's anger like a drowning woman and let it light my own passions. My fury grew, and as it did it suffocated the fear that stalked deep down inside me. Since I could not stand to go near Frank again, my anger turned toward Owen Sheridan. I marched into Joe Shields's office and asked him outright where Owen was. He gave me a queer look.

"Not that it's any of your business, missus, but he's away to England these three weeks."

"When will he be back?" I demanded.

"How the feck should I know?" he said. "I'm not his feckin' secretary. Now get yourself back to work."

So I had to bide my time. May came and went, and June dawned with the promise of a mild, wet summer. Theresa finally allowed me to make amends to her. I realized that she saw me as a rich source of information to fuel her need for gossip, and that outweighed my bout of bad temper toward her. She had let me cool my heels long enough. I smiled to myself. Poor Theresa was so innocent, you could read her like a book. I was glad for her company, though, since the other women still would not talk to me. I told her about how Frank had sold the Yellow House out from under me, and she seemed genuinely sorry.

"It's bad enough my brother stole your money," she said, "but for Frank to do that to his own sister . . ." Her eyes turned bright. "You say he turned Protestant? Changed his name and all?" I could see her excitement building. This was great gossip altogether.

ꙮ

ONE FRIDAY IN early July, I sat by myself at lunchtime on the wall that ran along the river near the mill. Theresa was out that day, nursing her ma, who thought she was dying. Old Mrs. Conlon had a bout of dying every few months. Theresa was made to stay home from work, the priest was sent for, and funeral arrangements were begun. But as they say, it's hard to kill a bad one, and the oul' bat always recovered. She would outlive the lot of us, I thought.

"Hello, Eileen."

The voice came out of nowhere, interrupting my thoughts. I jumped so that I nearly lost my balance on the wall.

"Christ almighty, would you not creep up on a body like that? I nearly fell in the feckin' river."

I looked up and saw it was Owen Sheridan himself. I choked into silence. I suppose, looking back, it was just as well I didn't see him at first, because I had no time to consider how I would react. He smiled down at me, his eyes glinting in the sun.

"Well, I am glad to see that you are doing well."

"And why wouldn't I be?" I snapped.

"Of course. It's a beautiful day, and I'm sure you are looking forward to your weekend."

"Aye," I said, finding my voice now. "I'll be kicking up my heels as soon as the horn blows tomorrow, dancing and carrying on until Monday rolls around again."

He ignored my sarcasm, sat beside me, and took off his cap. He wore his uniform, and I was grateful for it. The uniform put the distance between us—British soldier, rebel's wife—and it allowed me to set aside my earlier gratitude and vent my fury on him.

I stood up and towered over him, my hands on my hips.

"Haven't you the neck on you to be sitting down here beside me nice as you like and making small talk as if there wasn't a thing in the world wrong?"

He stared up at me in confusion. I thought I saw a fleeting smile, and it annoyed me more.

"There are a lot of things wrong in our world, Eileen," he said mildly.

I wanted to spit. "Stop the blarney right now!" I shouted.

People began to stare, but I ignored them. "You stole the Yellow House right out from under me. You stole it, even though you knew it was the only thing in the world I ever wanted. You took advantage of me and the situation. You . . ."

He stood up and took my arm firmly. "Let's walk a distance," he said. It was a command, not a suggestion. He led me away from the crowd of curious workers to a small park on the far grounds of the mill. He stopped and faced me.

"I did not steal it," he said firmly. "I paid your brother a fair price."

"Frank would never give anybody a fair price," I snorted. "But I suppose you would have paid anything to get back the family honor, and, and to spite me!" I finished lamely. I realized as I listened to myself that I sounded hysterical.

His voice was curt. "And just why would I want to spite you? Didn't I give you back your job?"

"Aye. And you made sure I had to grovel to the likes of Shields and Mary Galway. I suppose it amused you to think of me on my knees in front of them."

He did not crack a smile. "I doubt that anyone would ever have the pleasure of seeing that."

I broke down then. My accusations made no sense. They were petty and childish. But the pain was so great that it finally ruptured and tears flowed unbidden.

"But why?" I wailed. "Why did you do it? You knew how much I wanted it."

Suddenly his hand was on the small of my back. The old warm, safe feelings as before radiated through me. I did nothing to resist.

"Let's go over here and sit down."

He led me to a bench that stood on the edge of the park. I slumped down, and he sat next to me. He turned to look at me. His face was somber.

"I'm sorry to have caused you such pain, Eileen," he said. "I had no idea the house meant so much to you."

"But I tried to tell you," I said through my tears.

He nodded. "Yes, you did. But it did not register with me. After all, you said it belonged to your brother and that you had no money to purchase it from him. I'm sorry, but I did not realize how deeply you felt about it." He sighed and turned away, watching a robin frolicking on a tree branch.

"Mr. Craig approached me at the beginning of the year. He had been asked by your brother to find a buyer for the place. But, as you suspect, your brother was asking much too high a price, and buyers were scarce. Anyway, I had been thinking I wanted to buy a home for my wife and me, so that when she returned from England we would not be living at Queensbrook House with my family. I thought if we had a place of our own, well . . ." His voice trailed off. He turned back to me.

"So I bought the house—at an inflated price. Your brother seemed delighted to sell to me, some sort of inside joke that I did not understand. I began at once to restore it, and then I went to England to see Joanna."

He stopped abruptly. I waited. Then curiosity got the better of me.

"And?" I prompted.

"And, I brought her back here." He looked into the distance as if imagining a faraway scene. "I took her up Slieve Gullion. It was a beautiful day, and I thought she would love the view. But she complained about ruining her shoes." He looked at me with a rueful smile. "Anyway, I pointed out the house to her and she did not have much response. Then we came down and I took her closer to it. I pointed out all the renovations. I told her how I imagined the two of us living in it with our children—" He broke off.

For once I said nothing.

"Anyway," he continued at last, "she said she had already begun divorce proceedings. Nothing I could say would persuade her to change her mind." He looked straight into my face, his eyes sad. "So you see, Eileen, like you I had a dream that if I bought the Yellow House, my wife would come back to me and we would live there and raise a family and be happy ever after."

I pushed back a wave of pity that welled up in me. "You weren't meant to have it," I said quietly. "It belongs to the O'Neills."

He was silent for a minute. "Perhaps so," he said at last. "And I would gladly sell it back to your brother. But he would just turn around and sell it again."

"What will you do with it, then?" I said. "Will you live in it?"

He sighed. "I doubt it," he said. "Not now, at any rate. Perhaps in time."

He stood up and put on his cap. He gave me a little nod of his head.

"I'm sorry for your troubles, Eileen," he said, turned, and walked away from me. His limp was worse than before.

"I'm sorry for yours, too," I whispered after him.

❧

LATER THAT SAME month, Michael Collins and the Irish Republican Army signed a truce with the British government. It was the first step toward a treaty that would eventually give the South of Ireland its freedom from British rule. I, too, signed a truce that month: a truce with Owen Sheridan. In that moment when he looked at me with such sorrow in his eyes, I realized that the rich and privileged people can have their dreams shattered, too. We were not so different after all. As I look back now, I realize that moment caused a pinprick of light to shine on my soul, a light that would gradually illuminate a new understanding of myself and the world around me—an understanding that was shaped not by legacy or history, but by a knowledge of myself.

Passion

1921

18

Passion flames like a bright candle, but all the while it is melting into tears of wax. You want it to burn forever, but you know in your heart it will consume itself in the end. The wick will turn black and charred, and the wax tears will cleave into a cold, formless mass. The light and warmth and scent will dissolve into a wisp of smoke and you will descend into emptiness.

Besides betraying me, James had deserted me. He had not been near the house since the day he stole my money. I supposed he might be afraid I would try to kill him for stealing my savings—and he was right. My anger still boiled inside me, and I yearned for another chance to confront him. His desertion had only added insult to injury: the fact that he had chosen the Cause over me. There were times I wished James had died in the fighting. At least I could have held my head up as a proud widow. But as it was, I may as well have been a widow for all the company I had in my bed at night, and there was no pride to be had in that.

My anxiety had made its way into Aoife. The poor child cried every night and had to be coaxed and rocked to sleep. One August night in 1921, about a month after the truce had been signed, when I finally kissed her and left her in her bed, I went into my bedroom and sat in front of the mirror. My face looked thin and yellow in the low lamplight; the face of an old woman stared out at me. I winced and put up my hands and began unbraiding my hair. I picked up my brush and smoothed the hair with long, quiet strokes. Brushing my hair like this always calmed me down. I hummed the same tune to myself that I had just been sing-

ing to Aoife. The quiet was interrupted by an almighty bang on the back
door. I froze. Who could that be at this time of night? The B-Specials
again? UVF fellows bent on doing me and the child harm? I stood up and
gathered my long nightdress around me and went down the stairs. The
banging came again.

"Eileen!"

James's voice was unmistakable. I hurried over to the back door but
hesitated, frozen between alarm and anger.

"Jesus, Mary, and Joseph!" James cried.

Hurriedly, I released the locks and the bar.

"What took you so long?" James growled as he pushed his way past
me and into the kitchen. I closed the door and followed him in. He stood
rubbing his hands in front of the dying fire. Jesus, I thought, if I did not
know his voice, I would not know who he was at all. His hair was down to
his shoulders, and a scruffy black beard covered his face. He wore a dirty,
torn soldier's uniform and heavy black boots with no laces.

"Will you stop gawking and make me some tea," he barked. "I'm famished with the hunger."

I did not move. I stood, trying to get my bearings. How I had waited
for this moment of confrontation—but now that it was here, I was unable to move any more than if I had been turned to stone. James's eyes
burned into me.

"I said to get me some tea, woman!" he shouted.

Still I did not move. We stared each other down like bulls in a field.
Then James grabbed my arm and shoved me aside. He strode to the hob
and lit the gas under the teapot. He rummaged in the cupboards, pulling
out crockery and banging it down on the table. He reached for a loaf of
bread and turned in circles, looking for a knife. When he found the big
bread knife, I instinctively jumped back toward the door. Furiously, he
swung the knife at the loaf, slicing it into jagged wedges. He spread butter
in thick chunks on the bread, poured scalding hot black tea into a mug,
and sat down to eat. I watched him as he gulped everything down. Jesus,
he looked like the Antichrist, but I couldn't take my eyes off him.

"What are you feckin' looking at?" he growled. "You'd think you'd
never seen your husband before."

I bit back a sharp reply. Something in me put me on my guard. What
if he had come to pay me back what he had stolen? A faint wisp of hope
sputtered deep down within me. Be cautious, Eileen, I thought. Watch
your mouth.

"Terrence tells me things are worse than ever," I said quietly, "a lot more dangerous than before."

He put down his bread and bared his teeth at me in an ugly smile.

"And you are concerned about my welfare, I suppose?" It was said with a cackle more than a laugh.

"What do you mean?" I said, hanging on to my temper like a sail in a windstorm.

He leaned over and grabbed my wrist hard. "What do I mean?" he roared. "I mean you've hardly time to be thinking about me or anybody else while you're gallivanting around with the British Army!"

Ah, so that was it. I should have known that's why he came. He had not come to say he was sorry for leaving me and the baby destitute. And God knows he had not come to pay me back my money. He had come to vent his anger on me.

"I . . . ," I began, even though I knew there was no point.

"There's no point in denying it." He said the words for me. "You've been seen with him. And his car has been seen outside this house late at night."

"And what feckin' business is it of yours?"

James banged his fist on the table. "I came here to tell you to stay away from him."

Something snapped in me. The disappointment of my foolish, dashed hopes passed. Now anger rent my cautious guard and spilled out. Eileen O'Neill, warrior, was back. I walked over and planted myself in front of him.

"And who the feck are you to be telling me what to do?" I cried. "You who left your wife and child to starve. You who stole all the money I had in the world, money I had worked my fingers to the bone for from the time I was fifteen. How dare you waltz in here and try to give me orders?"

He jumped to his feet. His face had gone white. He looked like the devil.

"You're still my feckin' wife!" he shouted.

"You don't own me, James Conlon," I cried.

He reached up and slapped my cheek. The shock of it stung me into silence. James had never slapped me before. No matter how much we had fought, he had never laid a hand on me.

"You'll not disgrace me by informing," he yelled, "or God help me, it's more than a slap I'll be giving you."

I reached out and pushed him. I was blind with tears and fury. I wanted him out of my house. He shoved me back, pinning my arms behind my back. I spat in his face. "I'm no bloody informer," I cried, "and well you know it!"

It was then the old passion roared back. I felt its fire rushing through me, burning my insides. It struck James at the same time. He let go of my hands and grabbed my hair, forcing my head back. Then he brought his mouth down on mine in a fierce and brutal kiss. But I would not give in. I tried to fight him off. I bit back on his lips. I pounded at him with my fists, but his weight threatened to overpower me. It was Aoife's sudden loud cries that gave me the strength I needed. I tore myself away from James and grabbed the knife that still lay on the table.

"Get out!" I cried. "Get out now and don't ever come back."

James stared at me in astonishment. "This is my fecking house!" he roared. "You can't keep me out of it!"

"It's not yours anymore," I shouted, moving closer to him, the knife shaking in my hand. "It's mine. I'm the one still slaving up at the mill. I'm the one paying the rent on it. You have no right here. Now get out, or so help me I'll swing for you."

I lunged at him. Aoife's cries were deafening now. James stared at me, his eyes wary. He put out his hands.

"Now, Eileen," he began, as if trying to soothe a panicked animal.

I lunged forward again, and he backed up to the kitchen door. "Get out!" I cried.

Slowly, James reached behind him for the door handle, opened the door, and backed out. I advanced on him until he was well away from the house. I waited until he turned, leaped over the back wall, and was gone. Then I ran back inside and closed the door. I slid to the floor, my heart thumping in my chest.

૭૪૭

DESPITE MY FEARS, James did not come back to the house. For a time I jumped at every late night noise, and my anxiety continued to affect Aoife. We were both a bundle of nerves. I was glad I had stood up to him. I would do the same again. But still and all, I knew he was not a man to take rejection easily. He would have seen it as insubordination. He would have shot one of his followers for less. I knew I had not seen the last of him.

Meanwhile, the truce continued to inflame the Republicans in Ulster. In the negotiations with the British government that followed the truce,

Collins was the chief spokesman on behalf of the Irish. There was heavy pressure on him to recognize the two-parliament system that had been established the year before under the Government of Ireland Act. Would Collins be willing to compromise? Did he stand on the brink of betraying us? I thought of the night I had been mesmerized by Collins's speech in Dundalk. After all his lovely words about Irish freedom, would he really sell out part of Ireland? I did not want to believe it. But I had seen so many betrayals already—husband against wife, brother against sister—that I thought anything could be possible.

Terrence brought me word of the meetings above the Ceili House. James was fit to be tied, he said, but he still had faith in Collins. My immediate reaction was that I was glad. Now it was his turn to be betrayed. James, who had abandoned his wife and child, who had given up all hope of a decent life, who had set himself up to be shot at any time of the day or night—how would he ever go on if his great hero let him down? While orders had come to stop the fighting, James and his men not only ignored them, but stepped up their attacks. Railway lines were blown up and troop trains were derailed. The newspapers were full of similar stories. Part of me felt a strong urge to get back into the action. I was as angry as the rest of them. And once again anger, my old friend, saved me from brooding on my own rapidly decaying dreams.

Fergus kept up his visits. I told him what I had done to James, and he feared what James might do to me.

"He's not a fellow you cross, Eileen," he said.

"I know. But I had good cause."

"You did, surely, but all the same . . ."

According to Terrence, Fergus had become James's right-hand man and confidant. Some of James's men had abandoned the fight, and it seemed that Fergus was the only man James trusted. I wondered, not for the first time, whether James *should* trust Fergus. Ever since the night Fergus had been lifted by the police in the room over the Ceili House, his behavior had become more and more strange. He was jumpy and secretive, and there was, God help me, a hint of evil in his eyes that made me shiver when I looked at him. Was he informing? I wondered. Not that I could have blamed him after the way James and his mother had treated him all these years. Still, I feared for him.

"Terrence says James thinks there's an informer in the squad," I said, trying to sound offhand. "He says the police often seem to know where they are almost before they know themselves."

"Aye, but sure how do you prove it?"

"All the same, Fergus, it's terrible things they do to informers when they do find them. I worry about my brother Frank; bastard that he is, I would not like to see him dumped on the side of the road with a placard round his neck."

Fergus looked up at me, his eyes wary. "Aye, your brother needs to watch himself, so he does. He's taking mighty chances working with both sides."

"Aye," I said, and got up to stoke the fire.

 කල

AUGUST GAVE WAY to September, and October dawned, surprisingly bright and clear after the bleak summer. The good weather lifted people's spirits. I had fallen into the pattern of volunteering at the hospital. I baked soda bread and cakes and brought them up to the fellows on the ward. Jesus, I was turning into a right Florence Nightingale. I laughed at myself, but still and all I had to admit Owen had been right. I had a new sense of pleasure I had not known before when I saw their shy smiles and heard their grateful, "Thanks, missus. It's even better than me ma's."

I was careful at first to go to the blue medallions as well as the red, but after a while I forgot even to look. Those boys were all the same, except for a few rough blackguards. They had all been caught up in the excitement, and yes, the hate. I tried not to see myself in them, but at times it was like looking in a mirror. I suppose they had all seen themselves as warriors—and look where it had landed them. I thought of Owen's letter from France. I recalled his words: *All I can be sure of now is that there is no glory in war.* Looking at these boys, I began in a small way to understand what he meant. And yet surely Ulster's fight was different. How else were the Catholics ever going to get their equal due in their own land? Wasn't the sacrifice worth that? And then I thought of Da, and I was ashamed of myself for my moments of doubt.

Sister Rafferty said she was delighted with the effect I was having on the young fellows.

"You're a real tonic for them, Mrs. Conlon," she said. "Mr. Sheridan was right to bring you. But then he would recognize a person of charity when he met one."

"Oh?"

"Aye. Sure Mr. Sheridan is a very giving man himself. The work that he does with those workhouse children . . ." She clasped her hands together, and her face lit up.

She saw my puzzled look and smiled. "Of course, he doesn't make a big show of it. He would not have told you. But he has arranged for apprenticeships for many of the boys and girls. He's even arranged for some of them to go to England for training at his own expense. He often looks in on them when he travels to England. And not a Christmas goes by that he doesn't come loaded down with presents."

Well, I thought, Owen Sheridan is a dark horse. Not for the first time, I realized I had jumped to too many conclusions as far as he was concerned. I was glad Sister Rafferty had told me. It put a new light on things and why making a difference always seemed so important to him.

I timed my Sunday visits so I could go and see Ma. I brought her flowers every time, but she no longer seemed interested in them. She turned her back and wouldn't even watch me put them in water. Nellie Leonard, the nurse in Ma's wing, eyed me with curiosity every time I went in. I knew she was looking over my shoulder for Owen, and I was glad to see her face fall when she realized he was not there. Occasionally, I ran into Terrence as I was leaving. Ma was not allowed more than one visitor at a time, so he would wait until I came down the stairs. Again, I was struck by how steady he had been in visiting Ma all these years. I don't think a week ever went by without him going to see her. I was grateful to him for it, and for the fact that I could find comfort in talking to him about her. He was the only one who understood.

I had not seen Owen in two months. His visits to the mill had stopped. Word was that his father was in ill health and Owen was spending a lot of time with him in England. Theresa announced that she had it on great authority that his divorce was final. The news left me with an unsettled feeling, but I didn't press her for details. I wondered if he would sell the Yellow House. Since he had been away so much, the talk about him and me had quieted down, and I was glad of it. I wanted to keep my head down and not draw attention to myself. Maybe he had heard the gossip himself and decided to put space between us. I told myself I didn't miss his company, but then I lied well to myself. The truth was that I thought about him more than was good for me. Glimpses of him making tea in my kitchen, his eyes searching my face, all jumped in and out of my mind. The images came when I was at my spinning frame, or doing the washing, or lying in bed at night. The ones at night were the worst. They left me agitated, my entire body on a state of alert. It was a state neither pleasant nor unpleasant. The more I tried to distract myself, the more intense the images became. I was sure I was going mad.

As I smoothed the threads on the bobbins one morning in October, another image came to me and I lost hold of the yarn. Flushing, I turned around to see if anyone had noticed. And there he was, standing behind me still as a statue. How long he had been watching me I did not know.

"Will you spare a body the shock of creeping up on them like that?" I said, but I could not help smiling.

He smiled back. "Forgive me, I did not mean to startle you."

I went back to my work. All heads turned to watch us, but if he was aware of it, he didn't show it. Sweat streamed down my face. I stole a glance at his left hand. His wedding ring was gone.

"I have been asked if you would transfer to the Fever Hospital for the next couple of weekends. They need help sorting out and updating their records, and"—he paused and grinned—"it seems you have greatly impressed Sister Rafferty not only with your kindness, but with your intelligence."

"You've no need to soft-soap me," I said, "but my sister, Lizzie, died in that place when she was a child. I'd rather stay with the lads in the men's ward."

"I'm sorry," he said, "I'd forgotten that you told me that." He looked at me with pity. "I'm sure Sister Rafferty will understand. But you know, Eileen, sometimes facing the past can be very healing."

I fiddled with the threads on the spindles and said nothing. I felt eyes boring through the back of my head, and I wished fervently that he would go away.

"They are very much in need of the help, Eileen," he went on. "It would only be for two days at the most, and I would take it as a great favor if you would reconsider."

Jesus, Mary, and Joseph, would he not give it up? Now he was trying to make me feel guilty. "I can accompany you there if it would make things easier," he said.

"I know where the bloody place is," I said sharply.

He nodded. "I just thought it might be helpful . . ."

"No," I said firmly, "it's best I go alone."

"Very well." He smiled again. "They will expect you this Saturday. Perhaps you can let me know when you are finished with the project."

"Look, I agreed to go. That's enough. If there's any reporting to be done, I'll talk to Sister Rafferty."

He looked at me with the old teasing grin I remembered from years ago. "As you wish, Eileen," he said. "Cheerio, then."

He left. I glared around at the others and went back to my work, tugging so hard on the yarn that I broke the threads.

ை

THE FOLLOWING SATURDAY was the weekend before Halloween. When I got off my shift at the mill, I collected Aoife and brought her down to Theresa's house. Theresa sewed up a fancy costume for Aoife and decorated the house with images of goblins and witches and banshees. She baked cakes and breads and laid out water and soda bread beside the hearth for the thirsty souls that would be wandering about all night. Tommy McParland, a great one for storytelling, sat around the fire with friends and relatives and their children, telling ghost stories that would make your hair stand on end. I was always sad on those nights. Tommy put me in mind of Da and the great stories and songs we used to have at the Yellow House on Hallows' Eve.

"Will you be down later?" Theresa asked, giddy with excitement.

"I don't know," I said. "I don't know how long this job is going to take."

Curiosity shone in Theresa's eyes. "Oh?"

"Aye," was all I said. "If I'm up to it after, I'll be down. But don't wait for me."

It occurred to me afterward that Theresa could easily think I was going to see Owen on the sly. Let her think what she likes, I said to myself. Sure she'll think the worst anyway.

As I rode the tram into Newry, I saw that people already had their Halloween decorations up. Soon buckets of water would stand outside on back steps for the thirsty souls to drink, candles would light up the windows, and children would be out going door-to-door, trying their best to scare the life out of their neighbors. I thought how we Irish still loved our pagan traditions, regardless of how much the priests had tried to beat it out of us. Superstitious lot, so we were.

When I arrived at my stop in Newry, it was still early afternoon, but the bright sun did nothing to drive away the dark, grim shadows of the workhouse and the surrounding buildings. Even though I had been going twice a week for almost a year, I could not still the shivers that came over me every time I set foot here. To get to the Fever Hospital, I had to enter through the main workhouse door into a big hallway. I imagined the thousands of poor souls who had collapsed on this floor at the end of their sad journeys. I imagined I could still hear their cries.

I hurried down the hallway and in through a door on the right that led to the Fever Hospital waiting room. I froze as if I were rooted to the floor. The room had not changed from that night fifteen years ago when we had arrived with Lizzie. Peeling paint still hung from the walls, and smells of urine and disinfectant still filled the air, but the wooden benches and chairs, which that time had been filled with wretched adults and hollow-faced children, were mercifully empty. I glanced at the stairway where I last saw the straight-backed nurse climbing away with Lizzie, and my ears echoed with the cries of sick children pried from the arms of their mothers.

I took a deep breath and walked across the room to a door marked "Office." I pushed it open and coughed from the dust that swirled up from the floor. An old man sat at a desk, hunched over a pile of papers. I wondered how he could read anything in the poor light. There was no window, and the small lamp on the desk cast ghostly shadows on his bent head.

"Who are you?" he growled when I walked in.

Fine greeting for someone who's come to work for nothing, I thought.

"I'm Mrs. Conlon. Sister Rafferty asked me to come and help with organizing the records here." I looked around at the piles of folders and dusty ledgers.

He followed my gaze, then waved his hand with impatience. "Och, there's no need for organizing things," he said. "Sure I could put my hand on anything anybody wanted."

I supposed he was telling the truth, but there again, the man looked as if he were already at death's door. Who would find things after he was gone?

"Nonsense!" he shouted. "Waste of time."

I removed my coat. "Worth a try, anyway," I said briskly. "Do you have any instructions for me?"

He rummaged around the desk, picked up a yellowed notepad, and shoved it toward me.

"The day girl left this for you. Lazy young bitch, needing somebody else to do her work for her."

He wiped his nose with his sleeve and stood up. "Well, I'll be away, then, and leave you to your own devices. Don't forget to lock the door behind you!"

As he made for the door, a sudden panic rose in me. He was an oul' git, but he was better than nobody. I didn't want to be in this room alone.

"Will you not be staying, then?" I cried.

"What for?" he said. "Organizing? Bah! No need for it. No need at all!" And at that he walked out. I listened to his boots scraping across the floor of the waiting room, and then there was silence.

I sighed and sat down behind the desk and rolled up the sleeves of my blouse. I leaned over and adjusted the lamp so it gave more light. Jesus, I could be blind by the time I was finished here. The instructions seemed easy enough. I was to take each ledger by year and copy out each name onto an index card, along with other particulars. Then the cards would be filed in alphabetical order, by year, and put in one of the new cabinets that had been purchased for this purpose. The day girl had got as far as 1904, she noted, and I should start with 1905. She had begun the first couple of entries so I could get the way of it. I looked at the cards. Her handwriting was large and clear, but the entries in the ledger looked as if a spider had scrawled them; they were almost unreadable. I sighed again. This job would try the patience of a saint—and I was far from a saint.

As I fell into the pattern of the work, I found myself wondering about all the names I was copying. Who was this child or that old woman? Sometimes it seemed whole families, brothers and sisters and parents, had all come down with the fever at once. I shuddered as I wrote down the dates of death, mostly of the youngest children and the oldest adults— the weakest and the frail. I shifted in the hard chair and straightened up my back and shoulders, which were stiff from bending over the desk. I got as far as the month of April 1906, and then I could stand it no more. I needed to get up and walk around.

I had not intended to reach for the 1908 ledger, but suddenly it was in my hands. I stared at it, afraid to open it. I held it to my breast and walked back and sat down. I laid it gently on the desk and ran my fingers over it, pushing away the dust. Lizzie's name was in here. Did I dare look? Could I stand to look? Could I bear not to? At last I opened the cloth cover and ran my index finger down the front page. I was trembling.

Get on with it, Eileen, I scolded myself, get on with it, or get up and leave. Don't be sitting here like an eejit.

Maybe it will tell you whereabouts she was buried, I answered myself. Maybe there'll be some description of the plot in the pauper's field, and you can get a headstone put there, and you can visit her once in a while.

Before I lost my courage, I thumbed through the pages. I held my breath as I came to October, the month Lizzie had been brought in. And there it was, Elizabeth Cecelia O'Neill. I never knew her name was Cecelia. I blinked away dust that pricked at my eyes. Elizabeth Cecelia O'Neill, aged 4 years, daughter of Thomas and Mary O'Neill of Glenlea. Diagnosis: Scarlet Fever. Condition: critical. I braced myself to read the next column, which would record the date of her death, which I knew was November 10, 1908. I expected to see the word *deceased*. I could hardly bring myself to read it. But read it I had to. I needed to see it all. I wiped my eyes again and brushed away the dust from the page. "10 November 1908, adopted out." I closed my eyes and opened them again. I moved my finger up and down the page to make sure I was reading the right line. But there it was: "adopted out." I took in a stab of breath. "Mother of God," I whispered. "I thought she was dead." There was more writing beside that: "Alfred and Lydia Butler, Belfast."

How long I sat there, I don't know. No thoughts or feelings ran through my brain or body. I sat mute and cold as marble, staring at the writing in front of me. Then with an eruption that rocked me to the core, I sprang up and furiously tore the page out of the ledger. I crumpled it and shoved it into my bag, grabbed my coat, and ran out of the room, leaving the door swinging open after me. I ran across the waiting room, past Nellie Leonard's desk, and up the stairs to the ward for the insane.

19

I took the stairs two at a time. Nellie Leonard's protests floated up the stairs with me—I was too early for visiting hours. I ignored her cries and pushed through the doors into the ward for the insane. I ran down the aisle between the rows of iron beds. Images of half-dressed, disheveled women rode past me as if in a dream, their taunts and cries silent as mimes. I had to get to Ma. I had to tell her the news.

I pushed open the door to Ma's room, and I came to a halt. Ma was not in her bed, as I had expected, but was standing by the window, absorbed in the activity in the courtyard below. She wore a pink dress I had not seen before, her long hair tied back in a matching ribbon, and she wore her brown velvet hat. She turned around, a broad smile on her face. She was wearing rouge.

"Ma?" I could hardly get out the word.

As soon as I spoke, her smile dissolved into disappointment. The smile was not meant for me. For a moment, I was again the abandoned child. Then I remembered why I had come. I ran to her and threw my arms around her.

"Ma!" I cried. "Ma—I have news!"

I hugged her tight. She did not resist me, but neither did she hug me back. She stood passive as a doll. I put my arm around her shoulders and led her over to the bed.

"Sit down, Ma. I have something to show you."

Obediently, she sat down, smoothing out her pink dress, and waited. I sat beside her and reached into my bag, fumbling for the crumpled page

I had stuffed in there. I pulled it out and smoothed it with trembling hands.

"Listen, Ma," I whispered, "listen."

I read the entry slowly. "Elizabeth Cecelia O'Neill . . ."

When I had finished I grabbed Ma's hands in mine. They were cold and stiff.

"She's alive, Ma," I cried. "Lizzie's alive. She did not die after all. All these years—oh, Ma, can you believe it?"

Ma stared back at me, her rouged face showing no emotion, not even confusion. I tried again. I placed the paper on her knees and took her fingers and traced the words, repeating them aloud. Still silence. Fury filled me then, and I took her by the shoulders and shook her.

"You have to understand, Ma. You have to. Lizzie's alive. You don't have to be insane anymore. Your sin did not cause her death. God never took her away from us. Oh, God, Ma. Please say you understand. Please listen!"

"Eileen!" A male voice startled me. I looked up. Terrence stood in the doorway, Nellie Leonard hovering behind him. "Eileen! What in God's name are you doing?"

Terrence strode toward me and pulled me away from Ma and lifted me to my feet. His eyes blazed with anger. I realized in that moment that Ma's smile had been meant for Terrence. I put up my fists and beat him away from me.

"Have you lost your senses, girl?"

The head nurse, in a white starched cap, appeared in the doorway, shoving past a frozen Nellie to demand an explanation.

"Mr. Finnegan! Miss O'Neill!" She looked from one of us to the other. "You will both leave immediately. You have upset my patient."

I looked down at Ma. Tears streamed down her face, smudging the rouge into red blotches. She had removed her hat. She was trembling.

My frustration exploded. "Feck the lot of you!" I cried. "I will not leave until Ma understands. I will stay here all night if I have to."

I tore the paper from Ma's lap and waved it at Terrence. "Lizzie's alive, Terrence," I shouted. "Lizzie's alive. Ma's not responsible for Lizzie's death. She has to understand!"

"Miss Leonard, go and call the guard," snapped the head nurse, and Nellie scurried away.

Terrence snatched the paper from my hand and read it. Then he looked from me to Ma and back again, his face pale.

"It's best you leave now, Eileen," he said. "I will talk to her. Wait for me downstairs, and then I will drive you home. Please."

I looked over at Ma. Her eyes were large with fear and confusion. A wave of sorrow washed over me, and my whole body sagged in exhaustion. I nodded at Terrence and dragged myself past the head nurse and out into the main ward. Now the ward came alive. The catcalls and cackles of the women rang in my ears. The smell of disinfectant, stale urine, and old women burned my nostrils. Grotesque faces hidden by Halloween masks blocked my way, spitting on me, taunting me like angry ghosts. At last I reached the stairs and staggered down into the hallway. Nellie Leonard waited for me.

"Are you all right, love?"

I did not answer. I made straight for the door. I had to get outside. I gave no thought to waiting for Terrence. I had to get away from this place. I pushed open the door and stumbled out into the courtyard and out the gates into the street.

୨୦

I WAS SO distracted, I didn't know where to go. I couldn't go home to my empty house, and I couldn't go to Theresa's house. I couldn't face all the questions and curiosity just now. But I could not be alone. Da, I thought wearily, why in God's name are you not here this night?

My feet kept walking. Dusk gathered. Children laughed and shouted as they banged on doors and jumped in and out of shadows. Halloween was coming, the night when the dead get up and walk again. I shivered and kept going. How I got to Queensbrook House, I don't know. I have no recollection of making a decision to go. I just ended up there at the front door. I lifted the knocker and let it fall. Piano music, low and melancholy, drifted out. A light was on in Owen's study, but the rest of the house was dark. I supposed that even the bravest of children would not rap on the Sheridans' door, threatening tricks. The piano playing stopped and I heard footsteps in the hall. Owen's voice called out as the door opened.

"I'm sorry, children, I was not expecting you. Can you wait while I see what we have in the kitchen? Apples, maybe, or . . .

"Eileen?" There was a rough catch in his voice. I got the vague impression that he had been weeping. But he smiled then in the dim light. "Come in, come in," he said. "I am delighted to see you. Forgive me, I gave Kathleen the night off, and my family is away for the weekend. It's only myself here. I didn't hear you at first."

As he talked he held the door open wide for me. It did not occur to him that I had said nothing, and he had obviously not noticed the state I was in. I brushed past him and trudged down the hall into his study. He followed me in and turned up the lamp.

"How is the project coming?" And then, "Eileen, what is it?"

He took my arm and led me to a chair beside the fireplace. He leaned down and raked the dying embers into a faint blaze. Then he went to his sideboard and poured a glass of whiskey. The man always seemed to be giving me whiskey, I thought idly.

He waited until I had drunk the whiskey. It coursed through me like a hot knife. Tears spat from my eyes. I blinked and put down the glass. Owen came over and knelt on the floor in front of me. He took my hands in his and rubbed them gently to warm them. The gentleness of it made me want to weep again.

"Tell me," he whispered.

"It's Lizzie!" I blurted out. "Lizzie's alive. She's been alive all this time. And all these years I thought she was dead!" The tears flowed now, running down my cheeks and dropping on my coat. I made no attempt to stop them.

"Oh, Eileen," he breathed, "that's such wonderful news!"

I nodded. "And I don't know why I'm crying like an eejit," I stammered. "It's dancing for joy I should be, but I'm so sad I just can't stop. And I went to see Ma, but she wouldn't listen." I looked up at him. "I thought the news would make her well again. I thought . . ."

He put up his hand and brushed the tears off my cheeks. "Ssh," he whispered, as if to a child. "It's all right. Of course you are sad. All these years you have grieved for your lost little sister, and now you discover your grief was misplaced. You are mourning now for all that grief you endured."

In an odd way, his words made sense. I had to mourn the grief before I could accept the happiness that had replaced it. He understood so completely that my gratitude was enormous. I began to cry again. He moved up and sat on the arm of the chair. He enfolded me in his arms. I laid my head against his chest and sobbed. I smelled the starch in his linen shirt and the sweet odor of his tobacco. I pressed my face close into his chest and lost myself in the oblivion and comfort of his presence.

"As for your mother—it will take time," he whispered. "In time she will understand. Perhaps when you are able to bring Lizzie to her . . ."

I looked up at him then. It had not even occurred to me that since

Lizzie was alive, I could find her, touch her, bring her to Ma. My heart leapt with sudden joy.

"Will you help me find her?"

"Of course."

My sobs gradually subsided, and I gave him a weak smile. He had not moved from the arm of the chair. He smiled down at me. "Better?" he said.

I nodded. "Yes." I thought I must look a sight, and I smoothed my coat and hair, my hands fluttering nervously about myself. "Thank you," I whispered.

He got up again and pulled me out of the chair. "Come over here and lie down," he said, indicating the daybed.

Wordlessly, I let him lead me to it and I sat down. He picked up my feet and swung me around so I was half sitting and half lying. Then he sat at the edge of the bed and began undoing the laces of my boots. I watched him, as if from far away. The dying flames painted gold streaks on his pale hair. His fingers were nimble as they uncrossed the laces. I wished I had polished my boots that morning. Slowly he unbuttoned my coat and slipped it off from underneath me, the way I did with Aoife when she fell asleep in her clothes. He undid the top buttons of my blouse and his fingers brushed against my throat. A flush rushed up to my face. I closed my eyes briefly.

He stood up. "I think this calls for Champagne. We must celebrate Lizzie's resurrection. What do you think?"

I nodded. "Yes," I murmured. "I'm ready now."

He left the room and I heard him rummaging about in the kitchen. I heard cupboard doors open and close and the tinkle of glassware. I was in a daze, warm and wonderful and yet not real. It was a dream I was going to be unhappy to wake up from. He returned carrying a silver bucket with a bottle inside it. Two glasses sparkled in his other hand. Pure crystal, I thought. He set everything down on the sideboard.

"Now," he said, smiling. I watched as he put a white cloth around the bottle and rocked it back and forth. When the cork popped and the golden liquid spilled out over the rim, I jumped a mile.

"Jesus, Mary, and Joseph!" I exclaimed.

He laughed. "A wonderful sound, isn't it, Eileen?"

He filled the two glasses and brought them over and sat beside me on the daybed. I sat up, bracing myself with one elbow. He handed me a glass and then clinked his against it. "A toast to Lizzie," he said.

"*Sláinte!*" was all I could think to say.

When we had sipped, and I had sneezed from the bubbles, he said, "And now you must tell me all the details."

"There's not much to tell," I began. But to my surprise, there was. I told him not just the notation about Lizzie and who adopted her out, but the whole experience, from the memories when I walked into the Fever Hospital to the names of all the poor children recorded in the ledgers. I told him about Ma and her velvet hat and the fear in her eyes. When I had finished, I looked up at him.

He drew his face close to mine. I smelled the Champagne on his breath. I waited. His lips covered mine in a long, soft kiss. Pure, it was, I thought. Chaste.

He drew back. His eyes shone violet in the firelight. "Eileen," he whispered, "I want very much to make love to you. But I do not want to take advantage of your condition. I could never forgive myself for that."

I smiled. "No man has ever taken advantage of me against my will. You should know that by now."

He smiled back. "Aye. How could I have forgotten that?"

My arms rose and wound around his neck. I pulled him closer. His lips pressed hard on mine, and he forced my mouth open. Gently his tongue caressed mine. I jumped a little from the shock of it. James had never kissed me like that. Owen smoothed my hair. His breathing became hard. Images of James and the priests and the cackling mill women all swam in front of me. A shiver rolled down my spine, but still I did not push him away. I had all my senses about me, and I knew in that moment I wanted Owen Sheridan as much as he wanted me.

He leaned back and looked at me.

"You are so beautiful." There was a choke in his voice.

Slowly he unbuttoned the rest of my blouse, his fingers caressing each small button. I trembled. "Ssh," he whispered, "ssh, my lovely Eileen. I will not hurt you."

Then his hands were on my breasts, warm and urgent. They rose beneath his hands like gently kneaded dough. Then he was kissing them, teasing my nipples. Oh, the lovely pain of it. I moaned. He drew back and reached for the bottle of Champagne. Slowly he drizzled the golden liquid upon each nipple, as if anointing them, and then he licked them dry. The tiny bubbles tickled me into a state of mad arousal. I moaned again and called his name.

In time he was on top of me. Skin upon skin. My clothes and his lay crumpled on the floor. The harvest moon outside the window lit our limbs white as ghosts, but our passion burned with a life force. His lips moved down over my belly to my groin. He pushed my legs apart, and I offered myself up to him. I writhed under his tongue, arching myself back and forth. All sense of the outside world, this house, this room, left me. The only reality was the fire concentrated in the core of my being. When he raised himself up and slipped inside me, I screamed. The scream released all the spirits inside of me—an exorcism so raw and powerful that I thought it might kill me. And maybe it was killing the old Eileen. I wanted to kill her, to erase all her fears and anger and pain. I writhed beneath Owen. "Yes," I called out. "Yes." I called out for my sweet executioner to bring me to the brink of oblivion and beyond.

At last it was done. I saw myself lying on the strand of the sea, my arms and legs outstretched. I had washed up on the shore, torn and sore from the sharp stab of the rocks. But I was smiling. I was alive and peaceful as a newborn. I laughed aloud.

"Eileen?" Owen's voice brought me back to him. I opened my eyes and was startled to see him.

"Owen?"

"Yes, my love."

He rolled to my side and took me in his arms. The dim fire had long since extinguished itself, and the moon had risen out of sight.

"Stay with me tonight," Owen whispered.

He reached for my coat and covered our bodies with it. I sank into his arms, my body a lead weight from pain and pleasure. I slept as I had not slept since I was a child.

လ၀

I COLLECTED AOIFE from Theresa's house early on Sunday afternoon.

"I slept late," was all I said.

Theresa eyed me. She knew better, of course. I had never slept late in my life. I was not even up to telling her the news about Lizzie. My thoughts were tripping over themselves in my head, and no straight sentence could have come out of me.

"Your brother Frank was here last night," she said offhandedly.

I was startled. "Was he?"

"Aye. He said he was up at your house but you weren't there. He said all the lights were out."

"I . . . I went out for some air," I said. "I turned the lights out so the children would not be banging on the door."

Theresa rubbed the dishrag across the kitchen table. "I thought you'd be here earlier to take her to mass in Newry. Now she's missed going and that's a mortal sin—"

"Will you whisht!" I said. "Sure she's only a baby. You sound like your oul' ma."

Theresa sniffed and rubbed the dishrag harder. I had forgotten all about mass. Paddy and the Mullens must be wondering what happened to me. I had never missed a Sunday before now. Inwardly I cursed myself.

"Come on, Aoife," I said sharply. "It's time to go."

When we got home I told Aoife to go out to play—something I rarely did—but, stubborn child that she was, she refused to go. Instead, she sat on her little chair and stared at me. She had an old woman's head on her shoulders, that child. I brewed a pot of tea and tried to ignore her.

I was taut as a cat waiting to pounce. I couldn't relax. I was sore from the places where Owen had been, and part of me wanted to caress them. Instead I boiled water on the hob and dragged out the tin bath. Aoife squirmed.

"Not bath," she cried. "Clean."

I had bathed her yesterday before taking her to Theresa's. What a lifetime ago that seemed now. "It's not for you," I said more sharply than I meant.

It occurred to me that I had never taken off my clothes in front of the child. I had always bathed late at night when she was upstairs in bed. But I undressed now, slowly and deliberately. I had already exposed my body to a man I hardly knew, so what was the sin in exposing it to my own child? Aoife watched my every move. I sank into the hot water and rubbed myself raw with carbolic soap.

I made no excuses for myself as I lay there and thought about what I had done. Sure I could have said it was the shock of hearing about Lizzie or the upset about going to see Ma that had left me not in my right mind. Or I could have said it was out of loneliness I did it. I could have said I deserved a little comfort after the life I had been through. But I would have none of it. I had done what I did deliberately. I had wanted to do it. No one had forced me. I had knowingly committed a sin, and a mortal one at that. I had slept with a man who was not my husband. I had disgraced myself and God. I wondered idly why I cared about what God thought. I imagined having to tell the sin in confession. I imagined a young priest having to give me absolution. I wondered how many desperate women such a priest would have to absolve in his life.

The water grew cold, and still I lay there. Every time Owen's face appeared in front of me, I turned away and closed my eyes. I would not let myself remember any of it. No matter what punishment others might think I deserved for this, it was nothing to what I knew I would inflict on myself. The truth could not be escaped. I was as much a prisoner of guilt as any other Irish Catholic woman. I laughed. "You thought you were so different, Eileen O'Neill," I said aloud to myself. "The rules never applied to you! Well, look at you now. Your knees will be as red and raw as oul' Mrs. Conlon's saying novenas for the rest of your days, begging forgiveness from the Virgin."

Aoife lost her composure and began to whimper. I had frightened the life out of her with my outburst. I got out of the bath and dried myself. Still naked, I picked her up and held her close.

"Ssh, child," I whispered. "It's only a woman's sadness you are seeing. You'll have plenty of it in your own time."

I climbed the stairs, undressed her, and put her into my bed. I slipped in beside her. The warmth of her small body, innocent and pure, was such a comfort that I wept silently until we both fell asleep.

ॐ

LATER THAT EVENING, P.J. and Terrence came to my door, along with Paddy.

"Terrence told me the news," P.J. burst out as soon as he had seated himself beside the fire. "The bastards!" he cried. "Stealing the child from right under our noses. They should be drawn and quartered. That matron has a lot to answer for. I'll bet it's not the only time it happened. If it's the last thing I do, I'll track her down and . . ."

P.J.'s face was scarlet, and his breath came in small spurts. Terrence put up his hand.

"Ah, sure it's all water under the bridge now, P.J. That matron is long dead and gone. It's tracking down Lizzie we should be—and thanking God for the miracle that she's alive."

P.J. sniffed and relit his pipe. He didn't like being crossed by Terrence.

I had almost forgotten about Lizzie in all the events of the last night. Now I smiled for the first time.

"Aye, it's a miracle all right, Terrence. Although I wish the miracle could have rubbed off on Ma."

Terrence looked at me. "Ah, give her time, Eileen. Perhaps she needs to see Lizzie in the flesh before she grasps the meaning of it at all."

It was what Owen had said. I put the thought out of my head.

"We'll track her down, Eileen," said Terrence. "Between us all we'll find her. Won't we, P.J.?"

P.J. nodded.

I turned to Paddy. "I'm sorry I missed mass with you this morning, love."

He looked at me, grave as always. "It's no bother, Eileen. Terrence and P.J. said they wouldn't have expected you today. They said after what happened last night that you would need your rest."

His young face was solemn as an old man's.

P.J. rose. "Well, speaking of rest, we should let you get an early night, love. We'll be going, will we, Terrence?"

Terrence nodded and stood up. Paddy didn't move. "I'll stay over with Eileen," he said. "I don't want her to be alone tonight."

We stared at him.

"Sure I have wee Aoife, love," I said.

He shook his head. "No. I think you need somebody older."

I looked over his head at P.J., who winked at me.

"What about school, young lad?"

"I can take an early tram home in the morning and still be in time for school."

P.J. took a long draw on his pipe. "Well, I'll have quare explaining to do to the missus, but you can stay if your big sister agrees."

I nodded. "Of course. It'll be lovely to have a fine young man protecting me."

When P.J. and Terrence had gone, I took Paddy upstairs to Aoife's room. Aoife was awake again and delighted to see him. I let them play. At almost thirteen, Paddy still loved to play with Aoife and make her laugh. After a while, I took Aoife into my bed and Paddy fitted himself uncomfortably into her small bed. Later, I climbed in beside Aoife, who was already asleep. Joy and love mingled with fear in my mind as I fell again into a deep sleep.

20

I was with Owen again, pulling him so tight around me that not a thread of light could weave its way between our bodies. I locked him inside me and held him there, my fingers clawing his flesh. I cried his name aloud, urging him to fill up every empty chamber within me. Sweet, wet sweat cooled my skin, and I cried out loud. Somewhere, thunder clamored, waves of urgent sound matching the rhythm of our bodies. The images faded into mist, but the sound remained, louder now, insistent. A thumping on my shoulder brought me awake.

"Mammy, Mammy, bogeyman!"

Aoife was shaking me. I sat up. The thundering stopped.

"Bogeyman," Aoife whispered. "He has no head." The child's wide eyes glinted in the darkness. I cursed Tommy McParland for frightening the life out of the child with his ghost stories about bogeymen and headless horsemen and the like.

"Ssh," I whispered. "It was only a dream."

"No, Mammy," she cried, shaking her head from side to side.

"All right," I said. "Just stay here."

Then a thought occurred to her, and she smiled. "Da," she crowed, clapping her hands.

I thought to myself I would rather it be a headless horseman than James at this moment. I got out of bed and pulled on my dressing gown. Slowly I crept downstairs and opened the front door and looked out. Frank's face stared back at me. I flinched at the sight of him.

"Did you not hear me?" he hissed. "I banged loud enough to wake the dead."

"I was asleep," I murmured. "I must have been tired out."

"Aye, from your gallivanting last night. Where were you, at all?"

"Out."

"Sure I know that. Wasn't I here banging on the door like an eejit, and all the lights out in the house. And you weren't at Theresa's, either." Accusation filled his voice. "Are you letting me in or am I to stand on your doorstep like a stranger?"

I wanted to say that he was indeed a stranger, but I opened the door and let him into the parlor. He looked around.

"It's not a palace, is it," he said.

I ignored him. "Come into the kitchen. I'll make tea."

As I busied myself with the kettle, he sat in an armchair beside the fireplace and stretched out his legs, boots up on the fender. He did not take off his cap. Aoife and Paddy had crept down the stairs. They stood in the kitchen, Paddy holding Aoife by the hand, and stared at Frank. Frank looked from one to the other.

"Is this the child?" he said gruffly, pointing at Aoife.

"Sure who else would she be?" I snapped.

Aoife piped up. "Who are you?" she said.

Frank snorted. "Cheeky as her mother, I see."

I placed the kettle on the hob and pulled down cups and saucers from the cupboard.

"He's your uncle Frank, pet," I said, "come to visit his poor relations."

Paddy let go of Aoife's hand. He stared steadily at Frank. Frank shifted in his chair.

"And who's this other nosy fellow?" he said.

"That's your brother, Paddy," I said.

Frank's mouth dropped open. He stared at Paddy. "It can't be," he said at last, "sure Paddy's just a young fellow—a baby."

I swung around. "Time doesn't stand still, Frank. Our Paddy is almost a young man now, and a fine one at that, no thanks to all the thought you ever gave to him."

Frank did not take his eyes off Paddy. "He's the image of Lizzie," he whispered.

I wanted to tell Frank the news about Lizzie, but something made me hesitate. Instead I said, "And what brings you here away from your fine farm?"

Frank swung around to look at me. "It's glad you should be I put myself out to come here and warn you!"

"Warn me about what?"

He took his time with the tea I had handed to him, spilling it into the saucer and blowing on it to cool it. He slurped it up from the saucer and sat back in the chair. "Good and strong, at least," he said, "the way Ma used to make it."

I thought as I watched him that he might have plenty of money but he had no manners.

"Well?" I said.

He looked over at the children. "Maybe they shouldn't hear this," he said.

I would not humor him. "They'll stay where they are," I snapped.

"Suit yourself." He cleared his throat and stood up. His bulky presence filled the kitchen as he paced back and forth like the country squire.

"You've been seen with that Sheridan fellow."

I shrugged. "That's old news," I said, sweat prickling the back of my neck.

Frank's face turned red. "So you admit it! How the feck do you think it looks for a sister of mine to be seen gallivanting about with the likes of Sheridan? Is it informing you are?"

I jumped from my chair. "Informing? And what is it to you what I'm doing? Sure you don't give a feck about the Cause. From what I hear, you're too busy feathering your own nest!"

Frank came over to me. His face was inches from mine. "You're right, I don't give a feck about the Cause, but I do give a feck about staying on the right side of your husband's friends." He backed away slightly. "We have certain agreements between us, and I can't have my sister carousing with the British Army. It casts suspicion on all of us. Now, I don't know what you're up to, my girl, but you'd better stop it right now. I forbid you to go near him again."

I was too flabbergasted to speak. Forbid me? What in God's name gave him the right to forbid me to do anything?

"I'll live my life as I please," I shouted at last. My whole body trembled.

Frank raised his hand and slapped me hard across the face. Aoife screamed. The pain of the slap brought tears to my eyes. I was too shocked to speak.

"Leave her alone! Leave her alone!" Suddenly Paddy was behind Frank, tugging on him, his fists locked around his arms. The boy's devil had returned.

Frank swung around, his hand raised to slap Paddy, when it seemed to freeze in the air. He let his hand drop and instead took him by the shoulders and pushed him away. He stared at him.

"Jesus, he's the image of Lizzie," he said again.

Something softened my heart. I reached over to Frank.

"Come and sit down," I whispered, "I have something very important to tell you."

Frank allowed me to lead him back to the chair by the fire. He sat down and looked into my face. In that moment, I caught a glimpse of the wounded young boy who rode off in the cart from the Yellow House years ago.

I knelt in front of him and took his hands in mine. "Frankie," I whispered, "Lizzie is alive. She never died after all. She was adopted out of the Fever Hospital by a couple in Belfast. We're going to find her, Frankie. We're going to bring her home."

Tears softened Frank's eyes, and he wiped them away quickly. "Are you sure?" he said.

"Would I lie about something like this? I only found out myself last night. I still haven't swallowed the news yet."

Frank sat frozen in the chair for a long time. Emotions that only he could identify crossed his face. He looked around my house and at Aoife and Paddy. Then he stood up.

"I'm sorry I slapped you," he said. And then the old Frank was back. "But mark my words, Eileen, there'll be trouble if you keep being seen with that fellow. Don't say I didn't warn you."

And then he was gone. The roar of his motorcar filled the street and then died away to a low whine. I steered Paddy and Aoife to bed and went back downstairs to clean up the kitchen. Slowly, I washed dishes and stoked the fire. I would have to be up early to take Paddy down to the tram. Paddy! I shuddered at the anger I had witnessed seething out of the boy. It had stopped Frank in his tracks as well. I had hoped that he might have outgrown it by now; he was almost thirteen. Da would have said he was a true O'Neill—another young warrior. But somehow the thought brought me more distress than pride. I switched my thoughts to Frank. What would be going through his head just now? Would news of Lizzie change him? Would coming face-to-face with his lost family soften him, or would it make his sense of loss even greater? Lizzie had been the only one who could make our Frankie smile. I prayed that we could bring her home.

∽

ON MONDAY MORNING, I stood at my spinning frame whipping the trestle back and forth like a demented woman. Shields came past a few times and paused to watch me.

"The place isn't on fire, you know," he said. "You can slow it down a bit before you break the machine altogether."

"Never known you to worry about a body working too fast," I snapped.

He shrugged and went away about his business. Theresa eyed me from the other end of the room but said nothing. I was caught in the chaos of my own thoughts. I had slept poorly after Frank left. Aoife had fretted as if she knew something was wrong. She'd sweated and tossed and whimpered in her sleep. By dawn, all sleep driven from me, I'd gone down and made tea and waited until it was time to take Paddy to the tram. I realized that the news about Lizzie had been buried under the commotion of the last two days. It was hard to think about her without thinking about Owen, and I did not want to think about him at all. I didn't even dare look over my shoulder in case he was in Shields's office. What in the name of God would I say to him? How could I look at him without the whole world knowing what had gone on? I had to take hold of myself, I realized, or I would go stone mad.

At lunchtime, I went to sit on the wall outside the mill. It was freezing, and I sat there shivering, but I had to get some air. He must have been waiting for me. He approached wearing a greatcoat over his uniform. At least he's not freezing his arse off, I thought. He sat beside me.

"Hello, Eileen," he said.

I nodded.

"Are you all right?"

"And why wouldn't I be?" I said sharply. I could feel the flush warming my cheeks despite the cold.

"I miss you," he said simply.

I sat up straight. "Look," I blurted out, "the other night was a mistake! I wasn't in my right mind, what with Lizzie and all. So don't think I'll be making a habit of it. I'm a respectable woman, and I'll not be . . . be seduced again by your sweet talk or anybody else's. So just leave me alone before people start to talk more than they already are!" My words punctured the frigid air. Small wisps of cloud from my hot breath floated in front of his face.

He watched me in silence for a moment. "It wasn't a mistake," he said.
"It was!" I shouted.

"I don't believe you, Eileen," he said. "How can you say this? How can you say that what we had was not real, and passionate—and loving? You don't believe it was wrong any more than I do."

I looked around to see if anyone was listening. My whole body trembled.

"Did someone threaten you?" Owen's voice cut in sharply.

I swung back to face him. "No," I cried again.

He looked at me. His eyes were clear and gentle, and I saw an understanding and a pity in them that angered me.

"And I'm not needing your pity, either," I snapped. I took a deep breath. "Please," I said softly, "give me what's left of my pride."

He nodded. "I love you, Eileen," he said, "but I don't want to make things hard for you. I have heard some of the rumors. The mill workers are judging you harshly, I've heard, but no harsher than my own family and friends are judging me. If it was up to me, I would have us both ignore them, but I realize it is not that easy." He paused and let out a long sigh. "Do you love me, Eileen?"

His eyes riveted mine. I began to sweat. How could I answer him? Of course I loved him. But how could I tell him that and then ask him to leave me alone? I took a deep breath.

"No, Owen. It was a mistake, as I said. I was just in need of some comfort."

I could hardly stand the look of pain that passed over his face. I wanted to take him in my arms and tell him that I was lying and that I loved him more than life itself. But how could I? I was a married woman and a Catholic. And he was a Quaker and the son of the mill owner. I could not encourage this anymore. And so I said nothing.

"Forgive me, then. I misunderstood. "

He stood up. His voice and manner became more formal. He was the polite but distant soldier once again.

"I would still like to do what I can to help locate Lizzie."

"Thank you. But it's best if I do it myself."

"I understand. Good-bye now."

He left. I knew I had hurt him. But sure hadn't I hurt myself more? As I watched him go, tears stung at my eyes. I rubbed them with my sleeve. Bloody love! All it ever caused was heartbreak. I was as well off without it, even if I had to cut it out of my heart the way a butcher cuts meat.

⚮

THAT EVENING, TERRENCE came to the house. Billy was already there, playing with Aoife. I was glad of the distraction. For a while, I could ignore the pain in my heart that had been there all day since I saw Owen. I tried to focus on the good things.

"Isn't it wonderful news about Lizzie?" I said.

The excitement I had wanted to feel began to build inside me. I was giddy.

Terrence nodded slowly. "Aye, Eileen. God works in unexpected ways."

"We'll find her, won't we? You must have connections in Belfast?"

"I do. We'll leave no stone unturned. Trust me! I want it as much as you do. I want your mother to see her in the flesh."

I wondered again about the other evening when Ma had been all dressed up and waiting for Terrence. But this did not seem the right time to ask.

I leaned back and sighed. "Isn't it grand, Terrence? I always knew one day we could all be back together. Now wouldn't that be the real miracle?" I knew I sounded like a silly sod, but I couldn't help myself. "Now if only we could get the Yellow House back, we could bring Ma and Paddy, and me and Lizzie, and maybe even Frank . . ."

The words trailed off.

"So you still have the same old dream," Terrence said gently. "It's a lovely idea, but not very practical now, is it?"

"Not everything has to be practical," I said. "And you of all people should be a believer in miracles. After all, you're still hoping Ma will get better."

Terrence rubbed his hands together. They were square and brown, not at all like Owen's. God forgive me, I thought. I have to get that man out of my mind.

"I told you I will be delighted to search for Lizzie," Terrence said. "She may not remember much about you, but she's your sister, and she should know your family."

"Aye," I said, "such as it is."

For the first time, I had a pang of doubt. Would Lizzie really want to know our family? What was she like, anyway? She'd be almost twenty by now. What if she was reared in style by well-to-do people? Would she want to know that our da was a dreamer who almost forced us into poverty? Would she want to know that her ma was astray in the head, and her sister was an adulteress, and her brother Frank . . . well, God only knew what was in Frank's heart. Holy Mother of God, would I be opening a hornet's nest best left untouched? I think Terrence was reading my mind.

"Don't worry, Eileen. I am sure she will want to know the truth anyway. And then if she wants to meet you, it will be her decision."

"But, the Yellow House . . . ," I began.

"That's your dream, Eileen, not hers," Terrence said quietly.

∽

FOR THE NEXT weeks, I kept my head down. I said little to anybody. My production at the mill broke all records.

Theresa came over to me. "I don't know what's got into you, Eileen," she said, "but the devil himself must be driving you. You'll slow down if you know what's good for you. The workers are starting to talk. You're making them look bad."

"I don't give a feck about them," I snapped. "It's a sad day for them if they can't keep up with me!"

"Watch yourself," she said. "They haven't forgotten the other business."

She was right. Ever since Fagan and his cronies had tried to stop us from coming in for our shifts that morning, they had gone out of their way to aggravate me. Little things, like cracks in the spindle or damp, tangled flax on my bobbin in the mornings. I knew it was them. But what was I to do? I ignored them and went on about my business. Eventually, they eased off, but I smelled their resentment every time I walked past. The truth was that I was not on a tear to make money or show anybody up. Cranking up my machine to the breaking point was the only way I could make it through the day. My nerves were shattered, and I could not relax enough to look sideways.

There had been little sign of Owen. A couple of times he nodded from the other end of the floor, but I showed him no encouragement, and he went about his business. My heart broke at the sight of him. I told myself he didn't matter—he was a mistake born of my weakness. But on the long, lonely nights when I lay in bed, sweating and tossing, images of his sweet face calling to me, I realized the truth that I was in love with the man. An odd thing, love. No one ever teaches you how to recognize it. I supposed I must have been in love with James. After all, I liked him well enough to marry him. It must be love, surely. It was no different from the way the mill girls prattled on about their boyfriends. No different from how Theresa felt about Tommy McParland. It was a matter of choosing someone—the best of the available men—and marrying them before you were written off altogether as an old maid. Is that how it was with James? I liked to think there was something more than taking myself off the shelf before it was too late. I found a kindred spirit in James, restless, yearning. It matched my own feelings. Surely, then, this must be love? But Owen. Owen was not restless. Instead he was a lovely, safe harbor into which I could sail and pull anchor, a harbor where I could find shelter from the storms that battered my life. And more than that, a man who knew me to my core, no matter that we had exchanged few words. When I came to Owen, I knew instinctively I had come home—a home more secure than even the Yellow House. A home that was eternal.

I pushed aside such thoughts and kept working. I had no news from Terrence or P.J. yet on Lizzie. I was mad to find her. I pestered them every time I saw them. I had not seen James since the night I threatened him with the bread knife. The newspapers still carried stories: IRA GUNMEN IN A PITCHED BATTLE WITH ULSTER FORCES OUTSIDE NEWRY. I waited for news. I wondered how long he could survive. Once in a while, there would be a quote from Captain Owen Sheridan. Would Owen and James ever confront each other? I wondered. The question troubled me so much, I put it out of my mind.

❦❧

THE CHRISTMAS SEASON came, but there was little joy in it for Ulster Catholics. In December 1921, Michael Collins signed the treaty that amputated part of Ulster from the rest of Ireland. We were stunned. Even though all the signs had been there, we had refused to believe it would happen. And now the ultimate betrayal had taken place. We had been left to the mercy of the Unionists. They had yet to redraw the border that would eventually redefine Ulster, which left us in a sad and uncertain limbo. Our dream of freedom for Ulster was over, and our future could not yet be imagined. The country was plunged into a civil war, with pro- and antitreaty forces fighting each other. Men who had fought together were now bent on killing one another. There was a tinge of sadness when you looked at the Christmas candles that glowed in cottage windows. "We need to keep it up for the children," people said, but their hearts were not in it.

My body felt heavy. I dragged myself to the mill and back. I lost my appetite, and the smell of Aoife's morning porridge turned my stomach. I lived on strong tea and bread. I had missed my monthly curse two times in a row. I put it down to the annoyances of all that had gone on since Halloween.

On Christmas Eve I went up to the hospital, bringing brightly wrapped presents and sweets for the young fellows in the ward. I brought Aoife for the first time. She cried when she saw the big stone building and pulled at my hand, refusing to go in.

"I know, love," I said. "I felt the same way when I first saw this place. But come on now. There are sick people in there waiting for presents."

Reluctantly, she let me lead her in through the big wooden door and up the stairs to the men's ward. My heart sank when I saw the poor lads, all scrubbed, waiting for the Christmas visitors. Sister Rafferty had changed the visiting rules for the holidays, but not even presents or visitors, I thought, could make up for the fact that these poor mites were in this cold place and not home by a warm fire.

I should have known Aoife would change her tune. When she realized she was the center of attention, she climbed up on each bed to hand over a present and get a big kiss or hug. She smiled and laughed more than I had ever seen her do. My heart filled with love as I watched her.

Christmas Day came and went. I tried to be cheerful for Aoife's sake. For once I was grateful for Theresa and her desperate efforts to have the perfect Christmas. Her house was choked with decorations—garlands, holly wreaths, a fine Christmas tree, and mistletoe. She sat up all night Christmas Eve wrapping presents and stuffing them into a big pillowcase that Aoife had hung up for Father Christmas. We all went to midnight mass. The service included a children's pageant. Aoife strutted on the altar in a lovely pair of silver angel wings Theresa had made for her. The Mullens came with Paddy. He would turn thirteen the next day. He had grown as tall as myself, and while he still had Lizzie's fair hair and blue eyes, he looked less and less like her as he grew. I realized as I looked at him that I hardly knew him at all. Would I ever come to know what was in his mind or his heart? He said little to anybody. Apart from the outbreak of anger I had witnessed with Frank, he was polite and well-behaved at home and at school, and he was very good with Aoife. The child adored him and trailed after him the way Lizzie used to trail after our Frankie. I sighed. Frank? Instinctively, I turned around to see if he was in the church, but there was no sign of him.

Theresa made a big Christmas dinner. But I hardly touched any of it. Oul' Mrs. Conlon eyed me sharply.

"You've not much of an appetite there, Eileen," she said.

I ignored her remark.

"If I didn't know better, I'd say you were in the family way," she said.

My stomach lurched.

"And how could that be," I snapped, "when my husband has not spent a night in the house this many's a month!"

"I was wondering that myself," she remarked.

Theresa looked at me closely, as if examining me. My anger rose.

"Will youse leave me alone!" I shouted. "I'm not hungry."

They went back to eating and drinking, and Tommy McParland, always the good host, called for a song.

"Did you bring your fiddle, Eileen?" he said. "I'll get out the old squeeze box and we'll have some music. Just like your old times at the Yellow House."

For some reason, I wanted to cry. "I didn't bring it," I said.

"No bother," said Tommy. "We'll have one of the lads run up to your house and fetch it. Give us your key, now."

I handed him the key. It was hard to argue with Tommy when he had his mind set on something. I was in no mood to be playing music, but at least it would get the conversation away from me.

The rest of the evening passed pleasantly enough. Paddy, it had turned out, had a beautiful singing voice, and he entertained the gathering with a couple of ballads so sad there wasn't a dry eye. I thought of Da and allowed my tears to flow as well. I had wanted to cry all day and was glad of the excuse to let the tears come. I didn't even know why I was so sad, but somehow I felt a great sense of loss. I was alone in the midst of all these people. I told myself it was because Ma and Da were absent and that I was lonely for the Yellow House, as I always was this time of the year. But deep down I knew it was more than that. I felt like half of me was missing. And that half, God help me, was Owen Sheridan.

❧

THE NEW YEAR of 1922 arrived, and along with it snow and ice the likes of which we had not seen in donkey's years. I sent Aoife down to Theresa's house with Billy for New Year's Day with a message that I had a bad cold and was going to stay in bed.

"But you're not sick, Mammy," she said. "Your nose is not red."

"Never you mind," I said as I pulled on her coat and hat. "Now off you go, and hold Billy's hand so you don't fall on the ice."

I watched them walk down the street. They made a comical pair: big, hulking Billy wrapped up in his woolly hat and muffler, and little Aoife in her red coat. Something tugged at my heart as I watched her. How my love for this child had grown since the early days when I had resented her very presence. Now she had become my lifeline—my wee warrior—and I knew I could never bear to lose her. A shiver crept over me, as if someone had walked over my grave.

I was never a great one for drinking, but that night I poured a glass of the whiskey I kept in the house for visitors and sat in a chair by the fire. The unthinkable skulked around me like an unwelcome ghost. Two months had passed since my curse had stopped, and there was still no sign of it. I was sick in the mornings, retching in the outdoor toilet before I could set foot toward the mill. I had lost weight, and my clothes hung on me like rags on an old stick. But that would change if . . . I could not bring myself to form the thought. I drank the sharp liquid, and it burned my throat. Mother of God, what was I to do? It had never occurred to me that this could happen. Hadn't I slept with James a hundred times since Aoife was born? I always believed there would be no more children. The thought that I could get pregnant ever again was as remote to me as the man in the moon. There! I had used the word! Fear and panic swirled inside me. I took another drink. How could I go to the mill with a swollen belly and everybody knowing it was not James's child? James! Mother of God, what would James do? He would destroy me. I had to get rid of it. Images of old crones with knitting needles in back alleys swarmed into my mind. The old mill women used to tell stories of them to us young girls to warn us of the dangers of lying with a man. Out of nowhere, I started reciting the rosary—"Hail Mary, Mother of God, blessed art thou among women, and blessed is the fruit of thy womb, Jesus . . ." Oh, how blessed is the fruit of my womb? The devil's child—conceived in passion and in sin. I drank some more. Owen's face passed in front of me. No, not the devil's child. Owen's child. Beautiful, like himself. Och, Owen—what will I do?

I awoke in the middle of the night. The fire was out and I was freezing with the cold. Outside, some drunkards were shouting, "Happy New Year!" I poured another glass of whiskey and carried it upstairs to bed.

Secrets

1922

21

Secrets are the cancer of families. Like tumors, they grow ever larger, and if they are not removed, they suffocate the mind and spirit and spawn madness. As long as they remain, they cast a shadow on every truth that is uttered, clouding it, constricting it, distorting it. Secrets hurt the secret keeper as much as the poor souls from whom the secret is kept. And even once the secret is out, its shadow echoes into the future, the remnants of its memory leaving us vigilant and fearful.

The spring thaw was a long time in coming. The mill reopened after the Christmas holidays, and the workers flocked in muffled up in coats and scarves. We shivered as we took off our boots and tiptoed onto the cold, damp floor to start up our spinning frames.

"We'll all die of pneumonia," they complained.

But we stuck it out. What else were we to do? There were plenty of people waiting to take our jobs. I caught the cold I had lied to Aoife about having a week before. God's justice, I suppose. Although I was freezing, I was pouring with sweat at the same time. Even Theresa broke down and showed me some sympathy.

"You don't look so well, Eileen," she said. "Sit down and rest. I'll cover for you."

She had a good heart. I patted her arm.

"Thanks, but I'll be all right. I've made it through worse, I can make it through this." I gave her a wan smile.

"You'd think the bloody bastards would find a way to get a bit of heat into this place before we all catch our deaths," she said, "but that would cost them money out of their pockets."

"Maybe there's not much they can do," I said. "The flax has to be kept damp."

"Oh, go ahead, defend them," snapped Theresa. "I forgot they're your friends."

I ignored the remark, and Theresa went back to her machine. I worked away, although my pace was a lot slower than in the past few weeks. Even Shields noticed it.

"I see you took my advice," he said. "But don't be slowing it too much, now. We still have our quotas."

I glared at him. Fat bastard thought the whole world revolved around him.

On the second day back, Owen appeared at my side. I jumped out of my skin. He had kept his distance so much since our last conversation that I had begun to believe he had heeded my words with relief. What did he want now?

"I didn't mean to startle you, Eileen. I just wanted to see how you are."

"And how would I be?" I snapped. "I'm freezing my arse off with the rest of them."

Owen sighed. "We are doing what we can to make the place more comfortable. I'm afraid—"

"Never mind the excuses," I said. "I've heard them all before."

I sneezed, and alarm crossed Owen's face.

"My goodness, Eileen. You are ill. You must come and sit down." He put his hand on my elbow. I shook it off.

"And who's going to take my shift if I sit down? And who's going to pay me the money I'll be short?"

"Your health is more important . . ."

"Aye—I'll be the healthiest pauper beyond in the workhouse."

He let the remark go. Then he said, "Speaking of the workhouse and the hospital, any word of Lizzie? My offer still stands, you know. I will be glad to help you locate her."

"I don't need your help," I muttered. "We are taking care of it."

He nodded. I was aware of the others slowing down their work to watch us. The familiar flush rose up my neck and burned my cheeks.

"I have work to do," I said sharply.

He disappeared back into Shields's office, although I had the feeling he was watching me from behind the glass window.

❧

I HAD TO tell someone. The burden was becoming unbearable. Oh, Ma, I wish you could hear me. But what good was herself sitting there like a statue? I decided to confide in Terrence.

"Any word on Lizzie?" I said when he came over not long into the new year.

"Not yet. You don't look so well, Eileen. Sit down."

He rummaged around the kitchen and found the bottle of whiskey and poured me a glass. "Here, drink this. It will ward off the cold."

Terrence sat down by the fire. He studied me while I sipped the bitter golden liquid. "There's something else, isn't there?"

"How would you know?" I snapped. "You sound like a priest ready to hear my confession." I didn't know what made me say that.

He waited. I took my time finishing the whiskey. A warm fire blazed in the grate. The room was cozy and warm. I felt sleepy.

"You can tell me whatever it is, Eileen."

If only it were that easy. I had known this man all my life. I had long supposed he was in love with my ma, just like poor Billy. He watched out for me now, particularly since James left. But I had always pretended to be strong. I didn't need anybody's protection. So how was I to tell him now that I needed his strength—me, Eileen O'Neill, Da's warrior? Suddenly I began to cry. Terrence came over and sat on the side of the armchair. He put his arm around my shoulder. It put me in mind of the time Owen had done that.

"I'm pregnant—and it's not James's child," I said.

There—it was out. I looked up at Terrence. "What will I do, Terrence?"

He got up then and walked to the fire. He stood with his back to it and looked at me. I could not read his face.

"Who is the father?" he said softly.

"Owen Sheridan."

"Does he know?"

"No."

"You must tell him, then."

"What good will it do?" I said. "I'm a married woman."

"He has a right to know, Eileen."

"Maybe."

"Have you told James?"

"Jesus, no!" I exclaimed. "He'd kill me."

"He'll find out sooner or later."

"Not if I get rid of it. I hear there's ways . . ."

"That would be a sin, Eileen." Terrence's voice was gentle but firm. I would get no quarter from him on destroying the child.

"It would be as well off dead!"

"That's not your decision," Terrence said simply. "Life and death are in God's hands."

I began crying again. "Then what am I to do?"

"Your obligation is to the child, Eileen. Owen Sheridan appears to be a decent man from what I've heard of him. He will not see you destitute. And then, of course, there's James . . ."

"Aye, well, James is a different matter. Not that he deserves any truth from me." I hesitated. "Maybe I can still pass it off as his," I began, but Terrence raised his hand to stop me.

"That would be wrong, and you know it. Those kinds of lies can destroy people forever. Besides, James is not stupid. Unless you have had relations with him in the past three months, he will know the truth."

I shook my head. "It's a year or more since I slept with him," I said.

"Then I suggest you tell him the truth sooner rather than later. And Owen Sheridan as well."

"But Jesus, Terrence, how am I going to go to the mill every day in this condition? I'll be disgraced."

Bless Terrence for not saying that I had already disgraced myself, if he thought it. Instead he said, "You're a strong woman, Eileen. You have come through much worse than this."

I nodded, still weeping. Terrence took my hand and pulled me up from the chair.

"Go to bed now, Eileen, and get some rest. You will find a way to tell Owen and James, and things will get clearer after that. I'm sure of it. And, I will pray for you."

I looked at Terrence's calm face. Without thinking, I reached up and kissed his cheek.

"Thank you, Terrence," I whispered. "Thank you for understanding, and not ridiculing me."

He squeezed my shoulders. "I am in no position to ridicule anyone. We all have our secrets. But I will do everything I can to help you. Good night now."

He left and I stared after him. What secrets? I wondered. But then we

had always known, ever since back in the early days of Glenlea and the
Music Men, that Terrence had his secrets.

⊘જ

I REASONED THAT I should tell Owen first. After all, when James found
out, he was likely to go after Owen with a gun. It was no idle thought.
James had shot men who had done him no more harm than being on the
other side of the sectarian divide. What was he likely to do to a man who
had impregnated his wife? Owen at least should be warned so he could
protect himself. The thought that James might want to kill me bothered
me less. I supposed that he might do it in his rage—but part of me felt
he would not kill the mother of his child no matter what she had done.
Perhaps it was false reasoning, but it gave me comfort.

I made up my mind to go see Owen at Queensbrook House. Terrence
was right—the best way was to come straight out with it. Telling Terrence had been the hard part. Once it was out, it was easier to accept the
truth of it. I had my coat and hat on, ready to leave. Aoife was down at
Theresa's, where she had been spending a lot of time lately. Theresa was
happy to take her. The excuse that hung between Theresa and me was
that I was too sick at the moment to care for her.

A rapping came at the back door. I paused on my way out the front.
Jesus. Could that be James? After all this time? Part of me wanted to go
on and pretend I had not heard him. I could not see him now. I was supposed to see Owen first. I cursed under my breath as I stood frozen in the
doorway. The rapping came again. Sighing, I turned around and went and
opened the back door. There stood James, smiling. He wore an expensive-
looking brown overcoat and trilby hat. How long had it been since I had
seen him dressed up like this, when he used to be such a dandy?

He eyed my hat and coat. The smile faded. "Going out?"

"Oh, aye. Just down to the corner for some bread. It can wait, I suppose."

He pushed through the door, took off his hat, and sat down. I removed
my coat and hat. "I'll make tea," I said.

"Leave off the bread"—he grinned—"you're a dangerous woman
around knives. But bring some whiskey."

I ignored his remark about the knives. "You never take whiskey," I said,
"unless you're in pain."

"Well, maybe I've developed a taste for it."

I took down the bottle from the cupboard and poured two glasses.

"And since when do *you* take it?" he said.

"Since it's been my only comfort on cold nights," I snapped. The words were out before I could stop them.

James smiled again. "Well, you can leave off it now. I'll be staying here for a few days. The boys and I have scaled back the operations for the minute."

I wanted to jump down his throat. How dare he come to my house and announce he was staying as long as he pleased? How dare he think he could waltz right back in here as if nothing had happened? But something made me swallow the words.

"What's going on? Have youse run out of steam finally now that the treaty has been signed?"

I knew this remark was like a red rag to a bull. To my surprise, he did not rise to the bait.

"We're planning a big job soon," he said calmly. "It's taking a lot of co-ordination. We can't afford to get distracted with too many other things. And we need to spend the time raising funds."

I looked at him. "Sounds like big doings."

"Aye."

I sipped the whiskey while the kettle boiled. "How do you know you'll be safe here? Wouldn't it be the first place they'd look for you?"

"In the past, yes, but I've been away for so long they'd hardly think to look here anymore. Besides, the boys are taking turns watching the house."

"Where's the child?" he said suddenly.

"Below at Theresa's. She's spending the night."

He looked disappointed. "Oh, I was hoping to spend this time with her. I don't want her forgetting who I am."

I shrugged. "I wouldn't worry on that account. Your ma has your picture up on the wall beside the pope, and she takes it down and shows it to Aoife every time she's down there."

James smiled and nodded. "Aye."

As the whiskey warmed my insides, a thought began to form in my head. It was the devil whispering to me. *Now is your chance*, the voice said. *This is what you were hoping for.* I tried to shake off the thought. I got up and busied myself with the tea. Suddenly James was standing behind me, his arms around my waist, his lips pressing against my neck.

"We have the place to ourselves," he whispered.

Panic rose in me. I knew fine well what he was getting at, and I wanted none of it. How in God's name could I sleep with the man now?

"Well, you'll get a good night's sleep and not be annoyed," I said.

He pulled me close to him. His heavy breath was in my ear. "Ah now, Eileen O'Neill, since when did you shy away from a good night in bed? Sure I thought you'd be aching for it after all this time. Unless you've been satisfying yourself somewhere else."

I stiffened. "God forgive you," I said. "And who would I be satisfying myself with—the likes of fat oul' Shields, is it?" I tried to laugh it off.

"Or maybe a rich Protestant," he said, still breathing in my ear.

I turned around to face him. "James, will you whisht. We've been through this before. If you want to believe the rumors, go right ahead."

I felt my soul getting blacker with every lie I told. I was so deep into it now, how was I ever to get out of it? The demon thought entered my head again. It was only just turned February. If I slept with James now, sure mightn't I go into an early labor six months from now? I was a big woman—it would take a while for me to show. Silently I thanked God for the chance.

☙❧

"I'VE MISSED YOU, Eileen. I've missed you so much."

We lay naked in bed in the dusk. In the distance, women's voices echoed as they called their children in to tea. Here and there a dog barked. James's body was leaner than I remembered, his muscles sinewy as rope. He smelled of the outdoors and musk and faintly of whiskey. His breathing grew ragged. Then he was on top of me, his lips pressing hard on mine, his body moving in a frenzied rhythm. I closed my eyes. Oh, Owen, my dear, gentle Owen, who made love to me with a fierce yet generous passion, whose kisses honored every part of my body and made me feel beautiful. How could I ever have enjoyed this brutal passion that was James?

When he entered me, I cried out. Not in passion, I realized, but in fear. There was already a baby in there. Could he feel it? Could he hurt it?

James took my cry for passion. He became rougher and more urgent.

"Eileen," he cried. "Jesus, Eileen. I love you."

When he was done, he rolled over on his back. He put his arm around my shoulders and pulled me close. We lay there, staring at the ceiling.

"What happened to us, Eileen?" he whispered.

"What do you mean? Nothing's changed."

"Ah, but it has. Too much has come between us. I mean the uprising—everything." He leaned over and kissed me. "But it will be all over soon. Our lives will be normal again."

I said nothing. Our lives would never be normal again.

He was silent for a while. "I hope for peace, Eileen. But who knows what will happen? I am a man with a price on my head. I've learned now to take it one day at a time."

And then I understood why he had come. James had finally accepted that he might die. He had come to spend time with Aoife and me in case these days might be his last. He had come dressed up and smiling and trying to pretend that everything was the way it used to be—and would be again. I shivered and pulled the blankets up over us.

ං

JAMES WAS GOOD to his word. He stayed for three nights. He confided in me the way he had done when we first met. He said he thought there was an informer somewhere. He did not seem to suspect Fergus, as I did, so I said nothing. He said he felt very much alone. Men were deserting him right and left. He cried when he spoke about Michael Collins and how by signing the treaty, he had let us down. We made love, and again I closed my eyes and thought of Owen.

Aoife was delighted to see him. He played with her, telling her stories, singing to her. They danced as I played the fiddle, fighting back tears as I watched them. I pushed down the regret that we never were, nor ever would be, a family like this: loving, happy. I had an awful feeling I was watching us all together for the last time.

On the fourth night, he left. He handed me a fistful of pound notes.

"Won't you be needing this for the Cause?" I snapped, the old resentment returning.

"We'll raise plenty more, never you mind."

I shoved the money in my pocket. Then on impulse I threw my arms around him and drew him close. "Be careful," I whispered into his shoulder.

He stroked my hair. His hand trembled a little. Then he turned and walked away. I watched his tall, straight figure disappear into the darkness. I heard his boots crunching over the frosted grass. Then there was only silence.

22

ℰ৯

The days at the mill wore on. I prayed Owen would not appear, and my prayers were answered. At the same time, I was worried. Was he off on a dangerous mission just like James? Would I be relieved if he was killed? Would I be relieved if James was killed? The thoughts made me dizzy. Of course I did not want to see harm come to either of them. But if I had to choose, what would I do?

It seemed to me I had made my choice already. My decision to pass off the baby as James's weighed on me, but it seemed the best of a bad bargain. Of course, Terrence would not agree with that. Well, it was none of his business.

I waited another four weeks or so. Then I said casually to Theresa, "You know your mother might be a fortune-teller after all."

Theresa eyed me. "Why?"

I held my head down in a shy sort of a way. Jesus, I was a great actress.

"Well—as I told you, James was home for a few nights—and now I've just missed me curse—and I'm feeling a bit queasy on top of it. I'm wondering if I might be—you know—pregnant."

Theresa stared at me. It was hard to read her eyes. Then she shrugged.

"You'd think you'd know better, Eileen. You seem to have your hands full taking care of one child, let alone two."

It was not the response I'd expected. But then it dawned on me. Of course. Poor Theresa was jealous. She wanted a child of her own more than anything.

"Well then, you'll have to help me with this one, too," was all I could think to say.

"I'm not your servant," she snapped, and turned on her heel and left.

My clothes began to feel tight. I stopped wearing belts. Fortunately, the big work apron hid many a sin. I was actually beginning to feel well again. My cheeks bloomed and my skin shone. Of course, I had to make a show of running away from my machine in the mornings, pretending I was sick. Word got around, and a few of the women congratulated me. Most of them just stared at me and whispered among themselves. Shields came over to me.

"I hear you're in the family way."

"Aye."

"And how will you be supporting yourself?"

"That's my business."

"But you'll not be able to work for a while," he persisted.

"Who says so?" I snapped. "I'm as strong as a horse and you know it."

"There's plenty of women out of a job would be glad of a chance."

"Aye, Protestant women, no doubt. Well, I've no intention of stepping aside for the likes of them. I'll be here until the baby drops, and then I'll be back."

I sounded more confident than I was. Inside, I was worried sick about what would become of me. James had not supported me in years. I was dependent upon myself alone. I prayed I would stay well enough to work up until my time.

Terrence came to the house one night at the end of March.

"I have news about Lizzie," he said. To his credit, he did not inquire if I had told Owen or James about the baby.

I dried my hands on my apron and pulled him toward the table. "Well?" I said. "Don't keep me in suspense."

He sat down. "It seems she was reared by a well-to-do family in Belfast."

"Och, I knew it!" I exclaimed.

"They were Protestant."

I stared at him. "Protestant?" It had entered my head that the name Butler could be Protestant, but I had shoved the thought away. "Protestant? Are you sure?"

Terrence nodded. "Aye. The father was a banker. He died some years ago. Seems the mother was active in society, but she took to her bed after the husband died."

"And what about Lizzie?"

Terrence hesitated. "Seems she ran off to America with some Catholic soldier she had nursed in the hospital."

I clapped my hands. "Och, she's my sister after all. A mind of her own."

But my delight dissolved as quickly as it came. "America?"

"Aye. About three years ago. They think Boston."

I sat down. "So she'll not be back," I murmured.

Terrence leaned over and patted my hand. "Now don't give up hope, Eileen. We might find an address for her. Maybe she'll be persuaded to come—for a visit, at least."

I was doubtful. "Maybe," I said.

Then Terrence switched the subject. "You're looking better," he said.

"Aye."

He laughed. "Amazing what clearing your conscience will do."

I said nothing. Terrence looked at me closely. "Jesus, Eileen, you haven't told them, have you."

I shook my head. Terrence sighed. "You'll have to do it soon. You are starting to show."

Instinctively, I looked down at my belly.

"I am not!" I shouted. "And what would you know about these things, anyway?"

"I have eyes."

"All right. I've told everybody I'm pregnant except James and Owen, so it will be no surprise to anyone."

"Except to them! Jesus, Eileen, how can you do this?"

"That's not the worst of it," I cried. "James came home a few weeks back and I slept with him. I'm telling people the child is due in the autumn."

Terrence gaped at me. "But it's due sooner than that, surely."

"End of July," I said. "But many women in the mill have had premature births—they say it's the conditions there that cause it . . ."

Terrence stood up and paced around the kitchen. He ran his fingers through his hair.

"Eileen! For God's sake. Who will believe you?"

"I'm a good actress."

He drew in a deep sigh. "Och, Eileen."

I looked up at him. "You'll keep my secret, won't you, Terrence? Say you will."

He was silent for a minute. At last he said, "I won't volunteer anything, Eileen. But I won't lie for you, either."

He left then. Well, that was that. I was on my own, as usual. A da killed in the fighting, a mother in the asylum, and a sister who had run away to America. One brother sitting on his backside beyond on a big estate, caring about no one but himself, and another brother raised with a stranger's family. It was a sorry state of affairs. Look what had happened to the great O'Neills!

∞

I AWOKE THE next day with a cold, empty feeling inside me. Anger and fear snarled at the edges of my heart. I had to face the world alone. Well, I was up to the job. Hadn't I always been forced to make my own way? A new resolve settled over me. I'd do what I had to do to get through this thing no matter what anybody thought, no matter who had to suffer— and let the devil take the hindmost.

I was only in the door of the mill when Shields came bustling over to me.

"You're wanted in the office."

"What for?"

He glared at me. "Get in there and mind your mouth."

I took my time removing my boots and putting on my apron. Shields stood like a general beside me, hands on his hips. When I was good and ready, I walked past him and into the office. Owen sat behind the desk. A strange rage rose up when I saw him.

"Yes?" I said sharply. "What is it you want?"

He looked surprised at my reaction. He nodded toward a chair. "Sit down, Eileen. This will not take long."

I sat. He walked over and closed the door, leaving Shields standing outside.

"I understand you are pregnant," he said, sitting down.

"That's old news now," I said. "You must be the only one didn't know weeks ago."

He studied me. "Is it mine, Eileen? I must know."

"Yours?" I laughed, although my heart was thumping to beat the band. "And where would you get an idea like that?"

"You know very well," he said quietly.

"Well, don't flatter yourself. It belongs to my husband." I was ashamed at the lies I was telling. I was hurting him with every word—I could see it on his face.

He put his head down and studied his hands in front of him. I wondered what he was thinking. Disappointment? Relief? Most likely relief, I told myself; what would he want with a child by a penniless Catholic worker? And he had already said the Quaker community was judging him. If they found out he'd had a child by a mill worker, they'd disown him surely.

"So you have seen your husband recently?" His eyes turned a dark violet. There was accusation in his voice and something else. I realized it was jealousy.

"Of course I have," I snapped, glad to have his anger to respond to. "He's my husband, isn't he? And he has his rights. So you can relax. You had no part in it."

"Rights!" Owen shouted. "What rights can that man possibly have? He left you and the child destitute, for God's sake."

"It's not your business!" I cried. "Stay out of it."

He stood up. "I just don't understand how you could have . . . have slept with him, so soon after . . ." His voice was quiet. "I thought the time we had together meant as much to you as it did to me. Apparently I was wrong."

His eyes searched my face. Pain stabbed at my heart.

"I told you that was a mistake," I said. "Is that all? I need to get back to work."

"Of course."

Before he could say more, I stood up. As I reached for the door, his voice came from behind me. "I would have been proud to be its father, Eileen."

I rushed past Shields, nearly knocking him down, and went to my spinning frame. I started it up with a loud rattle and furiously pressed the trestle so that the threads spun in the air like bullets.

Well, I'd had my chance to reverse all the lies, and I did not take it. Why would I? Just because Terrence said it was a sin? What did I care? What did I owe God, anyway? As I pressed away at the trestle, I thought about James. I would have to get word to him. He should have no reason not to believe me. I looked down at my belly. There was a rise beneath the apron. How was I to convince people I was only three months along? Well, I'd worry about that when the time came.

Owen's words came back to me all day. *I would have been proud to be its father*. Och, Owen, how could you mean that? Did he really love me as much as he had claimed? Or was he just lonely like myself? I recalled what he had told me about his hopes for his wife to come to the Yellow House, where they would raise a family. He had been sad when he told me, and my heart had ached for his sadness. Was he hoping that at last he would have a wee son or daughter? I tried to put the thoughts out of my head. I didn't owe him his happiness. A whisper sounded in my head: *What about your own happiness, Eileen? Is what you're doing going to make you happy?* I shook off the thoughts and kept working.

෨෬

MY CHANCE TO tell James came the next night. He showed up at the back door out of the blue. He was in his uniform and unshaven.

"What happened to the dandy fellow was here the last time?" I said offhandedly.

He pushed past me into the house. "Make some tea. I'm famished."

As we talked over tea, it came out that things were not going well for him. More of his battalion had deserted. A couple of them had been rounded up and were in prison.

"And the money's slow in coming," he said. "If it wasn't for your brother Frank . . ."

I slammed down my cup. "Frank? What in the name of God has Frank to do with anything?"

James looked puzzled. "I thought he had told you," he said. "We have certain arrangements with him."

"What kind of arrangements?"

"Transportation," said James. "We are so close to the border here, we're able to transport goods back and forth with little bother. Frank pays us a cut of what he earns."

"Smuggling? You mean Frank's smuggling?"

James laughed. "Och, get over it, Eileen. Sure there's plenty of them at it. Frank just happens to have the brains to set up a big scheme. He's buying up land with the profits like a drunken sailor."

"But . . . but he said he didn't give a feck about the Cause. He turned Protestant!"

"He doesn't. He doesn't care where the money goes. If the Volunteers could do a better job for him, he'd sign up with them in a minute. Frank's a hard man. Business comes first with him."

So Frank had not changed. How I had hoped seeing Paddy and hearing the news about Lizzie had softened him. But how could you soften a man like Frank, who needed his hard edge to mask the pain he had suffered?

"Jesus," I mumbled. "Whatever drove him in that direction?"

"Well, he got little enough guidance from your da, now, didn't he? Frank had to learn to make his own way."

I realized that in the past I would have jumped to my father's defense. But now I said nothing. James was right, after all.

"Stand up," James said suddenly. It was a command.

I did as he said. "Well, I see the rumors are true," he said. "I'd say it's six months along if it's a day."

"No," I cried. "It's three. The last time you were home. That's when it happened. I was as shocked as anybody."

"Me ma says you were feeling sick long before that."

"Och, what does she know, the nosy oul' bitch. Troublemaking, that's all she's doing." I wondered suddenly how often he went to see his mother. It had not occurred to me he'd be going to her house as well as mine.

I sank back down in the chair. "It's yours, James. Who else's would it be?"

"That's not hard to guess, Eileen. I'm not stupid. And I hear things."

I said nothing. Sweat poured down my neck and drizzled down between my breasts. My hands were clammy. I twisted them in my lap under the table. Please . . . please, God, I prayed silently, let him believe me.

"I'd have thought you'd be happy," I said at last. "Maybe it's the son you've always wanted."

"Aye."

He ate the rest of his food in silence. Then he pushed the chair away from the table and stood up. His face was dark.

"I've to be going," he said. "We've an important meeting tonight."

I put my arms around him, and he pushed me away.

"I've no time for any of that now," he said. "Just pack up a few sandwiches and I'll be away."

I packed the sandwiches as fast as I could. I felt his eyes boring into my back as I worked. I tried to hold in my stomach, but a sudden, sharp pain made me let go. The pains had been coming on me for the past week or so. Maybe it will abort itself, I thought, and this mess will be over. Then I blessed myself in shame at the thought.

"What are you doing?" said James.

"Och, sure I'm just saying a wee prayer for your safety," I said. I turned toward him and put a smile on my face. "Can't have any harm coming to a fellow about to be a new da."

There was no answering smile. He took the sandwiches.

"I'll be back when I can."

I watched him go, as I had done so many nights in the past. His shadow trudged across the grass and disappeared into the blackness. I stood at the door for a long time. A wind rose up and whipped at my skirt. I shivered slightly, but still I stood there, willing him to come back. I wanted to replay the entire scene. I wanted it to be different. Had I been foolish enough to think he would take me in his arms and swing me around the floor out of happiness? I went back inside, and instinctively I turned toward the wall, looking for the photograph of the Yellow House. But it gave me no comfort this night. The dream was almost destroyed, like so much else in my life. I sank into a chair by the fire and hugged myself, trying to get warm.

☙☙

TERRENCE CAME THE following Sunday evening.

"Just to see how you are," he said as he ducked his head in through the door.

"I'm not an invalid," I snapped. "I'm just pregnant! You've no need to include me in your sick rounds."

Terrence smiled. "Hasn't sweetened your temper any, has it?"

I shrugged.

"Where's Aoife?"

"Theresa took her to mass, and then took her back home with her for her dinner. I wasn't up to bringing her to mass in Newry today."

Terrence sat down and stretched out his long legs, his feet up on the fender. "At least someone's looking after the child's soul."

"Aye."

He took the cup of tea I gave him in his hand, blowing softly to cool the hot liquid. He looked tired, as if he had a weight on his shoulders. Well, no more than my own, I thought.

"Have you seen James?" he said casually.

I stiffened. Here came the questions again.

"Yes! And yes, I've told him the child is his, if that's what you're asking," I snapped. "And no, I'm not sure he believes me."

Terrence opened his mouth to reply but thought better of it. Instead he stared into the fire, sipping his tea. I stared into it with him. For a while, we were both lost in our own thoughts. Then he set the cup down on the floor and reached inside his jacket. He pulled out an envelope and held it out toward me. A smile lit up his face.

"I have a surprise for you."

"What is it?"

"It's a letter from your sister, Lizzie." His smile was radiant.

"What . . . ," I breathed. "How? When? You found her!"

"Aye. I was able to find her address in Boston." He smiled. "I asked Father Dornan to write to the archdiocese to make inquiries about her and her husband. They wrote back that her husband had died, but they gave me her address. So I wrote to her."

My heart did a small lurch. "Och, the poor thing. So she's widowed."

"Aye. Sad story. He was wounded in the war, and it left him weak in the chest. Apparently the hard work and the dampness over there caused him to take pneumonia. He was only in his twenties."

"Were there any children?" I breathed.

"Apparently not. Lizzie stayed on to work as a nurse."

"You'd have thought she'd have come home."

"Aye. But it seems Belfast does not hold a great draw for her anymore."

Terrence reached over and handed the letter to me. "It's short, but I'll leave you to read it by yourself. I must be going."

I took the letter with trembling hands and clutched it while I showed Terrence out. When I heard the sound of his car die away, I sat down by the fire and opened the letter. The handwriting was not flowery, as I would have expected from a well-to-do girl who would have had a fine education. Instead it was clear and neat, not a flourish in sight.

Dear Mr. Finnegan,

I was of course surprised to receive your letter. At first I thought it must be a prank of some kind, but Father Hebert here in Boston assured me of your legitimacy.

Aye, she was well schooled. Look at the size of the words. Ma and Da would have been proud.

The shock that I have another family has not yet settled in. I confess I have no memory of it and I am not sure what to think of it. I will need some time. I appreciate your forthrightness in setting out all the details, distressing as they are. I confess I am glad to know that I have a sister. I always wished for a sister when I was growing up. As to your inquiry as to whether or not I shall be visiting Ireland soon, if you had asked me last week the answer would have been no. I am not on good terms with my mother, and I have made a life for myself here in Boston. I am happy and satisfied to give my life to nursing. It is what I have always wanted to do. However, now that I have your news, I will give the matter some thought. In the meantime, I invite you to write to me whenever you wish. Having a second family is something I certainly never expected.

Yours sincerely,
Elizabeth Butler Donnelly

I read and reread the letter until the words swam in front of my eyes. "Och, Lizzie," I whispered, "I always wanted a sister, too."

23

That night, after Terrence left, I fell immediately into a sweet, deep sleep—a sleep I had not known in months. I had brought Lizzie's letter upstairs with me, read it once more, and slipped it under my pillow before drifting off into the hazy memories of childhood. Lizzie and I had joined hands, and we were swinging each other round and round, laughing with delight. Frankie watched us, smiling at first, and then he rushed toward us and tore us apart, shoving me to the ground and snatching up Lizzie in his arms. "Frankie," I called after him. "Frankie, come back!" But he ran with her toward the barn, kicking buckets and milk pails as he went, sending them clanging to the ground. I woke up with a start, but the noise persisted. I looked around me and realized it was coming from the street below. Rough voices mixed with the clank of metal and the blasts of a horn. Then tires screeched and a car sped away. A cold hand gripped my heart.

As I leaped out of bed and raced downstairs, I knew in that moment something awful had happened. As soon as I was outside, I knew I was right. A crush of neighbors stood staring down at something in the road, while others came streaming out of their houses, wiping their hands on their aprons and trousers.

"Mother of God!" I heard someone say.

Alarm rang through me. I pushed my way through the crowd, and then I saw him. My brother Frank lay in the road, his head and shirt covered in blood, his trousers torn off his legs. The crowd fell silent and parted to let me through. I sank down on my knees beside him.

"Oh, Jesus," I cried. "Oh, Jesus, Frankie?"

He stared up at me with feverish eyes. He tried to speak, but only groans came out of his bloodied mouth. His arms and legs were black, and the skin was peeling in tatters. He had been burned. I smelled the singe of fire on his skin. I put my fist over my mouth to stem my vomit. Suddenly I was aware of Terrence kneeling beside me.

"God of Mercy," he breathed.

"Look at the sign," someone said.

It was then I focused on a white placard tied around Frankie's neck. The word *traitor* was scrawled in black block letters across it. I stared at it in horror, the letters dancing before my eyes. *Traitor*. It was a reprisal. Images flooded my head. Frankie's smug smile as he proclaimed his new name and religion—Francis Fitzwilliam, Protestant gentleman, at your service; James's sly smile when he told me my brother was a smuggler; Frank's tears when he heard Lizzie was alive.

I knew these incidents happened all the time. Hadn't I seen enough of it when I had been out in the fight with James? But those men were faceless strangers lying beside a ditch as we passed. Now here it was on my own doorstep.

"Och, Frankie," I cried, putting my hand on his damp hair.

"Let's get him inside," cried Terrence, standing up. "Make way, and give us a hand with him."

But the neighbors only backed away and stared at us. They would not touch Frankie. Whether it was out of fear or a belief he had brought it on himself, I did not know. All I knew was Terrence and I were on our own.

Terrence took Frank under the arms and I took his feet and together we half carried, half dragged him into the house. We laid him on the parlor floor and I ran into the kitchen to fetch water and towels.

"Mammy! Mammy!"

I swung around. Jesus, I had forgotten all about the child. She stood at the kitchen door, staring up at me with huge eyes.

"Stay here!" I shouted, and her wee face crumpled up. But thank God she did not cry.

I bent over Frank. I rinsed towels in cold water, and when I laid them on his arms and legs, he screamed aloud with the pain. Then I mopped up the blood as best I could. There were gashes around his head and neck, but it didn't look as if he had been shot. Silently, I thanked God.

"We have to get him to hospital," I said to Terrence, who knelt beside me.

Terrence had a strange look on his face that I could not read. It was neither fear nor anger, but something else. He stood up.

"There's something I need to do first. Stay here."

He was gone. I mopped Frank's forehead and whispered soothing words. "Ssh, love, it'll be all right. You'll be all right."

Terrence returned carrying a small wooden box he must have taken out of his car. He knelt down, the same strange look on his face. He opened the box and took out a purple stole, which he placed around his neck, a bottle of oil, and a missal. I stopped tending to Frank and stared.

"What . . . ?" I began, but Terrence put up his hand to silence me.

He opened the bottle of oil and poured a drop on Frank's forehead as if anointing him. Then he opened the missal and began to read aloud in Latin, making the sign of the cross over Frank. Jesus, he was giving him the last sacrament!

Suddenly Frank came to and began to flail about. He raised his arms and pushed at Terrence. "No!" he cried. "No feckin' priests. Get away from me!" It was obvious he did not recognize Terrence. Terrence paid him no attention but continued chanting the Latin words and making a sign of the cross with his thumb on Frank's forehead.

"No," Frank cried again. It was weaker this time, more like a sigh.

Terrence took off his stole, kissed it, and folded it away in the box along with the oil and the missal. He stood up.

"We'll take him out to my car now, and bring him to hospital," he said softly. "Do you think you could find someone to help us? I'll get some blankets."

Something in his quiet command jolted me into action. I ran out the front door. The crowd of onlookers had grown larger. I stared at them, blind with fury.

"Will one of youse come and help us carry him to the car?" I shouted. "Or are youse all bloody cowards? Are you hoping my brother will die on my doorstep? Would that be the kind of sport you're after?"

At last a man I didn't know came forward, and then a few more followed him. "We'll take care of him, missus," they mumbled. A woman I knew only by sight from down the street came up to me.

"I'll mind the child," she said, "so you can go with your brother."

Tears stung at my eyes.

"Thank you," I said.

⤫

LATER THAT NIGHT, Frankie lay in the main ward of the Newry Hospital along with many of the young fellows I knew. Little did I ever think I would see my own flesh and blood lying there. Sister Rafferty put a red Catholic medallion above Frankie's bed without asking me. I looked at it and said nothing.

"We'll look after him," she whispered, putting her hand on my arm. "Go and get some rest, love. You look exhausted."

I went down to the waiting room with Terrence and sat down. I was not ready to leave Frankie alone just yet. As I sat, I became aware of the pains that tore at my stomach. How long had they been there? I wondered. I looked over at Terrence.

"I suppose you want an explanation?" he said.

I nodded.

"I was on my way home from your house when I passed the car speeding the other way. Something told me it was bad. I don't know how I knew, I just did. I turned around and followed them."

"That's not what I was asking," I said. It had not even occurred to me to ask why or how Terrence had arrived back at my house. "I want to know about the other thing."

Terrence straightened his back and looked at me intensely. "I'm a priest," he said, "or at least I used to be one long ago."

I smiled faintly. "We always wondered," I said.

"Aye, I think we must give off some kind of a smell that's hard to disguise," he said lightly. "Must be all that incense."

"But were you not defrocked?" I asked, my curiosity building.

"No. True, I was expelled from my parish long ago, but I was never officially drummed out."

"And why were you expelled?"

Terrence looked away from me. "Because I fell in love with a woman and fathered her child."

I gasped aloud. "Well, *you're* a dark horse, aren't you?"

I smiled, but the look on Terrence's face wiped the smile away. Jesus, I had offended him with my sharp tongue.

"The woman was your mother, Eileen, and the child was Frank."

The words hung like smoke in the air. I had an image of myself standing somewhere apart from the two of us, watching us have this conversation. It was unreal. It must be a dream.

"I was very much in love with your mother, and"—he smiled—"I believe she with me. But it was an impossible situation. She said she would go away with me, but I could not let her do that. So I left instead."

I sensed anger rising in me. I swung around to face Terrence. As I did so, my stomach clenched in pain. "So you left her alone after you'd enjoyed yourself with her? What kind of a man does that?"

"A very troubled man, Eileen. But at the time, I thought it best. And your father had already proposed to Mary a number of times. I encouraged her to accept his offer."

"Did my da know you then?"

"No. And I don't believe in all the years since that he ever suspected me."

We were both silent. The empty waiting room was full of dull brown shadows from the flickering gas lamps. In the distance, footsteps crept up and down the stairways, like ghosts. It all made sense to me now—the way Terrence had always looked at Frankie when he thought nobody else was watching. I even saw the similarities. Frankie's dark eyes belonged to Terrence, not to my ma, as I had always thought.

"Do you realize what this did to Frankie?" I blurted out. "Do you realize how this ruined his life?" I fought back tears of anger and pity.

Terrence nodded. He reached over and took my hands in his. "I know, Eileen, God forgive me, I know. And I know what it did to Mary. It breaks my heart every day." He looked at me intently. "And that is why you must tell Owen Sheridan about this baby. Please, Eileen, do not make the same mistakes I did."

෯

I LAY AWAKE all night thinking over the events of the evening— Frankie's brutal beating and burning, Terrence's confession. Thoughts swirled around in my head, and the pains in my belly bored into me as if the child wanted its say. Aye, child, you need the truth, I know. In the morning Terrence came back, and together we went to see Frankie. Sister Rafferty slipped us in, even though no visitors were supposed to be allowed. Frankie lay unconscious. I smoothed his hair and held his hand. Then I looked at Terrence.

"I've decided to tell Owen and James the truth," I said.

He nodded. Then a wan smile appeared on his face. "It's as well for you not to be going against a priest's advice."

"Aye," I said.

P.J. came up to the house later in the day, along with Terrence.

"I heard they burned down the whole Fitzwilliam house, and your grandfather with it," he said, blessing himself.

I winced with shock. Even though there was no love lost between me and the old man, still, the thought of somebody being burned alive sickened me.

"Frank got out just in time, I hear," P.J. went on. "But then the bastards beat him to a pulp."

"Why did they not shoot him? And why did they throw him on my doorstep?"

They were the questions that had been rolling around in my head all day.

P.J. made the great show he always did when somebody asked his advice. He tamped the tobacco into his pipe and took a long draw, slowly exhaling the smoke and staring up at the ceiling.

"Well, I've thought about that, love," he said at last, "and I think it may have to do with the fact that you're his sister, and you're James's wife. I'm not saying James did it, although it could have been on his orders. Your brother was smuggling—for both sides, as it turns out—and money that should by rights have gone to the Cause was going to the Ulster Volunteers."

"But James wouldn't . . ." I did not want to believe it, but I knew James was capable of worse.

"Whether it was James's orders or not," P.J. continued, "I believe it was a warning to yourself, girl, not to cross them. I don't know why they didn't go so far as to shoot him, which is why I think it's James may have spared him. But there's no doubt that when they left him on your doorstep they were sending you a message."

"What would that be?" I whispered, but I already knew the answer.

"That the same could happen to you if you're not careful." P.J. leaned over and put his hand on my knee. "Take my advice, darlin', stay away from the Sheridan fellow." He paused and cleared his throat. "Of course, the warning could have been meant for him as well."

Terrence nodded. "P.J.'s right, Eileen. After last night I made some inquiries of my own. Seems Frank was double-dealing both sides. But it was our side that burned and beat him. I was told but for James they would have killed him. James spared his life on account of you. You owe him that."

"I owe James nothing!" I shouted. "If my brother doesn't die now, he'll be an invalid for the rest of his life. It would have been better if James had killed him."

"Och, now, love," said P.J., "you don't know what you're saying."

I was in tears now. I rocked back and forth on my chair like a child. What was I to do? If I let the word out that Owen was the father of my child, would James torture him, too, and myself along with him? Terrence stared at me as if reading my mind.

"You can't go back on what we talked about, Eileen. You have to be brave for the child's sake."

"And who are you to lecture me?" I shouted. "Weren't you the coward of the first order?"

Terrence bowed his head. "I was. And look how much suffering I have caused."

"There'll be suffering either way," I said.

ॐ

I MIGHT HAVE weakened in my resolve to tell the truth, but I was given no time. No sooner had P.J. and Terrence left my house than a knock sounded on the front door.

"Come in," I shouted without thinking. I assumed it was Terrence or P.J. back again, or maybe Theresa looking for gossip.

I went into the parlor, and there standing inside the door in his army uniform, with his hat held stiffly under his arm, was Owen.

"Jesus, Owen, you can't be here," I blurted out. "Don't you know the place is being watched? They'll kill you."

Owen looked hurt at the harsh reception. "I don't care," he said, "I came to make sure you're all right. My God, Eileen, what a terrible thing for you to witness."

The look of concern on his face was genuine. He put out his hand to touch me, but instinctively I backed away. "You'd better come in," I said.

I turned and went back into the kitchen. He followed me. Aoife came over and stared up at him with wide eyes. Owen smiled down at her.

"Hello there, how are you? Here, would you like my hat to play with?" He offered her his hat, and she took it in her chubby hands and grinned.

"That may be the last you'll see of that," I said as I filled the kettle and put it on the hob to boil. I needed something to do with myself to avoid meeting his eyes. I felt him watching me as he pulled out a chair and sat down at the table.

"I'm very sorry about your brother, Eileen. It was barbaric of them to bring him to your door like that."

"Aye. Even if it was my own side did it."

"So I'm told," he said. "But the other side would most likely have shot him."

"P.J. says it was James saved him," I murmured, "but he may as well have let them kill him. He'll be an invalid if he lives. Frankie would hate that."

Owen fell silent as I made the tea and brought two cups to the table. I pulled out the chair across from him and sat down. My heart thumped in my chest. Aoife sat on her little chair, wearing Owen's hat. She looked so comical, I had to smile. He followed my gaze.

"She's a beautiful child, Eileen," he said, "and I'm sure the next one will be just as beautiful."

It was now or never. I sucked in a deep breath. "The child is yours!"

There—it was out. There was no taking it back. Owen put down his cup and stared at me. His eyes clouded like a soft sky. As tears stung my own eyes, I blinked them back. "I'm sorry," I said, "I should have told you sooner, but . . ."

He put out his hand and clasped mine. "It's all right, Eileen. I believed from the beginning the child was mine. I just knew it. Dear God, I just knew it."

A broad smile creased his face and he jumped up and dragged me to my feet. He put his arms around me and began to waltz me around the kitchen, singing and laughing like an eejit. Aoife watched us in astonishment. Then Owen leaned over and took her up in his arms and waltzed all three of us.

"I'm so happy, Eileen!" he shouted. "You have made me the happiest man on earth! I love you!"

"And I love you," I whispered. "Och, Owen, I'm sorry I lied to you."

I had never seen him like this. He had always been calm and confident, except when he showed a bit of temper. Now he was like a child at Christmas. I laughed along with him, and in that moment my heart leapt with love for him. We fell back exhausted into our chairs, but then a sudden panic gripped me.

I grabbed his hand in mine and looked at him in alarm. "You can't be telling anybody, Owen," I cried. "If this gets out, it will ruin both of us."

He frowned. "You can't possibly mean that. I am its father, why should I keep it a secret?"

"What about your family?" I said. "If they find out, you'll be disinherited. I don't want that on my conscience."

"They may want to at first," he said, "but I doubt that they will follow through. I am their only son, and in the end they would only want to see me happy. But it doesn't matter. You, Eileen . . . you and our child are all that matters to me. God, I want to shout it from the rooftops."

I had no choice but to tell him the rest of it.

"You don't understand," I cried. "After I found out I was pregnant, I slept with James. I wanted him to think the child was his. I know it was wrong, but I couldn't bear the thought of going to the mill every day carrying an illegitimate . . . I mean, carrying your child. God, Owen, if James or his people find out, they'll kill you, or me, or the both of us."

Owen stood up and stared at me for a long time. A cloud passed over his face. A muscle in his jaw twitched, and I waited for his anger to explode. Then he was the calm, confident soldier again. "No!" he said. "I will not have you let James Conlon go on thinking this child is his. It's not fair to either of us. You cannot tell half a truth, Eileen, you must tell it all."

"But . . ." My tears escaped and I put my head down on the table and sobbed. Aoife came over and put her hand on my head. I cried even harder.

"I'm afraid, Owen," I said between sobs. "I'm afraid for all of us."

He came over and stood beside Aoife and stroked my head along with her.

"Ssh, Eileen," he said. "Nothing will happen to you, I promise. I love you."

He leaned over and gently lifted me to my feet so that our faces were level. "You have made me the happiest man in the world, Eileen. Do you not know that? Do you not realize how beautiful you are and how much I love you?"

He kissed me gently on the lips. I stood trembling. His arms tightened around me. Then his lips roamed over my face and my hair, leaving a trail of sweet kisses. I felt his body tensing as his passion rose.

"Oh, Eileen," he whispered, his voice ragged, "I'm sorry I was angry with you. I was so jealous of James—and God help me, I still am. But I understand why you did what you did . . ."

He buried his face in my hair, and his shoulders heaved.

I put my arms around him then. "Ssh," I whispered. "Och, Owen, I love you, too. I'm so sorry I hurt you. Please forgive me."

We stayed that way for a long time, until Aoife tugged at my sleeve. I let go of Owen and reached down and lifted her up. She still wore Owen's hat. I lifted it off her head.

"You have to give this back now," I said.

She took the hat and placed it on Owen's head. Grinning, he saluted her. Then he leaned over and kissed her cheek and then mine.

"I don't want to leave you," he whispered, "but I'm on duty. I'll be back as soon as I can."

"Aye. Be safe."

He pulled me to him and kissed me again—a long, hard kiss filled with passion. I felt the child move in my belly as I pressed against him. At length, he gave out a long sigh and let me go. He reached in his pocket and pulled out a fistful of pound notes. "Here," he said, "it's all I have on me at the moment."

I shook my head. "I don't want your money," I began. "That's not why I told you."

Before I could get up a head of steam he smiled. "I should have known better," he said. He turned and handed the money to Aoife. She snatched it from him with tiny fists. I watched him as he turned and went out into the parlor. I did not move. I heard the front door close gently behind him. I pulled Aoife close to me. She squirmed in my arms.

"Let go, Mammy," she said.

"No, I'll not let you go," I said.

When I had put her to bed, I went back downstairs to clean up the kitchen. I took the dishcloth in my hands and waltzed around the room. I smiled as I hummed the tune Owen had sung. I felt lighter than I had in years.

೧೦

THE IRISH HAVE a great respect for logic, but an even greater respect for things beyond logic. Superstitions, premonitions, and apparitions are all part and parcel of our everyday reality. And so in the days following my confession to Owen, when the child inside me churned with agitation, my skin tingled with strange sensations, and my dreams were filled with taunting ghosts. I recognized the omens of approaching danger. On the surface, all was quiet. Right after Owen's visit I got a note from him saying he had been called away to England. His father was in hospital there and had taken a turn for the worse.

I went to the mill each day and did my work in silence. No one spoke to me. Even Theresa swallowed her thirst for gossip and kept her distance. It was as if they were all waiting. I waited, too.

ఞఴఴ

TOWARD THE END of June, I sat in my kitchen drinking tea with Billy. Aoife played on the floor with her tin whistle. She was coaxing sounds out of the instrument that were almost tuneful. Billy beamed at her.

"She's going to be a great player one of these days, aren't you, Aoife?"

Aoife smiled up at him. She loved Billy.

I leaned over and took another slice of the cake Billy had brought. Jesus, I was getting as big as a house. I stroked my belly. How had I ever thought I could pass this child off as premature? I had a month yet to go, but I looked ready to deliver any minute. Billy watched me, a tender smile on his big, round face. I smiled back at him. How glad I was that I had forgiven him long ago. He was as innocent as a big child. Da's death had not been his fault.

A sudden loud thud at the front door made us all jump. Aoife dropped her tin whistle, and Billy instinctively caught the child up in his arms. His eyes bulged with fear. My own heart thudded as I stood up and walked through the parlor. Somehow I knew my waiting was over.

James burst into the room. He was wearing his IRA uniform. Fergus and two of James's men stood behind him. They were all armed.

"Have you never heard of knocking?" I said to James.

He elbowed past me into the kitchen. "I want none of your lip," he said.

I followed him. "What is it you want?" I said, trying not to let fear creep into my voice. Billy sat clutching Aoife. They both stared at us. James planted himself in front of the fireplace. I'd forgotten what an imposing figure he made in his uniform. The years of fighting had given his body a sleek strength, and his handsome face had lost all the soft traces of youth. But his eyes still burned with the same passion, and they bored through me now. I stood riveted to the spot.

"I need to know once and for all," he said, "whose is it?"

A chaos of emotions ran through me. It was time. I could lie, and cry, and carry on, or I could stand up to the truth like the warrior I had always believed myself to be. I put my shoulders back and tilted my chin toward him in defiance.

"Owen Sheridan's," I said.

My words echoed like a gunshot around the room. James did not

move. I did not move. Billy tightened his grip on Aoife. We all held our
breath and waited. The evening sun painted the kitchen with an unreal
golden light. Then, like an unleashed animal, James sprang forward.

"I knew it!" he cried. "You fuckin' harlot! You fuckin' traitor! You're
worse than your fuckin' brother. Cowards, the lot of you, including your
precious da."

In one movement, James swept all the crockery off the table. It crashed
in smithereens on the floor, sending sugar and cake and tea everywhere.
Aoife screamed, and Billy leaned back in terror. Then James stood in
front of me. He put out his hand to hit me but thought better of it. His
face turned dark. He looked at me with such contempt that I felt my
insides curling up as if from the heat of a fire.

"I can't stand even to touch you," he said.

His words hurt more than if he had assaulted me.

He reached instead for Aoife, snatching her from Billy's arms.

"What are you doing?" I screamed.

"I'm taking her away. You're not fit to rear my child, you bloody
whore."

Aoife squirmed under James's hold. I leaped forward and thumped my
fists on his arms and shoulders. "You can't take her. You can't!" I cried.

"Will you look at the cut of yourself," James shouted, "standing there
bold as brass swelled up with another man's child? Och, I always knew
you had nerve, Eileen. But I never thought you had no shame."

He swung Aoife around. "Come on, Mary Margaret, I'm taking you
out of this house."

The child screamed and fought as James carried her toward the door.

"Mammy! Mammy!" she cried, her small arms thrust out toward me.

I ran outside after them, Billy behind me, carrying the tin whistle,
which he pressed into Aoife's hands. Then he ran back inside. The noise
roused the neighbors, and a group of them stood in a huddle out in the
street, watching us. I didn't care what they thought. I screamed and
pulled at James's clothes to get him to release his hold on my child.

"No!" I pleaded. "No!"

Fergus came over and pulled me away from James. "Let it go, Eileen,"
he said, "it's best."

I swung around. "How can you say that, Fergus? For God's sake, she's
your godchild. How can you let him take her?"

Fergus had me in his grip, my hands pinned behind my back. "Let me
go," I screeched, "for God's sake, Fergus! Why don't you stop him?"

Fergus shook his head. He had the look of a defeated man, a man who had given up entirely on life. "It's best, Eileen," he whispered. "If you don't let him take her, he'll do worse. He's lost his head entirely."

"Start the car," shouted James, and one of his men jumped in and started the engine. The other waited outside, his rifle in his hand. Fergus maintained his grip on me.

What happened then took place in slow motion. One of James's men raised his rifle and took aim at something behind me. I turned around. Billy Craig stood there with my rifle aimed at James.

"Give Eileen back the child!" Billy shouted. His face was red with emotion, and his hands trembled.

"No, Billy, it's all right," I heard myself cry. I had already seen what was going to happen.

"Feckin' Prod bastard," said the second soldier as he fired at Billy.

I broke free of Fergus and spun in circles, screaming like a madwoman as I watched the car speed away, my wee Aoife's face pressed to the window, and watched Billy collapse on the ground, bleeding from his chest. As I spun, the images melted into one another. Hands took hold of my shoulders, but I shook them off. I spun until I was exhausted and dropped down beside Billy.

"Ah, Billy," I cried. "Ah, Billy."

I remembered another time years before when I knelt over my dying father as Billy tried to pull me away. "Poor Billy . . . Poor Da."

Later, when the ambulance had taken Billy's body to hospital and the neighbors had melted into the darkness, I stood alone in my kitchen. I reached up and took the photograph of the Yellow House down from the wall and removed it from its frame. It was dog-eared and scratched from the number of times I had clutched it in my hands. As I looked at it, tracing each beloved face with my finger, tears of self-pity began to fall.

Your heart holds on to dreams long after your head tells you they're foolish. I'd known for years that I should have outgrown my dream of reuniting us all at the Yellow House. I studied the photograph again, taking in every small detail. Then I leaned over and slipped it into the fire. Flames flared brightly, warming my hands and face, and then it fell in a shower of cinders into the ashes.

Choices

1922

24

In the days after losing Aoife, and poor Billy's death, I was unable to sleep. I sat beside the empty fireplace not moving, not eating, not talking, even though Terrence and P.J. and Mrs. Mullen took turns sitting with me. They sat in silence as well. After they assured me that Aoife was being well cared for at Theresa's house, what else was there for them to say? Poor Billy was gone, God rest his soul. My wee warrior was gone, too. It never even occurred to me to go and plead with Theresa to give her back. In my grief and guilt, I believed I had deserved what I got. I had dealt James the worst betrayal of all. He had been justified in taking the child; anyone would have said so. As I told myself all these things, I clawed at my soul in sorrow and despair and self-loathing. I deserved it all. I was an exile, wandering in darkness in my own country, with only my bastard child to keep me company.

Owen was still in England. Apparently, his father had taken another bad turn. He wrote me every day, lovely letters full of passion and hope and talk of the baby. But I craved more than letters. I wanted him with me to help me face the world.

At last I went to bed and sank into a long, deep sleep. The child came to me in a dream. She had red hair and Owen's eyes. She reached out her hand to me and smiled. "It will be all right," she whispered. "I will take you home." When I awoke, my pillow was drenched with tears. I felt for the child in my belly. Thank God, she was still there. And in that moment, I knew I wanted this child more than I had ever wanted anything in this world. This child had come to save my life.

And so I found the strength to get out of bed, get dressed, and walk to the mill. I knew the reception that waited for me, but I did not fear it. I had found a new courage. It was no longer the warrior courage of Eileen O'Neill, preserving her da's legacy, fighting the injustice that had killed him. Nor was this a courage that was conferred upon me by the urgings of others or fired from rage against the acts of others. No, this courage had come from a place deep down inside me: It was mine alone, more powerful than any force I had ever felt.

It was like walking through a gauntlet. The mill workers stood on each side of the aisle, arms folded, watching me as I made my way toward my spinning frame. I carried myself as stiff as I could, my head high, looking straight ahead. Shields waited for me, Mary Galway behind him, her thin lips pursed in prim disapproval.

"I never thought you'd have the nerve to show your face," Shields said. His tone was gruff, but I thought I heard a hint of admiration in it. I ignored him and began setting up my tools.

"It will not go easy for you," he said. "Even the doffers are refusing to service your frame. I had to threaten them with the sack."

I nodded. "They'll have no choice, then."

"No. But you'd better watch yourself."

He walked away, and I began to thread the bobbin. I felt their eyes piercing my back. I heard their tongues clucking against the roofs of their mouths.

"Will you look at the cut of her marching down the aisle as nice as you like?"

"And do you see the belly on her?"

"Adulterer!"

"Aye, and the mother mad as a hare, and the brother a turncoat."

"She's no shame at all."

"Aye. She was always the brazen one."

I kept my back to the women for the rest of that first morning, but when the lunch horn blew, I was forced to stop and turn around. I caught Theresa's eye. She stared back at me. I could get no hint of her mood; there was neither anger nor sympathy in her face. She turned and walked away before I could even ask her about Aoife. I noticed Theresa's bad foot for the first time in ages. She seemed to be dragging it more than usual. An ache shot through my heart at the thought of my daughter. Would it always be like this, I wondered, like the ache that lingers long after a limb has been amputated?

I made it through the first day. When the final horn blew, I put on my boots and coat and walked out the gate. I was tired as a ditch digger. I wondered how long I would be able to keep it up. But I was not about to give in. I had to keep going for the child's sake. I would not let the bitches drive me out. I would not give them the satisfaction.

ഇൽ

THE TWELFTH OF July came—the beginning of the marching season, when the Orangemen celebrated the victory of the Protestant king William, Prince of Orange, over the Catholic king James at the Battle of the Boyne in 1690. It was always a great night at the Ceili House. Each year, as the evening grew late, we would play our loudest to drown out the Orangemen's big *lambeg* drums that began to sound at midnight on that day. The *lambeg* drums are so big they often dwarf the drummers. Weighing up to forty pounds and carried by a neck harness, they are said to be the loudest acoustic instruments in the world. I can well believe it because the echo of the drums from the town of Scarva could be heard far and wide for the next twenty-four hours.

The Ulster Minstrels would be down at the Ceili House, setting up for the evening. I had given up playing months ago, and I heard they had found another fiddle player to replace me. I was so distracted that it hardly bothered me at all. But today—today was special. Ever since I had begun playing with the band, I had always played my fiddle on this night. And it was always brilliant. When I was performing, I went into another world. I soared with the music, hovering somewhere up there with the angels. Even after I came to Queensbrook, music had been my escape from the hardships that plagued me. I realized now that these last few months, without the music, had been like a long drought. I hadn't taken up the fiddle since last Christmas Day, and even then it was in order to let out my tears. Now I missed the joy of it.

It was already dark when I put my fiddle in its case and boarded the tram for Newry and the Ceili House. I did not know why I had all of a sudden taken the notion to go, but something inside was driving me. Maybe it was the child, I thought. She had a mind of her own, this one, just like her sister. I could imagine the cut of me: a great ugly lump puffing away with the effort of climbing on the tram with a fiddle case under her arm. But I ignored the stares of the other riders.

As I walked down the street from the tram station toward the pub, the sound of the music drifted out and my heart jumped in my chest. They were playing a reel. I started humming, imagining the people up dancing, banging their feet in time to the music. I was filled with the old joy again just at the sound of it.

I put my hand on the door handle to pull it open, and then I hesitated. Would the band want me back? What would be the reaction of the crowd when they saw me, bold as brass and nine months along? I would have lost my nerve entirely if the door had not opened and P.J. come out to light up his pipe.

"Is it a ghost I see now?" he roared. His voice was ten times the size of him. "Or is that Eileen O'Neill, along with her fiddle?"

I smiled. "Ah, it's no ghost, P.J. It's myself, big and ugly as ever." Without thinking, I touched my swelled belly.

"Ah now, there was never a handsomer woman in all of Armagh," he said.

I laughed. "And there was never a man with worse eyesight than yourself, P.J."

The repetition of our old greeting gave me comfort, and I relaxed.

"Do you think I could come in and watch from the back?" I said.

"No!" shouted P.J.

I was startled. "No?"

"No! You'll only come in if you're going to put that thing in your hand to use."

"But you have a fiddle player already."

"Aye, and there's always room for one more, and particularly for Eileen O'Neill." He approached me and took my hand. "Eileen, darlin', d'you not know how much you've been missed? The crowd will be delighted to see you."

He turned his face up to mine. I saw the tender look beneath the light of the lamp. Then he winked at me. "I told them what drove you away was that you were mad in love with me and I had to reject you on account of having a missus already at home. I told them you were above in Queensbrook nursing a broken heart."

"And they believed you, I suppose."

He raised an eyebrow. "And why wouldn't they? Amn't I the handsomest fellow, and haven't I broken a hundred hearts before yours?"

"I wouldn't be surprised." I laughed as I took his arm and he led me inside.

It was just as P.J. had predicted. Terrence and Fergus jumped up when they saw me and hugged me. The new fiddle player, a lad named Seamus from above in Camlough, almost got down and licked my boots. It was such an honor to meet me, he said, his face as earnest as an altar boy's. I felt as if I had come home.

I started playing a reel called "The Siege of Ennis." A crowd got up in the middle of the floor and formed their lines. I was aware of the sour looks I was getting. I recognized some of the women from the mill. Well, I was already the talk of the town. At least I was doing what I loved. So bad cess to them all!

People shuffled into the pub—men mostly, but also a few couples out for an evening pint. Old, toothless Granny Larkin perched on her usual stool, smoking her tobacco pipe, but women seldom came in alone. A few younger fellows came in and nodded toward me. I knew them from the times I had drilled with James. Most of them had given up the fight, but there was still a bond among them and, I supposed, between them and myself.

Traditional music has a strong effect on people, particularly during troubled times on an Orange night in a small pub in the south of Ulster. When it is played loud and lively, it fills the loyal Irish heart with pride. Whatever resentful thoughts the people had when they first saw me walk on the stage disappeared under the power of the music. They clapped and yelled out my name as they called for tune after tune. When we finished it off with "The Soldier's Song," there wasn't a dry eye. Last rounds were called for and drunk, and people drifted out into the night air.

We laid down our instruments, and I got up and went outside for a breath of air. The heavy smell of the Guinness and tobacco was turning my stomach.

"I'm sorry, Eileen." A voice from behind made me start. I swung around. It was Fergus. "I thought it would be the worse for all of us if you stopped James from taking the child."

"How could it be worse?" I snapped. "He took all I had."

"I was afraid he might kill you," Fergus said softly.

He lit a cigarette and took a long draw on it. He puffed out a stream of smoke slowly and deliberately as he gazed up and down the street. I studied him. He looked sick, thinner than ever, with dark rings under his eyes.

"Theresa is taking great care of her," he said.

"So I hear. That's a great consolation!" My voice was bitter. "I have to go."

Fergus put his hand on my arm. "Wait!"

There was something in his voice that alarmed me.

"I need to talk to you, Eileen." He looked around quickly to make sure no one was listening. "I've information that's eating me alive. I have to tell somebody."

A sudden panic rose in me. Whatever Fergus had to tell me, I knew I did not want to hear. I laughed a bit too loud.

"If you're about to tell me you're after murdering your mother, Fergus, I'm not sure I can keep your secret—even though Mrs. Conlon was always a bloody oul' bitch. You'd be better off going to a priest."

"Jesus, Eileen. For God's sake, this is serious." Fergus sounded desperate.

"Are you going to stay out there all night, Miss O'Neill, when all decent people should be home in their beds?" P.J.'s voice bellowed through the air.

Fergus jumped like a rabbit. I looked back toward the Ceili House door.

"Aye, P.J.," I said, "I'm coming now."

Taking my cue, Fergus stamped out his cigarette and called out to P.J., "I have to be getting home myself. My oul' biddy mother will raise ructions if she has the tea ready and I keep her waiting. Good night now!" He picked up his mandolin case. "I'll come to the house," he whispered, and then he was gone.

That night, I lay awake as the beat of the drums from Scarva echoed in my ears. They beat a tattoo of trouble to come. Whatever it was Fergus had to tell me, I did not want to know. It would mean trouble. And I had trouble enough.

25

L ater that week, I heard that Owen had returned from England. I couldn't wait to see him. I knew he would be over to the house as soon as he could get away, so when I heard his familiar knock on the front door I flew into the parlor, opened the door, and threw my arms around him. Then I froze. It was almost midnight. He wore his uniform, and his face was blackened with dirt. His hands were bloody, and he had a wild look in his eyes. I almost thought he was James by the cut of him.

"What in the name of God happened?" I said as I pulled him into the house. "Look at the state of you."

"A bit of a skirmish," he said. "Nothing serious."

I didn't believe him. I boiled water and tore up some clean rags. I knelt in front of him and bathed his hands. He watched me. I thought I saw tears in his eyes, but I couldn't be sure if they were just aggravated from the dirt. He seemed jumpy, too, looking over his shoulder.

"Did you lock the door?"

"Yes."

"Put out the lights, Eileen." It was a command. I dimmed the gas lamps and went back to bandaging his hands by the light of the fire.

"Something happened, didn't it," I said.

He put his bandaged hands around the mug of tea I had set in front of him. "Yes."

I waited. He would take his own time telling me.

"Our unit ambushed some of James's men tonight. We had information they were planning an attack on a train at the Newry Viaduct. We were waiting for them when they arrived. We killed several of them. Others got away. Two of my men were shot and killed."

I sucked in my breath. "Was James there?" I had to know.

"Yes. James was there." Owen's voice was flat.

Something strange had come over him. Where was the man who had danced me around the kitchen, smiling and happy? A shiver of fear ran through me.

"Did you kill him?"

I sank to the floor and looked up at Owen. His face was buried in the shadows of the firelight, and I could not read it.

"Is he dead?" I whispered again.

Owen let out a long sigh. "He should be," he said at last. "I had him in my sights, but I let him go." He looked straight at me. "You see, it occurred to me in that moment that maybe you still loved the man, in spite of everything he has done to you. And if I killed him . . . well, you might never forgive me. Would you have?"

I stood up. "What kind of a question is that?" I shouted.

"A fair one, I would say."

"Well, it's not fair. I love you. I will always love you. You know that."

"Do you still care for James?" Owen's eyes blazed in the firelight. "Answer me, Eileen, would you have forgiven me if I had killed him?"

"I don't love him," I cried. "I hate him for all the things he has done to me. But you're right, Owen, I could not have forgiven you."

We sat in silence for a while, staring into the dying fire, both of us lost in our own thoughts. Owen had let James live on my account. How much he must love me to do that. I wanted to hold him in my arms and tell him how much I loved him, too, but the look on his face held me back.

"I'm sorry, Owen. You've tarnished your reputation on my account. You'll have no loyalty now from your men. You'll have lost their trust— or worse! Och, Owen, they might kill you—shoot you in the back and say you were a coward or an informer!"

"Yes, they well might. They would only be following the rules of this ugly war." He smiled, an odd little smirk with no mirth behind it. "It was worth it, though, wasn't it, Eileen? It was worth putting a price on my head to save your beloved James for you?"

"That's not fair!" Tears pricked at my eyes. "I didn't ask you to spare his life. You made that decision yourself."

Owen's temper flared. "What would you have had me do? You just admitted that you could not have forgiven me."

"No, I would not have. But what do you want from me now, Owen? Do you want me to get down on my knees and thank you for saving the life of the father of my child?" I sank to my knees in front of him. "Is this what you want?"

Owen stared at me. A muscle in his jaw twitched, and his eyes turned dark. Something cold wrapped around me, as if all heat had left the room.

"There is no need for that," he said. "Anyway, I have decided to retire from the army immediately. I don't belong there. It was a mistake for me to reenlist."

He pushed back his chair and stood up.

I reached over to hug him. "I'm sorry, Owen," I cried.

He pushed me away. "I must be going now," he said. "Both sides will be looking for me. My men will be eager to avenge the deaths of their two comrades, and I am as likely a target as one of the Republicans. And of course, James has lived to fight—and kill—another day. I shall have to watch my back at all times."

He looked down at my belly. "Take care of yourself, Eileen."

"I'm so sorry, Owen . . . ," I began, but he was already out the door.

I realized that Owen had come to the house hoping against hope that I would say I didn't care if he had killed James as long as he himself was safe. Jesus, I wanted to make myself say those words. But I could not. Much as I hated James for everything he had done, God help me, I was still not ready to see him dead—and certainly not by Owen's hand. How could I live with Owen knowing he had been the one who killed Aoife's father? Owen had given me his gift of James's life, but it had cost me his love. It was a price I did not think I could bear.

☙❧

THERE WAS TALK at the mill about the gunfight at the Newry Viaduct. The story was in all the newspapers. The names of the dead were noted in the articles. James's name was mentioned along with the fact that he had escaped. Theresa's face shone. Again, she was the center of attention. The people around Queensbrook and elsewhere took a morbid interest in these reports. Old men recounted the events as if they had been there themselves. Most of the Catholics loved the notion that the fight for freedom was still going on, though few of them were willing to lift a finger to help the Cause. The Protestants praised the army and the Ulster

Volunteers and the B-Specials for their bravery. They had no doubt that
the IRA would give up eventually. After all, Collins had turned his back
on them. No part of Ulster would ever be united with the Republic, they
said; the fellows that kept fighting were eejits at best and murderers at
worst. I said nothing. I had paid a higher price than most for the Cause,
and I for one knew it had not been worth it. I had lost James over it, and
now I had lost Owen as well. I wanted no part of the fecking Cause.

Owen watched me from outside Shields's office. I felt his eyes on me,
but he made no attempt to come over and talk to me. I ignored him and
went on with my work. My heart hurt at the thought of his sadness—
and my own. There were no words I could say to him that would make
things better. He would have to deal with it by himself. And if he could
not . . . I didn't want to think about that. I was tired. I just wanted to lay
my head down somewhere and rest. I didn't want to think about anything. I wiped my forehead with my hand, leaned over my machine, and
closed my eyes.

"All right there, Eileen?" Shields's voice startled me.

I straightened up. "Aye," I said.

"You're pushing yourself too hard, girl. It's home with your feet up
you should be."

I looked at him. I opened my mouth to make a sharp remark, but
Shields put up his hand. "I know. You'll work until you drop or the child
drops, whichever comes first."

He walked away. I saw Owen disappear into Shields's office. If he had
heard the exchange, he said nothing. I shrugged and went on with my
work.

ର

ON THE FOLLOWING Monday night, Fergus appeared at my door. My
heart sank when I saw him standing there. I was hoping that whatever it
was he had wanted to tell me, he had thought better of it and decided to
keep silent. I tried to get rid of him.

"I'm dead on my feet, Fergus," I lied, "I'm not up to visitors."

But he was not to be put off. He pushed in the door and took off
his cap.

"This won't take long," he said.

I sighed. "I'll make tea, then," I said.

He followed me into the kitchen and sat in the armchair beside the
fire. He didn't even wait for me to make the tea.

"I . . . I have information that James and the boys are planning to set fire to the mill." He spat out the words as if ridding himself of a poison.

I slammed the kettle back down on the hob and swung around.

"What?" I cried. "When?"

"This coming Friday night."

"Who told you?"

"It doesn't matter," said Fergus. The old cautions about naming names never leave you.

"How do you know it's true?"

"It's true." His tone was matter-of-fact.

I stepped back and looked at him. He lit a cigarette and puffed away nervously.

"What do you want me to do about it?"

He looked at me in surprise. "Jesus, Eileen, you have to warn them. The Sheridans, Shields, the lot. They have to be warned."

"Why don't you go to the police yourself?" I snapped. "I have a feeling maybe you have friends among them."

Fergus gave me a sharp look. "That's not your business," he said. "But let's put it this way: If the police found out, they would let the mill burn first and enjoy the sight. There's no love lost between them and the Sheridans because there's still Catholics working at the mill. They'd stand back in the shadows, cowards that they are, and wait for the ashes to fall. Then they'd arrest James and his men *after* the deed was done."

I stared at Fergus. His words shocked me.

"Anyway"—he sighed—"I'm tired of the whole bloody mess. I just want it finished once and for all."

"Why are you telling me?"

Fergus shook the ash from his cigarette and stared at the ground.

"James and the boys are watching me," he said. "They'll know if I talk to anybody. But I can talk to you without any remarks being passed because we're in the band together." He looked up at me. "And I'm telling you because they'll believe you, Eileen. It's well-known you are close to the Sheridans." He looked sheepish as he said it. "I mean nothing by that, it's none of my business. But I don't want it on my conscience if every work-ingman and -woman from here to Crossmaglen lose their livelihoods—and worse. What if some of them working a night shift are burned alive?"

"And you take no pleasure in the notion that the Sheridans, the rich Protestant landlords, could lose their livelihoods as well? Surely you are not out for protecting them?" I could not explain my sudden anger.

Fergus moved back from me. "So you think I'm a Prod lover now? Bad cess to you, Eileen." He threw his cigarette on the stone floor and stomped his foot on it, twisting his boot back and forth on the smoldering ash. He was calmer when he looked back up at me. "I would be delighted to see the Sheridans and the likes of them get what's coming to them. Nothing would please me more than to see them taken down a peg or two and have to suffer like the rest of us. But the price the Catholics will pay will be far greater. My sister and I both work up there. Tommy's out of work at the minute, and I'm the only support me ma has. How will we survive with no jobs?"

He was right, of course. The Sheridans would be unlikely to rebuild the mill. They had plenty of other mills around Ulster. Then another thought struck me.

"James may be misguided when it comes to the Cause," I said. "You and I both agree on that. But why in heaven's name would he want to do this? His own sister and brother work there. Besides, he'd lose what support he has left among the Catholics around here."

Fergus nodded. "It's the same question I have, and some of his boys as well." He looked steadily at me. "There's some saying he's so determined to get even with Sheridan—on account of yourself—that he's lost his reason altogether." His face turned scarlet. "I'm sorry, Eileen, but that's the truth."

I couldn't exactly say why I believed it was the truth he was telling me about both the plan and the reason behind it. It had occurred to me more than once that Fergus was jealous of James and could be informing. And he had a right to be jealous. Hadn't he destroyed his hands working as a bleacher all these years to support the family, and the only thanks he got was his mother putting him out of the house when James came back home from the war? James's words came back to me: *The police often seem to know where we are almost before we know ourselves.*

"You're the informer, aren't you, Fergus," I whispered.

At first I thought he was going to deny it. But then he looked up at me with tears in his eyes and nodded.

"I didn't mean for it to happen," he choked out. "Remember that night the police lifted me in the room above the Ceili House?"

I nodded.

"Well, they gave me an awful beating. That's when I snapped. I was sick and tired of taking it on the chin for James my whole life. By God, I thought, if this is the way it's going to be, then I am going to get something out of it!"

His voice grew stronger as he spoke, and I felt the torrent of his rage and resentment roll over me.

"I thought there'd be money in it," he went on, "but I know now that what I really wanted was revenge on James."

He lit another cigarette and stared into the fire. "Anyway, once I started informing there was no getting out of it." He sighed. "I just want it all to be over," he said again. "I'm sorry, Eileen."

I nodded. What was I to say? There was a time I would have exploded at Fergus for his cowardice, but now . . . well, now I understood that circumstances can drive us all to things we would never have believed we would do.

"We all make our own decisions, Fergus."

Fergus looked up at me, smiling like a child. "We had grand times in those days, didn't we? Before it all went wrong, I mean."

I nodded. "Aye. We were all so full of hope."

"Hope's the province of the young, I suppose. We all grow out of it. Except for James. My brother's a stubborn bastard. He'll not give up no matter that a blind man could see we'll never get our freedom in Ulster."

Was there a grudging admiration in Fergus's voice? I didn't know. Poor Fergus—always the short end of the stick. I made the tea, handed him a cup, and sat down opposite him.

"Tell me more about this plan," I said.

"There's not much to tell. James has been planning it for weeks now. None of us—his men, I mean—think it's a great idea. But you know James. Nobody opposes him."

Fergus gulped down his tea and stood up. "I have to go."

He reached out and grasped my hands in his. I looked down at his poor hands, scarred and misshapen from the bleaching chemicals. A wave of sorrow washed over me.

"You must warn them, Eileen. For God's sake, you must."

I watched from the front door until Fergus was out of sight. I had been right. What he had to tell me would mean trouble. And I wanted no more of it. I dragged myself up to bed for the first of what would be many sleepless nights.

26

When I went to the mill the next morning, it was like walking into a strange new place. I looked at the workers in a way I had never done before. I knew something about all of their families and circumstances. Molly Hanlon's husband was a cripple from the war and couldn't work. They had six children. Mary Toal's husband was a lazy brute who beat her unmercifully, particularly after he had the drink taken. He could not hold down a job. What would become of her if she was home with him all day long and no money coming in? Even the few Protestant women there worked out of necessity because their husbands had no job or did not earn enough to make ends meet. The Protestant men in the mill had the better-paying jobs. If they lost them, the wives would have to go out and try to find work or take in sewing or washing. The men would be disgraced. Alcoholism and brutality—the two things men seemed to turn to when they were down and out— would likely increase. Were all of their futures really in my hands? It was too much to think about, so I tried to put it out of my mind.

My production slowed down—although I was still keeping up with the slowest of them. Mary Galway sniffed in disgust as she made a big show of counting my pallets. I ignored her. Shields just shrugged.

"You'll not be living in style anytime soon with this kind of a show," he said. "There'll be no pay rises or promotions. You'll be buying no houses, yellow or otherwise."

"I'm doing just grand, thank you," I said. "Not that it's any business of yours."

I regretted the young fool that I was years ago, begging Shields for the job so I could buy the Yellow House and bring my family back together. I wondered if I had been stupid to refuse money from Owen. Time and again I had told him no. And I could hardly go begging to him now—the way things were. What an eejit he must have thought I was. Now I wondered how long I could keep going. I went home every night with my legs swollen like sausages.

The nights were the hardest. I wanted to ask Terrence what I should do, but I could not betray Fergus. Anyway, I knew what Terrence would say. He would tell me to do the right thing. And the right thing was to warn the Sheridans and to go to the police.

Owen's face danced in front of me. I did not want to think about him. Did I owe him anything now? He had not spoken a word to me since he had come to my house that night expecting gratitude for the fact that he had spared James's life. It was an ultimatum—James or him. He wanted to force me into a choice, and God help me, I was not sure I was ready to make it even after all that James had done.

I tried not to let the thought creep into my head that if people's lives were ruined, it would be my fault. Even though it was James who was planning to torch the mill, if I did nothing to stop the fire, the blame would be on me. I cursed Fergus Conlon for telling me just so he could clear his own conscience.

Anyway, it was only property we were talking about—nobody would be working there on Friday night. It was just stone and wood and glass. Good riddance to it. We would all be better off without that horrible oul' place with its smoke and dust and disease. I reasoned my way into a restless sleep that night and the next and the next. Each night, the words sounded more hollow in my brain. I became paralyzed with doubt and fear.

☙

ON THE MORNING of the Friday that Fergus had predicted the fire was to happen, I stood at my frame idly oiling the flax. I knew I must look a sight. Black circles hung beneath my eyes. My hair was unkempt and my hands shook as I tried to load the bobbin. Even Theresa came over and expressed concern.

"You look awful, Eileen," she said.

"Tell me what I don't know," I shot back.

"Well, pardon me for caring," said Theresa, her defenses up as always.

I shrugged. I had no energy for this ritual anymore.

"I'm all right," I said. "Just tired."

She shot me a look. I saw pity mixed with suspicion. Then she walked away.

"I have lovely ham sandwiches for lunch," she said over her shoulder. "I can never finish them all by myself."

It was an invitation—Theresa's way of offering me some comfort without coming right out. I was suddenly grateful to her. The thought surprised me, but God knows I desperately needed some company at the minute.

I joined her on the low stone wall that ran along the river. It was a lovely late July day. The sun shone and the water smelled fresh as spring. I breathed it all in. It cleared my head. I took one of the sandwiches she offered and munched on it. I realized I had hardly eaten anything this whole week.

"How is Aoife?" The words caught in my throat.

Theresa's face lit up in a smile. "Ah, she's grand. She talks a streak, although she seems very serious for a child her age."

"She was never one for laughing," I said. "She has an old head on her shoulders."

Theresa's expression changed. "She doesn't mix much with the other children on the street. But, sure Tommy says he and I are company enough for her. He plays with her like a big child. And you should hear her on that tin whistle!"

I smiled. "I'm sure you are taking great care of her," I said. "As long as she's happy."

The words hung in the air. I did not say that I missed her more than anything, and I was weighed down with guilt at causing James to take her away. I did not inquire if she was asking for me. Theresa did not say that there was a shadow on her newfound happiness because it had come at my expense.

"Aye." Theresa nodded. "She's happy, Eileen."

I went back to my work. For a while, when I was talking to Theresa, I was able to put the thoughts of the fire out of my mind. But now the panic came roaring back. Fergus had said they would do it tonight. When? I wondered. How long did I have? I went about my work, mechanically pushing the trestle back and forth, smoothing the threads, unloading the bobbins. The room was filled with idle talk of the women: the young ones' plans for the night—a dance beyond in Banbridge or the new moving picture at the cinema in Newry; the older ones teasing them about this or that young fellow. There was laughter. Even the men joined in, some with dirty oul' talk about the things they did when they were young, while the women told them what grand imaginations they had. It was the light mood of a late Friday afternoon. The week was over except for those who had to work the Saturday morning shift. The hard work was done, the money earned, and now it was time to have a bit of fun. I usually paid no attention to their blather. It was all the same to me what plans they had in mind. It was well for them, I usually thought, but I would be going home to my own silent house and sitting by the fire. Now their banter overwhelmed me. What if they knew there would be no job to come back to next week and no more money for the pictures or the dances? Would they be laughing and carrying on then? Oh, Jesus, what was I going to do?

I was packing up my tools when Shields walked by. Owen was with him. I looked down, focusing all my attention on putting my chisels in my bag. Shields pointed out some machines to Owen.

"We have some here that are in a bad way," Shields said. "They'll not be holding together much longer."

"And the mechanics will be in this evening to repair them?" Owen's tone was all business.

"Aye. They may have to work all weekend. I thought it was as well to get them started as soon as we could. A few of the managers will be here as well to oversee things. I'll be back here myself after my tea to get them started."

I stiffened. *No!* I wanted to scream out. Stay at home!

"Good man," said Owen. "I can come over later to see how things are going if you need me."

"Sure not at all, Mr. Sheridan, sir. I can take care of it."

The scream filled my head again. Stay at home! All of you!

"Very well, Joe. My mother has arranged a dinner party tonight and expects me to attend. I would not want to disappoint her. So as long as you think you can manage . . ."

"Indeed we can, sir."

I trembled as I picked up my tools, took off my apron, and shoved them all into my bag. I hurried over to the cloakroom, sat down and dried my feet, and pulled on my boots. My feet and legs were so swollen that I couldn't lace them. I didn't care—I had to get away from there. I shuffled out of the gate and down the street toward home. I did not look back.

When I reached my house, I went in and banged the door closed behind me. I sank down in a chair and stared into the empty fireplace. I didn't bother to turn on the lamps.

You hear that drowning people see their whole lives flash in front of them. Vivid images of the Yellow House crowded my mind. Suddenly, Da's face appeared in front of me.

"You're an O'Neill, my darling Eileen. Their brave blood runs through your veins. You will be as great a warrior as your ancestors, my lovely girl. You'll save your people from oppression. You'll do great deeds!"

"Get away, you oul' eejit," I cried. "Great deeds my arse. You always had my head turned with your nonsense."

"You have your chance now, Eileen darling. You're an O'Neill. You know what you must do."

"Och, will you whisht!" I shouted at the ghost. "Leave me alone. What do I care if the mill burns? Good riddance to it."

"But what about the workers, Eileen? Your friends?"

"They're no friends of mine, Da. They'll be down off their high horses now. They won't be so busy ridiculing me when they have no food on their tables. Serves them right."

"And what about the men who will be there tonight? What about Joe Shields?" Da said.

"What about him? It's him has made my life miserable all these years."

"It was Joe Shields gave you your start."

"Aye, and I've earned that job every day since. I've worked my arse off."

Da's face drew closer to mine. "You can't stand by, Eileen, and let him and the others die."

"They mightn't die," I whispered.

"But they might."

Da's ghost disappeared. I stared into the empty fireplace. Rays of light from the dying evening lit the gray cinders. It was that time of gloomy half-light that hovers like limbo between sunshine and darkness. The child was quiet in my womb, as if lost in her own thoughts. I began to hum "The Spinning Wheel," the soft lullaby I remember Ma singing to Lizzie when she was a baby. I used to kneel on the floor beside her and watch her, marveling at the gentle light that shone from my mother's face. I rocked myself back and forth now as I hummed, sinking into the comfort of my memories. I closed my eyes.

I must have drifted off into sleep. When I opened my eyes, I could see nothing but blackness. It was a minute before I realized where I was. My back was stiff and my swollen feet, still thrust into the unlaced boots, were throbbing with pain. I got up, went to the door, and opened it a crack. I could hear nothing. The silence was unsettling. Not a dog barked, nor a child cried. It was as if the world had stopped.

I lit the gas hob and boiled water for tea. I put extra tea in the pot and steeped it until it was strong and black. I sat down and sipped it.

Take a hold of yourself, Eileen, I said to myself. It's time to make up your mind.

Reason was returning, revved up by the strong tea. Men were going to be up there at the mill tonight. I had to warn them. And God help me, I couldn't let all those people lose their jobs. I'm sorry, James, I can't let you do this. I can't.

My decision made, I trembled as I laced my boots as best I could and pulled on my coat. Then I looked up at my rifle on its shelf. Images of poor Billy leveling the rifle at James swam in front of me. I thought I would never touch it again. Now . . . well, now I needed it to protect myself and the child. I lifted it and held it under my coat. I went out without closing the door behind me and ran as fast as I could up the street and around the corner. I stopped to catch my breath. Pains spiked my belly. I held on to a tree, breathing hard. I had to keep moving. I started up the hill. I could see the mill in front of me. The lights were out. Strange, I thought, there were supposed to be people in there working. I got as far as the gate and stopped. Something was not right. Then I smelled it. Acrid smoke filled my nostrils. Jesus, no! Maybe I was too late.

I started off at a run, my coat flying behind me, my bootlaces flapping. I ran in through the main door. The smoke was thick now, and I thought I would choke. My foot kicked something in the dark. It was a body. I bent down. The man was barely breathing. His face was blackened with smoke. I did not recognize him. I struggled up the stairs and down the main aisle toward Shields's office. More men stumbled toward me, handkerchiefs over their faces. I rushed past them. The office door was hot to my touch. I pushed it open. Another man lay on the floor, groaning. I knelt beside him. It was Shields.

"Joe!" I shouted.

He opened his eyes. "Get the fire brigade. Sound the alarm!"

I stumbled back out into the main room. The smoke grew thicker. The fire was somewhere—I could feel it—but I could not yet see the flames.

I had to get back down into the main hall and sound the mill horn. I ran down between the machines toward the stairs, and then something exploded behind me. I turned around to see a blinding ball of light. It was fire, rolling down the factory aisle. I watched fascinated as the fire licked at the wheels of spun thread. The thread glowed briefly and then erupted in flames. I saw men holding lighted torches running crisscross between the machines. Were they real? Images of men with torches running toward the Yellow House flooded my mind. I saw my da aiming his old rifle at the shadows in the dark. In a daze, I raised my own rifle and fired at the torches as they arced through the air. Then there was silence. How long I stood there I don't know.

At last the spell broke and I ran toward the stairs. I had to sound the horn or the whole place would be destroyed. Jesus, I thought, what a joke that we stand up to our ankles all day in enough water to drown a village, and now there's nothing but dry thread and tinder feeding the flames. I raced down the stairs and doubled back behind them to the wall where the handle was mounted. I pulled the handle and the deafening sound of the horn pierced my ears.

I ran to the main door. I was desperate for air. I pushed it open, and there, a few feet away, stood James. He stood with two of his men, all three carrying lit torches. He grinned at me, a grotesque sneer, white teeth flashing in his soot-covered face.

"So you came to save your lover! I knew all along what you would do."

"Owen's not here," I shouted. "I came to save the others, and the mill."

James snorted and coughed. "I knew Fergus would tell you, the bloody coward. I suspected him as the informer all along. My own bloody brother! This was as much a test of his loyalty as yours, and you've both showed your true colors this night."

"I had to save the mill, James. What else was I supposed to do?"

"Even if it meant turning against your own husband?"

"You took that chance when you told Fergus," I snapped. "But you had to get your revenge on the Sheridans, and on me!"

James's eyes bored into me. They shone with madness. He moved closer. "We're coming in. We have to finish the job. The bloody fire brigade will be here any minute now, thanks to you."

"No!" I cried. "There are men dying in there. You'll do no more damage, James."

Slowly, I took out the rifle from underneath my coat and aimed it squarely at James. My hand was steady. I knew what I must do. My head was clear, and I understood that I was about to destroy a part of myself along with him. But the sacrifice had to be made.

"No, James," I said quietly. "Back away now."

A low, guttural sound roared out of his throat, and he rushed toward me. I closed my eyes and squeezed the trigger just as a hand gripped my arm.

"Eileen, no! Don't do this!"

Owen's voice cut through the whirring in my head. My elbow jerked up and the bullet must have flown over James's shoulder. The men behind him scattered and ran, dropping their torches. James stood as if frozen to the ground, his burning torch still in his hand.

Owen stepped in between James and me. "Go and get the water buckets, Eileen," he said over his shoulder. "Go and start the pumps."

His voice was quiet and firm. I slid out from behind him, backing along the wall, never taking my eyes off the two of them. I moved a few yards and stopped. I could go no farther. James brandished the torch at Owen, and Owen reached for it. I tried to scream but made no sound. Owen and James rolled on the ground, the torch now abandoned near a stack of wooden crates. The flames from it licked the crates, and soon the blaze roared to the heavens. James got to his feet and stepped backward, reaching in his belt for his revolver. As he did so, the stack of crates fell over, pinning him underneath. I screamed again. Owen's name formed on my tongue, but again no sound came out. Owen appeared to move in slow motion. He plunged into the flames that engulfed James, pulling the crates off him and flinging them aside. Then he lifted James under the arms and dragged him to safety, laying him on the ground a few yards away. The bullets from James's revolver exploded in the fire like fireworks. Owen knelt on one knee, gasping for breath. I ran toward him.

"Water, Eileen," he choked, "start the pumps."

I raced back along the wall and around the corner to where the water pumps stood. I lined up tin buckets and started filling them, pumping with all my might. Suddenly hands were all around me, taking buckets and running back and forth. I left and rushed back to find Owen. He came staggering out of the mill, dragging a man behind him, then went back in. Several men knelt on the ground, coughing and spitting. Owen must have pulled them all out. Joe Shields was among them. He looked up at me.

"You did well to sound the horn, Eileen. Or we would all have been done for."

I looked around, suddenly remembering James. He lay where Owen had placed him. I walked over and knelt beside him.

"I'm sorry, James," I whispered. "I had to do what I did."

He had passed out. I could not say rightly if he heard me.

The factory horn still blew, like a cry from the deep. In the distance, the bells of the fire brigade wagons cut through the night air. Smoke and flames poured out from the upper floor of the mill. Owen was nowhere in sight. I could not even cry out for him. *Please, God. Please let him be alive*. The silent prayer was the last thing I remember before the blackness.

Home

1922

27

Flowers filled my hospital room—bouquets of roses, lilies, foxglove, all colors and shapes, some from friends, more from strangers. The child lay in a bassinet beside the bed. I stared at her for hours. She had my red hair—a true O'Neill. I thought how proud Da would be if he could see her. Her eyes belonged to Owen, though, heather blue in the daylight, changing to dark violet in the evening.

I remembered little about the birth. She had arrived at the height of the fire as I lay sprawled on the ground outside the mill. Owen had been there, and Theresa, and Nellie Leonard, the nurse from Newry Hospital. The whole village had turned out to watch the fire when the mill horn began blaring. Fire bells clanged while people ran about, shouting and whistling. Others cheered as if watching a fireworks display. And there was screaming—loud, shrill screams. I realized now the screams had come from me.

We did not name her immediately. Owen had a liking for poetic, English-sounding names like Emily or Charlotte. But I was having none of it. She would have a good Irish name, and that was that. Owen gave in eventually and left it up to me. I supposed if she could talk, she would tell me exactly what she wanted to be called. She was a child with a mind of her own; that was clear even this early. I thought of naming her for my mother, but I decided she should have her own name. That way, she would have no expectations to live up to. I wanted her to be free.

Ah, there it was! I would call her Saoirse—the Gaelic word for *freedom*. Saoirse Elizabeth. The second name would please Owen and would be a reminder of my dear Lizzie. I laughed, picturing Owen trying to get his tongue around the name Saoirse. "Seer-sha," I could hear myself saying. "It's pronounced SEER-SHA. Now that's not so hard, is it? . . ."

"Saoirse Elizabeth Sheridan," I said aloud to the baby. "What do you think of that now? Isn't it a grand-sounding name?"

She gurgled in response and looked up at me with wide eyes.

Owen brought in the newspapers. They were filled with the story of the fire at Queensbrook. Photos of the fire brigade dousing the building were splashed across the front pages. The papers called it a foiled IRA plot. There was mention of James's arrest. Miraculously, no one had been killed in the fire. But most startling was the headline that blazed across all the front pages in big block letters:

WOMAN CREDITED WITH SAVING MILL. EILEEN CONLON LAUDED AS HEROINE.

"Jesus!" I exclaimed to Owen. "Where did they get that story at all?"

Owen smiled. "But it's true. Joe Shields gave a statement to the reporters and the police. He says if it wasn't for you, they would all have died and the mill would have been completely destroyed." He paused and looked around the room. "Where do you think all these flowers have come from? They're from people grateful to you that they still have a job to go to."

Owen had told me that while the mill was badly damaged, the damage had not been structural. It would be closed for a while, but the Sheridans had every intention of opening it up again. In the meantime, the workers would be paid a small stipend to tide them over.

"But the fire brigade would have come eventually," I protested. "And besides, if I was really a hero, I would have come to you with the information sooner."

I had told Owen that I had known about the fire for almost a week.

"It was not an easy decision for you, Eileen. But you made the right one in the end. You are a hero to me as well as to many of the townspeople."

I shrugged. "I'm sure there's them will say I turned against my own husband."

Owen nodded. "There will always be those who will find some fault."

"I wasn't looking for any glory," I said earnestly. "I just wanted to do what was right."

"I know."

Owen had explained that he'd left the dinner party early to check on the men at the mill. He'd had a strange feeling, he said, that something was wrong.

I hesitated for a moment, then asked him the question that had been haunting me since the night of the fire. "Why did you stop me from shooting James?"

Owen took my hand and kissed it, then looked straight at me. "You know why. You would never have forgiven yourself if you had killed Aoife's father, no matter what the reason."

"I was aiming for his arm," I said, "the one that held the torch."

"Even so, what if you had missed and caught his heart?"

I smiled. "You weren't to know what a great hand I am with a rifle. I wouldn't have missed," I said lightly. But he was right. In my condition that night, I could easily have missed my aim.

"He'll be dead either way now," I said, thinking of the execution that awaited James.

Owen nodded. "At least he'll get a soldier's death. He would have wanted that."

Owen had made no mention of that awful night when he had walked out of my house and not come back. It was understood between us now that I had finally been forced to choose, and I had chosen him.

I reached over and took his hand. "You are a rare brave man. You showed it the night of the fire. You risked your life to save those men. And James, too. Thank you."

Just then Saoirse woke up and started bawling with the hunger.

ᘯᘰ

I HAD NO shortage of visitors. Mrs. Mullen came with Paddy, who looked down at the child and smiled. P.J., Terrence, and the lads from the band arrived and pronounced Saoirse beautiful. Fergus was with them, but we said little to each other—the looks that passed between us said it all. Father Dornan from Newry Cathedral came in while they were there and brought out his flask of whiskey. They all drank a toast and then another one. They kicked up such a commotion, singing and carrying on, that the nursing sister had to come and throw them out, priest and all. Oul' Mrs. Conlon came, just to sniff around and tell me how hard she was praying for my soul and for the child conceived in sin. Joe Shields came, all dressed up in a black suit two sizes too small for him and carrying a bunch of flowers. He was so comical looking, I almost laughed.

"Jesus, you look like an altar boy, Joe," I teased.

"Aye," he said gruffly. "The wife made me put on the monkey suit." He dropped the flowers as if they were contagious. "I came to thank you, Eileen."

"Och, sure I've had enough thanks to do me the rest of my life," I said. "You've no need to say more."

Nobody from Owen's side came. It did not surprise me. I was sure Owen had told them, but I did not press him on it. I knew it hurt him. Forgiveness from that side, it seemed, would be a long time in coming.

I thought of Ma. I wished she were here with me—and Da and Lizzie, too. And Frank, poor Frank. His burns had healed as well as they could, so Sister Rafferty said, but he was still in the coma. How long he would stay in it no one knew.

What did surprise me was that there was no sign of Theresa. I would have thought she would be the first one in, not just to see me and Saoirse, but to get all the gossip she could. When she came in on the third day, holding Aoife by the hand, I realized why she had stayed away. It was time for her to give Aoife back.

I had not seen Aoife since the night James took her away. My heart swelled at the sight of her and I reached out my arms, but she did not move. Instead, she stared at the child in the bassinet.

"That's your wee sister, Aoife," I said softly. "Isn't she lovely?"

Aoife's face curled up in the pout I remembered so well. She looked directly at me, accusation in her eyes. Theresa edged the child forward.

"Och, she's your sister, love," she coaxed. "Give her a kiss, now."

Aoife shook her head. She tugged on Theresa's hand. "No," she said.

Theresa looked at me. "I suppose you'll be wanting her back now," she whispered.

A spike of anger shot through me. Of course I wanted the child back. I looked over at Aoife. She stared back at me, fierceness in her small face.

"I love you, Aoife," I said, ignoring Theresa's question. "I love you just as much as that baby there. I want us all to be together now."

I put out my hands toward her again, but the child balled her fists and gave me the defiant look I was so used to.

"Mary Margaret!" she declared. "Not Aoife."

A sudden, desperate fear that I had lost her drove my anger to the surface. I glared at Theresa.

"How dare you?" I cried. "How dare you steal my child?"

I knew it was unfair—it was James who had stolen Aoife—but I didn't care. Memories of Aoife's christening day came flooding back. I saw old Mrs. Conlon's triumphant face as she told me the child was to be called Mary Margaret. James's family had wanted to steal her from the beginning. Had they succeeded? Had I already lost her?

"Give her back to me, Theresa," I cried. "She's mine."

Sobs burst out of me. The noise frightened Aoife, but I couldn't stop them. She whimpered and hid her face against Theresa's coat.

Theresa came over and put her arms around me and rocked me like a child. "Sure I know she's yours, Eileen," she whispered. "It's just . . . well, Tommy and I have become so attached to her, and . . ." Her voice trailed off.

I was suddenly filled with pity. Poor Theresa, desperate for a child, had smothered Aoife with love. Inwardly, I cursed James for putting all of us through this.

"I'm sorry, Theresa," I said. And then I added, "Aoife can stay with you and Tommy until I'm home from hospital and settled in. But after that . . ."

"It's all right, Eileen," Theresa whispered, "I knew all along I could never keep her."

When they had gone, I got up and lifted Saoirse out of her bassinet and cradled her in my arms. I nestled my face in the warm fuzz of her head. She let out contented little sounds. "I'll be the best mother I know how to be," I whispered. "God help me I will."

☙

I HAD BEEN home only a day when a car pulled up outside the house. I sighed. Owen had just left, Theresa was not due back with Aoife until the next day, and I really didn't want to see anyone else right now. I had just put Saoirse down in her crib and was enjoying a quiet cup of tea, lost in my own thoughts. I got up and went over to the window and drew back the curtain. A black taxi idled in the road. A slightly built young woman with blond hair got out and seemed to say something to the driver, who turned off the motor. She turned and looked up at the house. I dropped the curtain and hoped she had not seen me peering out like some nosy oul' bitch who couldn't mind her own business. By the looks of her finery, I supposed she was a visitor from England looking for her poor, unfortunate relatives. Well, good luck to her. She probably wouldn't be staying too long once she found them.

A gentle knock on the front door startled me. I strained to listen. The knock was so quiet, I wondered if I had heard right. Then it came again, a bit louder this time. What would she be wanting with me? I hardly knew my neighbors, so it was unlikely I would be able to help her. Annoyed, I got up and opened the door.

"Yes?" I said sharply.

She stepped back from the doorstep. "I am sorry to disturb you, ma'am, but I was looking for a Mrs. Eileen Conlon."

Her voice was soft and well-bred. Not English, I decided. There was an Irish accent there all right, and something else as well.

"I'm Mrs. Conlon," I said warily. "Who's asking for her?"

She smiled, a lovely wide smile that showed dimples in her pale cheeks. She put out both her hands to clasp mine. "Oh, wonderful," she said, "I've found you." She looked genuinely happy to have found me. I waited.

"I was hoping to find you before I left. You see, I'm leaving tomorrow. I was here two weeks ago and no one was home. Then I had to go to Belfast. I thought I would give it one more try and stop here before going home. And here you are . . ." She was breathless with the words running out of her like a river.

"But who are you?" I said.

"I'm your sister, Lizzie," she cried.

I could get no words out. I stood frozen in place on the doorstep.

She raised a gloved hand to her mouth. "I'm sorry, I realize you were not expecting me, I just took the chance that you'd be here, and—"

I found my voice then, and I opened my arms wide.

"Lizzie!" I cried. "Oh, my lovely Lizzie!"

ҩҩ

WE SENT THE taxi away and talked through the night, stopping only when the first rays of dawn spiked through the windows. We drank tea and took turns holding Saoirse as we talked. I began at the beginning and traced the whole story for Lizzie, starting with the Yellow House. She smiled as I spoke, remembering dreams, she said, that all made sense now: a house with a garden, children laughing, a dark-haired woman calling her name. She flinched at the account of Ma going away into herself after she lost Lizzie. Tears filled her eyes. "Poor woman," she whispered. Of course I knew she would never think of Ma as her mother— she would be a stranger always. I told her about how Da was shot the night they burned the Yellow House, and how Paddy and I ran to Newry in the middle of the night. I told her about our grandfather and how poor Frank lost himself. I told her about the mill and James and his passion for the Cause of Irish freedom. I cried when I told her about Aoife and how James had taken her away. I told her that Owen was Saoirse's father— and how torn I had been between James and him.

"And what about the future?" Lizzie asked. "What will you do?"

I shook my head. "I honestly don't know," I said. "At one time I had this dream of bringing us all back together at the Yellow House. It was what kept me going for the longest time. But I finally saw how foolish it was. I gave it up." I looked at her, tears stinging my eyes.

Lizzie put her arms around me and hugged me. "It was not a foolish dream," she whispered.

I held on to her for a while. As I held her, a warmth, sweet and smooth as honey, filled me, a sensation I had never felt before, not even with Owen. I felt a gap in my soul, empty these years with longing, fill up and close. At last I pulled back.

"Well, now that you have heard the whole story of the O'Neills, what about Lizzie Butler Donnelly? What kind of a life did she have?"

Lizzie smiled. "It was nothing like yours, Eileen. Not nearly as dramatic, or sad, or tormented. Certainly not on the outside. But on the inside . . ."

Lizzie had indeed been brought up with a well-to-do Protestant family in Belfast. She was never told she was adopted, even though she faintly remembered another family she had lived with out in the country. The Butlers had told her that she had been sent to those people for a short time while Mrs. Butler recovered from an illness. They were of no consequence, she was told. But still, Lizzie said, she always felt like an outsider.

"I was the replacement child," she said, gazing at me with shadowed blue eyes. "Their only child, also named Elizabeth, had died at the age of nine. They took me because I looked like her, but I could never live up to their idealized image of her. I found myself competing with a ghost."

"Jesus," I murmured.

"Oh, I was comfortable enough," Lizzie said briskly. "I wanted for nothing. My father was kind, and my mother . . . well, I suppose she did her best."

Lizzie paused for a moment, then her face lit up with an impish smile. "I got my own way in the end, anyway. I became a nurse at the hospital, despite my mother's objections, and I ran off and married Eugene Donnelly, a Catholic farm boy. Mother was so scandalized, she took to her bed!"

"Aye, you've the O'Neill stubbornness, so you do," I said.

"I see that now," said Lizzie. She pulled the shawl around her shoulders and shivered slightly. We let the silence creep around us for a while, each absorbing what the other had said.

"And Boston?" I ventured. "What is there for you now in Boston, with Eugene gone?"

Lizzie hesitated before she spoke. "I suppose my future is as uncertain as yours, Eileen." She smiled. "Funny, how we should both end up at the same place after all."

"Aye." Then I whispered, "Must you go back tomorrow?"

"Today, now." She smiled. "Yes. I have obligations—the hospital, friends. And I have a life there, even without Eugene."

"And you have family here."

She nodded. "Yes."

We held each other's hands. My eyes filled with tears. "I will not lose you again, Lizzie," I said. "Not after all this time."

"And I will not lose you, either, Eileen."

The sun was rising as I walked her down to the taxi rank at the end of the street. There was a taxi all right, but no driver to be seen. "This isn't Boston." I laughed. "It could be hours before John Hurley gets his arse out of bed. He's a lazy bugger."

I knocked on the door of Hurley's grocery shop. Mrs. Hurley came down the stairs in her slippers, gruff as an oul' bulldog, but she sweetened up when she saw Lizzie.

"Och, I'll be after getting John now so he can drive you over to the hotel and then to the train station. He told me he dropped you off last night with Mrs. Conlon here, and then you came back out and told him to go on home." She was out for the gossip, I could see, but I gave her nothing.

"If you'll be so good as to get him, then," Lizzie said sweetly, but I could see she was used to giving orders.

As John Hurley shuffled to the taxi and started up the motor, Lizzie and I gazed at each other. We were both in tears. At last she came forward and hugged me. She was small and slight as a winter leaf. I had an awkward awareness of my own height and strength compared with hers. But yet I felt a steel core in her equal to my own.

"I'll be back, Eileen," she whispered. "Just give me some time."

She got into the taxi and rolled down the window. "Give my love to darling Saoirse," she said as the car sped away.

I stepped back onto the pavement, tears still in my eyes.

I forgot that Mrs. Hurley was still standing there. She pounced.

"Saoirse? Is that what you called the wee one, love? Saoirse Conlon, now isn't that a grand name?"

"It's Saoirse Sheridan," I said, and turned on my heel and left.

28

I badgered Owen to set it up for me to visit James in jail. I could not explain why I needed so much to go. I just had this gnawing feeling that my future could not move forward until I had seen him and talked to him. At first, Owen tried to talk me out of it.

"What is the point, now, Eileen?" he said, exasperated. "What will it achieve? It will only upset you. The man will be executed—there is little doubt of that. Why don't you just wait until it is over?"

"I can't," I cried. "I can't explain it, but I have to go."

Owen gave me his familiar look that said he knew once my mind was made up there would be no talking me out of it. He sighed. "I'll arrange it, then."

THE VISITING ROOM was a small rectangle with barred windows set high up in whitewashed walls. It reminded me of the Newry Hospital. Even the smell of stale urine was familiar. I sat at a wooden table and waited. Owen had arranged for me to meet James at a time when there would be no other visitors. Keys clanged in a lock and the heavy metal inside door squealed open. James stood there. I could not believe my eyes. I hardly knew him. He was stooped like an old man, and his face was pale and flecked with stubble. A dirty bandage covered his right arm where he had been burned. I thought back to the blinding white bandage he'd worn when I first met him. Only his eyes showed any sign of life. They blazed when he looked at me, reminding me of the holy pictures of martyred saints the nuns gave out to frighten children.

"What do you want?" he said.

The guard shoved him toward the table and ordered him to sit down. He went over and stood beside the door. I recognized him as a lousy oul' turncoat named Mulcahy—a Catholic who had taken a job with the Royal Irish Constabulary. He'd have his ears wide open for information. There would be no privacy after all.

"I came to see you," I said.

James eyed me up and down. "I see you had the bastard."

I nodded. "Aye, a girl."

His anger filled the room. Its power crowded in on me. Sweat drenched my hands and face.

"How are you?" It was a stupid thing to say, but I could think of nothing else. "Are the burns healing?"

James laughed aloud. "Aye. Sure I'll be the healthiest man ever to stand before a firing squad!"

"Och, James," I said. I put out my hand to touch his, but he pulled it away.

"What do you want?" he said again. "Why are you here? To gloat, is it?"

"No, you know it's not for that."

We sat in silence. As I looked at him, I tried to bring into my mind the young James I had fallen in love with—the tall, dashing, passionate James with his glorious plans for a free Ireland! How I had loved his restless spirit and his courage. He was so different from the other lads at the mill. I remembered how we sat and talked long into the night. I was caught up in his fervor for freedom and for justice. It was what I had wanted for myself. But it turned out James wanted freedom and justice on a much grander scale, while I yearned for it only in my own life. I supposed now that I had known it all along, but at the time I believed James was my savior. I never would have imagined the price I would have to pay for his vision. It was not his fault, I realized. He had never misled me. I believed only what I wanted to believe.

"I did love you, James," I said softly.

"Fine way of showing it. You would have shot me dead if Sheridan hadn't stopped you."

"Aye, I could have. And I would have been in the right. You had no business trying to burn down the mill. It had nothing to do with the Cause. It was jealousy. You lost your head altogether."

James attempted a smile, but there was no mirth in it. "I made the biggest mistake a soldier could make. I let my own emotions get in the way of the real fight. But it was you that drove me to it. No man would blame me for what I did. Och, why did you do it, Eileen?"

"What did you expect after the way you treated me?"

"You knew what you were getting into."

"No! I didn't," I shouted. "How could I know you would abandon me and take my money? How could I know you would steal my child and turn her against me? And how could I ever have guessed it would go on this long, you still fighting after everybody else in Ireland gave up? Why, James? Why did you have to keep it going?"

His eyes blazed. "We had to keep it going for Ulster's sake. Who else was going to do it?"

"You did it for your own bloody stubbornness. Even Collins and the other leaders gave it up!"

"Aye, bloody double-crossers," he shouted. "They got what they wanted and stranded the rest of us here with the Volunteers and the B-Specials and the rest of the Protestant gits. What kind of future do you think the Catholics here in South Armagh are going to have with the Protestants in charge? You see yourself how they are taking away our jobs and our rights. They want to drive us out or kill us. Then they'll trample those of us left into the ground."

I sighed. James would never admit there was anything more important in his life than the Cause. And he had always been ready to pay the price.

"But you have nobody behind you now, James. Even the commander of the Northern Division gave the word to stop the fighting. It's over!"

"It will never be over. Mark my words, Eileen, there'll be them that will come after me. There'll never be peace in Ulster until it's part of a united Ireland."

He shook with the effort of talking. His burns had weakened him something terrible. I almost cried at the sight of this strong, vigorous man trembling like an invalid. I put out my hand again. This time he did not pull away.

"They'll give me a grand funeral, anyway," he said with a small smile. "The Irish are great ones for that. They love burying their heroes."

I nodded. The tears escaped now. I wiped them from my cheek.

He watched me. "I'm not sorry about taking Mary Marg— Aoife, Eileen. I was justified. And I'd do it again. But I wish I hadn't had to take your savings—I know what the money meant to you—but there was no choice. The Cause needed it."

I realized that was as close to an apology as I was ever going to get from him. This was the first time he had ever called our child Aoife. That was apology enough. We sat, both of us lost in our own thoughts. There was nothing more to say about those things. They were in the past. The future was what mattered now.

I smiled up at him. "Lizzie came to see me. Och, she's as lovely as I remember her."

He nodded. "Aye, Terrence told me. That's grand news, Eileen." He gave me a small, tender smile.

Mulcahy took out a pocket watch and made a big show of looking at it.

"Time's almost up," he growled.

James laughed. "Don't I know it." The smile faded. "What will you do, Eileen?"

"What do you mean?" I said, knowing full well what he meant.

"Will you marry that Sheridan fellow?"

"I don't know," I said honestly.

"I'll never understand you wanting a Prod like him. I hate the thought of him rearing Aoife."

"He's a Quaker," I said automatically.

"It's all one and the same." He hesitated. "But I suppose you should marry him, if it's what you want."

"Jesus," I cried, anger spiking my voice. "Did you think I was waiting for your bloody permission? For your blessing?"

Another small smile crept across his ashen face. "I see nothing's dampened the temper in you. I hope Sheridan is man enough to stand it." He reached over suddenly and squeezed my hand. "You've had a hard enough life. God knows I didn't make it any easier. You deserve a bit of happiness." A sudden thought struck him. "The bastard is willing to marry you, isn't he? He's not leaving you stranded? Because if he is . . ."

I smiled in spite of myself. "No. He wants to marry me. I just don't know if I'm ready . . ."

James stared into my eyes. He had the melancholy expression he always wore when he was listening to sad Irish songs. "Do you love him, Eileen?"

I nodded. The tears flowed freely now. "Yes, James, I do."

"Then what's holding you up? I know you don't give a rat's arse about what other people think. And you said yourself you're not waiting for my permission. So what is it at all?"

I did not answer. He stood up then and banged his fist on the table.

"Jaysus, Eileen. Will you take a bit of happiness when it's offered to you? Will you stop worrying about everybody else in the world and take pity on yourself for a change? Will you lift the weight of the world off your shoulders? The world will go on well enough without any of the great O'Neills out there helping it. You say I sacrificed myself for others. Well, darlin', you're doing the same thing."

The effort of talking was too much for him. He sank back down in his chair.

"Time's up!" Mulcahy came over and pulled James up.

"Wait," I cried. I stood up, put my arms around James, and kissed him gently on the lips. They were cold and trembling. "Good-bye, James," I whispered. "God bless."

"Pray for me, Eileen," he whispered back. "And kiss Aoife."

I nodded.

Mulcahy shoved him toward the door.

"Will you hold your water?" James shouted, the blaze back in his eyes. "This is no way to be treating a hero of the Revolution!"

"Hero my arse," grumbled Mulcahy.

"He's a braver man than you'll ever be, Mulcahy," I said. "You and the rest of them never deserved the likes of him."

☙

THE DAY JAMES was buried, August 22, 1922, was the same day Michael Collins was shot. He was ambushed at the side of a country road in his native Cork. Some said it was his own side killed him, but no one knew for sure. Collins had predicted his own death the day he signed the treaty with Great Britain. "I have just signed my death warrant," he was reputed to have said. Those loyal to Collins damned de Valera for having sent a soldier to do a politician's job. I thanked God that James had not lived to see him killed.

As James had said, the Irish are great ones for funerals. He was buried with the full honors of the Irish Republican Army. His coffin was draped in the Irish tricolor, and the six pallbearers were IRA soldiers in full dress uniform. The procession route from the church in Glenlea where we had been married to the graveyard in Newry was lined with silent mourners holding Irish flags. A solitary drumbeat was the only sound. The soldiers fired volleys of rifle shots into the sky over the graveyard as the coffin was lowered, while a lone bagpiper played "The Minstrel Boy," a sad, haunting lament. In the distance, Slieve Gullion stood stately, as if at attention herself.

The town was black with people. They came down from Belfast and up from the South. Dignitaries of de Valera's government were there, along with top brass of the IRA. Aye, they all came out all right. But where were they when James was fighting alone, coming home to me at night scarred and bleeding? If the Ulster Volunteers and the B-Specials were there, they kept out of sight. Only the RIC men stood at each corner and halted traffic as the procession passed.

Owen did not come. We agreed it was best. I walked behind the coffin, along with Fergus, Theresa, Tommy, and Aoife. James's mother placed herself bold as brass in front of the coffin, just behind the priest. The oul' hypocrite! This was her wildest dream come true: her son a martyr, people singing hymns and saying prayers, and her at the head of it with a look of shining agony on her face. Father Dornan blessed the coffin. Many's a priest would not have dared show himself in such a situation. James had murdered people. He was a wanted man—a revolutionary. But Father Dornan said James was a soldier and deserved a decent burial.

The day was warm and the sun shone its hot rays down on the proceedings. Birds sang in the trees as we passed, and hedge flowers bloomed in glorious color. It was a beautiful day for such a sad occasion. Appropriate enough for James, I thought. He always had a mixture of joy and melancholy about him—like most of the Irish.

The reception was held at the Ceili House. P.J. and the boys played traditional music while porter and whiskey flowed. I sat in the corner with the rest of James's family. Many of the dignitaries and the IRA men came over to shake my hand. The head man handed me the folded tricolor from James's coffin. The local people were a different story. Those that knew the truth about James and me nodded silently but kept their distance. James's mother had made herself the center of attention anyway, bawling and carrying on, so it took the notice away from myself. For once I was grateful to her. Father Dornan came over and sat beside me.

"By the way, there was a young woman came looking for Terrence a week or so ago. Didn't say who she was. Unfortunately, Terrence was away at the time." He looked at me with his eyebrow cocked. I smiled.

"Aye, that would have been our sister, Lizzie, from America," I said, pride filling my voice. "She came to find us."

"Well, isn't that marvelous," Father Dornan exclaimed. "What a miracle." He winked at me. "I helped Terrence out with that bit of detective work, you know."

I smiled. "Yes, I know, Father."

Eventually, the crowd began to thin out. The diehards would be there all night, as long as the drink was free, but the rest of them would be drifting off before evening. I was anxious to get home to Saoirse. Owen was minding her, so I knew she was being well cared for, but suddenly I missed the both of them more than I could say. I got up to go.

"Will you be coming down to the house?" Theresa asked.

"No," I said. "I want to get home to Saoirse. Anyway, you'll have your hands full without me." I nodded toward Mrs. Conlon, who had started carrying on again now that she saw the party was winding down.

Theresa rolled her eyes. "Aye," she said, "it's well for you has somewhere else to go."

I patted Theresa's arm. "Thanks," I whispered.

"For what?"

"For being a friend through all of this."

She blushed. "Sure what have I done, compared to what you've done for me?" She reached over and grabbed Tommy's hand. "You see, once we'd had Aoife for a while, we realized what a blessing children are no matter that they're not your own. And so we've decided to adopt one."

She beamed at me. "Of course me ma's against it," she said. "She says you never know what you're getting when it's some other woman's child. She says just look at our Fergus!"

I laughed aloud. "Och, well, now James is gone, it will give her something new to pray over."

I shook hands with Father Dornan and with P.J. and the band.

"No, I'd rather take the tram," I said to their inquiries about a lift. "It's a fine evening. I would like to be by myself."

I walked out of the pub and started up the hill. It was one of those lovely August evenings in Ireland when the light lingers until late and the world is suspended between day and night. I was lost in my thoughts when a hand touched my shoulder. I spun around. It was Fergus. I had not seen him since he came to the hospital. And today I'd had no chance to talk to him since his mother hung on to him for dear life. I stopped and looked at him.

"Well?" I wanted to say, "Are you satisfied?" but I held back.

He must have read my mind. He lit a cigarette and took a long drag on it. "I didn't mean for him to be caught and killed," he said.

"And what else did you think was going to happen? Did you think they were going to give him a medal?"

Fergus hung his head. "I just wanted to save the mill, Eileen. That's all."

"Aye." I shrugged. "So did I. But in some ways I wish you had never told me, Fergus."

"I know. But I didn't have the courage to do anything about it myself. You always were braver than most of us." Fergus looked at me, anxious as a rabbit. "Anyway, James would have died sooner or later. He would never have given up. He was bent on his own destruction. It's what happens to people who never question themselves. They all destroy themselves in the long run."

29

On the last Sunday in August, Owen's car pulled up outside my house. Aoife opened the door wide to run out and greet him, and I came out behind her. There, bold as brass and looking like the cat that got the cream, was Theresa. She stepped out as daintily as she could, despite her crippled foot, while Owen held the door open for her. I laughed.

"Well, what brings you here, missus?"

Owen grinned from Theresa to me. "She has come to take care of our daughters while I take you out to lunch."

I was taken aback at the words *our daughters*, but they had a sweet ring to them just the same. "And what's the occasion?" I said.

"Surprise. Now go in and put on something wonderful."

Theresa hurried up and pushed me into the house. "Upstairs!" she said breathlessly. "Let's see if you have anything in your wardrobe fit to be seen in."

She took the stairs to my bedroom as fast as she could, threw open the wardrobe door, and pulled out what few clothes I had, clicking her tongue as she did so.

"Jesus, Eileen, anybody would think you were a pauper!"

"Well, I'm not far from it," I said, annoyed.

Theresa swung around, her eyes glinting in her small face. "Well, you'll not be one for long," she cried. "I think he's going to ask you to marry him!"

"What? Did he tell you that?"

"Well, no. But I don't know why else he'd be making such a big palaver. Here, try this on!"

Theresa bullied me until I was dressed to meet her approval—a long fawn linen skirt and pale pink high-necked blouse—presents from Mrs. Mullen long ago that I had never worn. I had lost the weight quickly after Saoirse's birth, and they fit well enough. Theresa found some pearls, a ribbon, and a belt.

"Go on now," she said, stepping back and admiring her handiwork, "don't keep the man waiting."

I tried to smile at Owen as he talked away on the drive to Newry, but I could not let go of what Theresa had said. It made me nervous. I hoped she was wrong. I wasn't ready to face the question.

"What's the occasion?" I said at last.

He turned and smiled at me. "Well, not that we need an occasion, but it occurred to me that I let your birthday pass and did nothing to celebrate it."

I smiled back, relieved. Theresa was wrong. I would have no decision to make.

It was a bank holiday weekend, and crowds were out enjoying the warm late summer weather. Little flags fluttered on boats in the canal—a regatta of some sort—and in the town square a band played. The pall that had hung over all of us the past few years seemed to be lifting. I felt my heart grow lighter as well. We parked and walked to Morocco's Café on Hill Street. How long had it been since the last time I had walked there with Owen and Paddy? Nine years? Jesus, it seemed a lifetime ago.

The place was packed, but we managed to find a small table in the corner. Owen went up to the counter to greet Mr. Morocco and order some food and drinks. Again, I was surprised at his ease in a place like this. Mr. Morocco seemed delighted to see him. Owen came back to the table grinning, holding a tray loaded with sandwiches, cake, and ice cream.

"You're worse than a child," I said, laughing as he set everything on the table.

"I told you I had a sweet tooth."

"Aye."

As we ate, I looked around. I always loved Morocco's Café with its feel of mystery and the enchantment of faraway places. I looked back at Owen. How he had changed since the last time we sat here together, just before he went off to war. The restless, earnest young soldier was gone, and in his place was a mature man at ease with himself and the world.

His hair, once the color of corn, was woven with gray. Time had engraved more tiny lines on his forehead and around his mouth. He wore a white linen shirt with no collar, open at the neck, and tan trousers. I had not seen him in his uniform since the night he had left my house after the run-in with James. He had left the army just as he had said he would. A wave of love swelled in me, and I reached out and took his hand.

"We've seen a lot of life since the last time we were here," I whispered.

He must have been thinking the same thing. "Yes. I was off to find my life's meaning, and you were still a young girl with a passionate dream."

"And you still haven't found your meaning, and my dream's in tatters." I shrugged.

"Maybe I've not yet found my meaning," he said thoughtfully, "but at least I know it does not lie in war." He smiled then. "However, you, young lady, you can still have your dream. You can move to the Yellow House. I have told you before I will give it to you."

"And I've told you I won't take it. If I ever want it—which I don't—I will get it under my own steam."

"Stubborn, independent girl." He smiled. "But then, you always were."

"Do you remember when we first met?"

He nodded and smiled. "How could I forget? Nobody had ever had the cheek to talk back to me like that."

My cheeks reddened. "Aye, I had an awful tongue in my head back then."

"Still do." He grinned.

His eyes clouded—a look I had come to know well. "Why did you never write to me, Eileen? If you had, I might not have married Joanna. Things might have been a lot different."

I shrugged. "Och, Owen. I was just a young girl, and believe it or not, I was shy. I couldn't imagine going to Queensbrook House with letters addressed to you." I laughed then. "You should have seen the cut of Joe Shields when he handed me your letter, though!"

Owen laughed back. "I can only imagine."

"I still have the letter," I whispered.

We were silent for a moment, lost in our own thoughts.

"I was hurt when you took up with James," he went on, serious again. "I know I had no right to be, but deep down it hurt. And then after you and I . . . after we made love, the thought that you had slept with James again nearly drove me to distraction. I never knew I was capable of such jealousy."

I wanted to stop the direction of the conversation. What good was to be had from it all now?

"And what about your life's meaning?" I said. "I think maybe it's been staring you in the face all along."

He looked at me, confused.

"Sister Rafferty told me all the wonderful things you do for the children at the workhouse. And the Sheridan mill is the only mill around here that has not sacked all the Catholics, and I know you had a hand in that. I think all the meaning you need is right here."

Then a thought occurred to me. "Unless they've disinherited you, on account of me?" I cried.

He smiled. "On the contrary, they are urging me more than ever to take over the mill." He let out a small laugh and shrugged. "But if they had disinherited me, I might have made a fine gentleman farmer." He looked up at me and grinned. "All water under the bridge," he said briskly. "Now, about your birthday . . ." He reached into his pocket and took out a small velvet box tied up in a ribbon. I stared at it.

"Go on, open it."

Before I could do so, Mrs. Morocco came over to our table. She beamed down at Owen.

"Oh, Mr. Sheridan," she said, "my husband told me you were here. I had to come out and see you—and thank you."

I looked from her to Owen. He waved his hand. "No need, Mrs. Morocco."

She grabbed his hand in hers. "Oh, yes, Mr. Sheridan. Without your help we would have lost the shop—and after my husband had worked so hard . . ."

Tears lit the corner of her eyes. Owen took his hand away from her. "You both worked hard," he said softly. "I only did what anyone would have done."

She nodded and wiped her tears with her apron. "More tea?" she said.

We both shook our heads no, and she moved away. I looked at Owen, waiting for an explanation. He shrugged. "I worked out a small loan for them. Their business dropped off during the war years. I just helped them get back on their feet. Now, open your present."

I pulled the box toward me and untied it slowly, my large fingers awkward on the delicate ribbon. I removed the lid. There on a bed of satin lay a lovely ring with an emerald stone. I dropped it as if it were on fire.

"Emerald," said Owen, "to match your eyes. Of course, if you don't like it . . ."

"Like it?" I cried. "What woman wouldn't like it? But I can't take it."

Owen's eyes widened. "For heaven's sake, why not?"

"Because I'm not ready to marry you," I burst out. "Not you or any-body else. It's too soon. Don't you see? I've only just buried a husband. For the first time in years I have my freedom. Och, Owen, I must be mad in the head to be refusing you now, but I need time. There are too many pieces of unfinished business in my life now, Frankie, Lizzie, Paddy, where I will live—all of it."

I realized he was laughing. He threw back his head and laughed louder than I had ever heard him do before. "Oh, Eileen," he said finally, "my darling Eileen. Do you not think I know you well enough not to spring something like that on you? I don't know what Miss Theresa told you, but this ring is to celebrate your birthday and the birth of our darling Saoirse!"

I stared at him, my mouth open. "You mean you don't want to marry me?"

He leaned forward and took my hands in his. "Of course I do, my love. I would run away with you this minute if you would let me. But I realize you need some time. I cannot say that I am in no hurry, but I want the decision to be yours. I want you to come to me openly and willingly and without any doubts. That is the only way I will marry you!"

I didn't know whether to laugh or cry. Where did I ever find a man who knew me to the core as this man did? Where did I ever find a man as understanding and unselfish as this man was? Och, Da, did you send him to me after all?

Owen took my right hand in his and slipped the ring on my finger. It fit perfectly. I had a feeling Theresa had helped him with the size. I looked down at it and smiled through the tears that clouded my eyes.

"It's beautiful, Owen," I whispered.

When we arrived home, Theresa made a big show of taking the girls out for a long walk. If she noticed the ring on my right hand instead of my left, she said nothing—I would be in for the inquisition later. I smiled and closed the door behind her. Owen and I made love sweetly and passion-ately. Afterward, he told me he would be going back to England shortly. His father would not last much longer, he said, and wanted Owen's deci-sion as to whether he would take over the mill. If he said yes, he would need to spend time learning at similar mills in England. He did not know how long he would be gone, he said, but probably into the next year.

"Long enough," Owen said, "for you to make your decision as well, Eileen."

೧೦

WORD CAME FROM Sister Rafferty that Frankie had woken up from his coma. Terrence came for me, and together we rode to the hospital. I left Saoirse and Aoife with one of the young nurses and rushed to where Frank lay. I trembled as I looked down at him. His eyes were closed. I sat down and clutched his hand. Sister Rafferty came over.

"He goes in and out of it, love, but it's a good sign. He'll be back with us for good soon."

I nodded and looked up at Terrence. It was hard to read his expression. What would happen when Frank came to and saw him? Would he spit at him again the way he had done the night Terrence had prayed over him? I sensed Terrence's anxiety, and he sensed mine.

"It's all right, Eileen," he whispered. "I just want him well."

We sat waiting. Terrence murmured quiet prayers. I said a few of my own. I had not prayed in a donkey's age. God had not been kind to me. But now I wanted so much for Frank to be back with me, I actually slid off my chair and got down on my knees beside his bed.

"Sweet Jesus," I murmured, "please help Frank. I know he sinned. I know he turned against you, the way I did myself. But it wasn't his fault, Jesus." I looked up, defiant. "If I can forgive him, why can't you?"

As if he heard me, Frank opened his eyes.

"Frankie," I screeched. "Frankie!"

Frank examined my face. He looked puzzled. Could it be that he didn't remember me? Oh, Jesus, no. "It's me, Frankie," I cried, "Eileen."

Frank stared at me and then at Terrence. His brown eyes were bright, as if he had a fever. I held my breath and waited. Terrence said nothing.

"I'm your sister, Frankie," I said. "Eileen. Don't you remember me?" Tears of frustration pricked at my eyes. "Please, darlin'," I said.

Then a grin spread across Frankie's face. It was a cheeky, smug grin. It was the same grin he'd flashed when we were children and he had just won a game against me.

"Eileen," he muttered.

My heart leaped. "Aye, Frankie, Eileen."

He noticed Terrence then, and his eyes blazed. "Music," he cried, "Music Man."

Terrence nodded. "Aye, Frank," he whispered, "Music Man."

"Play a tune," said Frankie. "Lizzie wants to dance."

A weight as heavy as Slieve Gullion herself settled in my belly. I could hardly breathe. I looked at Terrence, but he looked away.

"Play!" shouted Frankie, his voice demanding.

I tried again. I stroked his hand. "Do you not remember what happened, love?" I whispered. "Do you not remember the fire? Grandda Fitzwilliam?"

He gave me a puzzled stare and shook his head, rolling it back and forth violently on the pillow. "I want to go home now," he cried.

"Where's home, Frankie?" I whispered.

He sighed in exasperation. "The Yellow House, you eejit," he said.

Sister Rafferty came up behind us. "I think that's enough for now," she said, I heard the pity in her voice.

"But he doesn't remember," I cried. "He thinks he's a child. God help me, he thinks we're all still at the Yellow House."

Sister Rafferty patted my arm. "Sometimes it takes a while for the memory to come back," she said softly. "We just have to be patient."

"And what if it never comes?" I cried. "What if he's . . . he's left like Billy Craig?"

"We'll just have to wait," she said. "At least you have him alive."

Terrence and I hardly said a word in the car all the way back to the house. When we arrived, I put Aoife and Saoirse to bed and poured Terrence and myself each a glass of whiskey.

"Well, so much for feckin' prayer!" I said.

Terrence drained his glass, then looked at me. "God works in mysterious ways, Eileen—"

"Och, don't give me that blather," I cut in. "The O'Neills are going to have another mad one in the family, and that's the size of it."

Terrence winced at the reference to Ma. He never liked to talk about the fact that she was insane.

"Well, we'll have to give it some time," he said. "But if he doesn't change, I suppose we should be thinking about arrangements."

I looked up. "What arrangements?"

"Well, he won't be fit to run your grandfather's farm."

"He can come and live with me!" I said, annoyed at the turn of the conversation. No matter what had passed between Frankie and me, he was still my brother, and he needed me. I would not abandon him now.

Terrence nodded. "That's not entirely what I mean. Someone will have to step in and take care of his affairs. The Fitzwilliam estate and the other lands will have to be sold. And you would have been the next in line, as I understand things. So the proceeds should go to you."

I rounded on Terrence. "Feck you!" I cried. "Frank's not even in the ground and you're talking as if he was dead. How can you be so cold, and him your own flesh and blood?"

Terrence stared at me and then looked over at Saoirse, who was sleeping peacefully in her crib.

"I'm just thinking of you, Eileen—and the children. In time you will see that I am right."

After Terrence left, I sat by the fire, seething with anger. How could he talk like that? How did he know that Frankie would not wake up tomorrow and be right as rain? God knows I would rather have the angry old Frankie back than this child that lay in his bed. But what if he didn't change? I could hardly bear to think about it. I got up and dragged myself up to bed.

☙

IN THE END, it was Terrence who arranged everything. Frankie was brought to my house. There was nothing more the hospital could do for him. He learned to walk with crutches on his poor, damaged legs, but his mind did not heal. He was a ten-year-old boy. He played happily with Saoirse and Aoife. Terrence brought him a bodhran drum and he beat on it while Terrence played the pipes. Sometimes I brought him to the Ceili House, and the boys would let him come up and play onstage. He grinned like a big child. His temper was so sweet that in time it was hard to remember the angry, brittle man he had been.

The property was all sold for a good price. I now had enough money to live without having to work again. Terrence planted the notion in me that I should buy my own house. After all, he said, you can't live in a mill house when you no longer work at the mill.

"They'd hardly throw me out," I cried, "after what I did for them."

But Terrence knew me too well. He had hit a nerve of pride. I knew I could not stay.

"The old Yellow House is up for sale again," Terrence said casually one night.

My whole body tensed. "Owen's selling it?" I whispered.

Terrence nodded.

"Well, good luck to whoever gets it now. It won't be me. I don't give a rat's arse about that place. It was always bad luck."

But the seed had been planted. Did I dare even think I could go back there? Was the dream still alive? Could I trust God this time? Had this been His mysterious way of answering my prayers, or were the evil ghosts still waiting for me? That night, Slieve Gullion appeared to me in my dreams. "Come home, darlin'," she said, "come home."

30

We moved in the week before Christmas 1922. The house had been transformed. It smelled new and fresh. Theresa had sewn flowered curtains for all the windows, bright rugs covered the floors, and a pair of brass andirons shone beside the fireplace. The walls had been painted a soft cream, and Ma's pictures hung on them. Shane Kearney had been good to his word and kept everything that had been salvaged from the fire. I cried when I went into the back room of his pub with Theresa and saw Ma's sewing machine, the desk with inlaid marble that Da had made for her, and her paintings. The "ghost chair" that always stood empty beside the fireplace for Great-Grandda Hugh was there as well.

The outside of the house was still a bit drab. The whitewashed exterior was stained and chipped. Maybe in the spring I would paint it. I wasn't quite ready for it to be yellow again. Maybe I would never want it yellow again—it might bring bad luck. I decided to leave the decision until spring, after the garden was planted.

Word came from Lizzie that she would be home for Christmas. I was delighted. She did not say if it was to be for a visit or for good, but no bother, I would be happy to see her either way. I decided to throw a party for her on Christmas Eve, and I wanted everybody there.

I sent a note to Owen. I tried to sound offhand in it, but the truth was I was desperate to see him again. I had cursed myself more than once for having let him go.

Terrence and I got permission from the hospital to bring Ma home for the holiday. She sat beside me in the backseat of Terrence's car, shrunken like a frail doll. She gazed out the window at the houses and fields as we passed. It was a dozen years since she had been outside. I squeezed her hand. When we pulled up in front of the house, it was hard to know if she recognized it. She got out and stood and stared up at it for a minute, but I could read nothing in her eyes. We brought her in and sat her down in an armchair beside the fire. Theresa had tea made and handed her a cup.

"Thank you," she said in the polite way I had come to know.

Her hand trembled as she held the cup. Aoife toddled over to her and sat on the floor beside her, holding on to the arm of the chair.

"Hello, Granny," she said.

I supposed Theresa had told her who was coming, but Theresa looked surprised.

"How did you know she was your granny, love?" she said.

Aoife said nothing but leaned closer to the chair. Ma looked down at her and smiled. She reached a thin hand down and stroked the child's hair. I swallowed a lump in my throat.

೧๏

THE WORD WENT out to everyone that the ceili was on at the Yellow House for Christmas Eve. I looked around the big kitchen. Theresa had decorated it as well as she had ever decorated the Temperance Hall in Queensbrook. She bustled about now, adjusting this and that. Ma sat in the armchair by the fire, Aoife on the floor next to her. Saoirse crowed in her cradle, and Frankie sat in a corner, occupied with a new puppy Terrence had brought him. We called it Cuchulainn, after our faithful old dog. The turf fire burned bright, while loaves of soda bread baked in its ashes. Bottles of porter stood like soldiers on the kitchen table along with a big bowl of apple cider. I looked out the kitchen window. A few flakes of snow swirled in the evening sky.

"We're having a party, Mrs. Gullion," I whispered as I stared out toward my beloved mountain, "just like old times. What do you think of that? Aye, I know, it's about time."

P.J. and Fergus were the first to arrive, stamping their feet from the cold and admiring the house. They had brought Joe Shields with them, along with his accordion. One by one they went over and took Ma's hands in theirs and greeted her. She smiled a shy, thin smile but said nothing. Then they settled themselves on stools in the kitchen with bottles of porter, their instruments on the floor beside them. Terrence put a glass of porter beside Great-Grandda Hugh's chair, and wee Cuchulainn bounded out of Frankie's arms and settled himself on the empty chair, where we all knew an invisible hand petted him. I turned away before I would begin crying and making an eejit of myself.

More people streamed in, and the music began. We had moved the furniture back against the walls so people could dance, and the jigs and reels were soon in full swing. Mrs. Mullen and Paddy had arrived with P.J. We were almost all there now. I kept watching the door. Where was Lizzie? And where was Owen?

Lizzie arrived with Father Dornan, stamping her feet like the others and dusting the snow off her coat. She put out her small hands toward me, and I ran to her.

"Lizzie," I cried. "Och, Lizzie. Welcome home!"

The music and dancing stopped. Everyone watched us. Lizzie smiled her lovely calm smile, tears edging her blue eyes. I took her by the hand and led her over to Ma.

"Here's Ma, Lizzie," I whispered.

Lizzie stood very still and gazed at the old woman in the chair. I wondered what she thought of this frail creature. Surely she looked nothing like the woman in Lizzie's dreams—the tall, young, dark-haired woman with the beautiful eyes. Lizzie knelt in front of Ma and took both her hands in hers. Aoife moved away, and silence hushed the room.

"Hello, Mammy," she whispered, "it's me, Lizzie. I've come home."

Ma stared at Lizzie. She said nothing, but her face crumpled and tears flowed down her thin cheeks like a stream thawing over gray, frozen rocks. Lizzie began to hum "The Spinning Wheel." Then suddenly Ma began to hum with her, a small, frail sound like a baby bird. Frankie and Paddy came to stand beside me, watching their ma and their sister. I squeezed them both close to me.

"Thank God," I whispered. "Thank God."

The party went into full swing. I played Da's fiddle and people danced. P.J. played tunes in memory of Da and Billy Craig, as he called on God to give rest to their souls. Lizzie went over to Frankie and brought him to the middle of the floor to dance with her. This time it was poor Frankie and not Lizzie who shuffled on unsteady legs. I watched them with a joy and a sadness that threatened to break my heart wide open. Later, Lizzie took Saoirse on her lap and sat next to Ma. Tommy McParland brought the local children around the fireplace and told ghost stories. The *craic* lasted well into the early hours of the morning. People kept arriving, but no one left.

I imagined myself standing on top of Slieve Gullion, looking down on the house bright with lights, the merry sounds drifting across the fields and valleys. I thought of Da and Billy Craig, and I knew they were watching us, too, and James as well—poor James. But despite all the warmth and joy of the evening, there was a hollowness inside me. Over the last weeks, the kindness of everyone around me had chipped away at my old armor. I was a changed woman now. I was happier than I had been even as a child. I had peeled away all the defenses I had built up over the years. I was naked as a newborn, ready to love and allow myself to be loved. And I had no shortage of love. My family was around me again. I had friends. I was back at the Yellow House, and like the Yellow House, I had been returned to life.

Och, Owen, I thought, where are you? Why did I ever let you go?

Terrence came over and put his arm around my shoulder. "Owen?" he whispered.

I nodded. "I sent him word about the party, but he didn't come."

"Give it time, Eileen," Terrence said gently.

"I know."

ogo

IT WAS NEARLY dawn when the house finally emptied, leaving Ma, Frankie, Saoirse, Aoife, and myself—our own wee family—to ourselves. Paddy asked to stay as well. He would celebrate his fourteenth birthday the next day. I had wondered how he would react to the sight of Ma again—and she to him. She stared at him, but there was no repeat of the screams she had let out when she last saw him. I didn't know if she even recognized him now—I prayed that in time she would, and that the wound that was still buried deep inside Paddy's heart would be healed.

The Music Men left, and Father Dornan drove Lizzie to the hotel in Newry. I took Ma up to bed in my old bedroom and left the curtains open so that she could see Slieve Gullion in the moonlight. Aoife insisted on sleeping with her granny. I leaned over to kiss them good night, but they were already asleep, arms curled around each other. Paddy and I helped Frankie up the stairs to bed. He was exhausted from all the doings of the night, but happier than I had ever seen him. I almost envied him his innocence. Saoirse was out like a light. She had been passed around from lap to lap all night long, smiling and crowing with pleasure. How I wish Owen could have seen her. I leaned over her cradle and kissed her. "Dream of angels, darlin'," I whispered.

I put on my coat and slipped out the kitchen door into the damp, dawn air. It was Christmas Day! I climbed the gentle slope at the back of the house toward the graveyard where Da was buried. The smell of smoke from our turf fire mixed with the fragrances of wet earth and grass. The snow had left behind a thin frost delicate as icing on a wedding cake. My boots crunched on it as I drew near Da's grave. A rustling startled me, and I swung around. Cuchulainn came panting up to me. I was glad of his company. We had built a low stone wall around the graveyard and put a small iron gate at one end. I swung open the gate and entered the sacred ground. Lizzie's headstone with the angels was still there; I had not had the heart to remove it. I knelt and ran my hand over Da's gravestone.

"It was a grand party, wasn't it, Da? Did you see we found Great-Grandda Hugh's chair, and did you see the cut of Cuchulainn here sitting up on it? I think Hugh was petting him. Och, sure I didn't think to put out a chair for you, Da, but of course if I set up a chair for every one of the dead, there'd be no room for the living at all." I chuckled softly.

"Aye, I know, Da. Sure it's only a symbol. What did you think of Lizzie and Ma singing, Da? Wasn't it grand?"

I brushed back a tear. "I'm only crying because I'm happy, Da. We're all back here, aren't we? One way or the other, we're all back together. Didn't I tell you, Da? Didn't I say we would be one day? . . . What's that? . . . Aye, sure why wouldn't I be happy, Da? What more could I want? What I have will do me. It's more than most have."

I stood and walked toward the stone wall and sat down. I looked out across the dark fields. Dawn was beginning to break. In the distance, I heard the metal clang of buckets echo as farmers trudged to their milking sheds. Lights, like tiny stars, twinkled in cottage windows. A halo formed around the shoulders of Slieve Gullion as the darkness greeted the light. A sudden breeze made me shiver, and I shifted against the coldness of the stone wall beneath me. A sound from somewhere in the distance startled me, and I rolled off the wall and crouched behind it. Was it ghosts?

Jesus, Eileen, I thought, catch yourself on. You're too old to be frightened by headless horsemen anymore. But a child of the country has that odd mixture of practicality and superstition. Maybe it was the echo of Tommy McParland's stories that was playing on my mind or the fact that I was in a graveyard, but a shiver of fear went through me that I couldn't shake. And so I lay still and peered out over the wall. The sound of a car motor growled as it drew closer to the house. Then it stopped. I watched the car door open and a shadowy figure get out and stand looking up at the house. I held my breath. The figure walked around to the back of the car and lifted something out of the boot. Without warning, Cuchulainn sprang from my side and raced toward the car. The stranger bent down and petted him. Well, it was no ghost, I thought. Slightly embarrassed, I stood up, straightened out my clothes, and opened the gate. As I made my way down the hill, my heart began to thump in my chest. Darkness had finally given way to light, and there stood Owen, the golden dawn light haloed around him. I began to run toward him, and with each step a stone weight lifted from me. He stopped and swung around, the soldier in him wary. Then he laughed.

"I thought you were a ghost."

I was breathless. "I thought you were, too."

"I'm sorry I missed the party," he said. "The ferry from England was held up on account of the weather."

We stood in silence. Cuchulainn ran around both of us, barking in joy.

"I see you haven't painted yet." Owen inclined his head toward the house.

"No. The time didn't seem right."

"Maybe it is now?"

"It is," I said.

He bent and picked up a metal tin he had taken out of the car and handed it to me. "Canary yellow, as I recall," he said.

"Aye."

Epilogue

1924

In the summer of 1924, a boundary commission was formed that ultimately agreed to the border drawn earlier by the 1920 Government of Ireland Act. With the skill of surgeons, the politicians had amputated part of the province of Ulster from the rest of Ireland. Glenlea was imprisoned within that border. Slieve Gullion spread her robes and welcomed home Ulster's warriors and dreamers. The warriors now lie in her bosom in a restless, bitter sleep, while the dreamers pen their songs and laments for their lost land.

I, too, have drawn my own borders around myself. I have drawn close to me those things that matter—love, family, and home. I have left outside the borders anger, fear, and regret. I am at peace now for a time, just as is my beloved Ulster. Now my warrior sleeps while wisdom stands watch. Wisdom is my new companion, a wisdom forged from the fires of battles fought and lost, and life lived. And my dreamer lies awake, guarding memories past and memories yet to be born.

And so the summer has come again to Glenlea, and time hovers between day and night like a gift from heaven.

A brief historic overview of events leading up to the
establishment of Northern Ireland

In 1897, when Eileen O'Neill was born, the island of Ireland was divided into four provinces—Munster in the south, Leinster in the east, Connaught in the west, and Ulster in the north. The entire island was under English rule and governed from Westminster in London.

The two main religions in Ireland were Roman Catholic and Protestant. Catholics formed the majority in all provinces except Ulster. In three of the provinces, the Protestants were predominantly aristocratic families that had received land grants for generations since the sixteenth century. Ulster Protestants were different. They consisted mostly of Scottish and English agricultural workers and tradespeople who had been "planted" there by the English government, beginning in 1610, for the purpose of heading off future rebellions in Ulster—that having proved the most resistant of the provinces toward English rule. All Irish-owned lands in Ulster were confiscated and redistributed to the "planters" whose allegiances lay with the British government. There were also a number of Quakers throughout Ireland. The Quakers (the Society of Friends), separate and distinct from the Protestants, played a role in Irish social and economic issues for centuries.

The Irish famine years 1840–1860 were still vivid in people's minds when Eileen was born. During those years, death and emigration had shrunk Ireland's population from eight million to four million. The famine had also caused massive displacement of Catholics from their land in the provinces of Munster, Leinster, and Connaught.

In Ulster, where the concentration of Protestants was the highest, political and economic power rested in their hands. In 1690, the Protestant king

William III of England, also known as "the Prince of Orange," had won a decisive battle over the Catholic king James of Scotland at the Battle of the Boyne. Protestants in Ulster showed their loyalty to the British Crown by donning orange sashes and lilies each July 12 to begin their marching season celebrating the victory. Marches were led by members of the Orange Order, Orange being the region in Holland that was originally William's seat. A major facet of the celebration was the reenactment of the Battle of the Boyne in the town of Scarva each July 13, to the accompaniment of the beat of *lambeg* drums—a practice that continues to the present time.

The main industries in Ulster in Eileen's time were linen manufacture, in which Quakers like Owen Sheridan's family played a prominent role, and shipbuilding, which was controlled by Protestants. Although Quakers did not discriminate against Catholics in entry-level hiring, the skilled jobs generally went to Protestants. In Protestant-owned industries, preferential treatment in employment generally was given to Protestants.

At the time of Eileen's birth, while Protestants and Catholics were coexisting in relative peace throughout the land, a movement known as Home Rule for Ireland had begun to gain traction after having been started in 1870. Home Rule would have given Ireland its own parliament within the United Kingdom of Great Britain and Ireland. The outbreak of World War I in 1914 brought the Home Rule movement to a halt. Irish Protestants in general opposed Home Rule, but none more vigorously than the Ulster Protestants, who feared they would be subordinated to a Roman Catholic regime as well as lose their political and economic advantages. As early as 1905, Ulster Protestants began to take measures to defend and protect their position with the organization of the Ulster Unionist Council. By 1913, the Ulster Volunteer Force was formed and at its height was hundreds of thousands strong.

With the advent of World War I, it was widely thought that the Home Rule movement would be stayed. Meanwhile, a movement proclaiming an independent Irish Republic took hold in the south. It consisted of groups called the Irish Volunteers and the Irish Citizen Army, and on Easter Sunday in 1916, these groups took their cause to the streets by capturing the General Post Office in Dublin, holding out for almost a week against British troops. At the time, this movement did not have great support among Irish Catholics. However, when the British government executed the leaders of the rebellion as traitors, the tide of public opinion turned sharply in favor of the Republicans, or Sinn Féiners, as the rebels became known. As violence began to escalate all over the country, the Republican movement found its military leader in 1918 in the charismatic Michael Collins, and the movement gained strength. While most of the characters, including the O'Neills, Sheridans, and Conlons, are fictional, Michael Collins was a real person, though his actions and dialogue in this novel are used fictitiously. Irish Republican Army brigades were formed all over the country, including Ulster. Men fought under the IRA banner, and women enlisted in the auxiliary corps, known as Cumann na mBan. Eileen and James were members of these organizations.

When World War I ended in 1918, negotiations were renewed with Westminster to establish a separate parliament for Ireland. While violence raged in the streets, politicians negotiated, and in December 1920 the Government of Ireland Act was passed in Great Britain. Under pressure from Ulster Unionists, the act effectively partitioned six of the nine counties of the historic province of Ulster from the rest of Ireland, and Northern Ireland came into existence. However, the new Irish government, called the Dáil, refused to take their seats in the British House of Commons, setting up instead an independent Irish parliament called the Dáil Éireann. Thus, the battle raged on. Finally, in July 1921, Collins reluctantly agreed to a truce and in December of the same year signed a treaty that gave quasi-independent status to the twenty-three counties in three provinces of Ireland (Munster, Leinster, and Connaught), as well as three counties from the province of Ulster. The "Twenty-six" counties became known collectively as "the Free State." The Free State gained complete political freedom from England in 1949 and became known as the Republic of Ireland. The treaty was unpopular everywhere in Ireland, and violence raged not only between Republicans and the British Army, but within the Republican ranks as pro- and antitreaty forces fought the Irish civil war. In August 1922, Collins was shot to death on a country road in County Cork. The identity of his assassins has never been confirmed. Even after Collins's death, Republicans in Ulster, like James Conlon, continued to fight a guerrilla war, but little by little they were rounded up or driven out of the country with prices on their heads.

In 1998, following a peace accord known as the Good Friday Agreement, Republicans and Unionists in Northern Ireland formed a power-sharing assembly with the freedom to legislate a wide range of issues not reserved specifically for the British Parliament in Westminster.

Coming soon,
from the author of
The Yellow House

The Linen Queen

I

From Monday to Thursday we sang to break the monotony; on Friday we sang to celebrate. In the four years I had worked at the Queensbrook Spinning Mill in County Armagh in the North of Ireland, the singers were mute on only three occasions—the day Bridie McCardle's child was buried; the day Lizzie Grant caught her hair between the rollers of her spinning frame and was carried out on a stretcher; and the day after England declared war on Germany.

On this particular Friday in late March of 1941 we sang as usual to celebrate the upcoming two days of freedom from the mill. I stood barefoot, just as I had every weekday since I was a fourteen-year-old doffer, the water from the condensing steam swishing around my ankles, and forced a hank of flax through a trough of hot water to soften it. As I guided the flax down through the eye of the flyer and on to the yarn bobbin we finished up "My Lovely Rose of Clare" and paused for breath.

My friend Patsy Mallon called out to a young lad who stood in the aisle near her frame. "Would you ever come over here and piece me threads together, Danny? There's a good lad."

I looked up, wiping the sweat from my forehead with the back of my hand. Patsy was a big, bold girl with a large bosom and a salty tongue. She scared the wits out of young part-timers like Danny who went to school in the mornings and worked in the mill in the afternoons. Patsy would lean over them, pressing her breasts against them as they worked to tie the threads or replace the empty bobbins on her machine. I shot a glance at my other friend Kathleen Doyle, who worked two spinning frames at the stand next to mine. Kathleen's face reddened as much as Danny's had done and she bowed her head. Kathleen was the most innocent girl on the floor.

The late March day was drawing in. Soon darkness would sift through the grimy windows, which were set so high up on the walls you couldn't see out of them. I looked over the enormous room with its dim light and orderly rows of wet spinning frames extending the length of it, separated by narrow aisles called passes. I felt small in here, dwarfed by the room's size, and timid in the face of the rows of bobbins that grinned like misshapen teeth and spat and hissed like devils. I sighed. At least it was Friday. I would have two days off before I had to return to this cave.

Just as the Friday afternoon singing resumed—a rough chorus of spinners and doffers murdering the gentle, plaintive notes of "The Croppy Boy"—the doffing mistress, Miss Galway, marched down the middle aisle between the rows of spinning frames and blew her whistle louder than a banshee's scream. Miss Galway was an ancient woman—some said she'd been there as long as the mill itself—but she still had a fine set of lungs. Every time she blew her whistle to get the attention of the young part-timers we all winced. Today she blew it longer and louder than usual and we knew something was up. Without a word we all pulled the handles on the sides of our frames and our machines shuddered and fell silent.

"Ladies, we have a visitor today. Mrs. McAteer wishes to make an announcement of some importance."

We all turned toward the door as Mrs. Hannah McAteer entered on cue. She was a tall, grim woman with a long, narrow face and black hair flecked with gray. She was the widowed sister of Mr. Carlson, who owned the mill, and the mother of Mary McAteer, who worked in the mill office. Patsy said the *craic* was that Hannah, a Quaker, had married a Catholic farmer who'd been killed in the First World War and left her penniless. She and her daughter were at the mercy of her brother, Patsy said, and that was why she always looked as if she'd just smelled shite.

"Good afternoon," Mrs. McAteer began, looking around as if she indeed smelled something bad. Well, who could blame her for that? The smell of oil and grease and sweat in the room would choke a horse.

"I have some very good news for you."

We left our machines and edged closer to her.

"I assume you have all heard of the Linen Queen competition that takes place every year at a linen mill in Northern Ireland. Well, this year it is Queensbrook's turn."

She attempted a smile as a cheer went up from the spinners. She raised her hand for silence. "Now, this is a very important honor for us here in Queensbrook. Mr. Carlson has asked me to head the committee to choose those girls lucky enough to be asked to enter the competition. I shall take this responsibility very seriously in order that Queensbrook may stand the best chance of winning. Six girls from Queensbrook will be given the chance to enter. That's four more than usually allowed, since we are the host mill. To be fair we will choose three from the weaving shed and three from the spinning mill."

Kathleen and Patsy stood on either side of me, each one clutching my arm.

"Well no harm to the weaving girls," Patsy said, "but they all look like ghosts over there what with the heat and the noise and the dust. They'd be no competition at all. At least the spinners all have great complexions on account of the steam."

"Can you believe this, Sheila?" whispered Kathleen.

I wanted to believe it. A strange flutter took hold of my heart. I had heard about the Linen Queen competition in which girls from mills all around the North competed for the title. Talk was that the winner was awarded prize money as well as a crown and a sash. Winning the crown would be nice, I thought, but the money might be enough to buy a ticket to England. My throat went dry.

"Of course you must understand that the Linen Queen competition is not merely a beauty competition."

Was Mrs. McAteer looking directly at me, or was I imagining things?

"A girl's fitness to represent the mill—good attendance, solid work habits, a respectable family, and above all, good character—will be considered above looks. And of course she must be between eighteen and twenty-one years of age."

This time I was sure she glared at me when she spoke of character. True I had mocked her daughter, Mary, more than once and Mary had caught me at it. Well, Mary had deserved it. She'd called me names to my face and accused me of being loose with boys. How could I help it if the young eejits followed me out of the mill every day calling foolish oul' blather after me? It was Patsy who asked for that kind of thing, not me. But I was sure Mary had told her ma all about it. I hadn't cared until now. As if she read my thoughts, I turned to see Mary, a plump girl with black hair, standing in the doorway taking everything in.

"The competition will take place on Saturday night, April 12."

Mary's ma continued speaking to the hushed crowd. "The entrants will be announced one week from today, which will give the lucky girls a fortnight to prepare. Frocks will have to be festive, but modest. Those chosen will be given a list of rules. Good luck to all of you."

A festive frock, I thought. How in the name of God would I ever afford such a thing? The earlier flutter in my heart turned heavy.

Mrs. McAteer swung around and walked toward the door. No one moved. Then as if she'd suddenly had an afterthought she stopped and turned. "Oh, and the prize money this year is two hundred pounds."

A gasp went through the room.

"Jesus, Mary, and Joseph, that's a fortune of money," shouted Patsy. "I could move out on my own, and I could buy as much finery as I liked, and I wouldn't have to give that tight-fisted bastard another penny."

Patsy was talking about her da, who took all her money off her, and had been beating the daylights out of her since she was a child.

"It would be like a miracle," Kathleen whispered. "Think what my ma could do with the likes of that."

Kathleen was the oldest of ten children. Her da was disabled and her ma had taken the consumption after years working in the weaving shed. The family depended on Kathleen's wages.

I said nothing. Thoughts collided in my brain. If it was based on looks I knew I'd stand a fair chance. And I hadn't missed a day's work since I started at the mill. I'd even fought off the mill fever that most youngsters suffered from when they first started. I'd kept going in those first few weeks even though I was hardly fit to stand. My attitude could be better I knew, but it was hard to smile all the time when you hated the mill as much as I did. And I had turned eighteen shortly after the previous competition had been held in Lisburn and so now I could qualify for the first time. As for character—well I realized that was in Mrs. McAteer's hands. Would she hold me back on account of the gossip that surrounded me?

A twinge of guilt crept over me when I thought of Patsy and Kathleen. We'd been friends since our school days and to tell the truth they were the only friends I had in the mill. They each deserved to win the prize. What if I was picked to enter and they weren't? I pushed the thought aside.

As we left the mill that night, all the talk was about the competition. I'd never witnessed such excitement. Even the older women who would have no chance of being picked encouraged the young ones. They were all delighted for us. I couldn't wait to talk to Ma.

ক৹

I SAID GOOD-BYE to Patsy and Kathleen at the tram station. They both lived out in the country and came and went every day on the electric tram that the mill had laid on for workers from outlying towns. I lived in the mill village itself and had only a short walk to my house on Charlemont Square, one of two squares in the village with identical houses built around a green, all of them occupied by mill workers and their families. Well it wasn't my house, exactly. It was the house where my ma and I lodged with my father's sister, Kate, and her husband, Kevin. We had lived there since the time my da left on his boat when I was ten years old and never came back. Aunt Kate had taken us in, but she never let us forget her charity. Kevin was a big, burly customer with a bad temper. I stayed away from him as much as I could, particularly when he was on the drink.

My ma and I slept in the granny room at the back of the scullery in an old iron-frame bed covered with flour sacks. It wouldn't have been so bad if it hadn't been for the fact that there was a perfectly good bedroom up the stairs that had been standing empty for years. It had belonged to Kate and Kevin's only child, Donal, who had left home five years ago when he was seventeen and had not been seen since. I was school when it happened, but according to the neighbors, when he left he had said he was never coming back. He'd fought with his parents for years and was always saying he couldn't wait to get away from them. I completely understood his need to escape. But Kate refused to believe he was gone for good and so she kept his room like a shrine—his clothes clean and pressed and hanging in the wardrobe, his copy books laid out on the small desk, his bed made up every week with fresh linen sheets. It was comical and eerie at the same time.

I slowed my step as I neared the house. Doubt began to taint my earlier excitement. Could I dare to hope that I'd even be picked to enter, let alone win? Maybe Ma would be in one of her good moods and would encourage me the way the other women in the spinning mill had done—but I was no sooner in the door when I realized it was a foolish hope. Ma was in one of her desperate bad moods. I could tell by the fact that she still wore her stained work apron and hadn't bothered to comb her hair. Ever since I was a child I never knew which Ma I was going to find when I walked into the house. There were days when she sang like a lark, all smiles and kisses. And there were days like this when she looked like an old woman with the life drained out of her.

"Don't go getting any ideas in your head!" she began. "There's girls all over the country better looking than you are, Miss," she said. "And we've no money for fancy frocks and all the rest of it."

"Don't start, Ma," I said wearily. "I haven't even been picked yet."

"And you won't be!"

Ma worked in the weaving shed as a cloth passer where she checked the woven cloth for faults. It was a good job, but a hard one. Most of the weavers hated her because she was so critical. It didn't seem to bother Ma. She was only forty years old, but sometimes she looked twice her age, as she did now. I felt a rush of sympathy for her. She'd had a hard time of it since my da had left. And it was no easy matter for her living in another woman's house and having to slave at the mill like the rest of us. But I shook the feeling off as quickly as it came. None of this was my fault. Why should I have to suffer as well?

Ma sat in the armchair beside the fire.

"I know what you're thinking, Miss," she went on, her voice ragged from coughing and cigarettes. "You'll win this competition and then you'll be too good for the rest of us. You'll forget where you came from. And you'll go off gallivanting and forget about your duty to me. And me not a well woman."

Ma always added the last part to nail my guilt securely in place. I sighed.

"I don't want to talk about it, Ma."

I tried to push past her toward the scullery, but she reached over and grabbed my arm. "I don't know where you got this notion that you're better than the rest of us," she said, "but you're not. If it wasn't for me you'd be out on the street."

"If it wasn't for you I'd have finished school by now, and I'd have a good job and we'd both be better off!"

Ma's grip tightened on my arm. "We needed the money," she said. "And you needed to find a husband to support us. How were you going to meet a chap locked away in that convent school?"

I sighed. There was no talking to her when she got like this. I waited for the rest of it.

"What about Gavin O'Rourke? He's a fine chap and he makes a good living with that boat of his."

"He's a sailor," I said. "I thought you'd have no time for sailors after what Da did to us."

"Besides," I finished, "it's just not like that between us."

Ma swore under her breath. "Love," she said, "what good does it do you? You can make a marriage without it. I never loved your da."

"And look how you ended up," I snapped. "I'm tired. I'm going to lie down."

I pulled my arm away from her and went into the granny room and lay down on the bed. All the earlier pleasure of possibility had drained out of me. Ma always managed to do this, I thought. Why did I even listen to her? I sighed. Well, when you lived together and slept together, it was impossible to escape. I closed my eyes and welcomed the darkness.

☙

THE NEXT MORNING, Saturday, Ma refused to get out of bed. When she was in one of her down moods she would lie there all day, refusing to open the curtains to let any light in. If I moved, she complained I was keeping her awake. After a while I could stand it no longer. I jumped out of the bed and drew back the curtains.

"You can't stay there all day, Ma," I said.

Ma turned over and hid her head under the flour sacks.

"I'm not well," she moaned. "Why don't you go down to Mulcahy's later and get the bread?"

"Och, Ma," I said. "You know I hate being around that man."

"It's your imagination," Ma said. "You think every man is after you. You've got a quare bob on yourself, my girl."

Ma turned over to face me. "There's money on the dresser—what few shillings we have left—and it's our turn to buy the bread. So go on now and get in the queue early."

It was twelve noon when I left the house. To tell the truth I was glad of an excuse to get out. The place smelled so musty I could hardly breathe. I took in a few gulps of fresh air the moment I closed the door behind me. Pulling my coat close around me I walked back down the hill to wait for the tram into Newry, the main town in the area.

By four o'clock I was stuck in the bread line outside Mulcahy's bakery on Hill Street. Myself and the other women there had been queuing up for hours. Just before closing time on Saturdays the bakery sold off the leftover bread and scones for next to nothing. They would be stale by Monday, so better for Mulcahy to get a few pennies for them than throw them out. The women with money would never have been caught dead in such a queue—those well-dressed ladies with their baskets had come and gone by now—hurrying away for fear they would catch a disease from the rest of us. I was mortified to be seen there, but today it was better than being stuck in the Queensbrook house.

I stood now, shivering in the chill March air. The other women wore coats and mufflers and old boots, but I wasn't going to be caught dead in a getup like that. Instead I wore my best coat, thin as it was, my bare legs freshly stained with tea, and high-heeled shoes. And, as usual, I had forgotten my gloves. I was freezing. I recognized many of the women from Queensbrook. The young ones chatted away, but the older ones looked dreary and defeated like my ma. We all carried empty canvas bags, hoping to fill them up with bread.

"What passes for bread these days is a disgrace," said one.

"Aye, nothing but water in it. No good for the children."

"And still they make you queue up and beg for it like dogs."

The line moved slowly. Darkness fell, and the wind picked up. I wrapped my coat tighter around me. Just as I reached as far as Mulcahy's the shutters came down on the windows and door. Mulcahy himself, an oul' boy with a red face, came out to confront us.

"Sorry ladies. We're closed. You may go home now. And come back on Monday."

Groans and curses erupted from the line. Some of the women turned and left, a look of resignation on their faces. Others pleaded and coaxed, but Mulcahy shook his head.

"Go home now," he said again. "The bread's all gone. And I haven't all night to be arguing. Why hello, Sheila. I didn't see you in the crowd."

His voice turned sweet when he saw me. He grinned broadly exposing yellowed teeth. "And how's your mammy, love?"

"She's not well at all," I lied. "She'll be desperate when I arrive back with no bread for the tea."

I knew exactly what I was doing. Some of the women watched me with mouths open. Mulcahy came over and put a hairy arm around my waist.

"Och, I'm sorry to hear that, love. Come with me now, sure I might be able to find a bun or two for your poor ma. Lovely woman, lovely woman."

I didn't know which of us was the bigger hippocrite. We both knew Mulcahy wanted to get me in the shop so he could press himself up against me and blow his hot, stale breath on my cheek. I shrugged. I could tell him to feck off, or I could go in and put up with him so I could get the bread and not have to listen to Ma complain. I tossed my head at the women who were gaping at me.

"See you Monday, girls," I said. "Safe home."

"So I hear the Linen Queen competition is at Queensbrook this year," Mulcahy said as he shoveled the bread into my bag. "A pretty girl like yourself should stand a grand chance of winning."

I shrugged. "I haven't been picked yet," I said.

"Och you will, love," Mulcahy said.

I thought if I kept the conversation going I could keep him at his distance.

"Besides," I said, "even if I'm picked, I have no money for a frock, so there's no point getting my hopes up."

It was the worst thing I could have said. Mulcahy laid down the half-full bag on the counter and pressed in close to me. "If it's just a matter of a frock," he whispered, "sure I'll be glad to see you right on that, love. I'd be happy to do you the wee favor."

I felt his heavy breath in my ear and the weight of his thick body pressing against me. I swallowed down the bad taste that rose in my throat. Soon his lips moved across my cheek and found my mouth. I stood paralyzed while his lips slobbered over mine. He pulled back. "I'd want nothing for the favor, except for you to be nice to me, love."

He pulled away and winked. "Now let's fill up the rest of this bag."

He finished pushing in the bread and buns and scones and handed the bag back to me. "You just let me know when you need the money, love."

I backed out of the shop without answering him and hurried down Monaghan Street in the direction of the tram to Queensbrook. I let one tram go. I wasn't ready yet to go home and face Ma. I sat down on a bench and leaned forward, my elbows on my knees and my palms on my cheeks. I thought over what Mulcahy had said. What if I was picked and needed money for the dress? Would I take his offer? The thought sickened me. But there again, how badly did I want to get out of this place? Shouldn't I be willing to do anything? The thoughts gave me a sore head and I closed my eyes.

It was well after seven in the evening as I stepped off the tram in Queensbrook. A cold, spitting rain hit me in the face like needles. My hands and feet were freezing. I opened the door quietly, hoping Ma was still in bed and that Kate and Kevin were out. But Ma was waiting for me in her armchair beside the fire.

"It's about time, Miss," she said.

"I'll put the bread in the scullery," I said ignoring her bad temper. "I got the last of it."

"We were all waiting for it for the tea," Ma complained. "It's probably stale by now."

"Well, we have some now," I said wearily, "and don't ask me what I had to do to get it."

ABOUT THE AUTHOR

Patricia Falvey was born in Northern Ireland. She was raised in Northern Ireland and England before immigrating to the United States at the age of twenty. Formerly a managing director with an international financial services firm, she now devotes herself full-time to writing and teaching. She divides her time between Dallas, Texas, and County Down, Northern Ireland. *The Yellow House* is her first novel.